Worth Dying For
&
She Left Me Breathless
Two Book Bonus Bundle

by
Trin Denise

Worth Dying For

Have you ever asked yourself, "Is this worth dying for?" FBI Special Agent Rheyna Sorento must answer that question when she gets the assignment of her life and how she answers, may very well put her in the ground. When three key government informants connected to the Massino crime family turn up dead, all signs point to an internal leak and FBI Deputy Director Kyle Edwards decides to take action. He creates a new covert operation dubbed, Pandora's Box. His plan is simple: Find the mole and bring down the mob.

With the death of her lover three years earlier, still fresh in her mind, Rheyna jumps at the opportunity to join Pandora's Box and the chance to escape the painful memories of what used to be.

Using friendship and deceit, Rheyna soon finds herself deeply immersed in the family of Anthony 'Big Tony' Castrucci, the man slated to become the next Under Boss. Over the course of several months, a rising body count and countless hours of mind numbing surveillance, Rheyna jeopardizes the mission, her life, and those of her team when she unexpectedly falls in love with Caroline, the mobsters all too beautiful and very *straight* daughter. If Rheyna thinks things cannot get much worse, she is sadly mistaken when the mole releases her identity, setting Big Tony on a path of destruction like none the bureau has ever known, a path that in the end will produce the unlikeliest hero.

ISBN-13: 978-1-908822-21-5

(Ragz Books)

ISBN-10: 190882221X

Cover Art by Claire Chilton

Editor: Janet Brooks

Structural Editor: Claire Chilton

Ragz Books

Contact the Author

Twitter: @trin_denise

http://www.trindenise.com

http://trindenise.blogspot.com/

http://www.facebook.com/trindenise

http://www.Ragz-books.com

Acknowledgements

A special thanks to Claire Chilton for doing such a great job on the cover – I love them!

A special thanks to Eileen Gormley – You are the queen of creating book blurbs and I appreciate your help immensely!

A special thanks to Margaret Farrell for all your hard work and for also convincing me that WDF would make a great novel.

Author Bio

Sneak peek – Listen To Her Heart

A Note from the Author

Free Signed copy of WDF or SLMB Contest

Chapter 1

Using the cover of darkness, several figures dressed in black moved stealthily around the perimeter of the building. At first glance and to the outside world, the warehouse nestled between groups of smaller buildings conveyed the outward appearance of years of neglect and abandonment. Located just a short distance from Pier 38 along San Francisco Bay, the Danco Steel warehouse provided the perfect location for the covert activities going on inside the building.

Special Agent Carl Stevens took his position next to the entrance door. He inhaled deeply and waited for the last members of his team to take their places atop the four-story roof. He was tired of this. After thirty years of service with the FBI, he should have been the one sitting in a posh cozy office in Washington. He should have been the one directing the raids, not running them. Since the implementation of affirmative action, he had seen agents of color and sexual orientation promoted over him. His time of service and dedication meant nothing to the suits in Washington. Instead, here he was again, running another piss-ant raid. He tried to look on the bright side.

Reputed Mob Boss Capo Anthony *Big Tony* Castrucci owned the warehouse, and his foot soldier, Johnny Scala, had been the one to provide the tip leading to tonight's raid.

Johnny, a longtime FBI informant, had relayed a message to his handler that Castrucci was expecting an important shipment tonight. Johnny didn't know what was coming, but he knew it was big, and depending on what they found, it might just be enough to get Stevens his promotion. As far as he was concerned, it would be a promotion long overdue.

Inside the warehouse, a flurry of activity was taking place as several heavily armed men unloaded wooden crates of Florida oranges from the back of a tractor-trailer. Nearby, two forklift drivers took turns stacking the crates along the wall closest to Eugene Vega and Johnny. Each man, with a crowbar in hand began prying off the lids. Johnny pushed the straw packing material over to the side, revealing a stack of new military-issued AK 47 rifles.

Eugene carefully removed a military concussion grenade and turned it over in his hand. He held it up for Johnny to see. "Isn't this the prettiest little baby you ever saw?" he asked.

"Yeah and be careful with it. If that pretty little baby goes off in here, you'll blow us to smithereens."

Eugene chuckled and tossed the grenade back into the crate. He turned toward a group of workers standing near the tractor-trailer. "Get the rest of these crates opened and repacked. We're already behind the deadline, and they go out on the boat tonight no matter what!" he yelled loud enough for everyone in the warehouse to hear.

Outside the building, Stevens raised his hand to the tiny microphone attached to his headgear. He nodded at the agent standing opposite him as he spoke into the microphone. "On my mark: one, two, three, mark!" On his command, the agents on the ground and roof simultaneously launched their bodies through the windows and doors, sending wood and glass flying.

"FBI, Freeze!" Stevens yelled from a crouched position just inside the door.

In a flash, the warehouse erupted in an earsplitting hailstorm of gunfire. Stevens dove for cover behind a stack of skids. He glanced to his left and saw the agent closest to him stagger, drop to his knees, and fall forward onto the concrete floor.

Stevens flattened himself against the floor and crawled over to the agent. He reached out and grabbed the agent by the wrists. In a half-crouched position, he gave one big tug, and pulled the agent safely behind a stack of oil drums.

He peered around the drum before hurrying back to his original position. He leaned back against the crates and took a deep breath. Using his sleeve, he angrily wiped off the sweat running down his face. He peered around the crate and fired off several rounds, striking two workers.

A glance at the agent told him that it was not good. He forced his mind to focus and made his way to the far side of the skids so he could look out into the warehouse. Through the haze of smoke, he saw Eugene reach into a crate and pull out a grenade. Without hesitation, he pulled the trigger—striking Eugene just below the ear.

Eugene stumbled; his body fell forward, covering the crate. He raised his head, turning slightly to look at Stevens. He smiled and pulled the pin.

"Ah, shit!" Stevens yelled as the pin hit the floor. Instinctively, he turned and lunged forward, covering the wounded agent's body with his own.

He glanced up just as the grenade tore through Eugene's body like paper, instantly igniting the contents of the crate and those next to it in rapid succession.

"Retreat, retreat," Stevens yelled into the microphone, though doubtful anyone could hear him through the roaring sound. He slid his arms under the agent's shoulders and pulled him through the open door just as the side interior wall exploded.

Stevens looked around the parking lot, now littered with chunks of wood and glass. He dropped his head as another explosion blew out the back wall near the dock doors. Through the drone, he could hear the pinging sounds of ammunition igniting inside the building. He wrapped his fingers around the outer edges of the agent's Kevlar vest and tugged with all his might. His leg muscles strained with each step as he drug the dead weight across the parking lot. Just to his right and less than two feet away, a piece of leg, torn off at the knee with its shoe intact, landed on the ground with a thud. He turned his head to keep from hurling on the spot.

He glanced back at the building, now engulfed in flames. Large billows of smoke poured into the sky, effectively casting an eerie glow over the parking lot and he knew there would be very little to salvage from the building. *It's a total loss*, he thought as he continued dragging the agent to safety. All around him, the scene was utter chaos. Charred bodies littered the ground and those who were lucky enough to survive the explosions scrambled to get out of the way of falling debris. He involuntarily gagged when he spotted the owner of the missing leg.

Off in the distance, the sound of thumping grew increasingly loud. Stevens looked up to see a helicopter come into view. It circled above the parking lot, its spotlight making large sweeps over the pavement. The pilot swung around and hovered above a group of workers standing with their arms behind their backs, their wrists in handcuffs.

Stevens cradled the agent's head in his lap and looked

at the nametag affixed to the front of his vest. "Ah, Jesus; Rollins, hang in there buddy. You hear me? Where's a medic? Damn it, get a medic over here now!" he yelled, half sobbing. He removed Rollins' headgear and knew instantly that he was gone by the fixed position of his eyes. He used his thumb and forefinger to pull down the agent's eyelids.

Stevens got to his feet, jerked his headgear off, and slammed it to the ground. He looked around the parking lot. He shook his head in disgust. It never ceased to amaze him how quickly reporters arrived on scene. Half the time, they were there before the ambulance. He watched them set up their equipment as fast as they could. He knew each one wanted to be the first with the latest breaking story and it made him sick.

His attention turned to a young woman talking with a uniformed officer. She was dressed in a skirt that was too short for his taste. They turned and looked at Stevens and then she, along with her camera operator, started across the parking lot toward him.

"Agent Stevens, can you confirm that an anonymous tip led to the raid on this warehouse tonight?" she asked, cramming the microphone in his face.

"No comment."

Undeterred by his brusqueness, she asked, "Is it also true that this building is tied to Mob Boss Anthony Castrucci?"

"I said no comment," he snarled and brushed her aside with his arm. He walked over to two uniformed officers chatting next to one of the news vans and stopped in front of them. "Do you two think you can get these goddamn reporters back behind the lines?" He clenched his fists so tight that his nails were digging into his palms.

Chapter 2

Johnny Scala sat with his hands tied behind his back, his body shaking uncontrollably against the rickety wooden chair. He looked around the dingy, windowless room, and tried to remember how long he had been there. It could have been as short as one hour or as long as ten hours. He couldn't remember.

Sonny Valachi grabbed Johnny's hair. He snapped his head back, causing Johnny to groan unconsciously.

Johnny's eyes darted fearfully back and forth between the two men. It had been a few weeks since the warehouse explosion, and he had made a grave mistake in thinking he was in the clear. He couldn't have been more wrong, and he knew there was no way out. He was going to die—period! It was the La Cosa Nostra way of life. He broke the number one rule. He broke Omerta—the vow of silence.

Big Tony knelt down in front of him. He reached up and patted Johnny on the cheek. His voice was low, controlled, and tinged with the slightest Italian accent. "What's the most important thing to me, Johnny? I'll tell ya. It's loyalty. Fucking loyalty." He stood upright. His six-foot-two-inch frame towered over Johnny.

"I … I am loyal to you, Mr. Castrucci," Johnny said, his voice quivering with fear.

With well-manicured hands, Big Tony slid his hands down the front of his tailored jacket. He clicked his tongue against the back of his teeth. "I treated you like my own son and this is how you repay me?"

"I swear, Mr. Castrucci, I would never betray you,"

Johnny protested as tears ran down his bloody cheeks.

Sonny leaned against the wall and laced his arms across his chest. He tried to remember how many times he had seen grown men cry and beg for their lives. *Too many times to count*, he thought as he watched Big Tony pace back and forth in front of Johnny.

Big Tony stopped and leaned forward. He brought his face within an inch of Johnny's. "Don't lie to me, you little cocksucker!" he yelled in Italian, all niceties gone.

With a move quicker than Sonny thought possible, Big Tony slammed his fist into Johnny's mouth. The impact sent blood spewing against the wall.

Johnny coughed and spit his front tooth out. His head dropped against his chest, his eyes closing as he drifted in and out of consciousness. He wished he could do it all over again. He thought about that night four weeks ago and remembered how he felt standing in the warehouse with Eugene. He had been on edge. He shouldn't have done it. If only he could take it all back.

Big Tony's voice snapped him from his thoughts. "What do we do with rats? Huh, Johnny, what do we do?" he calmly asked. It was a question that Johnny undeniably knew the answer too.

Sonny, unable to control himself, doubled over with laughter. He pointed at Johnny's crotch. "The little shithead pissed his pants." He continued to laugh as the dark spot spread rapidly across the front of Johnny's jeans.

"I need to know what else you told them, Johnny."

Johnny shook his head vehemently back and forth. "I swear, I didn't tell 'em anything."

Big Tony ran his fingers through his hair. He looked at Johnny. It was crucial that he know just how much damage had been done. He smiled. "That's not what I heard, Johnny. I heard you had plenty to say. I want the fucking truth. If you tell me everything, I'll think about giving you a pass. I'm not promising anything, but I just might be inclined to cut you a break, but that solely depends on how truthful you are." He watched Johnny's facial expression begin to change. He almost had him.

"Please, Mr. Castrucci, please!" he begged. "I only told about the shipment at Danco. That's all, I swear!"

Big Tony looked at Johnny with dark, cold, and unfeeling eyes. He took a couple steps back, turned and nodded to Sonny before turning back to Johnny. "Thank you, Johnny," he said casually.

Sonny pushed away from the wall and walked over to Johnny.

Johnny sobbed loudly as he watched Sonny reach inside his jacket pocket, remove a semiautomatic, and then slowly screw on a silencer.

Very calmly and without any emotion whatsoever, Sonny pulled the trigger. The gun made a swoosh sound as the bullet—along with pieces of Johnny's brain—exploded out the side of his head. With the same calmness, Sonny pulled a knife from his pocket and clicked the blade in place. He pried Johnny's mouth open and pulled out his tongue. With a flick of his wrist, he sliced it off. He pulled Johnny's shirt pocket open and dropped it in.

Chapter 3

A knock on the door caused FBI Assistant Deputy Director Kyle Edwards to look up from the stack of papers on his desk.

"Come in," he said and closed the cover on the top file.

Ron Astor pushed the door open. "I'm sorry to bother you, but I have the documents you asked for."

"No bother at all. Please have a seat," Edwards said, motioning toward the chair. He took the folder from Ron's hand and laid it down on the desk.

"How are you doing, Ron?"

"Some days are better than others."

"How's Lynn?"

Ron shook his head. "Not too good. Six months, maybe a year at the most."

"I'm so sorry, Ron. If there's anything I can do, just let me know," Edwards said with sincerity.

"Thank you. I appreciate it more than you know."

Edwards looked at him thoughtfully. "Are you sure that you want to be included in this? Because if not—"

Ron held his hand up to stop him. "Really, Kyle, I'm fine and yes, I'm sure. Right now, this job is the only thing helping me keep my sanity."

Edwards nodded and opened the folder. "Okay, Ron. I won't ask again, but I do have one other question I'd like your opinion on."

"Sure."

"What do you think about Agent Sorento? Do you

think I made the right decision?"

"I think she's the perfect candidate for this assignment," Ron answered without hesitation.

"Good. I was hoping you'd say that, because I think she is, too." Edwards glanced down at the papers in the folder. "Is there anything in here I should be worried about?"

Ron shook his head. "Not really. I did an extensive check on their bank accounts, credit ratings, past job reviews, just like you asked, and anything else I could find. They're all clean. The only thing worth noting is Artie's wife, Alice. She's an alcoholic, which I'm sure you already know."

Edwards nodded. "Yeah, I've heard the rumors." He leaned back in the chair and laced his hands behind his head. "Do you think it's enough to scrap him?"

Ron shook his head. "Maybe Artie needs his job as much I do right now."

"All right, but keep an eye on his situation and let me know if you change your mind about him."

"I will."

"Okay, how about our other matter?"

"I finally received the corresponding data tied to the informants and let me tell you, we have tons. It won't be an easy task."

Edwards massaged the sides of his temples with his index fingers. "What's your plan of action?" he asked.

"I've written a new program to search for a common link between the men."

"And how long will it take before you have answers?"

"Days, maybe weeks," Ron answered.

Edwards frowned. "That long?"

Ron nodded. "Like I said, we have tons of data. Most of the informants have been on our payroll for years." He leaned back in his chair and crossed his legs at the ankle. "I hope you don't mind, but I expanded our initial blueprint a little."

"How so?" Edwards asked, his eyebrows rising slightly.

"I decided to include suspicious deaths as part of the equation. So far, I have four accidentals spanning two decades. Each one had been an informant with the bureau at one time or another. Two died as a result of a car accident, one from electrocution, and the other from a home invasion gone bad."

"Okay, Ron. I don't care how small it appears. You keep me posted on anything relevant you find."

"You got it," Ron said as he stood to leave.

Edwards glanced at his watch. "I'll see you in twenty."

As soon as Ron left, Edwards jerked off his tie and tossed it on top of the paper-strewn desk. Normally, he didn't drink while on duty, but decided to make an exception. He grabbed a beer from the small fridge and twisted off the cap. He walked over to the window and took a long swig. He looked out onto Pennsylvania Avenue and his thoughts turned to the meeting he would be having in twenty minutes.

He was determined not to lose a member of his team on this operation. The Director had given him full control, allowing him to handpick each member of his team. He should be excited to get the chance to nail Castrucci, to put a huge dent in the armor of the Mafia operating in the California region. Bringing down Massino's family would no doubt cause a ripple effect on the New York bunch. However, for some reason he couldn't shake the uneasy feeling in his gut. He had learned to trust his gut early on in the first days of his illustrious career with the FBI, and so far, it had served him well.

He had applied for a job with the bureau and to his delight was accepted at the tender age of twenty-two, and he was one of the first African-American men to graduate from the academy. Now, at the age of fifty-five, he had been with the bureau for thirty-two years.

He was promoted to Executive Assistant Deputy Director three years ago and was now in charge of the Organized Crime Division. Normally, someone in his position wouldn't be directly involved in an undercover assignment, but this case was different. He knew all the players, and the possibility of an internal leak made his decision that much easier. He was confident it wasn't any of the members he picked for this operation, and that's why he chose them.

He glanced at the personnel folders on his desk and sat down in the leather chair, propped his feet up on the desk, took another swig of beer, and opened the top folder. On the inside flap, a paperclip held a photo of Rheyna.

She stood five-foot-nine with black, shoulder-length hair, piercing grey eyes, and mocha-colored skin. He laughed out loud as he thought of the words often used to describe her by men in the department—probably a couple of women, too. 'She's built like a brick shit house' pretty much summed it up. He never understood where the expression came from and reasoned that a brick shit house was superior to a wooden one.

He admitted to himself that Rheyna's looks had played a small part in him choosing her for this assignment, but it wasn't the only factor. She was Italian and spoke the language fluently, which was an added benefit, but more importantly, her record within the bureau spoke for itself. Over the past fifteen years, she had received several commendations for her work in the field, including one for bravery when she took a bullet in the leg while shielding a child with her body during a pornography sting.

With all that factored in, the recommendation by Special Agent Laura Forrest had more than cemented his decision and an easy one it had been. He knew that both women were lesbians and didn't care. As a black man in a white man's world, he had dealt with discrimination in one form or another all his life, and he would be damned if he would tolerate it by anyone under his command.

He grabbed another beer from the fridge and tossed the cap in the wastebasket. Ah, Forrest, what a firecracker—what she lacked in size, she more than made up for with heart and attitude. After graduating from the academy, she had been assigned to the Forensic Unit in Quantico, Virginia and reported directly to him. That was over twenty years ago.

In addition to her duties at Quantico, she was also responsible for the FBI recruiting at the local colleges. To this day, every person she recruited had excelled and prospered in the bureau. Over the years, they had become very good friends. Edwards trusted her judgment, but more importantly, he trusted her with his life.

He picked up the next folder and opened it. He looked at the photo of Special Agent Carl Stevens and laughed. Stevens looked just like Herman Munster. The resemblance was so uncanny they could have been brothers.

Stevens had been with the bureau as long as Edwards had. They were in the same graduating class, their wives were friends, and their children attended the same schools. He felt bad for Stevens when he was promoted over him but Stevens took it like a man—took it in stride. He reminded Edwards of a duck when it came to dealing with life—he just let everything roll off his back without giving it another thought. It was a trait that he had always admired about Stevens and secretly wished that he himself could let things go as easily.

Stevens was also a good friend, and he knew he could always count on him. He had chosen Stevens for this assignment because no one in the bureau, next to the Deputy Director, knew more about the Mob and its inner workings than Stevens did.

He pushed the folder aside, picked up the next one, and flipped open the cover. Arthur Janson was an odd sort, to say the least and he laughed as he looked at the picture of Artie, and the signature red and white bow tie the bespectacled little man wore. He wondered how many times Artie had been beaten up in school.

He was your typical nerd—complete with pocket protector but Artie was a good agent. He had been with the bureau for almost as long as he and Stevens and spent most of his career in counter-terrorism, with the last two years in drugs. He thought about what Ron had said earlier regarding Alice and hoped that Artie would be all right.

He picked up the last folder and glanced at Ron's photo. The man had been through a lot in the past year and a half. He didn't know how Ron was getting through it all and wondered how he himself would deal with the news if he were told his wife; Tess had less than a year to live. He shuddered at the thought.

Like everyone else on the team, Ron joined the bureau right after college. He started his career in Civil Rights where he worked for almost ten years before transferring to Investigative Support to become the Sr. Programmer. Besides Edwards, Ron was the only African-American on the team. If anyone could find the leak and a possible common denominator between the deaths of the bureau's informants, it was Ron.

He glanced at the clock on the wall and sighed. He knew Tess would be waiting up for him when he got home, just as she always did. He thought about his wife for a moment and smiled. They had an anniversary coming up next month—it would be thirty-five years on the fourteenth. As far as he was concerned, Tess was the most amazing woman on the planet. She knew what the life of an active FBI agent entailed and not once had she ever made demands on his time or questioned his loyalty to the bureau. No matter how late or how long his job kept him away, she was always there waiting, always loving him. He glanced at the clock again and realized it was almost time for the meeting. He grabbed his tie off the desk and headed out the door.

Artie Janson stepped out of the conference room and walked briskly down the hallway. He hit the men's bathroom door, knocking it into the wall with a bang. He jerked his cell phone off his belt and walked into the open area lined with urinals and looked around. He listened for sounds coming from the stalls. Confident he was alone; he hit the redial button and waited for the voice to answer on the other end.

"Damn it to hell, Alice! What've I told you about calling me on the job?" he yelled. "I don't care what your reason is. You don't call me at work." He brought his foot back and kicked one of the bathroom stall doors. "Are you drunk? Of course, you are. Why I would think otherwise is beyond me. You're going to put us in the poor house. Do you hear me? Do you hear me, Alice?"

The hard expression on his face softened. "Now don't cry. You know I hate it when you cry. I'll be home in a couple hours. We can talk then, okay?" He slammed the lid shut on the phone and clipped it back on his belt. He looked up with a startled expression when Stevens stepped out of the last stall. "I'm sorry, Carl. I thought I was alone," he said with a nervous laugh.

Stevens walked over to the sink and washed his hands. "It's all right, Artie, no big deal," he said as he ripped a towel off the roll.

Artie leaned against the sink and shook his head.

"Are you okay?" Stevens asked.

Artie continued to shake his head. "It's Alice. I don't

know what to do about her."

"What'ya mean?"

"Come on. You heard the conversation. I just don't know how much more I can take."

Stevens laid his hand on Artie's shoulder, giving him an affectionate squeeze. "Is there anything I can do?"

"I don't think so, but thanks."

"Are you sure?"

Artie nodded. "Just do me a favor and please keep this to yourself. I don't want Edwards or the others knowing about my problems."

Stevens looked at him thoughtfully. "Artie, we've been friends for how long—fifteen, twenty years?"

"Yeah, something like that."

"Then you should know by now that I won't say anything to anyone. Your business is just that—yours."

"Thanks, I really appreciate it."

Stevens opened the bathroom door. "Come on now, we don't wanna be late."

Edwards glanced around the room. His eyes stopped at the two empty seats. "Does anyone know where—" Before he could finish, the door opened and Stevens, followed by Artie, walked into the room. Edwards gave them a disapproving look. "It's nice of you two to grace us with your presence."

"Sorry, bathroom emergency," Stevens said and sat down in the seat next to Laura. Artie took the seat opposite Rheyna.

"I assume everyone knows each other?" Edwards asked. Without waiting for an answer, he flipped off the lights. "Then let's get down to business."

It took several minutes for Rheyna's eyes to adjust to

the darkness. She looked at the photos up on the screen positioned near the far end of the room and felt excitement racing through her veins. Her heart was pounding so hard in her chest, she was sure the others in the room could hear it. She still couldn't believe she was sitting with her new team in the Strategic Information Operations Center command room, commonly referred to as Sigh-ock.

She turned her attention to the next image on screen. They were looking at a detailed outline of the Massino Crime Family tree. The tree had so many branch shoot-offs, it took up the entire length of the document. Sitting at the top of the tree was the big boss himself, Carlos Massino, followed by the name and title of every known member of his family.

Edwards cleared his throat and displayed a picture of Johnny Scala on the screen. "Until last week, Johnny Scala had been a Castrucci foot soldier."

He used a handheld remote to bring up two more photos. The first showed a car with the trunk lid open, the second showed a close up view inside the trunk where Johnny Scala laid dead, his body curled in the fetal position, his hands tied behind his back.

"As you can see, his body was discovered in the trunk of his car in the Danco Steel parking lot." He paused to take a drink of water. "He took a bullet to the head, and the coroner found his tongue in his pocket. Normally, we would chalk this one up to the mob cleansing one of its own. However, Mr. Scala had been one of our top informants for the past sixteen months."

He brought up two more photos. The first looked very similar to Scala, the bullet riddled body also in the trunk of a car. The second one showed police officers pulling a body from the water. The man's face was beyond hideous; his body was badly decomposed, bloated, and unrecognizable. "These two were also ours. Scala's the third informant to turn up dead in the last nine months."

Stevens shifted in his seat and turned to look at Edwards. "Maybe it's just coincidence."

"I don't think so," Edwards said, shaking his head.

"You think we have a leak, don't you?" Laura asked the question everyone was thinking.

Edwards thought for a moment before answering. "Yes, I do. It seems like the only logical explanation." He brought up several more photos in succession. They showed different views of a large funeral gathered outside a Catholic Church.

Rheyna recognized some of the faces.

"What you're looking at is surveillance photos taken two weeks ago at the current Under Boss, Salvatore Anastasia's funeral." The next photo was of Carlos Massino himself. He looked regal in his grey, custom-tailored suit. He appeared to be around sixty-year's old, give or take a few, with slicked back white hair. He had Mob written all over him, and ironically, he reminded Rheyna of her grandfather.

"The man you're looking at is Mafia Don Carlos, head of the Massino crime family. He was a no-show at Anastasia's funeral and that has me deeply concerned."

"Are you worried about who the next Under Boss will be?" Rheyna asked, puzzled by his statement.

Edwards took a seat by the projector and laced his fingers on top of his head. "We're pretty sure we know who the next Under Boss will be. I'm concerned about the backlash that's sure to come because Massino chose not to attend the funeral."

Rheyna shook her head. "I'm not sure I follow."

Stevens nodded in agreement with Edwards. He turned in his seat to look at Rheyna. "According to the La Cosa Nostra code, his lack of attendance showed the ultimate disrespect toward his Under Boss, and word on the street says Massino's right-hand man, Roberto Failla, is getting the nod for the position over Castrucci."

Edwards looked at Rheyna. "What's strange is that Massino gave no explanation for not being at the funeral, and from our experience, we know when a boss does not attend a funeral, he's afraid of one or two things: the first being a fear of arrest, the second being a fear of death. Massino had neither."

Stevens leaned back in his seat. "Our sources in L.A. are reporting that several members of his family, including some on the Commission, are upset and want something done about it. The same source also stated Massino is highly irritated with the rash of killings within the family, especially on Castrucci's crew. Castrucci, on the other hand, is making matters worse by rationalizing the deaths. He says he's keeping peace within the rank and file."

Laura made a disgusted sound in her throat. "What a freaking joke. Killing for peace is like fucking for chastity," she blurted out.

Rheyna busted out laughing, and so did everyone else in the room.

"Laura, I must admit, I've never heard anyone put it so elegantly," Artie said between fits of laughter.

"I'm glad I could amuse you all, but I'm dead serious. I mean, just think about. Look at the Middle East for example, and all the senseless killings that go on there every single day. They kill in the name of peace, and every one of us in this room knows it will never happen." Laura's expression was stern and it brought the seriousness of it all into perspective.

"You're right, Laura. It'll never happen, at least not in our lifetime," Edwards agreed. He took a sip of water and looked back at the screen. "Okay, back to the business at hand." He brought up the next photo, showing four men standing outside Bella's Café in downtown Los Angeles. Carlos Massino and Anthony Castrucci were standing to the left with Salvatore Anastasia and Roberto Failla to the right. They reeked of power and money, dressed in dark, tailored suits accented with flashy jewelry.

If Rheyna had to describe them, she would say that Anastasia reminded her of Fred Thompson, the actor-turned-Senator from the TV show *Law and Order*. Roberto was the total opposite: bald, short, stocky, and somewhat nerdy-looking with military-issued black-rimmed glasses.

Big Tony, however, was the dapper Don. He towered over the other men. Immaculately dressed in a dark blue pinstripe suit, he was quite handsome in a rugged sort of way. All of the men looked like your average Joe's, but appearances could be deceiving and in this case, they were deadly.

Edwards continued to describe the men in the picture. "As you can see, the man standing between Massino and Anastasia is Capo, Anthony *Big Tony* Castrucci. For the last seven years, Anastasia had been Castrucci's mentor." He stopped to take a drink of water before continuing. "It was expected that Castrucci would automatically become the new Under Boss when Anastasia died, but we now know that isn't going to happen. The man standing on his right is Roberto Failla. He *will* be the next Under Boss." He paused to look at the papers in front of him. "Right now, our biggest concern is with Castrucci. He's fueling a very large fire within the family and he's made it very clear that he's not going to stand idly by while they shut him out. We think he's planning to assassinate Massino and Failla for control."

"Doesn't he need the approval from the Commission to carry it out?" Rheyna asked.

"We think he's already begun seeking it," Edwards said as he brought up another photo of two men standing outside Anastasia's funeral. The man on the left was anything but handsome. His thick black moustache and goatee did very little to hide the deep pockmarks etched in his face. Edwards used a laser pointer to identify the men, starting with the goateed man.

"This is Jay *Marbles* Farino, Castrucci's hitman. Farino is definitely not the smartest guy on the planet, and ignorantly leaves his calling card with the bodies, a single marble. We think he's responsible for more than twenty hits, but we can't prove it. Standing next to him is Sonny *Pretty Boy* Valachi, Castrucci's trusted right-hand man. He currently oversees several different crews of soldiers working in the San Francisco Bay area and Los Angeles. Some of their business is legit, some not."

He brought up several more photos showing aerial shots of a very large and lavish estate.

Stevens let out a loud cat whistle. "Who says crime doesn't pay?"

The large sand-colored mansion was surrounded by large, black, wrought iron fencing that stretched out toward the ocean and ended with a fabulous view overlooking the bay. It was breathtaking, if you could ignore the heavily armed men patrolling the grounds.

The house was approximately two-hundred feet across at the front with a large covered entryway porch leading to the edge of the circular driveway. The grounds in the front of the house and surrounding areas were completely covered with lush flowers of every kind imaginable.

Rheyna surmised that the upkeep for the landscaping alone probably cost more than she made in a year. The front part of the house was deceiving, and from the driveway, it appeared to be a single story ranch, but halfway toward the back, the building raised another two floors.

This meant that the overall size of the house was three stories high. The rear of the house was unbelievable. Set in a horseshoe design, the ends stretched out across a large cement patio. Each side was identical, with balconies leading out from the upstairs windows. Directly in the middle, the house recessed into the shape of a Greek

Coliseum.

Rheyna looked at the photo, thinking it reminded her of something she had seen before. She thought for a moment and then it dawned on her—the back of the house looked just like the front of the White House. It was identical, right down to the last detail.

At the edge of the patio, knee-high concrete pillar railings separated it from the large L-shaped in-ground pool. The pool was something to behold all by itself. Standing at least fifteen feet tall and covering the entire small part of the 'L' was a gorgeous waterfall constructed from large slate-shaped rocks. Sitting to the right and less than forty feet away, was a small guesthouse.

Edwards continued to talk as he walked around the table. He laid a manila folder down in front of Rheyna. "Okay, ladies and gentlemen, that brings us to Operation Pandora's Box."

He pulled out a chair and sat down between Laura and Rheyna. "You five, me, and the Deputy Director will be the only ones with access to this information." He shuffled through the paperwork in front of him and handed a set of documents to the other agents. "We've decided to change directions and go directly after Castrucci. He's not as smart as Massino, and we're hoping that his arrogance will turn out to be his Achilles heel."

He brought up another photo. This one was of two women. Both had blonde hair and blue eyes. The older woman was attractive, but the younger one was insanely gorgeous. "The one on the left is Terasa, Castrucci's wife. The other is their only child, Caroline," Edwards said as he walked over and flipped on the light switch.

It took a few seconds for Rheyna's eyes to adjust, but it didn't seem to faze Edwards a bit.

"Rheyna, how're your photography skills?" he asked.

The question caught her totally off guard. "Uh … a little rusty, I haven't done much since college."

He looked at her thoughtfully for a moment. "Well, you'd better brush up. In two weeks, you will be the photographer shooting the family portrait at the Castrucci estate. While there, I want you to observe the inside of the house and the grounds. The one thing we've never been able to do is get inside. If you get a chance to plant wires, do it. More importantly, I want you to use whatever means you deem necessary to help bring this son of a bitch down."

Rheyna knew from past stings that the estate was guarded around the clock. Castrucci constantly had men doing electronic sweeps in the house and on the phone lines. Getting into Fort Knox just might be easier.

Edwards looked directly at Rheyna. "From the Intel we've gathered so far, Castrucci's nephew Rico, and Massino's granddaughter, Melinda Belotti, are planning their wedding at the estate. This in and of itself is not a big deal, except the informant indicated that the wedding is just a smoke screen for a meeting of the Commission." He glanced around the room as he continued to speak. "As you are all aware, there hasn't been a full Commission meeting since the one in Staten Island in 1984. What I'm hoping, Rheyna is that they like you and your work well enough to consider hiring you for the photo job."

"When do I leave?" Rheyna asked.

"Tomorrow morning at six and Laura will leave tomorrow evening. The rest of us, except for Ron, will be there by the end of the week."

He nodded toward the folder in her hands. "All the information you need is in there, along with photos of the main players. Commit it to memory and when you're satisfied, destroy the file. From here on out, your only contact will be with Laura or me." He looked around the room and smiled, showing a full set of straight, white teeth. "All right then. If everything goes as planned, starting tonight, and as far as the Massino crime family is concerned, Rheyna Sorento does not exist."

The sheet bobbed up and down in rapid succession. Big Tony closed his eyes and leaned against the headboard. He moaned, his body shaking from the orgasm.

"Jesus, Charlene. You ... are so damned good at that." He held up the sheet and peered down at the woman between his legs.

She sighed heavily and laid her head on his stomach.

"Come here, sweetheart," he said, stroking her long, bleached blonde hair with his hand.

She raised her head to look at him and then crawled out from under the sheet. She climbed over his legs and flopped down next to him on the bed.

"Hand me my cigar, honey."

Charlene picked up the half-smoked butt from the ashtray and handed it to him before grabbing a cigarette of her own and lighting it.

He watched her oversized tits rise and fall as she took a deep drag from the cigarette. With her head tilted back, she blew the large plume of smoke toward the ceiling. She laid the cigarette in the ashtray and reached down to pick her purse up from the floor. She unzipped a side pocket and pulled out a tube of lipstick and a small compact. She snapped open the lid and smeared the bright cherry red cream across her lips.

"Why you need that shit for?" he asked.

She grabbed a wad of gum stuck to the nightstand and tossed it in her mouth. Her lips slowly turned upward into a broad smile. "Because you rubbed it all off," she answered, sliding her hand under the covers to stroke him.

He grabbed her hand to stop the motion. "No more, Charlene. I need to get going."

The smile left Charlene's face. "Ah Tony, you just got here."

He swung his legs over the side of the bed and turned to look at her. "I got places to go, people to see," he said.

She slid up behind him and wrapped her arms around his neck. She laid her head on his shoulder. "But I haven't seen you for over two weeks."

He disentangled her arms. "Stop whining. You know I don't like it when you whine." He picked up his trousers and pulled them over his legs. "Why don't you make yourself useful and get me something to drink?"

She reluctantly got out of the bed and threw a robe on while he continued to get dressed. "Uh, Tony, I got something I been meanin' ta tell ya," she said with a nervous laugh as she poured him a glass of scotch.

He came over and took the drink from her hand. "Yeah, well, what is it?" He watched her pour herself a glass of orange juice. "What the hell you drinking juice for? You on the wagon again?" he asked, half smirking.

"That's what I been meanin' ta talk to ya about."

"Well, spit it out. I don't have all damn night."

"Um ... um, I don't know how to say this."

"Just fucking say it already," he said impatiently.

Charlene took two steps back, and bumped into a chair. "I'm ... I'm pregnant," she mumbled.

"You're what?"

"I'm pregnant, two months pregnant, to be exact."

"You stupid fucking bitch!" he yelled. He looked at the glass in his hand and then slung it against the wall, shattering it to pieces. He turned and grabbed Charlene by the shoulders and shook her. "How could you be so stupid?" he yelled, his voice shaking with rage.

"Please, Tony. It's not like that," Charlene protested.

"Please, Tony. It's not like that," he mocked. Without warning, his arm shot out, and the back of his hand made a cracking sound as it connected with Charlene's face.

She screamed and fell back in the chair. "I … I want to keep the baby!" she yelled back at him, tears streaming down her cheeks.

He took a menacing step toward her and brought his hand up to strike her again. She put her hands up in front of her face to block the blow. "Like hell you are. You're gonna get rid of it. That's what you're gonna do."

"But Tony, it's a living, breathing being growin' inside me. Can't I keep it?" she pleaded.

"I don't give a rat's ass if it's the King of Egypt." He grabbed her hair and yanked her effortlessly out of the chair. He brought his face within an inch of hers. "You listen to me, Charlene, and you listen real well, because I'm only gonna say it once. You get rid of this thing, or … I'll get rid of you!" he snarled, flinging her back down in the chair.

He grabbed his coat off the back of the sofa and jerked the front door open. "I meant what I said, Charlene," he said over his shoulder and then slammed the door shut behind him.

Sonny looked up from the magazine as the back limo door opened. Big Tony slid in the seat across from him.

"You all right, Tony?" he asked, frowning.

"Just take care of her and do it soon," Big Tony answered, slamming the door shut with enough force to rock the car.

Rheyna opened the refrigerator door and looked inside. "What do you want to drink?" she yelled.

"I'll have a beer," Laura yelled back from the

bathroom down the hall.

Rheyna grabbed two bottles, twisted off the caps, and tossed them in the wastebasket next to the stove. She looked at the assignment folder lying on the counter and felt a twinge of excitement. Although she knew the assignment could be dangerous, maybe even deadly, she was so looking forward to it.

The thought of getting out of Washington and moving to a new location was a welcoming thought. For the past three years, she had been safely coasting through life, not really living, and this assignment was her chance to start over.

She went into the bedroom and changed into an old pair of sweat pants before grabbing the folder and brown bag filled with cheeseburgers and fries off the counter. She laid the folder on the coffee table and unwrapped one of the burgers. She didn't realize how hungry she was until she sunk her teeth into it.

As she ate, she looked around the room. Her thoughts turned to Jenny, and how she had traded in the efficiency apartment for the little white house and picket fence. Well not exactly—the house was actually a two-story yellow row house in the 1700 block of Seaton Street near DuPont Circle and the picket fence was only twelve inches tall, and six feet long, counting all four sides. Jenny had used it to enclose a tiny flower garden she had planted in the backyard. Overall, the house was quite small, considering its hefty price tag. Hell, you could fit the whole house inside the Castrucci garage with room to spare.

The decision to purchase it was made six months after the two of them had met, and Jenny had been the love of her life for twelve wonderful years. They were introduced after Jenny had helped Stacie organize a gay fundraiser.

Stacie was Laura's better half, and the two of them had secretly conspired to fix Rheyna up with Jenny at their annual barbecue. She and Jenny had hit it off immediately, went on their first date shortly thereafter, and were inseparable from that day forward. She laughed aloud as she thought about lesbian dating etiquette. First date was dinner; second date was picking up the U-haul truck.

She lost Jenny to breast cancer three years ago. By the time they discovered the cancer, Jenny was already in the final stage of the disease. She would never forget the day Jenny died; it was the most excruciating pain she had ever felt in her life, and a part of her died that day as well.

She remembered it as if it were yesterday. Jenny had laid her hand on Rheyna's cheek and said, "I know this will be hard for you, Rheyna, but I want you to promise me you won't give up on love. Promise me that you will be open to loving someone else. You are the most wonderful woman I've ever known, and it'd be a shame for someone else to not know what I have known for all these years."

Rheyna didn't know who was crying harder—her or Jenny. With tears running down her cheeks, she had promised. She laid her head across Jenny's stomach. Jenny had stroked her hair and told her how much she loved her. She told Rheyna that everything would be all right, and then she was gone.

That was three long, hard years ago. After Jenny's funeral, Rheyna was so devastated she completely lost track of time. The next six months were and still are a haze. She went through life on autopilot. She had taken the obligatory three-day leave of absence for bereavement.

Laura had suggested she take a few weeks, or even a month off. She couldn't do it—she needed to work. It was her only solace. It offered her a temporary reprieve from her thoughts, and it kept her out of the house—Jenny's house and hers.

She was not sure what would have happened if it hadn't been for Laura and Stacie. They each took turns stopping by to look in on her. They made sure she was eating properly and getting enough sleep, but mostly, they stopped by to be her friend. She knew she made Jenny a promise that day and sometimes, she felt guilty because she didn't keep it. She tried at first, went out on a couple of dates, and finally gave up when she realized she was looking for Jenny in those women. It wasn't fair to them or her.

She looked around the room, at the pictures on the wall, and all she saw was Jenny. She hadn't changed anything in the house since Jenny died. Her clothes were still on the hangers in the closet, just as she left them. She also stopped sleeping in their bed. It was just too painful, so eventually, she moved her things into the spare bedroom. On most nights, she slept on the couch, finding comfort in the small consolation of having something familiar up against her back.

Laura dropped down on the couch beside her. "I can't believe you started without me," she said, the sound of her voice jarring Rheyna from her thoughts.

"Huh?"

"Dinner," Laura said as she took a sandwich from the bag.

"Oh, that. Sorry. I guess I'm a little preoccupied."

Laura dipped a fry in a blob of ketchup. "I have no idea why," she teased.

Rheyna finished her sandwich and went over to the fireplace. She busied herself with igniting the logs while Laura continued eating. She stared at the fire, mesmerized by the multicolored flames shooting up toward the flue, each fighting, and straining to drink the last bit of oxygen in the air. She personally thought that curling up on the couch with a book by Karin Kallmaker in front of a roaring fire was the ultimate in relaxation.

When Laura finished eating, Rheyna cleared the trash off the table and opened the folder. "Okay, let's see what we have here," she said and spread the contents out. She put the documents in one pile, photos in another, and the miscellaneous items off to the side.

Taped to the inside cover was a set of keys to her new home, along with a white envelope. She removed the keys and envelope, and laid them to the side. She picked up the set of photos and glanced through them before handing them to Laura. The photos were exact duplicates of the ones they had seen earlier.

Laura looked at the photo of Salvatore Anastasia's funeral and shook her head. "It must have been really bad."

"What?"

Laura tossed the photo down on the table. "The reason Massino skipped the funeral," she answered.

"Yeah, I'd like to know his reasons myself."

"Maybe you'll get a chance to find out."

Laura picked up the photo of Terasa and Caroline and shook her head. "She's just too Goddamned hot. Women who look that good should be illegal. If I were a few years younger, I'd—"

Rheyna laughed. "If you were younger, you'd what? You're happily married and you're not supposed to have thoughts like that."

"I'm not dead, you know, and I can still dream, whether I'm married or not."

Rheyna laughed at the expression on Laura's face and then snatched the picture out of her hand. She looked at the photo. She was instantly captivated by Caroline's eyes. "I wonder if there's such a thing as being too attractive."

"I don't know. I'm sure it has its perks, especially when you have brains and money to boot. I think I read somewhere that she's a doctor. She have her own practice yet?" Laura asked, reaching across the table to grab several sheets from the stack.

Rheyna rummaged through the documents she set off to the side. She pulled out the one with Caroline's information. "It says she graduated nine months ago and opened her own clinic one month later." For some reason, Caroline being a veterinarian didn't surprise her in the least. If anything, it made Caroline more attractive, if that was even possible.

"Okay, how you wanna do this? Do you want me to just go down the line and explain the terms, or would you just rather read them yourself?" Laura asked.

Rheyna looked at the document in her hand. "I'm pretty comfortable with most of them, but I think you giving me a verbal refresher will be good."

"Okay, next question. You want technical or laymen's terms?"

"I'll take laymen's terms for five hundred, Alex," Rheyna said in a deep voice.

"Very funny," Laura chuckled.

"Funny 'ha ha,' or funny 'queer'?" Rheyna asked.

Laura shoved her, almost knocking her off the couch. "You're not right, but since you asked, funny 'queer'."

"Lay it on me, teach," Rheyna said, pulling herself upright.

"Okay, here is the simplest explanation I can give you. You can sum up the entire organization's hierarchy by comparing it to a corporate business and the United Nations. The Boss, which would be Massino, is the CEO. Next is the Under Boss, who we think will be Failla, and he's the President or Assistant CEO. The Consigliere, that would be Valachi, is the In-House Counsel. The Capo, which would be Castrucci, is the Manager. The Soldiers and Associates are the worker bees—these guys are the nobodies, drug dealers, loan sharks, etc.—and the Picciotto, referred to lovingly as a hitman, is Farino, who we all know as Human Resources," she said with a laugh.

"As for the world famous Commission, they're like the United Nations, with each crime family boss equaling a foreign country. Is that simple enough for you?" she asked as she stood to stretch her legs.

Rheyna nodded. "I think that sums it up pretty well."

"Good. I'm gonna get another beer; you want one?"

"Yeah," Rheyna said as she picked up several documents and glanced through them. She skimmed over the detailed reports and tossed them into a pile.

Laura came back with two beers. She twisted off the caps and handed a bottle to Rheyna.

"Thank you," Rheyna said without taking her eyes off the photos.

Laura was silent as she watched Rheyna systematically go through each one and commit the faces to memory. After several minutes, Rheyna tossed everything into a neat pile.

Laura walked over to the fireplace. She bent down and picked up a piece of wood from the brass log holder, pulled back the fire screen, and tossed it in. She turned to look at Rheyna. "I wish I had that gift of yours."

Rheyna leaned back on the couch and took a long drink from the bottle. "Trust me when I say having a photographic memory isn't all it's cracked up to be. More times than not, you remember things you'd just as soon forget."

Laura eyed her without commenting. There was no need. She knew exactly what Rheyna meant. She sat down on the couch, and laid her hand on Rheyna's knee. "How are you doing?"

Rheyna looked at her. "You know, Laura, I've always known that La Cosa Nostra was run like a well-oiled machine, but—"

"I'm not talking about the mob, Rheyna." For emphasis, she poked Rheyna in the chest with her finger. "I want to know how you are doing and I want the truth and—"

"I'm fine, Laura." Rheyna laughed at the expression on Laura's face. "Why do you always do that?" she asked.

"Do what?" Laura asked, her right eye narrowing, her

left eyebrow shooting upward.

Rheyna pointed at Laura's eyes. "That eyebrow thingy you do."

"I don't know what you're talking about."

"Yeah, whatever, and you don't need to worry about me so much."

"I always worry about you, and if I didn't care so much, it wouldn't matter—now would it?"

"I know you do, and I love you for it, but believe me when I say I'm fine. To tell you the truth, I'm actually looking forward to a change of scenery." Rheyna reached over and pulled the envelope out from beneath the keys. She raised the flap and pulled out the contents. She looked at the copy of her new California driver's license. "This isn't too bad. At least they let me keep my first name, and I'm only twenty-eight."

Laura snorted. "In your dreams, you're twenty-eight. How old are you, anyway?"

Rheyna tossed her the driver's license. "Thirty-five and holding with a birthday coming up in May, smart ass."

Laura did a mock salute and curled her upper lip, doing her best Elvis impersonation and said, "Thank'ya, thank'ya very much. I'll be here all week."

Rheyna shook her head and laughed. "You're just not right. That's all there is to it."

Laura glanced at the driver's license. "That's not too bad, considering what name they could've given you. What's left?" she asked.

Rheyna skimmed through the other documents. "A college transcript from Oklahoma University for a B.A.S. in Photography and a Chequotah, Oklahoma police report showing that I was arrested as a juvenile for petty theft and vandalism." Rheyna felt the color drain from her face.

Laura must have seen it, too. "What is it? What's wrong?" Laura asked, taking the papers from Rheyna's hand. She looked at the documents and shook her head.

"You know these aren't real," she said, throwing her arms around Rheyna's shoulders.

"I know, but it's still a little unnerving." Rheyna gathered up all the documents and photos. "I think I've seen enough," she said and walked over to the fireplace. She knelt down on one knee, slid open the screen and tossed all the items into the fire. It didn't take long for the dancing flames to turn the papers into a pile of ashes. She thought about her parents and decided to give them a call before she left on her flight.

"I can't believe how late it is," Laura said as the cuckoo bird above the mantle signaled that it was midnight.

Rheyna closed the fire screen and turned to look at her. "I know, and I still have to pack."

Laura stood and brushed off her slacks. "And I have to go home and break the news to Stacie. I have a feeling she's not going to be too happy with me."

"If I know Stacie, she'll be up waiting for you and she'll handle it just fine," Rheyna said as she walked Laura to the door. "Thank you, and be safe driving home," she said, leaning forward to hug Laura.

"You're welcome, and I will. You have a safe flight and I'll talk to you sometime tomorrow night."

Rheyna watched her back out of the driveway. She stood there looking out the window for a good fifteen minutes before heading upstairs. Her thoughts turned to Anthony Castrucci, and she unconsciously shivered. She pushed the uneasy feeling out of her mind, thinking she would try to get a couple hours' sleep before packing her clothes.

Laura locked the door and turned off the lamp on the

end table. She tiptoed down the hall to the bedroom. She tossed her coat across the back of a chair and unbuttoned her blouse.

"Hey, baby, I was hoping you'd still be up."

Stacie sat up and stretched her arms over her head. She tried to stifle a yawn. "You know I have trouble sleeping without you next to me."

Laura pulled a t-shirt over her head and hopped on the bed beside her. "About that—you may have to get used to it for awhile."

Stacie frowned. "You have a new assignment, don't you?"

Laura nodded. "I leave tomorrow afternoon."

"How long will you be gone?"

"I'm not sure. It could be a couple weeks, or it could be a couple months. It all depends on how long the operation drags out."

Stacie wrapped her arms around the top of her knees and laid her head against them. "I don't want you to go."

Laura reached over and pulled Stacie down on top of her. "Oh, sweetheart. I don't want you to be sad." Laura ran her fingers through the long red curls flowing down Stacie's back. "I'll come home every couple of weeks for a night or two, if I can manage the time. I promise."

"Is it dangerous?" Stacie managed to ask as Laura began trailing kisses along the side of her neck.

"You know—"

"I know you can't talk about your cases," Stacie interrupted. "I just want to know if you'll be in any danger. You know how I tend to worry."

"Yes, it could be dangerous," Laura answered honestly.

Stacie's body tensed. She held Laura at arm's length to look her directly in the eyes.

"Sweetheart, I'll be there in a support position only." Laura squeezed her arms tight around Stacie's waist. "The real danger will be with Rheyna."

Stacie rolled over and leaned on her elbow. "Rheyna's on this assignment, too?"

"Yes, and I'm sorry honey, but I can't give you any more details."

"I hate this part of your job."

"I know you do and I hate this part myself."

"Can you at least tell me where you'll be?"

"I'll be in California."

"You tell Rheyna I said to be careful."

"I will. Now, come over here," Laura said, pulling Stacie down beside her. "I might not get to see you for awhile," she said, and then her mouth hungrily claimed Stacie's soft lips. Laura slowly made her way down to Stacie's breast. Stacie shivered as Laura's tongue made circling motions around her nipple before consuming it in her mouth.

"Don't think … think this makes up for you leaving," Stacie managed to say, her breath catching in her throat.

"No, but it's a good start," she whispered against Stacie's skin. Laura slowly made her way down her lover's body. God, *how I love the smell, the taste of this woman*, she thought as she kissed the inside of Stacie's thigh. She rubbed her cheek over the small tuft of hair, savoring the scent. Stacie moaned as Laura's tongue gently licked along the sides of her clitoris.

Stacie gripped the sheets with both hands. "You're slowly killing me, you know?"

"Am I?" Laura moaned as she explored the soft wetness now surrounding her fingers. Stacie's hips began to move against her fingers with slow, deliberate thrusts.

"Oh, God," Stacey groaned as Laura's soft, hot mouth paralyzed her. Without thought, her legs spread wider. Laura could feel Stacie growing harder with each tantalizing lick. She tightened her arms around Stacie's legs and drank in her lover's sweetness. Stacie reached down and ran her fingers through Laura's hair, holding her close as she began to climax, her back arching, her body shaking to the core.

Stacie fell back on the bed breathless, her chest heaving up and down until finally she pushed Laura away. "No more, baby, no more."

Laura laid her head against Stacie's wet belly and tried to calm her own uneven heartbeat. Like an aftershock, she felt Stacie's hips raise slightly, thrust forward and tighten before finally relaxing. She clamped her own legs together in an attempt to quiet the overwhelming ache settling in her groin.

After a few minutes, Stacie sat up and leaned forward. She reached down and grabbed the top of Laura's t-shirt. With one fluid motion, she pulled it over Laura's head and tossed it on the floor. "Jesus, Laura, I'm thinking you should go away more often."

Laura's voice was husky with desire. "I wouldn't go that far."

"If it's okay with you, I'd like to reciprocate." Stacie didn't wait for an answer and pulled Laura up to straddle her face.

"I'm not sure you need to touch—" A guttural sound escaped from Laura's lips as Stacie's warm fingers held her open. She held her breath for what she knew was coming next. She fell forward, grabbing the headboard for support.

"You're so wet and hard," Stacie murmured as she rubbed her lips over Laura's swollen clit. Laura moaned as Stacie took her fully in her mouth. Her hips moved back and forth, encouraging Stacie to suck harder with each thrust.

"Yes, yes, oh, God," Laura panted as Stacie's fingers massaged her opening. "Please, baby," she begged.

"Not yet," Stacie whispered as her mouth and fingers continued the tease.

"I can't take much more."

"Sure, you can," Stacie groaned, sliding her fingers through the wetness, and then she entered her.

Laura began a rocking motion with her hips against Stacie's fingers. "More, baby, please give me more," she cried out. "Harder, harder, oh yes, harder, yes!" Laura moaned, her back stiffening, her body shaking with orgasm before finally collapsing against the headboard in exhaustion.

Chapter 4

Rheyna's flight had been uneventful and long, but on time. After picking up her luggage, she stepped outside the American Airlines terminal at San Francisco's International Airport. The weather was perfect—a warm seventy-six degrees according to the Captain. She shielded her eyes from the sun, marveling at the blueness of the sky.

She crossed the street and headed toward the long-term parking area, weaving back and forth between the rows of cars until she came to the spot marked LGT4. She busted out laughing when she saw her car. She shook her head, knowing that she owed Laura a lobster dinner.

Sitting in the parking spot was a silver Jeep Wrangler Rubicon. She let out a whistle that could be heard around the parking lot. She flung her suitcase into the back and quickly removed the soft-top. It never dawned on her to look at the keys in the folder; otherwise, she would have realized that one set was for a Jeep. She smiled at the air freshener hanging from the mirror. It was a rainbow with a pot of gold at the end. Any person would be lucky to have a friend like Laura. At that moment, she realized just how truly lucky she was and silently prayed that her luck would continue.

She opened the glove box and pulled out a map of the area and the directions to her new home. According to the map, the house was located in Half Moon Bay, approximately thirty-five minutes from the airport and a short distance from the Castrucci estate. She didn't know what to expect of the house, but she knew it was bureau-owned property and untraceable. If Castrucci decided to check on her—and they were sure he would have by now—he would see that she purchased the house two months ago. She laid the map on the seat and backed out of the parking spot.

Thank heaven for MapQuest's easy-to-follow directions, she thought as she made her way out of the airport and merged onto U.S. 101, heading south toward San Jose along San Francisco Bay. The view was breathtaking, and with the wind blowing through her hair, she took every bit of it in. She was so engrossed in the scenery that she almost missed the Half Moon Bay exit.

According to the map, she would be on CA92 West for thirteen miles. Off to the right, a small minimart got her attention, and she decided to stop to pick up a few things. She was almost certain that the fridge would be stocked with food and other necessities, but she specifically wanted a pair of sunglasses, beer, and junk food—namely chocolate.

Her luck just kept getting better, she decided as she stopped in front of the beer section. Sitting on a shelf were several bottles of her favorite wine, Moscato Allegro. She picked up three bottles and headed for the checkout. She couldn't believe it. She had been ordering that particular wine from an online store for the last two years. It was by far the best wine she had ever tasted, and with little effort, she could polish off a bottle by herself.

She was even more excited to learn from the sales clerk that the winery was located in Paso Robles, a three-hour trip down the coast. The clerk assured her that the view alone was worth the drive. She thanked the clerk for the information and went back to the Jeep, thinking she just might have to take that drive.

With her new sunglasses on, she set off toward Half Moon Bay and before she knew it, she was pulling into the driveway at 22 Mirada Road. The house sat directly on the beach, overlooking the Pacific Ocean. It would be an understatement to say it was beyond her expectations. The folks in Washington were definitely taking care of her.

With bag and suitcase in hand, she let herself in through the front door and walked directly into the living room. She looked around in awe, thinking she must be one successful photographer.

The living room ran lengthwise from back to front, with a counter-topped bar separating it from the small, eat-in kitchen. She noticed a small package sitting on the counter. *No doubt, a gift from Laura*, she thought as she surveyed the room. The house was decorated with a southwestern theme, and the fabric print on the furniture reminded her of the Navajo Indian blankets that are sold at flea markets. She found the cream and mauve tones comforting. A stone fireplace reaching from floor to ceiling covered one entire wall.

She set her suitcase on the floor and walked over to the patio doors. She looked through the glass, her breath catching in her throat. She had a panoramic view that looked directly out into the Pacific Ocean. Without hesitation, she slid the door open and stepped outside.

The scene that greeted her was breathtaking. The entire deck was surrounded by knee-high wild flowers in various stages of bloom, but the yellow poppies were something else. They were everywhere, stretching down the beach as far as the eye could see. She watched a seagull dive down deep into the water, only to come up seconds later with a fish in its mouth.

She took a deep breath and allowed the fresh air to fill her lungs. She sat down on a lounger, leaned her head back, and closed her eyes. She could hear the waves slapping against the rocks and she imagined the sun setting in the evening. She looked forward to seeing it firsthand. After several minutes, she reluctantly opened her eyes. She had a job to do. She got up from the lounger and went back inside to put away the few items she picked up at the mini-mart.

She grabbed a beer from the fridge and took a long drink before making her way through the rest of the house. The bedrooms were located on the opposite side of the house. She tossed her suitcase on the bed of the first room she came to. It was not anything too fancy and was decorated in the same southwestern theme as the living room. It had a queen-size bed, dresser, and two obligatory nightstands with lamps. It did however, have a window that looked out onto the beach. She thought about unpacking and then changed her mind. She wanted to see the other rooms first. She went across the hall and poked her head into another bedroom. It was just like the one she had chosen, but without the view.

The next room she entered was set up like a state-of-the-art photo lab. Against the wall, sitting on top of a conference table, was a computer, printer, and Canon Rebel digital camera. She suspected the cost ran in the range of ten to fifteen grand for the computer system. The camera alone was worth at least two. She picked up the camera, thinking that they couldn't have gotten her a better one. It would have been her first choice. A low grumbling in her stomach caused her to look at her watch. She couldn't believe that it was almost seven.

She made herself a bologna sandwich, took it along with the package from the counter, and went out onto the deck to watch the sunset. It didn't disappoint. It reminded her of the Northern Lights. The sky was divided from top to bottom in a combination of blues and yellows and a red so bright, that the reflection on the whitecaps made the water look pink. She had never seen anything like it.

She ate the sandwich as she sorted through the box. She had some idea of what she would find inside and wasn't surprised in the least to see the 9mm semi-automatic. She hoped she wouldn't need it, but it was comforting to see just the same.

Being an ordinary citizen, at least on paper, meant that she couldn't take her service weapon on the plane. As for her trip, she knew Edwards would have her name erased from the flight manifest on the off chance that a background check would be done. She knew that by now, Castrucci would have done just that. Whoever did the check would see that she had arrived in Half Moon Bay two months earlier from Chequotah, Oklahoma when she bought the house.

She sat the gun and the box of ammo off to the side and looked at the cell phone. It was her direct link, her lifeline, to Laura. She turned the phone over and smiled. Taped to the back was a note reminding her to set the answering machine.

She laid the phone down and picked up the two envelopes sitting at the bottom of the box. The first one contained a stack of personalized business cards, along with the Castrucci estate address. The second envelope had a credit card with her new name on it, and money. She counted out three grand in twenty-dollar bills. She gathered up the contents of the box and went back inside to search out the answering machine. It didn't take long—she found it next to the toaster and coffee maker and recorded a message.

She took her gun and the box of ammo and went back to her bedroom. She sat down on the side of the bed and loaded the clip. She opened the top drawer of her nightstand and slid the gun beneath a stack of magazines.

Back in Washington, she hadn't been sure of what to pack and finally decided that it wouldn't be much, since she needed to update her wardrobe. Therefore, it didn't take long to put away the few things she had brought. She grabbed her favorite pair of flannel pajamas and a t-shirt and headed off to the bathroom for a much-needed shower.

Once dressed, she ran a comb through her hair, went into the kitchenette, and grabbed a beer out of the fridge. She took a swig and dropped down on the couch as she snatched the remote off the coffee table. She flicked through the stations until she found *Law and Order*.

She spent the next several days exploring the area and getting familiar with the camera equipment. At night, she would take the cell phone, along with her dinner, and go out on the patio to check in with Laura. After the phone call, she trolled the internet for area newspaper archives tied to Castrucci and the Massino crime family.

Tommy drove the limo down the trash-strewn street and past several buildings that were burnt to the ground. He stopped in front of one that should have been condemned years ago.

"We'll be back in a couple," Sonny said as he and Big Tony got out of the car.

Big Tony looked at the building with disgust. "This place is a dump. I don't understand how people live like this."

Sonny led Big Tony past an assortment of cars perched atop concrete blocks and stopped at the front door leading into the building. "Yeah, it's definitely not my cup of tea, but it's a diamond in the rough."

"It better be," Big Tony said as they climbed the creaking stairs. "It smells like piss in here," he grumbled. He took out a hanky and covered his nose, taking care to step over a drunk passed out on the second-floor landing. "What floor did you say he's on?"

Sonny glanced down at the paper in his hand. "Third."

"Figures," Big Tony said as he continued to climb up the steps leading to the third floor. "Man, I need to get in better shape," he said, gasping for air.

Sonny walked past him and stopped in front of the second door. "Here it is," he said, wrapping on the door with his knuckles.

Inside the tiny apartment, Billy Smith pushed open the bedroom door and walked over to the small blonde-headed girl sitting on the edge of the bed. He crouched down on the floor in front of her. "You sure are pretty, darlin'. You remember what Daddy told you?" he asked softly.

She nodded shyly and continued to play with the pink ruffle at the bottom of her flowery dress.

Billy laid his hand over hers. "These men are really important to Daddy, and I want you to be a good girl, okay? All right, I'll be right back and then we can get some ice cream." He left the room and walked back to the front door. He took a deep breath and opened it.

"It's about damn time," Big Tony said impatiently.

Billy ran his hand through a mass of greasy hair. "Sorry 'bout that," he said with a nervous laugh.

Big Tony brushed past him and walked into the filthy living room. "She better be worth it," he said, glancing around. He looked at the kitchen and the sink full of dishes, crawling with cockroaches. He shook his head in disgust. "Where is she?" he asked.

"Uh, uh, this way," Billy answered, leading the men to the little girl's bedroom.

Big Tony pushed the door open and walked over to the bed. He reached down and lifted the girl's chin. He turned her head from side to side. "How old is she?" he asked.

"She'll be seven her next birthday."

Big Tony looked at Sonny and grinned. "I've seen enough," he said. He turned and walked out of the room with the two men following close behind.

Billy crammed his hands in the front pockets of his jeans, shifting nervously from one foot to the other.

Sonny pulled out a yellow envelope from inside his breast pocket and handed it to Billy.

"Have her ready by noon. I'll send someone for her. Make sure she's wearing what she has on now," Big Tony said as he and Sonny watched Billy open the envelope.

Billy's eyes shifted nervously back and forth between the two men. "Uh ... um, there's only fifteen here."

Big Tony shrugged his shoulders. "Yeah, so what?"

"Uh ... the deal was for ... for twenty thou," Billy stammered.

Big Tony crossed the room in two steps. He shoved Billy, knocking him backward into a raggedy chair. He whipped out a gun from his waistband and crammed the muzzle against the side of Billy's head. "You piece of shit. You're lucky I gave you that much," he snarled through clenched teeth.

"Uh ... yeah. Uh ... this is plenty. Please, please don't hurt me," Billy begged.

Big Tony pulled the gun away. He spit on the floor next to Billy's chair and then laughed as he tucked the gun back inside his waistband. He jerked the door open and looked back at Billy. "You're pathetic, but if she's as good as you promised, I'll give you a little bonus next time. If she's not, you'll be the one paying me and make sure she's ready at noon."

Billy waited for the door to close and then slumped back in the chair. He let out a huge sigh of relief, smiling broadly, as his dirty fingers skimmed over the stack of one-hundred-dollar bills.

The voice of a woman with a slight Italian accent came through the answering machine, waking Rheyna from a deep sleep. She had an idea of who the caller was and her suspicion was confirmed as the message played.

It was Terasa Castrucci asking if it would be possible for Rheyna to come out today to take their photos. She apologized for asking on such short notice, since the appointment was set for next week. She wouldn't be asking, except her husband's business would be taking him out of town on the scheduled date. She left her contact number and said goodbye.

Rheyna took a quick shower and poured a cup of coffee before returning Mrs. Castrucci's call. Esther, the Castrucci's housekeeper, answered the phone, told her that Mrs. Castrucci was at the hairdresser, and requested she come between one and two today, if possible. Rheyna told her she would be there, and Esther then proceeded to give her directions to the Castrucci estate.

She loaded up her camera equipment and tossed it in the back of the Jeep. She knew her way to the house from one of her driving ventures earlier in the week, making a point to drive over to the Castrucci estate to familiarize herself with the surroundings. She figured she had time to grab a quick lunch before her appointment with Mrs. Castrucci and stopped and picked up a turkey club sandwich from a little sub shop on Magellan.

After finishing the sandwich, she headed for the Kelly Avenue exit. A half mile later, she turned into the Castrucci driveway.

The estate itself sat far back on the property, making it invisible from the street below. There was no doubt in her mind that it had been a calculated move by Castrucci when he built the house. She continued up and around the blacktopped drive and stopped in front of a large gate. She rolled down the window and pressed the intercom button. She glanced at the large row of trees in front of her. She recalled from the estate photos that the house sat just on the other side of the tree line.

"Yeah, what business do you have?" A deep male voice barked through the speaker.

"My name is Rheyna Moretti. I have an appointment with Mrs. Castrucci."

"Just a minute," the voice barked again.

After several seconds, the gate opened. She drove through the tree line and felt her breath catch in her throat when the house came into view. It was more beautiful than she imagined. Just as in the pictures she had seen, the only diminishing factor was the two heavily armed men walking toward her. She pulled the Jeep next to a blue Jaguar and turned off the engine. She had just unhooked her seatbelt when the driver's door was flung open.

The taller of the two men yanked the camera bag from her hands and rummaged through it while the other one proceeded to push her against the car and pat her down. Satisfied that she was okay, he nodded to the taller man to give her camera bag back. The shorter one motioned for her to follow him. Rheyna turned to see the other man inside her Jeep, searching through the glove box.

Without looking at her, the shorter one said, "Mrs. Castrucci is expecting you."

As if on cue, the front door opened and Rheyna instantly recognized Terasa Castrucci from the photos. She held out her hand to Rheyna and smiled warmly.

"Hello, Ms. Moretti. I'm Terasa Castrucci and I would like to start by saying thank you for changing our appointment on such short notice and," she nodded at the retreating figure walking down the driveway, "please accept my apology for their behavior. Personally, I think they're uncalled for."

Rheyna took Terasa's hand in hers and was pleasantly surprised by the firm grip. "You're welcome, Mrs.

Castrucci; please call me Rheyna, and there is no need to apologize." Again, Terasa smiled warmly at her and Rheyna thought she was every bit as lovely as her photo.

She was dressed exquisitely in a lavender floral print skirt suit. A few stray tendrils of hair had escaped from the perfectly coifed hair and hung loosely down around her ears and shoulders. The pearl necklace and earrings she wore added to her beauty. Rheyna had no doubt they were the real thing and very expensive. Terasa Castrucci was regal, yet personable.

Rheyna followed her into the sunken entryway and let out a gasp. She then proceeded to trip up the stairs leading into the foyer, nearly falling on her face. Terasa reached out to steady her and chuckled. Rheyna looked up, feeling like a complete idiot. All this time, she had been so impressed by the outside of the house that she hadn't given the inside a second thought. She hated to admit it, but she was awestruck.

Windows surrounded the entryway, covering the entire area from floor to ceiling. At the base of the entryway steps, a spiraling black wrought-iron staircase wound its way down from the second floor out into the foyer. The foyer had to be at least forty-feet wide in all directions and opened up into the upper level of the house. Italian marble covered the floor and its pattern reminded Rheyna of the color swirl one gets when mixing chocolate syrup with vanilla ice cream.

The room was naturally bright and warm, aided by numerous skylights located along the ceiling. Structural columns—made from hand-carved marble and accented with gold leaf-shaped inlays—framed oversized doorways.

Looking toward the back and upward, she could see where the room protruded outward, as in the photos. What was missing from the photos was the beautiful ornamental railing encircling a walkway, covering the entire second floor. She assumed that a series of hallways branching out from the walkway led to the upstairs bedrooms. From her position, she could see through the doors that opened to three separate balconies overlooking the pool and the ocean. She felt as if she were standing in a museum.

Terasa looped her arm through Rheyna's, snapping her from her thoughts. She led Rheyna into what she described as the sitting room. She poured two glasses of wine, handed one to Rheyna, and then sat down on a couch in front of a large picture window overlooking the bay.

"I want you to know how much I appreciate you altering your schedule for me on such short notice," Terasa said with sincerity.

"It was no trouble at all, Mrs. Castrucci. I was happy to do it." Rheyna glanced around the room with admiration. "This has to be the most beautiful house I've ever been in."

Terasa beamed at the compliment and smiled. "I'm glad you think so and thank you. I did all the decorating myself."

Rheyna held her glass up in a mock toast. "You did a fantastic job."

Just when she thought she couldn't be surprised anymore, Caroline Castrucci walked into the room, causing Rheyna to choke on her wine. Standing before her was the most gorgeous two-legged creature she had ever seen. Caroline wasn't just beautiful—she was narcotically stunning.

Rheyna tried not to stare, but failed miserably. Starting at the bottom of her white slacks, Rheyna's eyes traveled the entire length of Caroline's darkly tanned body before coming back to the area at the base of her throat where a bright silver chain hung just above her breasts. The clothing did little to hide her curvaceous body, and Rheyna wondered if all of her skin was that tan.

Rheyna felt a burning sensation in her cheeks and knew Caroline was watching her. She fought off an uncontrollable urge to shiver. She stared at Caroline's lips and wondered what it must feel like to kiss them.

Caroline's mouth curved into a smile, and Rheyna forced herself to meet her gaze. She found herself looking into the brightest and deepest pair of blue eyes ever created. She was overwhelmed with a physical desire so strong, that it rocked her to the core.

Caroline's right eyebrow shot up, and Rheyna blushed. Caroline's smile grew wider. She looked at Rheyna as if to say, "Do-I-meet-your-approval?" and by the look on Caroline's face, it was obvious that she was enjoying their little exchange. Caroline was the first to break eye contact. She walked over to her mother, bending slightly, and kissed Terasa on the cheek.

Terasa wrapped her arm around Caroline's waist and smiled. "Rheyna, I'd like you to meet my daughter, Caroline."

Caroline met Rheyna's gaze and held it as she walked over. She stopped directly in front of Rheyna. She was so close, Rheyna could smell the sweet fragrance of her cologne. She held her hand out and smiled. "Hello, Rheyna, I'm pleased to meet you."

Rheyna took Caroline's hand in hers and returned the smile. "I'm pleased to meet you, too." What surprised Rheyna was how much she meant those words.

"Where's your father?" Terasa asked, oblivious to the little exchange going on between the two women.

"He's on his way," Caroline answered, still looking Rheyna in the eyes.

"I was thinking that I would like the pictures taken in here. What do you think, Rheyna?" Terasa asked.

"I think it's a great idea," Rheyna answered as she began setting up her equipment, grateful for the distraction, and a few much-needed minutes to get it together. She was fully aware by the rapid beating of her heart that Caroline was still watching her. Something told her that if she looked up, she would see two bright blue eyes laughing at her.

"What in the hell is wrong with me?" she mumbled under her breath as she attached the camera to the tripod. "I'm acting like a schoolgirl with a crush."

She looked up just as Anthony Castrucci appeared in the doorway. His mammoth body swallowed the doorframe. He, on the other hand, looked exactly as Rheyna had pictured. He walked into the room with his right hand man, Sonny Valachi, following closely on his heels.

Sonny nodded his head at Rheyna and took a seat just inside the door.

"Anthony, this is Rheyna Moretti. She's the photographer I hired," Terasa said, looking at her husband.

He smiled and nodded at her. "Ms. Moretti, I'm all yours. Where do you want me?" he asked.

In a nice jail cell, she wanted to say, but bit her tongue. Instead, she said, "Here, in front of the picture window, please." She indicated the seat next to Terasa and then moved behind the couch. She pulled the cord to move the Venetian blind out of the way.

"Caroline, can you stand right here, behind your parents?" she asked before walking back over to her camera. As she bent down to peer through the lens, she had to admit that the three of them made a striking family. Caroline had obviously received the best of each parents' genes.

"Caroline, can you place your right hand on your father's shoulder? That's good, now hold it right there. Okay, smiles, everyone."

Rheyna snapped several photos in succession. "Okay, now, what I'd like to do is get a couple individual shots. I'll start with you first, Mrs. Castrucci, if that's okay with everyone."

"Of course, dear," Terasa answered.

As soon as Caroline and her father moved, Rheyna snapped the photos. "Okay, all done," she said.

Terasa stood and motioned for her husband to take her spot.

"Would you like me to sit in the same spot, Ms. Moretti?" he asked.

"That would be fine, thank you," she answered.

She bent to look through the lens and felt an uneasy feeling in the pit of her stomach. She quickly took the photos and stood upright.

Big Tony got up and turned to Rheyna. "If you don't need anything more from me, Ms. Moretti, I have a business trip to prepare for."

"Nope, that should do it. Thank you, Mr. Castrucci."

Caroline walked over and took a seat on the couch. "I guess it's my turn," she said, smiling at Rheyna.

"Yes, it is," Rheyna, answered. Once Caroline was settled, she snapped off more pictures than she needed. She looked up from the camera. "All done," she said as she began taking her equipment apart.

Out of the corner of her eye, she saw Caroline leave the room and felt a pang of disappointment. She was grateful when Terasa walked over and looped her arm through hers; otherwise, she would have stood there psychoanalyzing herself.

She smiled at the older woman. "When I get back, I'll get the proofs made. It shouldn't take me too long."

"Thank you, Rheyna, I appreciate that," she said as she walked with Rheyna to the front door.

"I'll call you in the morning," Rheyna said. Her thoughts turned to Caroline. "Or I can bring them over to you, if you prefer."

Terasa laid her hand on Rheyna's shoulder. "Are you sure it wouldn't be a bother? I've already put you out as it is."

Rheyna smiled at her. "Nonsense, I have an

appointment in the morning not too far from here. I can just drop them off after I'm done."

"All right, you win, but only if you're positive that it's not too much trouble."

"I promise you, it's not."

"I guess I will see you sometime tomorrow then," Terasa said, smiling at Rheyna. She stood in the doorway and watched Rheyna walk to her car.

Rheyna climbed into her Jeep and tossed the camera bag on the seat beside her. She waved goodbye to Terasa and headed down the driveway.

Later that night, after checking in with Laura, Rheyna sat down at the computer to download the Castrucci photos from the memory card. She loved technology, especially when it worked to her benefit. She loved the touch-up portion of the software, where she could literally erase tattoos or instantly airbrush on a ready-made tan. She opened the software and brought up the Castrucci photos. It took less than an hour to arrange the photos and print out the proofs.

She went back into the kitchen and grabbed a beer from the fridge. She twisted off the cap and took a swig. Her thoughts turned to the bureau and the technology in the field of criminal investigation. She vividly remembered the day Sigh-ock opened for business.

Dedicated by President George Bush in 1998, the twenty-million-dollar, high-tech operations center, located on the fifth floor of the J. Edgar Hoover Building was roughly the size of a football field and measured more than 40,000 square feet. It was specifically designed to accommodate up to 450 additional staff members or agents in the event of an emergency.

The center's main purpose was to provide crisis updates to the FBI using sophisticated computers and communication equipment. When and if a crisis began, the center sent out updates to the top people throughout the FBI, as well as other U.S. government agencies.

The glaring need for an updated center became evident in the summer of 1996 when bureau officials tried to manage simultaneous investigations regarding the explosions at the Summer Olympics in Atlanta, TWA flight 800 over Lockerbie Scotland, and the Saudi Arabia truck bombing at Khobar Towers. It was total chaos trying to handle it all. The crises left the FBI shorthanded on personnel and severely handicapped for space. There weren't enough rooms or telephones, and some of the bureau's best agents were assigned to makeshift desks throughout the hallways, reading confidential documents.

On the day of the dedication, FBI Director Louis J. Freeh introduced reporters to the new facility with a one-time-only tour. At the time of the dedication, the bureau's fastest growing sector was counter-terrorism. Between 1993 and 1998, the number of offices stationed in the U.S. and around the world had more than doubled.

As of January 2008, the FBI Headquarters in Washington provided direction and support to fifty-six field offices, roughly four-hundred satellite offices—commonly referred to as resident agencies—four specialty field installations, and over fifty liaison offices—or Legal Attaches—throughout the world.

The security at Sigh-ock was super tight. When exiting the elevator, the first thing one sees is a huge vault door, similar to the kind found in a bank. To the right, and affixed to the wall, is a keypad that requires a security key fob code for entry.

On each side of the doors are two large, red signs informing visitors that they have now entered a high-security area. Outside the doors, all activity is monitored and recorded by several strategically placed cameras twenty-four hours a day, 365 days a year.

Located directly inside the door and off to the right was a small galley kitchen with a microwave and coffee maker. She smiled as she thought about the first time she passed the room and saw the sign over the microwave that read, "Food and Drinks Prohibited."

She thought back about her illustrious career with the FBI and how it all began around fifteen years ago. She never dreamed about being a cop, let alone an agent with the FBI, and for as long as she could remember, she had wanted to be a photographer.

That all changed the day she met Special Agent Laura Forrest. They had met some sixteen years ago while Rheyna was attending George Washington University. She had seen Laura from a distance off and on the entire time she was in school. Laura was the one who conducted the FBI recruiting drive every semester outside the main entrance to the college.

Secretly, she had thought Laura was too small and too attractive to be a FBI agent. She was sorry to admit that she had a stereotypical view of what an agent should look like, and Laura definitely was not it. Laura stood maybe five-feet-four inches tall with heels on. With blonde shoulder-length hair and green eyes, she was what Rheyna would classify as a sweet piece of eye candy.

Her so-called 'gaydar' had gone into overdrive from the first moment she had seen her. Laura had grinned at her like a Cheshire cat, a grin that said, "I know your secret, too." Although they never spoke until the day she graduated, Rheyna had liked her immediately. After the ceremony, she was busy packing her things to leave campus for the last time, when Laura unexpectedly appeared at her dorm room with a recruiting pamphlet in her hand.

She introduced herself and asked Rheyna if she had

ever given a thought to joining the FBI. Not one to mix words, Rheyna told her, "Thanks, but no thanks."

What Laura said next surprised her: "What's the matter, afraid you can't hack it, don't have what it takes? I guess my instincts were wrong about you." Laura tossed the pamphlet on the bed and walked out of the room without another word, and that was all it took.

Laura had challenged her and she couldn't resist. She told herself at the time that it was just the Taurus in her. She sat down on the bed, leafed through the brochure, and was pleasantly surprised to read that one of the FBI hiring policies included a clause that protected people based on sexual orientation.

Later that night, while sitting in her newly rented efficiency apartment, she logged onto the FBI website and downloaded an application. To her surprise, she was accepted two weeks later.

She had driven by the J. Edgar Hoover building a thousand times without giving it much thought, but on the day she was to report for duty, she stood outside the front entrance marveling at its sheer size. It was enormous and took up a full city block. The building itself was located at 935 Pennsylvania Avenue between Ninth and Tenth Street, with the front of the building facing Pennsylvania Avenue. The building raised seven stories at the front, with a huge overhang at the back that added four more floors.

Laura told her that the building had been designed this way in order to bypass a city ordinance that restricted the height on all new buildings facing Pennsylvania Avenue.

The main reason for this had to do with the major parades that periodically marched down the Avenue. It was a requirement for all new buildings to have open second floors in order to accommodate parade spectators. The exterior part of the building was most interesting and was constructed out of crude concrete slabs. At first glance, they appeared to be riddled with bullet holes. She learned later that the holes were not from bullets, but were actually part of the architecture, designed to give it character. Not only did they look like bullet holes, the building looked unfinished to her, and she was not alone in that thought.

She couldn't recall how many times she had overheard a tourist taking the tour ask, "So, how much longer before the building's completed?" It was a standing joke around HQ, seeing that the building was completed in 1974.

When she entered the building, the first person she saw was Special Agent Laura Forrest. She had been waiting for her and again, she had that shit-eating grin on her face. All Rheyna could do was smile back. After she signed in at the front desk, Laura laced her arm through Rheyna's and took her on a tour of what would be her home for the next fifteen years.

The first area they entered was the visitors' lobby. The room was nicely decorated in neutral color tones and like any lobby, it contained several lounge chairs, a sofa and a large table littered with brochures and pamphlets. To the right of the entrance doors was the obligatory guard's desk where each visitor had to sign in. The wall nearest the entrance had a set of mirrors reaching from floor to ceiling and unbeknownst to visitors, a group of agents, along with security guards, sat on the other side, watching the lounge through two-way mirrors.

Sitting two floors down, directly in the middle of the building—and viewable from the lobby—was an open, outside courtyard with ivy-covered walls. All along the outside perimeter, gardens grew in the spring, producing the most vibrant flowers she had ever seen. Around the gardens, carefully laid pavers led to an enormous, flowing fountain located in the middle of the court, which was surrounded by wrought-iron benches. The benches were a nice touch and provided the ideal place to sit and collect one's thoughts, a place to escape, to get away from all of the terrible things that went on inside the building.

This was where she chose to eat her lunch on most days. She was amazed at the countless animals and birds that made their way in and milled around the flower gardens. They even had a groundhog for a mascot. She understood how the birds and groundhog got in, but to this day, she had no idea how all the others did, since the only way in was up or through the ground. She still tries to figure out where the tabby cat came from.

The colorful garden was very different from the bland colors inside the building. When entering a restricted area, one is slammed back to reality with the dreary décor. Every door is painted charcoal grey and every wall in the building is beige and bare. Not one wall has pictures hanging on them. The building's size and odd design, combined with the fact that everything looked alike, made it too easy to get lost. In fact, employees who worked there for years still did.

After sixteen weeks of training, Rheyna was assigned to the Criminal Investigative Division located on the fifth floor. The CID was by far the largest of the divisions, with seven individual sections, and those sections were responsible for employing eighty percent of all FBI agents.

That division alone investigated approximately seventy-thousand cases per year. For Rheyna, this meant that she was not likely to get bored. Although she didn't get to choose where her assignment would be, she had secretly hoped for Organized or Violent Crime. She was not surprised at all when she ended up spending the first three years of her career in the area, she wanted least— White Collar Crime. Fortunately, for her, the last twelve have been divided between Civil Rights, Counter-Terrorism, Drugs and Investigative Support, and less than forty-eight hours ago, she had been granted her wish: she was finally assigned to Organized Crime.

Chapter 5

Artie looked at the final disconnect notice for the water bill. He ripped it into little pieces and tossed it in the wastebasket. He turned his computer monitor around and started tapping on the keyboard. A light knock on his door caused him to stop.

"Come in," he said, quickly switching off the monitor.

Edwards opened the door and poked his head in. "I saw your light on and wasn't sure if you were still here."

"Yeah, I'm just wrapping up a few things before I head home."

"Okay, well, don't be too late. We have a big day tomorrow."

"Don't I know it," Artie said with a smile. "I'll see you tomorrow, bright and early."

"Good night, Artie," Edwards said before pulling the door closed.

Artie turned the monitor back on and continued tapping the keys. He ripped off a piece of paper, jotted down the information from the screen, and shut his computer down. He crammed the paper in his pocket and took his coat off the door hook.

Cecil Titus looked up from his newspaper. "Hiya, Artie. What brings you down to my neck of the woods at this late hour?" Cecil managed to ask between bites of a salami sandwich.

"Hello, Cecil. I just have a few things to check out before I head on home."

Cecil pressed the button to allow Artie behind the steel door separating the small lobby area from the evidence room. Artie slid his ID badge into the card reader, walked through the caged door, and shut it behind him. He pulled the door open that led to the evidence property warehouse.

"Let me know if you need any help!" Cecil yelled just before Artie disappeared between a set of wooden shelves used to hold the evidence bags and boxes.

Artie glanced at the numbers on the outside compartments and carefully navigated his way around the hordes of bicycles and other large items that littered the aisles. He scanned the metal ID tags at the top of each rack and turned down an aisle marked with the letters D through L. He stopped in front of several brown evidence bags and pulled the paper out of his pocket. He double-checked the numbers to verify that they matched. He reached into the pigeonhole and pulled out a brown bag. He glanced around and then nervously unrolled the lip of the bag and peered inside.

Cecil wadded up the wrapper, took aim, and lobbed the ball at the trashcan located several feet from his desk. "Ah, shit," he said as the paper ball clipped the rim and skidded a few feet away. He picked it up, and dropped it in the can. He inserted his ID badge into the card reader, let himself though the caged door, and headed down the first aisle. He walked in a zigzag fashion, glancing up each aisle as he weaved in and out between the rows of shelving racks that looked more like a maze than an evidence room.

"Ah, there you are," he said, spotting Artie at the end of the row. "I wanted to show you the picture of my new granddaughter, Chloe," he said, pulling his wallet from his back pocket.

Artie quickly closed the bag and shoved it back into the cubbyhole. He turned and walked toward Cecil.

Cecil took the photo out of his wallet and handed it to Artie. "Isn't she just the prettiest thing you ever seen?"

Artie glanced down at the small baby covered in pink. "Yes, Cecil, she is."

Cecil beamed with pride, smiling from ear to ear. "I'm telling you, Artie, this one's gonna be a real looker when she grows up." Cecil took the photo back and carefully inserted it into his wallet. He winked at Artie. "Probably gonna have to beat 'em off with a stick."

"I think you may be right," Artie said with a nervous laugh.

Cecil nodded toward the area where he saw Artie standing. "Did you find what you were looking for?" he asked.

"Oh, uh, yeah, uh, I just needed to see a document, that's all."

"So you don't need to check anything out, then?"

Artie shook his head. They walked up the aisle and back through the caged door. Artie opened the door to the lobby. "It was nice to see you, Cecil."

Cecil grinned and flopped back down in the chair behind his desk. "Come back and chat when you have a little more time."

"I will," Artie said and pulled the door closed.

Chapter 6

Fresh out of the shower and fully dressed for the day, Rheyna went back into the kitchen. She tucked the morning newspaper under her arm and then wedged a half-eaten bagel between her teeth. She grabbed her cell phone off the counter with her right hand and carefully picked up her cup of coffee with her left. She slowly made her way toward the patio door and, using her knee, slid it open.

Damn, I'm good, she thought as she set the cup of coffee down on the table without spilling a drop. She pulled the newspaper from under her arm and dropped it, along with her cell phone, next to the coffee cup. She sat down on the lounger and leaned back, propping her feet up on the table while she ate.

She finished the bagel and brushed her hands down the sides of her jeans. She took a couple sips of coffee and then picked up the newspaper, laying it across her lap. *Not only am I good, I'm nuts,* she thought as she glanced again at the article just below the headline. She grabbed her cell phone, flipped the lid back, hit the speed dial for Laura, and waited for her to pick up.

"Hey, girl, I didn't expect to hear from you this early. What gives?" Laura asked, stifling a yawn.

"Good morning to you, too, sunshine. Did I wake you?" Rheyna asked, jokingly.

"It's seven in the morning. You know damn well you did, and this better be good," Laura kidded back. "So what's up?" she asked.

"You're gonna think I'm nuts, but I've been thinking—"

"Oh, God no, say it isn't so," Laura teased.

"Anyway, since I took this assignment, I've been racking my brain to find a way to really get in with the Castrucci's and I don't just mean as a photographer or trying to plant a bug or two," she said, then added, "By the way, I'm ignoring your comment, in case you haven't figured that out."

Laura laughed. "I kinda got that. Okay, you've got my attention. I'm listening."

"You know how Caroline is a Veterinarian and—"

"Oh, so you're calling her Caroline now?" Laura interrupted.

Rheyna laughed. "Will you please stop and let me get this out, already?"

"Okay, okay. I quit. I promise. Go ahead."

"I'm gonna get a dog," Rheyna said bluntly before Laura could interrupt again.

"Excuse me? Did I just hear you say you're getting a dog?"

It was Rheyna's turn to smile. "Yep, you heard me correctly," she said, looking at the newspaper article and the photo of Caroline standing in front of the Haven Veterinarian Clinic. Before Laura could say anything, she continued, "There's a pet adoption today at Caroline's clinic and I'm gonna drop by and get one."

"You're right. I think you're nuts. Nuts, but brilliant."

"I don't know about the brilliant part. By the end of the day, I may just end up being a new pet owner in the state of California and nothing else."

"I don't know. Either way, I think a dog might be good for you."

"Well, I'll give you a call tonight and let you know."

"Okay, Rheyna, be careful and stay safe."

"I will," Rheyna said and hung up the phone. She took

the newspaper and her cell back inside. She stopped at the counter, grabbed her keys, the manila envelope with the Castrucci proofs, and headed out the door. She figured she might as well head for downtown Palo Alto. She needed to update her wardrobe and a glance at the clock confirmed that most of the stores were probably open by now. She would do some early shopping, maybe grab a bite to eat, and then head over to the clinic to get a dog before finally making her way back to the Castrucci estate to drop off the proofs to Terasa.

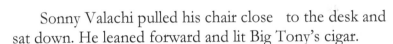

Sonny Valachi pulled his chair close to the desk and sat down. He leaned forward and lit Big Tony's cigar.

Big Tony inhaled deeply and blew out several smoke rings in succession. He pushed several haphazardly stacked papers off to the side and looked at the manila folder lying on the desk in front of him.

Printed neatly across the top tab were the words: *Rheyna Moretti*. He flipped open the cover and picked up a photo of Rheyna coming out of her beach house. "You were right, she's definitely a looker, and she's Italian to boot. Terasa did real good with this one," he said, tossing the photo off to the side.

Sonny picked up the photo and looked at it. "Yeah, in my younger days, I might have tried to tap that," he said with a laugh.

Big Tony flipped through the documents in the folder. He looked at Sonny. "What about a husband?"

Sonny shook his head.

"Boyfriend?"

Again, Sonny shook his head. "I've had Henry on her since you gave me her name and there's nothing. Hell, just this morning, he called, begging off. He said all she does is shop and hang out at the beach and that she's boring him to death."

Big Tony held up a copy of Rheyna's arrest record. He skimmed over the document and chuckled. "It seems she was quite the little hoodlum as a kid."

Sonny nodded in agreement. "Yeah, a couple minor skirmishes here and there, some vandalism and petty theft, but nothing too serious."

Big Tony picked up two document papers clipped together. "It's too bad about her parents, though," he said, looking at the death certificates. He put them in the folder and closed the cover. "What else you got?" he asked.

"From everything we could find, she seems to be on the up and up. Moved here about two months ago, bought the beach house. She got a degree in photography and started her own freelance business not long after graduating." Sonny paused to light a cigarette. "From what I could tell, she has no other family. Both her parents were only children and after they died, she was pretty much left alone."

Big Tony pulled open his lap drawer and tossed the folder in it. "Okay, you can go ahead and pull Henry off," he said, pushing the drawer closed. He took another drag from his cigar. "Did you take care of my other little problem?"

"Yeah, it's done, but I'm worried. I know they're gonna figure out she was preggers."

Big Tony's eyebrows shot up. "So?"

"It's only a matter of time before they tie her back to you, Tony."

"Like I said, so what if they do? Charlene was a whore. Hell, I don't know that it was mine and for that matter, we don't even know if she was pregnant at all."

"And what if she was telling you the truth and the baby was yours?"

"If you did your job, I don't have anything to worry

about, now do I?"

Sonny shook his head.

Big Tony tapped the end of his cigar in the ashtray. "How'd it go on Friday?"

Sonny frowned.

"The girl, I'm talkin' about the girl."

"Oh, yeah, she was a real pro. You'll be pleased with the results."

Big Tony smiled. "She worth fifteen K?"

"More like twenty-five," Sonny grinned.

"Good, good. Our Hong Kong clients will be thrilled. Maybe we'll charge them seventy-five next time."

Sonny laughed. "Oh, they'd pay more, I'm sure."

"She have any sisters or brothers?"

Sonny shook his head.

"Cousins?"

Sonny busted out laughing. He shook his head.

Big Tony leaned back in his chair. "Pity, we could've had a family affair," he said, blowing smoke toward the ceiling.

Rheyna got out of the Jeep and shut the door. She looked around the Haven Veterinarian Clinic parking lot. She couldn't believe how crowded it was. The lot had definitely reached its capacity. She made her way toward the crowd of people who were milling around in front of the clinic. As she got closer, she could see what was holding their interest—to the left of the doorway, along the whole front of the building, cages of various sizes set in a U-shaped design were stacked on top of each other. Each cage contained an animal as diverse as the size of the cage. She walked past a row that had a monkey, several different colored rabbits, a couple guinea pigs, and a very large box turtle.

Ah, this is what I am looking for, she thought as she walked up to the small cages. She walked slowly down the row, looking at the different breeds of puppies. She stopped in front of the last one. It contained a small black puppy with a cast on its right front leg. The little pup was curled up in a tiny ball, sound asleep and snoring louder than any human Rheyna had ever heard. She looked at the card stuck in the slot. It said the puppy was a female Labrador Retriever, approximately ten-weeks old, and could be adopted for $125.00. The card went on to say the price covered the cost of the puppy's shots, an electronic ID chip, and a $50.00 gift certificate toward spaying/neutering fees.

Rheyna stuck her fingers through the cage, scratching the pup's head. The puppy opened her eyes and then stretched her front legs out, arching her little body like a cat. She yawned while simultaneously licking Rheyna's fingers. Rheyna smiled. "Hey, girl," she said, continuing to rub the pup's head.

"She's a real cutie, don'tcha think?"

Rheyna jumped, startled by the voice coming from just over her shoulder. She felt her pulse quicken. She turned to face Caroline and smiled. "I think she's adorable." She nodded at the pup's leg. "Why does she have a cast?"

"Because her leg is broken in two places and she has a pin holding her kneecap in place."

"That must have hurt like hell. How'd it happen?"

Caroline opened the cage door. She reached in and caressed the side of the pup's face. She turned to look at Rheyna. "I think she had a run-in with a car and the car won. I found her lying against a curb not far from here."

Rheyna frowned. "So the person who hit her just left her there?"

Caroline nodded. "Unfortunately, it seems that way."

Rheyna shook her head. "People can be such

assholes," she blurted without thinking.

Caroline smiled at her. "Yes, they can."

Rheyna looked back at the puppy. "I'll take her," she said, turning to Caroline.

Caroline eyed Rheyna curiously, crossing her arms against her chest. "Most people don't adopt wounded puppies. From my experience, they're usually the last to go."

Rheyna laughed at the expression on Caroline's face. "Well, I guess you can say that I'm not most people."

Caroline smiled at her and nodded at the pup. "I can see that, but are you really sure about her? A pet is a lot of responsibility, especially one with a broken leg."

It was Rheyna's turn to smile. "I thank you for your concern, but I've already made up my mind. I've always wanted a dog. It's not the way I pictured getting one, but it'll work."

"All right, you win." Caroline smiled as she grabbed the cage card out of the slot. "Let's go get the paperwork taken care of and then I'll get a tech to help get your new puppy into the car."

Artie snapped off the bowtie and tossed it on the kitchen table, along with his briefcase. He picked up the stack of mail on the counter and tossed it next to his briefcase. He opened the refrigerator door and glanced inside. He shook his head at the bare contents and then grabbed a pack of lunchmeat from the crisper—a cold sandwich again. *What else is new?* he thought to himself as he rummaged through the cupboard for a loaf of bread. He pulled out a chair and sat down at the table. He tossed a few pieces of ham between the bread and flipped through the mail. He tore open the letter from the

Mortgage Company.

He looked at the typed form letter. They were now three months in arrears on the mortgage payment and if the bank didn't receive the back payments within one week, they would begin foreclosure proceedings. He took out a hanky and wiped sweat from his brow. He opened the next letter and shook his head as he read the final disconnect notice from the phone company. He pushed it aside and opened the next one.

"Artie, is that you?" Alice yelled from the bedroom. "Is that, is that you?" she asked again.

He pushed away from the table and walked down the hallway toward their bedroom. He stopped in the doorway and looked at the disheveled woman lying spread eagle across the bed in her bra and panties and wondered what happened to the beautiful woman he had married. He walked over to the side of the bed and looked down at the nightstand littered with whiskey bottles and an ashtray overflowing with cigarette butts.

Reaching down, he angrily snatched up a pile of gambling tickets. "What the hell is this, Alice?" he asked, slinging the ticket stubs at her. "You promised me you would stop gambling!" he yelled, his voice shaking with anger. He walked over to the desk sitting against the wall and jerked the computer plugs out of the receptacle. "That's the final straw."

"What, what are you doing?" she asked, pulling herself upright to look at him.

He ripped the computer monitor off the desk. "I'm taking this damn thing out of here!" he yelled.

"Artie, please don't be like this!" she cried.

He stopped in the doorway and turned to look at her. "I can't take this anymore, Alice. I don't know what else to do."

She fell off the bed and shakily got to her feet and followed him into the kitchen. "But you can't take my computer," she whined.

When he set the monitor on the table, she grabbed him by the shirt. He pushed her hand away. "I can take it and I will," he said and headed back to the bedroom with her on his heels. He jerked the hard drive out from under the desk. "I'm leaving on an assignment, I'll be gone awhile, and this is the only way I can be sure you won't be gambling."

She followed him back to the kitchen. "I don't, I don't really gamble that much, snookims." She made a halfway attempt to bat her eyes in what was supposed to be a seductive fashion.

He set the hard drive next to the monitor. "Like the hell you don't. Have you looked at our bills, Alice? Well, have you?" She started to sob. "And you can quit the crying crap. It doesn't work anymore."

She dropped down to her knees and leaned against the stove. "But I'm sick, Artie, I need help."

He knelt down on the floor next to her and smoothed the stringy hair back from her face. His expression softened as he looked at her. "I know you are, honey," he said, pulling her into his arms. "I don't know how to help you anymore, Alice. I've tried. You need professional help, honey. You need to be in a treatment center where they can help you, but you have to want it and right now, you don't. You don't even think you have a problem half the time."

She angrily pushed him away from her. "I'm not as bad as you make me out to be!" she yelled.

He stood up and looked down at what was once his beautiful wife. He shook his head. "Look at you, just look at you. When was the last time you combed that rat's nest mess of hair? When was the last time you took a bath and put on clean clothes?"

"That's not fair," she pouted.

"Not fair? Not fair?" His look was incredulous. "I'll

tell you what's not fair, Alice. You maxing out our credit cards on that damn online gambling site and drinking yourself into oblivion. Do you have any idea how much money we owe because you think you're not that sick—how about $275,000 dollars' worth?" He pointed at the bills lying on the table. "In that stack is two final disconnect notices and a letter of foreclosure on our home. I've worked my ass off for our home and now I don't even know if it'll be here for me when I get back."

Alice sobbed as she pulled her legs up and curled herself in a fetal position on the floor. "I'm sorry, Artie. I promise I'll get help."

"Either you get help while I'm gone, Alice, or I'm filing for divorce when I get back. I have packing to do." He stepped over her and headed back to the bedroom.

Caroline and Rheyna stepped to the side to allow the vet tech to lay the puppy on the back seat. Rheyna thanked him and slowly pulled the seatbelt across the pup's midsection. She took extra care to avoid hitting her front leg and clicked the belt in place.

"She won't break, you know," Caroline laughed.

Rheyna shut the door. "I know," she said, walking toward the front of the car with Caroline by her side. Rheyna climbed into the seat and closed the door. "But I don't want to take any chances," she said through the open window.

Caroline leaned against the door. She nodded at the envelope lying on the passenger seat. "I can take those to Mom if you like."

"I would really appreciate that," Rheyna said, reaching over to pick up the envelope. She handed it to Caroline through the window.

Rheyna glanced at the puppy lying on the back seat. She turned back to Caroline. "Do you make house calls, by any chance?" she asked sheepishly. Seeing hesitation on Caroline's face, she quickly added, "I'd be willing to pay you, of course. I've never had a pet before and with her leg and—"

"You don't have the foggiest idea what you're doing, do you?" Caroline interrupted.

"Am I that obvious?" Rheyna asked, making a pouting face with her lips.

Caroline placed her hands on her hips. "I think you're more pitiful than the pup is," she said, shaking her head.

Rheyna raised her eyebrows. "Does that mean your answer is 'yes'?"

Caroline grinned at her. "How about I give you a call first and then we can discuss my house calling fees."

Rheyna reached over and flipped open the glove box. She pulled out one of her business cards and handed it to Caroline. "Thank you," she said as she put the key in the ignition.

Later that night, after getting the puppy settled on the couch, Rheyna took a bottle of beer, along with her cell and stepped outside on the patio. She took her normal seat on the lounger and hit the speed dial. On the fourth ring, Laura picked up.

"Should I congratulate California's newest pet owner?" Laura asked, chuckling.

"Yes, ma'am, you should," Rheyna answered, smiling from ear to ear.

"So tell me, did it work?"

Rheyna took a swig of beer. "Oh, it worked all right— better than I thought it would—and Dr. Caroline is going to call me tomorrow so we can discuss her services."

"And why on earth would you need her services?" Laura teased.

"This is where the brilliant-but-nuts part comes into play. You see, not only did I get a dog, I got one with a broken leg and get this, she's still wearing a cast." As soon as the words left Rheyna's mouth, she wished she could take them back. The feelings of guilt blindsided her, guilt for using the puppy in this manner and guilt for taking advantage of a beautiful and caring woman.

The sound of Laura's voice snapped her out of her thoughts. "Yep, I have to agree. You are definitely nuts, but brilliant."

"Well, I better get off of here. It's about time for my new pup to eat dinner," she lied.

"Okay, give me a call tomorrow."

"Will do."

"Oh, and Rheyna…"

"Yeah?"

"Good job."

"Thanks. I'll talk to you tomorrow," she said and hung up the phone, relieved to end the conversation. She didn't want to think about what she had done, and although she knew she was just doing her job, it still didn't make her feel any better.

Chapter 7

Just as Caroline had predicted, the new puppy had slept the entire first day and only went to the bathroom after Rheyna carried her outside. Today, the little fur ball was a little more active. She let Rheyna know just how hungry she was when she chomped down on the fried egg sandwich in her hand.

Rheyna tore off a small piece and handed it to her. She then made a mental note to go out later and get some proper puppy food. She wasn't sure exactly what she needed, since she had never had a pet in her life, but she was sure the store clerk would be able to fix her up.

Even with a broken leg, her new pup was a bundle of energy and bounced off the couch. She hobbled over to the fridge where Rheyna had placed a water bowl. She raised her head and looked at Rheyna, oblivious to the amount of water spewing all over the floor from her jaws. Rheyna got up off the couch and grabbed a rag from the counter. She bent down to wipe up the floor when the phone rang. She looked at the caller ID and felt her heart race. She answered it on the second ring.

"Hi, Caroline," Rheyna said into the receiver, her voice shaking a little.

"Am I disturbing you?" Caroline asked, not seeming to notice.

"Not at all," Rheyna answered. She sat down on the couch and smiled as the puppy jumped up beside her.

"I'm calling as promised to see how you and the puppy are doing."

"Right now, she's being a good girl. If you had called an hour ago, I wouldn't have said the same thing. I think everyone but her knows she has a broken leg."

Caroline laughed. "You're in for a real treat. Just you wait. When she gets that cast off, you won't be so quick to call her a good girl. Seriously, though, how are you holding up?"

"I'm doing well, thank you, and I think I'm going to like having her around."

"Good. That's what I like to hear. Before I forget, I also wanted to tell you Mom loved the photos. She chose three from the proof sheet you sent."

Rheyna thought about Terasa and smiled. "Good, I'm glad she liked them."

"Well, I guess I'll let you go now."

Rheyna didn't want to hang up the phone. If she were honest with herself, a part of her was disappointed that the puppy was the real reason Caroline called. She thought about her motives for getting the puppy. "Aren't you forgetting something, Doc?"

"I am?" Caroline asked.

"House calls, fees, feeling sorry for me, etcetera. Any of this ring a bell?"

Caroline busted out laughing. "I'm not sure, but I think something may seriously be wrong with you."

"Does this mean you'll be my puppy's personal physician?"

"On one condition."

"And that is?"

"Instead of paying me, you take the money and donate it to the pet adoption fund at my clinic."

Rheyna let out a melodramatic sigh. "Is that all? Here, I thought you were gonna demand my first born."

"That comes with the next pup you adopt."

It was Rheyna's turn to laugh. "Okay, Doc. You got a deal."

"In that case, I will see the two of you tomorrow morning, if you're open."

"I have an appointment at eight, so any time after that is good," she lied.

"See you tomorrow then," Caroline said before hanging up.

Rheyna looked down at the puppy sleeping peacefully in her lap. She felt bad about using her—actually, only a small part of her felt bad. The logical side of her brain was forcing her to think about her true motive. Was she only doing this to find a way into the Castrucci household, or was she reacting to her own emotions? She ignored the last question. For God's sake, she was a FBI agent. If anyone knew what that job entailed, she did. She tried to push all thoughts from her mind that didn't pertain to her job. It was her job to gather as much Intel and evidence against Anthony Castrucci in order to put him behind bars. If it meant using his daughter for whatever means she deemed necessary, than that was exactly what she was going to do.

She got up from the couch and decided to take the puppy outside for a small walk. She stepped out on the deck, and an overwhelming pang of guilt rocked her. There was no need for her to question the feeling. She knew where it was coming from. She hadn't been attracted to any other woman since Jenny, and her mind was telling her the attraction she felt for Caroline had absolutely nothing to do with her job. Now faced with this truth, her logical side was working overtime, trying to convince her that the attraction was purely physical. She knelt down to ruffle the puppy's fur and for the first time in three years, she couldn't stop the tears from streaming down her face.

In a small apartment located in the downtown section

of Palo Alto, the recording tapes were spinning. Unbeknownst to the occupants inside Pal Joey's Bar and Grill, the Pandora's Box surveillance team was across the street, listening in on their conversation.

Mafia Don Carlos Massino's Consigliere, Roberto Failla, and Foot Soldier Mike *Little Mikey* Labruzzo sat at a corner table in the back of the bar with Castrucci's Soldier, Henry Venutti. Henry reached inside his jacket pocket, pulled out a thick envelope, and handed it to Roberto.

Roberto scowled deeply, his eyebrow raising as he opened it and peered inside. He skimmed his fingers across the thick wad of cash and then tossed it in his briefcase. He leaned menacingly over the table toward Henry. "Where the fuck is Sonny?"

Henry cowered back further into the seat. "I told ya, he had other business to tend."

"What the fuck is more important than this?" Roberto demanded.

Henry took a deep breath. "The Feds, that's what. He's had a tail the past couple days and decided to lay low."

Roberto jabbed his stubby finger at Henry and leaned in closer. "You tell him the Feds will be his least fucking problem if he doesn't clean up the Goddamn motherfucking mess over in L.A." Roberto stood up and gathered up his briefcase. He tossed several bills on the table. "You tell Anthony to plug the fucking leaks, capische?"

Henry slid out of the chair and followed him toward the front door.

Roberto turned to Henry. "You tell him the problem better be fixed before he leaves on business."

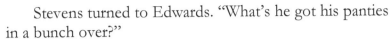

Stevens turned to Edwards. "What's he got his panties in a bunch over?"

Edwards reached across the table and turned the volume knob down.

"Two nights ago, we intercepted one of their boat shipments and confiscated over a hundred pounds of pure heroin," Artie said before Edwards had a chance to answer.

Over near the window, Laura continued peering through the camera lens. She snapped several photos of the men standing on the sidewalk. She stepped back from the camera and turned to Edwards. "From the sound of it, they definitely know that we're getting' inside information."

Edwards nodded in agreement. "And that makes it all the more dangerous for our informants. Do we know where he's going yet?"

Laura shook her head. "Nope, but they rescheduled the photo shoot with Rheyna because of it."

Stevens walked over to look out the window. "Our informant in L.A. thinks the shit's about to hit the fan. Massino wants his answers, yesterday." He paused to light a cigarette and took a drag before continuing. "We also intercepted a conversation between Roberto and one of his soldiers. Our Intel was dead on—Massino is demoting Castrucci for his insubordination."

Laura raised her eyebrows. "Wow, so not only is he being passed over as Anastasia's replacement, he's about to become a grunt."

Edwards rifled through the stack of papers lying on top of the conference table. He turned to look at Stevens. "We get the warrant for the wire tap yet?"

Stevens shook his head. "Nope, should be anytime now."

Edwards turned to Laura. "When is your next contact with Rheyna?"

"Nine-thirty tonight."

Edwards stood and pulled his jacket off the chair. "Okay. I'm flying back to Washington tonight to meet with the Deputy Director and Ron. In the meantime, Laura, you call me immediately if anything unexpected happens."

Chapter 8

Rheyna took a deep breath and pulled the door open. A large brown paper bag and a tight and sexy, stonewashed pair of Levi jeans greeted her. Caroline slowly lowered the bag from in front of her face and smiled at Rheyna.

"Well, hello there," Rheyna said.

"Hi, I hope I'm not too early," Caroline said, looking a little unsure of herself.

"Are you kidding? Please come in." Rheyna moved out of the way to let her through the door.

Caroline followed Rheyna into the kitchenette and set the bag on the counter. "I brought some things for the puppy. I hope you don't mind."

"Yep, I mind. I want you to leave and take everything back, right this very second." Rheyna laughed at the expression on Caroline's face. "I'm just kidding. Hell no, I don't mind. I was planning to go out later to pick up a few things for her and you just saved me a trip. So thank you and please tell me how much I owe you."

Caroline smiled at her. "First off, you're welcome and we can just add it to your donation and has anyone ever told you that you might be a little warped?"

"Personally, I think you have to be warped to survive in this world of ours. Makes things a little easier to stomach," Rheyna answered honestly.

Caroline started to respond, but the puppy got her attention. She limped happily over to Caroline with her tail wagging fifty times a minute. Caroline knelt down to her level and lovingly ruffled her fur. "She sure looks a lot better than the last time I saw her."

"Yeah, she's a real cutie. I think she and I are gonna get along just fine."

Caroline stood and crammed her hands into the front pocket of her jeans. "Have you thought of a name for her yet?" she asked.

Rheyna thought about it for a moment and then realized she hadn't given it a second thought. "No, I've been calling her puppy."

Caroline smiled as the puppy nudged her hand, wanting more rubbings. "You do know that you just got yourself a new best friend here and that she will love you with no questions asked?"

For some reason, Rheyna got the feeling Caroline was making the comment more to herself than to her. *I really, really like this woman,* she thought as she watched Caroline hug the puppy tightly against her chest.

Caroline looked up at Rheyna and smiled. "What do you think about Annie?"

"Annie?" Rheyna asked, because she only heard part of the question.

"You know, for her name."

Rheyna liked the sound of it. "I think Annie is the perfect name for her."

"Okay, then—Annie it is," Caroline said as she walked over to the counter. She opened the bag she brought and started pulling things out, laying them on the counter.

There were several cans of puppy food, a matching navy blue collar, harness, and leash, a couple of small bags containing tiny dog biscuits, and a rubber toy in the shape of a newspaper.

Annie must have known the items were for her. She limped over to Caroline and stood up on her back legs with her front paws resting against Caroline's legs.

Caroline reached down and scratched Annie's ears. "She is just too adorable," she said as Annie's tongue hung out the side of her mouth. She looked at Caroline with big, brown, expectant eyes. Caroline handed Annie the rubber newspaper. She and Rheyna laughed when Annie chomped down on the toy and it squeaked so loud, it caused her to jump several inches off the floor. She bit down on it repeatedly before trotting off to the couch with it hanging from her mouth. She looked at Rheyna and Caroline and chomped down again.

Caroline cringed at the sound and smiled. "I hope you don't end up hating me for that."

Rheyna wanted to say, "I don't think there is anything you could possibly do to make me hate you." Instead, she said, "I'll let you know in a couple days." Rheyna opened the fridge and pulled out a pack of ground chuck. "Will you stay for lunch?" she asked and immediately saw hesitation on Caroline's face. "Please, Caroline? It's the least I can do for your help with Annie."

"Since you asked so elegantly, how can I possibly refuse?"

"Do you like hamburgers?" Rheyna asked as she began the gross task of converting the meat into patties.

"One of my favorites, if you add cheese."

"Okay, then, it's settled—cheese it is," she said, thrilled at the thought of spending time with Caroline. She told herself that it was all in a day's work and that having Caroline stay for lunch to eat a hamburger was just a tiny needed piece of puzzle in the grand scheme of things. She intentionally ignored the little voice in her head and tossed the patties on a plate. She pulled a spatula out of the drawer and flung open the fridge door. She grabbed a pack of cheese slices and slid open the patio door.

Caroline, along with Annie, followed her out onto the deck. She lit the gas grill and tossed on the patties. Caroline, to her amusement, had already made herself comfortable. She had taken off her shoes and was sitting on the glider with her legs tucked up under her. Rheyna tried not to stare, but found it increasingly hard. "Would you like something to drink? A glass of wine, maybe?" she asked.

Caroline used her hand to shield her eyes. She smiled warmly. "A glass of wine would be nice, thank you."

Rheyna went back inside and pulled open the cabinet door. As she went to grab the glasses, she noticed her hands were trembling. She set the glasses down and leaned against the counter, trying to quiet her nerves. What is wrong with me? How in the hell am I going to pull this off if I can't handle being alone with her for more than two minutes? She took a deep breath and opened the fridge. She needed to calm down and get it together. She grabbed the bottle of Moscato. She used a corkscrew to pop out the cork and then took the glasses along with the bottle of wine outside.

Caroline graciously held them while Rheyna poured. Caroline raised her glass in the air for a toast. "To Annie, may she have a long, healthy life."

"To Annie and … to me surviving the squeaker," Rheyna said, clanking her glass against Caroline's glass. They both laughed when Annie, as if on cue, bit down on her new toy.

Sonny and Henry watched Big Tony meticulously unwrap and then light the illegal Cuban cigar. He blew several smoke rings into the air. The three of them were sitting at the table, having drinks by the pool, discussing business. Big Tony was agitated, and that was not a good thing, as they very well knew. When things didn't go right, it was the ones closest to him who felt the wrath.

"How much did they get this time?" he asked, directing the question at Sonny.

"Hundred pounds," Sonny answered without hesitation.

Big Tony slammed the glass of iced tea down on the table, spilling half the contents. "I thought you plugged the fucking leak!" he spat at the two men. The men grew silent as Esther approached the table with a pitcher to refill their glasses. Big Tony waited for her to leave before continuing. He turned to Henry. "Get me some fuckin' answers. I wanna know who the backdoor motherfucker is! You hear me, Henry?"

"Yes, sir," Henry answered as he scooted his chair away from the table.

The waves breaking along the edge of the sand created a soothing and romantic swooshing sound, and Rheyna found herself completely at ease. The sun was beginning to set over the ocean, sending a pallet of red, yellow, and orange hues cascading across the water's surface. The colors reflected back into a sky dotted in various shades of blue, creating a light purple haze across the puffy clouds. The effect was breathtaking and was only dampened by the low drone of boat engines as scores of skiers zipped up and down the coast.

Caroline took a sip of wine. "It's so quiet and peaceful. I wish it was like that at home, but I know it's just wishful thinking on my part. I honestly can't remember a time when someone wasn't at the house and to tell the truth, I don't understand how my mom takes it."

"Why don't you get your own place?" Rheyna asked.

"I will eventually, but for now, Mom wants me to stay until she knows for sure that Haven is a success."

"Well, I'd say from the looks of things, your clinic seems to be doing pretty well."

"I know it is and so does Mom. I think she's just using it as an excuse to keep me home. What about you?" Caroline asked. "I've done nothing but sit here and talk about me."

"What do you want to know?"

Caroline took another sip of wine. "Are you from California?"

Rheyna shook her head. "No. I moved here from Chequotah, Oklahoma about two months ago."

"Why here?"

Rheyna shrugged. "I guess I was tired of the cold and wanted to live in a place where the temperature didn't drop below thirty." Rheyna recited the words she had rehearsed umpteen times. She hated lying to Caroline and wanted desperately to change the subject. Out of habit, she glanced at her watch and instantly regretted it.

Caroline stood up and brushed off her jeans. "I'm sorry, I should go. I've probably worn out my welcome."

Rheyna didn't want her to leave. "You don't have to leave."

"Yeah, I do. My dad left for New Jersey today and Mom doesn't like to eat dinner alone."

Rheyna reluctantly followed Caroline to the front door. Caroline turned abruptly, causing Rheyna to lose her balance, and before either of them knew what happened, Rheyna fell against her. The force knocked Caroline back against the door. With her face only inches from Caroline's, Rheyna felt her pulse rate quicken. Her senses were assaulted with the sweet smell of Caroline's perfume, a mixture of honey and lilacs.

"I am so sorry," she managed to get out. She felt Caroline's hands on her forearms, trying to steady her. She felt Caroline's warm breath against her cheek and shivered. They were too close. Rheyna pushed against the doorframe, trying to upright herself.

"You don't need to apologize, Rheyna. I've been told a

time or two that I should add a set of brake lights. Although I'm not sure it would have mattered in this instance." Caroline winked at Rheyna, her eyes twinkling with amusement.

Rheyna was tongue-tied. "Uh … you can visit Annie anytime you like," she managed to say and felt her face flush. It was obvious that Caroline was enjoying Rheyna's discomfort, just as she had the first time they met.

Caroline busted out laughing. She smiled at Rheyna, which only made things worse. Her smile was truly disarming. "I was wondering, um … if you have any plans tomorrow?" she asked.

Rheyna realized happily, that she was not the only one a little unnerved. "I have a photo shoot in the morning," she lied. "But I'm free the rest of the day."

"How would you like to come for dinner? You can bring Annie along, too."

"Are you sure?"

"About you or Annie?"

Rheyna felt her cheeks redden. "Both."

Caroline grinned. "Yes, both of you, silly. Besides, Mom will want to show you the pictures she chose and … she loves dogs."

Rheyna opened the door and walked Caroline to her car. "In that case, how can I possibly refuse an offer like that?" she said, closing Caroline's car door.

Caroline started the engine and rolled the window down. "Dinner's at seven. I'll see you then," she said and then backed out of the driveway.

Rheyna waited for her to disappear from sight and then headed back inside to make her phone call to Laura. She hit the speed dial and slid the patio door pen.

"Well, good evening, Ms. Forrest," she said happily into the phone when Laura answered.

"You sure sound chipper," Laura said.

Rheyna was bubbling with excitement. She told herself

it was because her plan was working so well. If she were honest, she would admit that her excitement had more to do with seeing Caroline again. "I'm having dinner tomorrow night at seven with Caroline and her mother."

"Excellent. You've really outdone yourself this time and Edwards wanted me to tell you that he was impressed."

"Really? Edwards said that?" Rheyna asked, a little shocked.

"Yep, and you know as well as I do that impressing him isn't an easy feat."

"I hear you, but we can't get too excited yet."

"You're being modest, but okay. I'll try to contain myself."

Laura was silent for several seconds, and Rheyna could tell that she was digesting the information. Rheyna also sensed that Laura was thinking along the same lines. This was the opening they were looking for and hoped they would get. They just didn't expect it to happen so soon.

Rheyna was the first to speak. "Caroline said her father left for New Jersey. You know anything about that?"

"Yeah, just a few minutes ago, Stevens told me Artie picked up the tail at Newark's Liberty International Airport."

"Any idea what's going on?"

"Edwards thinks Castrucci's gathering support from the Commission, just as we suspected."

"There's a real surprise. How are we doing on the warrant?"

"Ron is working on it as we speak."

"Okay, I was just thinking that I might be able to get something in place before Castrucci gets back."

"I'll call you as soon as I get word. Talk with you soon."

Rheyna hung up the phone and went inside. She walked back to the camera room, grabbed her bag of toys, and took them into the living room. She knew that if the electronic gadgets in the bag were anything like her camera equipment, she was in for a treat. Thanks to modern-day technology and the creation of microchips, covert surveillance was on a completely different level, and because of this new technology, she didn't have to worry about anyone searching her house. If they did, they wouldn't find anything suspicious.

She emptied the duffel bag on the counter and sorted the items into two piles. She placed the cameras on one side and the listening devices on the other. "Not sure what they thought I'd do with this," she said as she picked up a smoke detector and popped open the lid. She had to look real close to see the infrared camera lens. She thought it would look a little bit out of place on Castrucci's ceiling or walls. She picked up a digital camera, masquerading as a matchbook. It was designed to take a picture each time the flap was squeezed. She looked at several items and decided that the ballpoint pen was the least likely to be discovered. She had no idea where she would leave the listening device. She would just have to wait and see what opportunities arose.

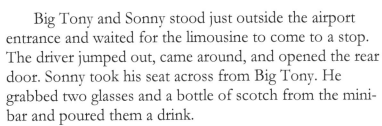

Big Tony and Sonny stood just outside the airport entrance and waited for the limousine to come to a stop. The driver jumped out, came around, and opened the rear door. Sonny took his seat across from Big Tony. He grabbed two glasses and a bottle of scotch from the mini-bar and poured them a drink.

Big Tony lifted the phone off the receiver and punched in a number. "Yeah, we just arrived and should be there within the hour," he said into the phone. "Okay … Got it." He placed the phone back in the cradle and took the glass from Sonny. A smile formed on his lips as he watched the liquid swirl around in the glass. He tilted his head back and emptied the contents in one gulp.

Sonny refilled the glass before taking a drink of his own. "If Carlos catches word of this, we'll both be floatin' in the bay."

Big Tony dismissed his concern with a flick of his hand. "Who's gonna tell him? Not Don Vitto, they all want him out, too." He reached over and patted Sonny on the side of his cheek. "You worry too fuckin' much."

Chapter 9

Rheyna glanced at the clock on the wall. It was nearly six P.M. She had risen early as usual, and to kill time, she and Annie had spent a couple hours sitting out on the deck, her with a book and Annie barking at anything that moved.

Afterward, they sat on the couch, watching TV. In all honesty, she had spent most of the time watching the clock slowly tick the hours away. She didn't think the day was ever going to end. Now that it was time to get ready, she felt a nervous energy.

She decided to take a quick shower and get dressed. Although she had shopped for more than two hours and spent over six-hundred dollars on new clothes, she couldn't make up her mind on what to wear. She stood in front of the closet for at least thirty-minutes, finally choosing a black pair of slacks, and a silk emerald green blouse. She completed the outfit with a pair of ankle-high, black boots that zipped up the side.

She looked at her reflection in the mirror and was pleased with what she saw. The California sun was already working its magic on her skin. She had turned a golden brown, which served to enhance the grayness of her eyes. She ran a comb through her hair and added a little eyeliner. *What am I doing? It's not as if this is a date or anything,* she told herself after deciding to add mascara.

Her cell ringing in the other room prevented her from probing the motive behind her actions any further. She laid the tube of mascara on the sink and ran to answer it.

"I just wanted to let you know that we got the warrant," Laura said on the other end.

"Great. I'll let you know how it goes."

"Don't take any unnecessary risks, okay?"

Rheyna could hear the concern in Laura's voice. "I won't," she said as a way of reassuring her. "If I get the chance, I'll try to get something in place."

"All right, and you call me as soon as you get home."

"I will," she said, and hung up the phone.

She was feeling a little on edge and decided to have a glass of wine. After she drank the last drop, she put the harness around Annie's little body. It had taken her several tries at first to figure out how the contraption worked, but she was now a pro at it.

She snapped the leash on and led Annie out to the Jeep. She settled Annie into the seat beside her, pulled the seat belt through Annie's harness, and buckled her in before securing her own belt.

Within a few minutes, she and Annie had safely arrived at the Castrucci estate. They were immediately granted entry through the gate. When she got to the top of the driveway, she frowned. The same two heavily armed men from her first visit approached the car. She stood there while the same man did his body search. This time, however, she didn't give it a second thought as she watched her Jeep go though the same treatment.

Caroline greeted the two of them at the door. "Hi, you two." She looked Rheyna up and down without any reservation whatsoever. "You look great," she said to Rheyna with a brilliant smile that made Rheyna's heart skip an all-too-familiar beat.

She thinks I look great, Rheyna thought as her senses were assaulted with the smell of Caroline's perfume. She also noticed the smell of something else—food. "Mmm ...something smells good."

"That would be Mom's cooking," Caroline said,

grinning. "When I told her you were coming, she insisted on giving Rosa the night off and cooking you a traditional Italian dinner."

Rheyna and Annie followed her through the foyer and past the room where Rheyna had taken their photos. They entered the second room off to the right.

The walls in the dining room were painted a deep burgundy color three-fourths of the way down. White Wains Coating covered the remainder. It was gorgeous, and Rheyna wouldn't have expected anything less. At the far end of the room, Terasa Castrucci was busy laying out tableware on a Henry the Eighth table that stretched almost the entire length of the wall.

Rheyna counted fourteen chairs and then turned toward the marble-encased gas fireplace. She thought it added a homey feeling to the room. Her eyes fell to the feast lying on the table and her mouth watered. Terasa finished what she was doing and smiled. *Now I know where Caroline gets it from*, she thought as she looked at the older woman.

Terasa walked over to them and took Rheyna's hands in hers. She surprised Rheyna by kissing her on the cheek and then she knelt down to Annie's level, just as Caroline had done. She held her hand out for Annie to smell. "And who do we have here?" she asked, smiling at Annie.

"Mom, this is Annie."

Terasa took Annie's head in both hands and planted a kiss on top of her head. The act of kindness caught Rheyna off guard. It was obvious that Annie was enamored as well. She kissed the older woman back before she had a chance to get out of the way. Terasa laughed and kissed Annie on top of the head again. It thrilled Annie so much, that if she wagged her tail any faster, she was certain to dislocate something.

"Caroline said you were a cutie, and I can see that she's right." She turned to face Rheyna. "I'm glad you decided to come for dinner, Rheyna. I hope you're hungry."

"I'm starving," she said, and she wasn't lying. The smell was killing her.

"I'm glad to hear that. Do you like Italian?"

"It's my favorite."

Terasa walked around the table and took a seat at the far end. She motioned for Rheyna to take the seat to her right. "Caroline, will you please pour us something to drink?"

They waited for Caroline to fill their wine glasses and then Terasa spooned a huge slice of lasagna on each of their plates.

Caroline came around and took the seat next to Rheyna and as she did, her leg slightly brushed against Rheyna's outer thigh. Terasa was speaking, but Rheyna found it hard to concentrate. Thank God for Annie. She wiggled her way in between their legs.

"Caroline tells me that you've only lived here for a couple months," Terasa was saying.

Rheyna nodded, taking a sip of the wine. "I just couldn't take the cold." She took a bite of the lasagna and thought she had died and gone to heaven—it was fabulous.

"What about your family?" Terasa asked.

"I don't have any," she managed to say between mouthfuls of lasagna. "At least none that I'm close to, my parents were killed in a car wreck when I was twenty two," she lied. She felt bad about deceiving this wonderful woman and her daughter, but she had no choice.

"I'm so sorry, you poor dear," Terasa said with sincerity, making Rheyna feel worse, if that was possible.

"Thank you. It's not as bad as it used to be," she lied again. She wanted to change the subject. "This lasagna is delicious, Mrs. Castrucci."

"Please, Rheyna, call me Terasa."

"Are you an only child?" Caroline asked.

Rheyna nodded her head. "Yes, I am."

Caroline's face flushed with embarrassment. "I'm sorry, Rheyna. I invite you for dinner and Mom and I give you the third degree."

"It's all right, I don't mind," she said, although she wanted to talk about something else besides her life. She knew when it came to telling lies, less said was the route to go. Otherwise, the risk increased of adding too much—or worse, leaving something out.

"Do you have any brothers or sisters, Caroline?" Rheyna asked the question, although she knew the answer.

"Nope, I'm an only child, " Caroline answered, then added, "but I'm sure my Dad wishes that I had been a boy. You know, to carry on the family name and all." There was no mistaking the sarcasm in her voice.

"Caroline, you know that your father loves you just the way you are," her mother interjected.

"Loving me and wishing I were his son are two different things."

For the next half hour, they chitchatted about the weather and the new stores that had opened in Palo Alto. Rheyna learned that the Palo Alto stores were Terasa's favorite shopping grounds. Terasa stood and gathered up the dishes. Rheyna stood to help.

"Oh, no you don't, you sit there and relax," Terasa scolded as she continued to clear the table. "Did you two save room for dessert?" she asked.

Caroline's eyebrows shot up. "Did you make what I think you did?"

Terasa nodded her head. "Of course I did."

Caroline grinned. "Oh ... my ... gosh ... her tiramisu is to die for."

"If it's going to kill me, I probably shouldn't have any," Rheyna said half joking, half-serious.

Caroline laughed. "You know what I mean."

"In that case, I guess I have no choice, then," Rheyna said as her thoughts turned to Caroline's comments regarding her dad. "Do you really think your dad wishes you were a boy?" she asked.

Caroline laid her fork down and picked up her wine glass. She thought about the question for a minute before answering. "Yes, especially where the business is concerned."

Rheyna could see the hurt in Caroline's eyes, and it made her dislike Castrucci all that much more. "What does your father do for a living?" she asked, just to see what Caroline would say.

"A little bit of everything." Caroline paused to take a sip of wine. "You know where Palo Alto is, right?"

Rheyna nodded her head.

"He owns a little eatery downtown called Pal Joey's plus several import and export warehouses down by the docks." She was silent for a moment. "I'm sure there are others, some that I don't know about."

Rheyna found it hard to believe that Caroline would be so ignorant as to not know the extent of her father's business dealings. However, it made all the sense in the world to her that Caroline wouldn't be inclined to share that information with a stranger and although Rheyna was having dinner with Caroline and her mother, she was, in effect, still a stranger.

"He sounds like a very busy man. Is that why he's out of town?" she asked.

Before Caroline could answer, Terasa walked in carrying a tray with the most delectable dessert Rheyna had ever seen. Terasa placed a huge plateful in front of her.

"Wow … I think I'm about to put on an extra ten-pounds," she laughed.

Clarence leaned back and stretched his legs lengthwise across the front seat. He skimmed through the pages of the Playboy magazine. The men had been inside the house for almost two hours. *It's a good thing I get paid by the hour*, he thought as he flipped to centerfold layout.

If he were more observant, he would have noticed Artie and another FBI agent sitting in a black sedan parked less than a hundred-yards away. The sedan was the same one that had followed them from the airport to Commission member, Don Vitto Lucchese's lavish estate.

Don Vitto sat next to the warm fire, a cigar between fat, stubby fingers. He contemplated Big Tony's request.

Sitting in the chair across from him, Big Tony continued to plead his case for support. Don Vitto looked at him curiously. His words were slow and measured, his voice thick with an Italian accent. "What you ask Anthony … could be misinterpreted as betrayal … in the strongest sense of the word and punishable by death."

"I don't mean any disrespect to the family, Don Vitto. I only came for your support," Big Tony said.

Don Vitto tapped the end of his cigar against the ashtray. "You do know that it would be a grave mistake to make a move without the full approval of the Commission."

"Damn it! His disrespect to Anastasia is unforgivable to me!" Big Tony's voice raised several octaves. Don Vitto cocked his head sideways and Big Tony immediately regretted the outburst. It was disrespectful, and he had done it without thinking. He patted nervously at his brow with a handkerchief.

Without a word, Don Vitto stood up from his chair,

and Big Tony knew their conversation was over. He got up from his chair and walked over to Don Vitto. He took Don Vitto's hand in his, bent slightly, and kissed the top of it.

"I will discuss your concerns with the other members of the Commission, Anthony," Don Vitto said, dismissing him with a wave of his hand

"Thank you, Don Vitto. That's all I ask."

Don Vitto waited for Big Tony to close the door behind him. He shook his head in disgust and then went over to his desk. He sat down in the oversized leather chair and looked at the phone, contemplating whether he should make the call or not. After a few minutes, he lifted the phone from its cradle.

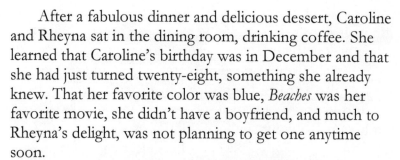

After a fabulous dinner and delicious dessert, Caroline and Rheyna sat in the dining room, drinking coffee. She learned that Caroline's birthday was in December and that she had just turned twenty-eight, something she already knew. That her favorite color was blue, *Beaches* was her favorite movie, she didn't have a boyfriend, and much to Rheyna's delight, was not planning to get one anytime soon.

Rheyna walked around the room, looking at the paintings hanging on the walls. She came to an abrupt stop in front of one in particular. She knew immediately that it was a van Gogh. It was the real deal and probably cost more than she would make in her lifetime. She could feel Caroline watching her as she continued to make her way around the room.

"Would you like to see the rest of the house?" Caroline asked.

"I would love it. I can honestly say that I've never seen

such a beautiful house in my life," Rheyna said as she followed Caroline up the staircase in the foyer. Her assumptions had been correct. All of the bedrooms were on the second floor, all seven of them. They were massive and decorated just as expensively as the downstairs rooms. She hadn't expected anything less. What she didn't expect was to see the spacious bathrooms each had. The enclosed metallic showers were at least seven feet long with jet showerheads strategically placed up and down the walls. She imagined that taking a shower in them would be like taking your body through a car wash.

The two back bedrooms were the best. Each had its very own veranda overlooking the pool and ocean. The view was stunning. She also learned that one of the rooms was Caroline's, which didn't surprise her in the least. The other belonged to her parents.

Before she knew it, they were almost back where they had started. The house was huge. In addition to the upstairs bathrooms, there were also three more located on the first floor. All in all, the house had fifteen rooms, counting the seven bedrooms upstairs, and three down in the finished basement. The foyer alone was the size of Rheyna's entire house. She stopped at a small table just outside the kitchen and picked up a small angelic figurine.

"Mom got that on her trip to Greece a few weeks ago."

"It's beautiful. Does she travel a lot?"

Caroline smiled lovingly as she thought about her mother. "She goes in spurts." She made a waving gesture with her hand. "All of the pieces you see in the house, including the artwork, she's picked up somewhere or another."

Rheyna set the piece back down on the table and continued to follow her. She had made mental notes of the layout, counting each step in her head as she toured the house.

Caroline stopped abruptly outside a room that, oddly enough, had the door closed. Out of all the rooms they had been in, it was the only one she remembered having a closed door. It sat directly across the hallway from the dining room and to the left of the kitchen. Caroline pushed the door open, and Rheyna thought it strange that she didn't go in. She joined Caroline in the doorway.

"This is my dad's cave," Caroline said, acknowledging what Rheyna was thinking. The room was dark and cold, nothing like the rest of the house. The first thing Rheyna noticed was the absence of windows. She looked around the room, not impressed by the décor in the least. Two of the four walls were lined from floor to ceiling with red cherry book shelving.

A small fireplace sat directly in the middle. To the left of the doorway and surrounded by dark leather, wing-backed chairs sat a huge desk. The computer sitting on the edge got Rheyna's attention. She was standing in the doorway of Anthony Castrucci's office. Caroline's description of the room was perfect.

"It's the worst room in the house," Caroline said, pulling the door closed.

"Definitely not my favorite," Rheyna agreed.

They turned to see Terasa coming toward them. "I just finished giving Rheyna the five-cent tour," Caroline volunteered.

Terasa smiled warmly. "Good. I hope she got her money's worth. I'm getting ready to turn in and wanted to tell you girls good night."

Caroline walked up to Terasa and hugged her. "Good night, Mom."

Rheyna smiled at Terasa. "Good night, Mrs. Castru—" Terasa wagged her finger at Rheyna. "I mean Terasa, and thank you for dinner," Rheyna corrected.

"You are most certainly welcome Rheyna, and you will have to come again soon." Terasa turned to leave and stopped. "I left the proofs in the folder by the door and I circled the ones I would like, along with sizes, and quantities."

"I'll get those done as soon as possible and give you a call."

"Or you can just bring them by the next time you and Caroline get together," she said over her shoulder before disappearing down the hallway.

Caroline turned back to Rheyna. "Would you like something to drink?"

"I would love it, but I need to check on Annie first. She's been awfully quiet."

"You go check on her and I'll get those drinks."

Rheyna felt her heart rate quicken as the first surge of adrenaline pumped through her veins. *If she catches me now, it's all over*, she thought. She glanced back out into the hallway and waited for Caroline to disappear from view. She made her way toward Castrucci's office. She turned the knob and pushed the door open, grateful that it didn't squeak. She walked over to the desk, pulled the ballpoint pen from her pocket, and mixed it in with the assortment of pens and pencils sitting next to the computer. To the untrained eye, it was just another fully functioning ink pen with blue ink, and she hoped it would just blend in with the others.

She made her way out the door and had just stepped into the dining room when Caroline appeared with their drinks. She felt another rush of adrenaline mixed with relief when Caroline smiled and held the glass out to her.

"I guess I should drink this and get Annie home," she said, taking the glass that Caroline offered, downing the contents in one large swallow to calm her nerves.

Caroline laughed, her eyebrows rising slightly. "Wow, I guess you really were thirsty."

Rheyna smiled. "I guess I was."

"Sure you don't wanna hang around and watch a

movie?" Caroline asked.

Oh, she wanted to, all right. More than anything, she wanted to hang out with Caroline, but she needed to check in with Laura and bring her up to speed. As much as she didn't want to say it, she did. "Can I have a rain check?" she asked.

"Sure, we can do it some other time."

Rheyna could see that Caroline was disappointed. She needed to get close to Caroline, but she needed time to get her game plan together first. The unexpected attraction she was feeling for Caroline was complicating things. She needed time to think, and being around Caroline made it practically impossible. For crying out loud, she was an FBI agent. She was trained to get close to people without getting emotionally attached to them. She would just have to force herself to stay detached, and she needed to not waste any more time. Time was of the essence and not a luxury she could afford to squander away.

This was her opening, and she needed to make the most of it. She wasn't sure if it was her heart or head doing the reasoning when she smiled at Caroline. "How about you come over to my house tomorrow night for dinner and a movie instead?"

Caroline's lips curved into a smile. "What do you want me to bring?" she asked.

"The movie," Rheyna said, and then snapped the leash onto Annie's harness.

Caroline walked Rheyna to the foyer. She was halfway out the door when Caroline grabbed her arm. Caroline picked up the manila envelope off the entryway table and handed it to her.

"Can't forget these now, can I? I'll see you tomorrow around six," Rheyna said, and then disappeared out the door.

She was on cloud nine as she drove home. The little voice inside her head was trying to convince her that it had nothing to do with Caroline and everything to do with the operation. Her heart was saying that it was the adrenaline speaking, but her brain knew better.

After getting Annie settled in, she did what she did every night—she took her cell phone out on the deck and called Laura. She was surprised how quickly the sound of Laura's voice brought reality crashing back.

"Artie followed Castrucci to the Lucchese estate in Newark. Castrucci was there for over two-hours and just left a few minutes ago. We also have surveillance tapes that picked up a conversation between Sonny Valachi and Thomas Grimaldi. They talked about major changes coming in the family."

"Did they say what kind of changes?" Rheyna asked.

"No. They stopped short, but we think it's because they're all a little worried about being recorded. However, Edwards and Stevens are pretty sure that it's connected with Castrucci's meeting in Newark."

"Well, on a good note, I was able to get one of the bugs planted in Castrucci's office tonight. ID two-six-four Victor. "

"That's great. I'll be sure to let Edwards know."

Rheyna thought about dinner at the Castrucci estate and the dinner date she now had planned for tomorrow with Caroline. She voiced her thoughts out loud to Laura. "The more I think about my plan regarding Caroline, the more I'm convinced that she's the way to go. Caroline is the key to me being on the inside."

"You be careful and don't forget for one minute that Castrucci's a very dangerous man."

She could hear the concern in Laura's voice and spent the next couple of minutes trying to reassure her. "With the way things are progressing, I'm not sure when I'll make my next call to you."

"All right, but no longer than forty-eight hours between contact, understand?"

Rheyna smiled. "Okay, Mom, got it."

She thought she heard Laura chuckle just before she hung up. She went back inside and sat on the couch beside Annie and propped her feet up on the coffee table. She opened the envelope containing the Castrucci photos and sorted through the proofs. She pulled out the ones that Terasa had chosen. The family was definitely photogenic, and the pictures had turned out very well. She looked at the photos with a sense of pride.

She held up one of Caroline by herself. After all these years, she still had it. She felt a tinge of guilt for wondering again how it would feel to kiss her mouth. She didn't know what was wrong with her. She was like two different people. It wasn't like her to have such sensuous thoughts for anyone, let alone someone she had only known for a short amount of time. No matter how she tried, she just couldn't shake it. She honestly hadn't thought about kissing any woman since Jenny.

The betrayal hit her in the gut like a boulder. Her guilt only worsened when she admitted she hadn't thought about Jenny very much since meeting Caroline. She pushed the thoughts aside, telling herself that nothing was going to happen between her and Caroline because she wouldn't let it. Caroline was off limits for two reasons: the first being, she was a very important piece in a much larger picture; and the second was that, in all likelihood, Caroline was straight.

She forced herself to think about Pandora's Box, the main reason for her being there. If she got close to Caroline, it would be for one reason and one reason only—to get her father. She realized she must have been thinking out loud because Annie was watching her intently, cocking her head to one side and then the other. Rheyna ruffled her fur. She looked at the picture of Caroline again and shook her head. "I just don't understand it, Annie— how someone so beautiful could come from something so ugly." She gathered up the photos and headed for the camera room to print up Terasa's order.

Chapter 10

Ron Astor set the vase of red roses on the windowsill and rearranged the small stalks of baby's breath. He glanced over at Lynn, his arms covered with purplish red-blotched lesions. Lynn's eyes fluttered open.

"Hi, gorgeous," Ron said as he slid one of the chairs over next to the hospital bed.

Lynn's voice was raspy and weak. "Hi yourself, handsome," he said and picked up the rag sheet covering his chest and laid it on the bedside table. His thin fingers grasped at the oxygen mask covering his face.

"Here, let me help you," Ron said, pulling the mask off. He nodded at the trash rag. "You know those things are gonna rot your brain."

"I don't have enough time for that to happen."

Ron covered Lynn's hand with his own, taking care to avoid the IV line. "Did you see Dr. Lane this morning?" he asked, purposely ignoring Lynn's comment.

"Two hours ago."

"What did he say?"

"He said my T4's are in the basement and that I'm not doing too well.

"How far in the basement?"

"White-counts at one-eighty."

As soon as he heard the number, Ron felt a horrible pit in his stomach. He laid his head across Lynn's stomach.

Lynn reached up and stroked the back of his neck. "It's okay, hon. I feel fine, despite those dumb old tests that say I shouldn't."

Ron tried to keep the anguish out of voice. "I don't wanna lose you. I'm just not ready to say goodbye."

Lynn used his thumb to wipe away the tears running down Ron's cheek. He caressed Ron's face with his hand. He said the words, knowing it was the last thing Ron wanted to hear: "I know, sweetheart, but you have to let me go."

"I ... I don't know ... I don't know if I can do this," Ron choked through tears.

"I've made my peace, Ron, and I'll be fine, but I can't do this without knowing that you'll be okay." He tilted Ron's face so he could look at him. "I need you to tell me that you're okay."

Ron shook his head. "But I'm not okay."

"Sweetheart, you have your whole life ahead of you, and I want you to live it as if you didn't."

Ron's lip quivered. "We were supposed to live it together. We were supposed to grow old together."

"Come up here with me," Lynn said, pulling Ron closer. "Just lay here with me for awhile."

Ron snuggled next to Lynn and laid his head on his chest. Lynn rubbed Ron's shoulders. "Shh, everything's gonna be okay," he whispered.

"I'm the one who's supposed to be comforting you, not the other way around." Try as he might, Ron couldn't stop the tears from spilling down his cheeks. He closed his eyes for a few minutes, hoping against hope that when he opened them, everything would be as it used to be.

Ron woke up to the sound of coughing. He must have dozed off. It took a few seconds for him to realize where he was. He slid off the bed and helped Lynn sit up. He grabbed the pitcher and poured a glass of water. He held the glass to Lynn's mouth. "Easy, just take small sips. You need to put this back on," he said, sliding the oxygen mask back over Lynn's head.

He looked at the frail man lying in the bed and it made

his heart hurt. He thought about the strong, virile man who had once been a professional baseball player at six-foot-two, 230 pounds. Back then, Lynn had been full of life, but now, he was just a man who had been reduced to a ninety-pound shell of his former self.

Anger replaced Ron's pain as he thought about this disease, how it was robbing him of the love of his life. He was angry with God, and he was angry with the people who had treated Lynn like a leper.

He remembered the hurt he saw in Lynn's eyes when the men in the clubhouse, the men that were supposed to be his friends, shunned him. He was angry at the hospital where Lynn had surgery in '82. It was supposed to be a simple procedure, they said. After all, gallbladder surgery was one of the easiest. They never anticipated him needing blood, blood that would come from a supply that was never tested for the HIV virus, because at the time, AIDS was a relatively unknown disease.

He was mostly angry with all those people who claimed Lynn deserved to die because he was homosexual. They had claimed that AIDS was a gay disease and that God had created it to wipe out the sinners. He was angry at the world and didn't know what to do about it. He didn't know what to do about the bills. Lynn's treatment had wiped out all their savings, and although Lynn had insurance, it was not nearly enough to cover everything they owed. He oftentimes found himself wishing that he had been infected, too.

He gently kissed Lynn on the top of the head and picked up his coat.

"Are you leaving?" Lynn asked weakly.

"Yeah, I'll stop in tomorrow morning."

Lynn smiled at him. "I love you, Ron."

"I love you, too, sweetheart."

Chapter 11

The day was warm and sunny, and Pal Joey's was bustling with the afternoon lunch crowd. Located in the business district of Palo Alto, it had quickly become a hotspot for the law-abiding—and not-so-law-abiding locals. In a booth at the far end of the bar, Big Tony sat with Sonny, eating lunch. Jay Farino sat at the bar laughing as he listened in on the argument between the two men. Jay Farino was not the only one listening in.

Directly across the street in their surveillance room, Laura and Stevens listened to the two men as they argued.

"And I'm telling you, the Lincoln has it over the Cadillac by a mile!" Sonny yelled back at Big Tony.

"How you figure?"

"Because the fuckin' Lincoln's longer."

Big Tony's look was incredulous. He scowled at Sonny. "You've got to be kiddin' me!"

Sonny busted out laughing. Big Tony smiled when he realized Sonny was screwing with him. He threw his napkin on the table and turned toward the bar. "Hey, Louie, how about another scotch over here?" he yelled over the lunch crowd noise.

Henry walked up to the table. Big Tony motioned for Sonny to slide over, and Henry plopped down in the seat.

"I gave Roberto the extra package, like you said," Henry whispered just loud enough for the booth's two occupants to hear. "He was a real punk about it, making threats about the last couple boat shipments." Big Tony raised an eyebrow, and Henry lit a cigarette before continuing. "The boys were talkin' shit about him being named Under Boss."

Sonny eyed him cautiously. "Who was doin' the talkin'?" he asked.

Henry nervously tapped his cigarette in the ashtray. "Paulie and Georgie."

"How'd you find this out?" Sonny asked, lighting a cigarette of his own.

"Card game at Nicky's the other night." Henry leaned his head back and blew the smoke up in the air.

Big Tony looked at Henry and then at Sonny. He clicked his tongue against the back of his teeth. "Is that right?" he asked. "They think they know everything and don't know shit."

Sonny nodded his head in agreement. "I'll tell ya, the young ones just don't have any manners like in the old days. They need to learn manners."

"Maybe we should get together for a dinner meeting— you know, to iron out our differences and all," Big Tony said.

Sonny took out another cigarette and used the one he had burning in the ashtray to light it. He looked at Big Tony. "In L.A.?"

Laura removed the headphones and looked at Stevens. "Do you think he's serious about dinner, or did he just order a hit?"

"I don't know. With these guys, you can never be sure."

"Should I contact the L.A. office and let them know, just in case?"

Stevens shook his head. "Nah, let's hold off and see if we can get something a little more concrete."

Laura shook her head too, but for a different reason. "Okay, it's your call," she said. It was up to Stevens whether suspicious information gained from the surveillance was acted on or not. Stevens might have been the senior agent when it came to decision-making for Pandora's Box, and he might have had a hell of a lot more experience than she did, but his answer just then didn't sit right. She had an uneasy feeling. This one was going to bite them in the ass, and she knew it.

It was dark outside by the time Big Tony returned home, and Terasa greeted him at the door with a kiss. "How was your trip, Anthony?" she asked.

"It was good, real good."

She followed him into the family room and watched as he poured a glass of scotch.

"Where's Caroline?"

"Over at Rheyna's."

He frowned, trying to place the name. "The photographer?" he asked finally.

"Yes. I think she found herself a new friend."

He hesitated, as if he were going to say something and then changed his mind. "I got some calls to make. I'll be in my study if you need me."

Terasa watched him retreat down the hallway. "I've been married for almost thirty years and have spent most of them alone. You'd think I'd be used to it by now," she said as she poured herself a drink.

The ending credits for the movie *Beaches* scrolled across the screen. Caroline wiped her eyes with a tissue. "I love that movie," she said between sniffles.

Rheyna tried not to laugh, but couldn't help herself. "You're such a wuss."

Caroline made a pouting look with her lips and playfully shoved her. "You can't tell me that you didn't cry the first time you saw it."

"I didn't say that, and for your information, I did. I just didn't cry the second, third, or fourth time," Rheyna continued to tease.

"Okay, smarty-pants, you pick the movie the next time."

"Okay, I will."

"I can only imagine what type of movie you'd pick."

"Really? And what would that be?"

"You probably like movies like *Terminator* or *Die Hard*, or one of those that blow up everything in sight," Caroline said smugly.

The woman was amusing, to say the least. "I do like those movies, but I prefer something more along the lines of the *Godfather* saga or *Scarface*," Rheyna said, wanting to see if she would get some kind of a reaction, and she did.

Caroline made a disgusted sound in her throat.

"What? How can you not like those movies, Caroline?"

Caroline took a sip of her wine. "I live it. Why would I want to watch it? I'm not stupid, Rheyna. I know what my dad does. I know what he is. I read the papers. I see what they say about him."

"You can't always believe everything you hear."

"All I know is that I don't want any part of it, and I'm nothing like him," she said, draining the rest of her glass before refilling it again to the top.

"Why don't we talk about something else, then?" Rheyna asked.

Caroline eyed her curiously. "I have a feeling that you and I could be very good friends."

"Me, too," Rheyna said, meaning it.

"Are you sure I'm not wearing out my welcome?" Caroline asked.

"No. You're not wearing out your welcome. I really enjoy your company, but it also helps that I don't know anyone else, so that kinda makes you a lock." Rheyna laughed at the expression on Caroline's face.

"I'm not sure if that was a compliment or a putdown."

"It's definitely a compliment."

"Do you like boats?" Caroline asked, completely changing gears on their conversation.

Rheyna nodded. "I haven't been on one since I was a child, though."

"Would you and Annie like to go out ... on our boat this weekend?"

Rheyna pretended to think about it for a second. "I think we could handle it," she said as her mind began to race with images of Caroline in a bathing suit. I need to stop this before I drive myself insane. It's the wine. It has to be, she told herself. She could also tell the wine was affecting Caroline. It was evident by how much her words had begun to slur in the last five minutes. The two of them had finished one bottle and were nearly through the second.

"I think it's about time ... I head home." Caroline set the empty glass on the table and attempted to stand and nearly fell sideways. Rheyna instinctively reached out with her hand to steady her. No doubt about it—Caroline was drunk.

"I don't think you should drive," Rheyna said, still holding onto Caroline's arm.

"I'm ... I'm fine," Caroline laughed just before she fell back onto the couch.

"Sure you are. You aren't going anywhere."

"I need to call my … Mom," Caroline said through a hiccup.

"I'll call her and let her know that you're here."

"Are you sure?" Caroline asked.

"Yes, I'm sure. How about I make you some coffee?"

"Coffee? Coffee would be nice." Caroline chuckled as she said the words.

By the time Rheyna scooped the coffee grounds into the basket, flipped on the switch and turned around, Caroline had fallen asleep. She got a blanket from the linen closet and covered Caroline with it. She sat down on the end of the couch and unlaced Caroline's shoes. She looked so peaceful. Without thinking, Rheyna reached out to smooth several strands of hair back from Caroline's face. She gently brushed the back of her hand against Caroline's warm cheek. She knew she shouldn't have, but she couldn't help herself. It felt like the most natural thing to do.

She went over to the counter, picked up the phone, and dialed the number to the Castrucci house. Their housekeeper answered. "Hello, Esther, this is Rheyna. May I speak with Mrs. Castrucci please?"

Within seconds, Terasa was on the phone. "Rheyna? Is something wrong with Caroline?" she asked, her voice full of concern.

"Everything's fine, Terasa. I just wanted to let you know that Caroline is spending the night. I'm afraid she's had a little too much to drink, and I don't think she should drive."

"I can send Vincent over to get her," Terasa offered.

"That's really not necessary," Rheyna said. She wanted to add, "Besides, I really don't want her to leave," but didn't. She liked having Caroline there, even if she was passed out on her couch.

"Are you sure?" Terasa asked.

Rheyna looked at Caroline and smiled. "I'm positive."

"Okay, Rheyna, thank you for letting me know and ... for taking care of my daughter."

"You're welcome."

She hung up the phone and checked to make sure that Caroline was still asleep. She went back to her bedroom and got her cell out of the nightstand. She took the phone and went back to the living room. She slowly slid the patio door open and stepped outside to make her call to Laura.

"I can't talk long. Caroline Castrucci is asleep on my couch," she said after Laura answered the phone.

"She's on your couch?"

Rheyna could imagine the look on Laura's face. "She had a little too much to drink."

"Uh-huh, sure she did," Laura teased.

"She did, I swear."

"Uh-huh, whatever you say, Rheyna."

"Laura, I think you know me better than that."

"You're right, I do."

"Good. Is there anything going on at your end that I should know about?"

"Nothing, really. Stevens is still going over the transmissions from Castrucci's office. So far, it's just been a lot of bullshit."

"Okay, well, I gotta go. I'll try and check in tomorrow."

After she hung up the phone, she stood on the deck for a little while. She thought about everything that had transpired over the past couple of weeks. They had flown by so quickly, but the past two had left a dark pit in her stomach. It was the same feeling she had in her stomach the night she and Laura had gone over the operation. She had a bad feeling, but she couldn't put her finger on it. She had similar feelings with other operations, but this one was different and not in a good way. She tried to justify her thoughts, thinking she was just being paranoid.

Chapter 12

Tommy Lapizzi was still half-asleep when Big Tony and Sonny climbed into the back of the limousine. He had been Big Tony's driver for the past two years and was hoping to become a soldier before too long. He hated days like this when he had to get up before the chickens. Fortunately, for him, he only did this two to three times a week when the Boss and Sonny made their warehouse rounds. He raised the glass partition as he drove the car down the driveway. Although he was an associate, he still was not privy to the business dealings going on in the backseat.

Big Tony lit his morning cigar. "How much you say he's in for?"

"Twenty Gs," Sonny answered.

"I think it's time you and the boys have a little talk with Richie."

Rheyna and Annie had risen early and set out for their morning walk along the beach. She was surprised to see that Caroline was still sleeping when they returned.

Annie finished her breakfast and then took her place at Rheyna's feet while she read the newspaper, or so Rheyna thought. She glanced up to see Annie standing eye level with Caroline's face, her tail wagging back and forth.

"No, Annie," was all Rheyna managed to get out

before Annie licked Caroline across the face. Caroline's eyes fluttered open, and she smiled.

Annie took this as an invitation. She stood up with her front legs on the couch and hovered above Caroline. Most people would have pushed her away, but not Caroline. To Annie's delight, Caroline grabbed her with both hands and leaned up to plant a kiss on the tip of her nose.

"And good morning to you, too, Miss Annie," she said, swinging her legs around to sit up on the couch. She ran her fingers through her hair and looked up to see Rheyna watching her.

"Would you like that cup of coffee now?" Rheyna asked.

"I would love a cup and maybe a couple of aspirins, too, please."

Rheyna poured her a cup and handed it to her before going into the bathroom to retrieve the aspirins.

Caroline took the pills, tossed her head back, and swallowed them. "Thank you," she said, her cheeks turning red. "I'm a little embarrassed. I don't usually drink that much."

"You were a good girl," Rheyna assured her.

"Are you sure?"

"Scout's honor," she said with a wink, holding up two fingers.

"That's too bad," Caroline said.

She's flirting with me, Rheyna thought, and this time, there was no mistaking the twinkle in Caroline's eyes.

Caroline picked her shoes up off the floor. "Damn. If my dad finds out, he'll make Joey drive me everywhere again."

"Who's Joey?"

"He's my driver."

"You have a driver?"

Caroline finished tying the laces on her shoes and stood up. "Yes, and I'm not supposed to go anywhere without him, except when I'm at Haven."

Rheyna tried to picture Joey. "I don't think I've met him."

"Yeah, you did. He was one of the guys who searched you when you came to the house."

Rheyna thought back to the two heavily armed guards and wondered which one of them was Joey.

Caroline grabbed her keys off the coffee table. "I've got to get going. I still have to shower and get to Haven. When's Annie's next appointment?" she asked.

"Next Tuesday."

"Depending on how well her leg's healing, we might be able to take that cast off earlier than we originally thought."

"That would be great," Rheyna said as she followed her out to her car.

Caroline opened the car door and slid behind the wheel. She rolled the window down. "It's usually not that quick for most. In Annie's case, she was extremely lucky, and her breaks were clean." She started up the car. "I guess I'll see you two this weekend." Caroline smiled at the surprised look on Rheyna's face. "Don't worry, I wasn't so drunk that I didn't remember our boating date," she said with a laugh.

"I wasn't thinking that at all," Rheyna lied.

"What were you thinking, then?" she asked.

"I was thinking that I'd like for you to tell Terasa that I'll drop the photos off tomorrow."

Caroline grinned at Rheyna as she backed the car out of the drive.

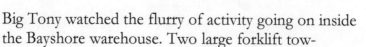

Big Tony watched the flurry of activity going on inside the Bayshore warehouse. Two large forklift tow-motors took turns unloading pallets of boxes from the tractor-trailer sitting against the dock door.

Sonny motioned for him to come over to a table where several men were busy opening large boxes and repacking them into smaller ones. Using his pocketknife, Sonny sliced the lid open on one of the small boxes and pulled out a six-inch ceramic owl. He handed the figurine to Big Tony. Big Tony turned the little figurine around in his hand. It looked like a tacky little "Made in China" knickknack that could be found at a local flea market for a buck or two. Big Tony ran his thumb over the owl's eyes—the glass balls were gone—replaced with diamonds.

He nodded his head in approval. "Very nice," he said, handing the owl back to the worker to be repackaged.

He and Sonny walked toward the office on the far side of the warehouse. A short, bald man sporting a black goatee came out from behind the desk to greet them. He grinned at the men.

"So what'ya think, Tony? Nice, huh?" he asked.

Big Tony patted him on the back. "Yeah, Charlie, they're real nice and definitely one of your best ideas yet."

Sonny dropped down on the seat near the door and lit a cigarette.

Charlie looked at Sonny and shook his head. "Man, those cancer sticks're gonna kill ya."

Sonny took a long drag from the cigarette and smiled. "If I could only be so fuckin' lucky."

Big Tony stepped around the desk and sat down in Charlie's chair. He looked through the paperwork. "What's our take?" he asked, looking at Charlie.

Charlie twisted his goatee hairs between his finger and thumb and calculated the numbers in his head. "After L.A., I'd say about 2.5 mil."

Sonny flipped off the ashes from his cigarette. "How soon's it shipping?"

"Tomorrow morning. I have two more shipments due

in on Friday."

"Same stuff?" Big Tony asked before lighting the end of his cigar. He reached in his breast pocket and offered one to Charlie.

Charlie shook his head. "One is. The other's rubies, coming from Sierra Leone. Both are worth about the same, though."

Big Tony stood up from the chair and tugged at the ends of his suit jacket. Sonny and Charlie got up and followed him out to the waiting limo.

Big Tony slid onto the backseat and rolled the window down. "Give me a call when the next shipment arrives."

"Will do," Charlie said, and then turned to go back into the warehouse.

Big Tony tapped on the window separating the driver from the rear of the car. Tommy lowered the partition. He looked at the men through the rearview mirror.

"Time for lunch, Tommy."

Tommy nodded and raised the partition.

Big Tony re-lit his cigar and turned to Sonny. "Speaking of food, what time's dinner?"

"Six sharp."

Chapter 13

Laura tossed a bag of hamburgers and fries down on the desk in front of Stevens. He smiled gratefully and removed his headphones. He jerked out the headphone jack and turned up the volume knob so they could both hear the conversation going on over at Pal Joey's.

"Anything good?" she asked.

"If you wanna learn about cars," he answered, taking a bite out of the hamburger.

"Are you serious? Cars again?"

He nodded and took another bite of the sandwich. "I swear, that's all they freaking talk about." He dipped a couple of fries in the ketchup. "Did you know that the frame for the 2006 Ford Sport Trac is the same one used in the 2007 model, except that its wheel base was extended 16.8 inches or that the 2005 Escalade has two recalls—one for the transmission and one for the second-row center seat belt or—"

Laura held up her hand for him to stop. "Okay, okay. I get the point. How long have they been at it?"

He glanced down at his watch. "Since noon and it's now six."

"Have we got anything from Castrucci's office?"

He shook his head. "Hell, no. They've been here all day."

Henry Venutti and Jay Farino sat at the corner of West First and Spring Street in silence, watching the front entrance to Little Vic's Delicatessen.

"Show time," Jay announced, nudging Henry's arm and nodding across the street.

A blue Chevy Blazer pulled up in front of the deli and came to a stop. Henry turned the key and started the engine. He put it in drive and slowly turned the corner, pulling the van up next to the Blazer's driver-side door before stopping.

Paulie and Georgie, the occupants inside the blazer, never stood a chance. The AK-47 bullets ripped through the car like a sheet of paper, creating a drone of noise so loud, it easily drowned out the screams of innocent bystanders, scrambling for cover on the opposite side of the car.

It was over in an instant. The van slowly pulled away and disappeared around the corner as quietly as it had arrived.

Rheyna had just finished printing off the photos Terasa had chosen and was inserting them into an envelope when a live-breaking news report on the TV got her attention. She turned up the volume to hear the man holding a microphone in front of his face.

"I'm James Styles and I'm at the scene here in front of Little Vic's Delicatessen, where two men were brutally killed as they sat in their vehicle."

Directly behind him was the blue Chevy Blazer. Part of the driver's side window had been shot out, and what remained was covered with blood spatter. The driver's side door and fenders were riddled with bullet holes. It looked like a slice of Swiss cheese. The driver's body lay against the steering wheel.

The camera operator zoomed in for a close-up view. Rheyna could see that he had taken several shots to the head and upper body. The camera then followed the reporter around the front of the car and stopped next to the passenger-side, where another man, still wearing his seatbelt, lay slumped against the window.

In the background, police officers could be seen cordoning off the area and pushing a group of curious onlookers back.

The reporter looked directly at the camera. "Witnesses claim that a grey panel van pulled up next to the men and opened fire with what sounded like a machine gun."

That would definitely explain the amount of bullet holes, she thought to herself.

The reporter continued speaking as a police officer pushed him outside the tape perimeter. "An anonymous source with the Los Angeles Crime Division stated that the two men in the vehicle were identified as George Fabrizio and Paul Moceri."

Rheyna recognized the names instantly. She knew what he was going to say next.

"Both men were suspected of working for reputed Mob Boss Carlos Massino."

She turned off the TV and leaned back against the couch. She knew this was a dangerous operation from the beginning, but hearing the news report brought home the crude fact of reality and the seriousness of her situation.

Once again, she felt that black pit in her stomach. There was no doubt in her mind that somehow, Castrucci was responsible for those two men's death. That proved he was willing to do anything to get what he wanted, and she was determined to be the one who nailed his ass to the wall.

Sonny sauntered toward the back of the alley and stopped beneath the street lamp. He rubbed the right side of his temple with his fingers as Henry and Farino dragged Ritchie into the alley.

They stopped in front of Sonny. Farino slammed Richie up against the wall, knocking the wind out of his lungs. Richie gasped for several seconds, trying to catch his breath.

Sonny grabbed him by the hair and lifted his head up to face him. "Where's my money, Richie?"

"I … I'll have it … have it in the morning, Sonny," Richie said, struggling to get the words out.

Sonny slapped him across the face, splitting his upper lip. "I gave you twenty-four hours. Where's my fucking money?"

Richie spit a mouthful of blood on the ground. "Please, Sonny … I swear I'll have it in the morning," he pleaded.

"Okay, Richie … you have til noon," Sonny said, running his hands through his hair in agitation. He started to walk away and stopped. Before Richie knew what was happening, Sonny slammed his fist into his gut. Richie let out a loud groan and slumped down to the ground on his knees.

He flinched as Sonny jabbed his index finger in the middle of his forehead. "If you don't have it by noon, I'm gonna cut your motherfuckin' fingers off. Capische?" Sonny drew his arm back to strike him again and then laughed as Richie cowered to the ground, his hands above his head.

Richie slowly moved his hands from in front of his face. "I swear I'll have it for you, Sonny," he said, his voice shaking.

"If you know what's good for you, you better," Sonny said over his shoulder before turning to leave.

Sighing with relief, Richie watched Sonny walk over to Henry and Farino, who had stopped near a trash bin close to the alley's entrance. He saw Henry glaring down at something and moved a little to the right to see what it was. An old bum was looking up at the men from inside a cardboard box.

"What ta fuck you looking at?" Henry yelled, kicking the man in the stomach as hard as he could. The old man groaned, slumped forward, and then fell back into his box. Henry high-fived Farino as if he had just scored a game-winning goal.

Chapter 14

The week had flown by, and before Rheyna knew it, she found herself and Annie on their way to meet Caroline at the Half Moon Bay Yacht Club. She thought about her conversation last night with Laura regarding the hit down in L.A.

They had found the abandoned grey panel van parked down at one of the docks. The van had been stolen the night before from a flower delivery service over on the south side, and just as they had expected, was wiped clean.

Laura told her about the conversation she and Stevens overheard at Pal Joey's between Big Tony, Sonny, and Henry. Laura was really kicking herself in the ass for not warning their people in L.A.

Rheyna tried unsuccessfully to convince Laura that it wasn't her fault. Stevens was the one who owned it. If anyone was responsible, it was him. He was the one who had to live with the consequences of his actions—or in this case, lack thereof. He was also the one who now had to deal with Edwards.

Rheyna pulled into the crowded parking lot and saw Caroline waving from the bow of a very large boat. From what she could see, Caroline was wearing a white t-shirt over a neon pink bikini. She had to stifle a laugh when she saw the name on the side of the boat. In big, red, cursive writing was the name '*Untouchable*'. Not only was it appropriate, but typical for Anthony Castrucci to be so openly arrogant.

She helped Annie over the rail and climbed onboard.

The red and white boat was impressive, to say the least. If she had to guess, she would say that it was at least thirty-feet long.

Caroline took off her sunglasses and perched them on top of her head. "Hi, there," she said with a big smile.

"Hi, there yourself."

"Are you sure you two are up for this?"

"Oh, yeah. I've been looking forward to it all week, and whatever I like, Annie likes."

Caroline grinned. "Is that a fact?" she asked.

"As a matter of fact, it is." Rheyna pulled her t-shirt over her head, revealing her own bikini. She slid one of the loungers around, so she would be facing Caroline. She didn't need to look up to know that Caroline was watching her. She knew where Caroline's eyes were by the warm tingling sensations traveling up her body.

"The color suits you. I think the black and teal goes great with your hair and eyes."

Rheyna felt her cheeks flush. She forced herself to look at Caroline, to meet her gaze. Her eyes went to Caroline's mouth.

Since the very first moment they met, she had sensed something different about Caroline, though not different in a strange or odd sort of way. Caroline was humanely different. "Marked by compassion, sympathy, and consideration for humans and animals," is the Merriam-Webster's definition of humane, and it described Caroline perfectly.

It was those attributes wreaking havoc on her emotions. Although she had wanted to leave Washington and looked at it as a chance to get on with her life, a big part of her was comfortable with her boring existence. Since Jenny died, she had avoided dating like the plague. The few times she had, it felt like a betrayal to Jenny's memory; the guilty feelings afterward didn't help, either.

She was falling for Caroline and falling hard. She didn't

want to be in love with any woman, especially if that woman happened to be Caroline Castrucci. It was something that could never be.

Annie barked, snapping Rheyna from her thoughts. She turned to look in the same direction as Annie. Just a few slips down, a young couple was boarding a boat approximately a third of the size of theirs. She turned back around and caught Caroline watching her.

"I really like the color of your suit," she said, immediately feeling like an idiot. Talk about a delayed reaction, she thought as she leaned back in the lounger.

Caroline smiled and pulled her glasses down over her eyes. "Okay, then. Now that we've got that out of the way, what'ya say we get out of here?" Caroline started the engine and expertly maneuvered the boat out of the bay.

Annie had found her place at the front rail, wagging her tail. She periodically barked at the passing skiers as Caroline steered the boat up the coast toward deeper water. They traveled at a steady, even pace, not too slow and not too fast, just fast enough to enjoy the breathtaking views along the coastline. They cruised for close to an hour before Caroline found a little out-of-the-way spot back in a cove off the main throughway.

She dropped anchor, pulled her t-shirt over her head, and then joined Annie and Rheyna on the bow. She pulled over a lounger and sat down next to Rheyna, swinging her legs over the side of the chair. She stuck her hand in the pocket on the backside of her lounger and pulled out a bottle of tanning oil. "I don't think we could have picked a better day to be on the water," she said.

Rheyna's senses were assaulted with a mixture of coconut and seawater. She watched Caroline spread the oil over her tanned legs. Her skin was the sweet color of honey and so rich in contrast with the blue of her eyes, giving them an almost iridescent glow. They were hypnotic. *It would be so easy to see her gracing the cover of Vogue magazine*, she thought as Caroline rubbed in the oil.

Caroline turned to Rheyna and smiled. "Is it awesome out here, or what?" she asked.

"Yes, and according to the wonderful weather channel, we're going to be in the high eighties all day."

"If you ask me, it feels more like ninety," Caroline said as she continued to spread the oil on her arms.

Rheyna glanced around the bay. "I think I could stay here for days."

"I have. It's just like having a little apartment on water, and it has everything you could possibly need. Dad bought it a couple years ago for business, but I use it more than he does," she said, holding the bottle of lotion out for Rheyna. "Would you mind putting some on my back?" she asked.

"I don't think that is such a good idea," Rheyna said the words in her mind.

Caroline didn't wait for her to answer and turned over on her stomach, stretching out on the lounger.

When Rheyna touched Caroline's skin, she half expected to hear a sizzle. She knew this was dangerous ground and quickly finished the task. She set the bottle on the table and leaned back in the seat, prepared to soak in the sun.

Caroline reached over her, her hand slightly brushing against Rheyna's stomach. She grabbed the bottle of oil and squirted a dab in her hand. "Your turn, now turn over and I'll put some on you."

What could she say? No, you can't possibly put your hands on me. What choice did she have, other than to comply? As soon as Caroline touched her, she felt all the stress leave her body. Her hands were so warm, and Rheyna was powerless to control the shiver that made her hair stand up on end. She hoped Caroline didn't notice. *No such luck*, she thought when she heard Caroline chuckle.

A little embarrassed, Rheyna turned over and pulled

her shades down over her eyes. She was grateful that Caroline didn't say anything.

Caroline stood up. She looked down at Rheyna. "I'm going to get a drink. Would you like something?" she asked.

"I'll have whatever you're having."

Caroline disappeared inside the cabin and came out a few minutes later with two glasses and a bottle of wine.

Rheyna peeked at her over the rim of her glasses.

Caroline held the glass out to her and laughed. "I promise not to pass out on you this time."

"That's not what I was thinking."

"What were you thinking, then?" she asked, pouring the wine into Rheyna's glass.

Rheyna motioned behind her. "I was thinking that boat is getting awfully close."

Caroline turned to look in the direction Rheyna was referring to, just as a horn blared. Annie's ears perked up, and she barked at the darkly tanned man in swimming trunks waving from the bow.

"Hey, Caroline!" he yelled as the boat came to a stop less than ten feet away from them.

She smiled with recognition. "Hi, Phil. What are you doing out here?"

"Same as you, honey—working on my tan."

Caroline frowned. "Where's Jesse?"

"Speak of the devil," Phil said, smiling at the gorgeous young man with blond highlights, coming from the other side of the boat.

Rheyna felt relief the minute she saw him. Her gaydar went off in full force. She had no doubt they were lovers.

"Hi, Caroline," Jesse said cheerfully with a wave of his hand.

"Hey, Jesse."

"Who's your friend?" Phil asked, looking directly at Rheyna.

"Oh, I'm sorry. Phil, Jesse, meet Rheyna Moretti." She turned to Rheyna. "Rheyna, I'd like you to meet two of my dearest friends. Doctor's Phillip Lowry and Jesse Kar."

Rheyna found it hard to hide the smile creeping at the corners of her mouth. "I'm pleased to meet you both," she said.

Jesse smiled at Rheyna. "I love your name. I don't think I've heard it before."

"Thank you. I have my grandmother to thank for it."

Rheyna knew they were sizing her up, and from the look on their faces, she was sure their gaydar had gone off as well.

Caroline lifted her glass to them. "Wanna join us?"

Phil shook his head. "I wish we could but we have to head back."

"We're both on call tonight," Jesse chimed in and then asked, "Why don't you two join us for dinner sometime next week?"

Caroline looked at Rheyna. Rheyna shrugged. "Sounds great to me."

"Okay, then. I'll give you a call later," Jesse said over his shoulder before ducking back into the cabin.

Phil winked at Caroline. "You'll have to bring Rheyna with you to our party."

"Oh, Phil, that's three months from now," she teased.

A big smile crossed his face. "Since when is it too soon to plan for a party?" he asked.

"You're incorrigible," Caroline laughed.

Phil smiled and put the boat in gear. "See ya soon!" he yelled as the boat took off toward the Yacht Club.

"They seem very nice," Rheyna said.

Caroline sat back down in her lounger. "They are."

"Have you known them long?" Rheyna asked after Caroline refilled their glasses.

"Since I was seventeen. Jesse and Phil encouraged me to become a veterinarian."

"They must be very good friends," Rheyna said as she watched their boat get smaller and smaller.

"The best anyone could ask for." Caroline took a sip of wine. "The party Phil was talking about is one they do every year to raise money for the Pediatric Aids wing at Children's Hospital." She set her glass on the table and stood up. "I'll be right back. I have a surprise for you." After a few minutes, she reappeared with an ice-cream cone and handed it to Rheyna.

Rheyna involuntarily groaned when she realized what flavor it was. "Moose tracks is my absolute favorite," she managed to say between licks.

"I know," Caroline said smugly.

"How do you know?" Rheyna asked, surprised at the revelation.

Caroline shrugged. "I overheard you tell Mom."

Rheyna tried to keep up with the ice cream, but the sun was melting it faster than she could lick it. Annie, on the other hand, was not minding it a bit. A steady stream ran down Rheyna's arm, falling off her elbow to the deck below, where Annie happily slopped it up. Rheyna grabbed the sides of her temple. "Oh ... brain freeze. I can't eat anymore," she said, giving the rest of the cone to Annie.

Caroline picked up a napkin and leaned toward Rheyna. "You missed some," she said softly, gently wiping off a small bit of ice cream near the corner of Rheyna's mouth.

The act froze Rheyna to the spot. Her heart raced into overdrive. The roaring in her ears was so loud; she was convinced that Caroline could hear it. *I really need her to stop touching me*, she thought, raising her head to look at Caroline. Something was telling her that Caroline was feeling it, too—she could see it in her eyes.

Caroline was the first to break the contact. She got up and walked to the helm.

Maybe I just imagined it. Maybe it's just wishful

thinking on my part. Just maybe Caroline really didn't know the effect she was having on me. Maybe you have a little too many maybes, she told herself. Maybe you should try focusing a little harder on the job you came here to do. "What's happening to you, Rheyna?" she asked herself. You need to stop screwing around and act like the FBI agent that you are. The roar of the engine forced her to stop talking to herself.

"We need to get going because the sun will be setting soon," Caroline said as she raised the anchor and put the boat in gear.

It took them a full hour to get back to the Yacht Club, and ten minutes after that, Rheyna and Annie were on their way home. She tried not to think about Caroline. She was fighting a losing battle. She had such a great time being alone with Caroline, and she hated for it to end. Once again, her thoughts turned to Jenny. "What am I gonna do, Jen?"

Don Carlos Massino, the head honcho of California's crime family, was sitting at his favorite table in the back room of Barecci's Restaurant. He listened intently to the voice on the other end of the telephone. His brow furrowed into a frown, his face and body visibly stiffened.

"I thought you should know," Don Vitto Lucchese said through the other end of the phone.

Roberto watched Carlos shake his head, his anger very much evident by the stern set of his jaw.

"I thought as much. Thank you, Vitto. I won't forget your loyalty," he said, slamming the phone down on the cradle. He looked at Roberto. "Can you believe the nerve of that man? How can he possibly be stupid enough to think that the Commission, the Commission I chair, would take sides with him over me?"

Roberto nodded his head. "Yeah, he's pretty ignorant and Henry told one of the boys he's getting worse. You not attending Anastasia's funeral has pushed him over the edge. He thinks you were disrespectful."

"I know what the hell started it and it goes to show that Tony should keep his fat mouth shut if he doesn't know all the facts."

Roberto saw the hatred dancing around in Carlos' eyes.

"I ought to go dig the son-of-a-bitch up and pump his rotting corpse full of holes. As far as I'm concerned, he and Tony are from the same fruit."

Roberto clearly understood his boss' rage. It would be a long, long time before he himself would forget the day Carlos found out the truth about his Under Boss, Salvatore Anastasia. The day he learned the truth was also the same day that Anastasia died.

Carlos' granddaughter, Melinda Belotti had come to see him later that evening after hearing the news. She told Carlos that she had been keeping a dark, terrible secret for years, and had lived in agony over it. She fell into his arms, sobbing, and he had comforted her. He reassured her that it was all right, that she could tell him anything. After some gentle prodding, he got her to open up.

She told him about a business meeting that had taken place at his estate late one night. She described the events in vivid detail. She said that later in the evening, a man had come into her room. He climbed into bed with her and placed his hand over her mouth to keep her from screaming. He whispered in her ear, and said that if she made a sound, he would kill her.

He pulled up her nightgown, removed her panties, and raped her. Afterward, he told her that if she ever said anything, he would kill her parents, as well as Carlos.

Although it was dark, she had recognized him by the

smell of his cologne. It was Salvatore Anastasia. Melinda was ten years old at the time. Carlos was speechless, enraged, and for the first time in his life, he was powerless. All he could do was sit and listen to his granddaughter's anguish and try to comfort her the best way he knew how.

Roberto knew that Big Tony was in a lot of trouble. It was evident by the look on Carlos' face. Roberto pulled out a chair and sat down across from him. "What do you want to do about it?" he asked.

Carlos slammed his fist down on the table. "I want to kill the son-of-a-bitch. That's what I want to do. I don't care about the details … and take care of Sonny, while you're at it."

Roberto pushed his chair away from the table and stood up. "I'll call Sammy."

Carlos held his hand up to stop him. "You know what? On second thought, let's hold off for a little while. I have something else in mind."

"Are you sure?" Roberto asked.

Carlos nodded. "Yeah, I'm sure."

Chapter 15

Rheyna couldn't believe how much time had gone by since Pandora's Box had begun, and the last couple of months went just as fast. It was frustrating, seeing they were still no closer to bringing down Castrucci then when they started. She was frustrated, as were the members of her team, but no one more so than Edwards.

The Deputy Director was on his back and getting restless. He wanted results and wanted them yesterday. The cost of the operation was mounting, and it took all of Edwards' energy to convince him they needed a little more time. So far, they had several hundred hours of useless surveillance tape and just as many photos, but nothing to link Castrucci directly to the killings or smuggling operations. Something had to give.

Her relationship—if you could call it that—with Caroline was growing, and so was Annie. She had long since had her cast removed, was sprouting up like a weed, and she and Rheyna were practically inseparable.

Rheyna continued with the ruse of running her photography business and her role in the operation felt more like that of a bystander. She and Laura concluded that surveillance alone was not going to cut it.

On most days, she was okay with her assignment and on others; it took everything she had in her to fight off the ever-increasing guilt for deceiving Caroline and Terasa. She and Caroline were spending a lot of time together in between her days at Haven. She found herself looking forward to the long walks she and Caroline took regularly along the beach with Annie. They even took the boat out several more times, and Rheyna actually drove it.

She felt no stress when they were on the boat, and for a few stolen hours, Rheyna felt at peace. She tried not to think about the time when it would all have to end, because if she did, she would also have to think about Caroline and how Caroline would hate her for what she had done to her and her family.

The thought of Caroline hating her tore her up inside. She dreaded seeing the disappointment in Caroline's eyes, a disappointment she knew was sure to come. She pushed the thoughts aside and decided she would cross that bridge when she came to it.

After her fifth or sixth visit to the Castrucci estate, the guards no longer searched her. She came and went as she pleased and she took full advantage of her liberties, gathering whatever information she could by eavesdropping on Big Tony's conversations out by the pool.

On one occasion, using a cool pair of sunglasses with a built in camera, she was able to get surveillance photos of two previously unknown members of the Massino crime family. She then passed the information on to Laura.

She and Caroline had gone to dinner with Phil and Jesse several times since their first boat trip. After spending time with them, Rheyna realized just what Caroline saw in them. They were kind souls, but most of all, they were genuine. They were also lovers, as Rheyna had first suspected. They had been together for almost nineteen years. Jesse was the cutup of the two and was heavy into joke telling.

She really liked Phil but she enjoyed Jesse's company the most. He was a riot to be around and was sure to lift the dourest of spirits. She also loved that he liked to shop and the two of them had went on several shopping sprees in the specialty shops down in Palo Alto. She was grateful for the friendship they had so easily offered her. Her only wish was that it had happened under different circumstances.

Chapter 16

Sonny looked at the shadowy figure standing in the recessed doorway. "You're taking a big risk meeting like this," he said.

"I didn't have much choice. The Assistant Deputy Director's getting too close."

Sonny lit his cigarette and laughed. "Well, what do you want me to do about it? Kill him?"

"I don't know but you need to do something and do it fast. He has some hotshot programmer back in Washington running some new computer program. It's only a matter of time before my name comes up."

"Don'tcha think you're overreacting a bit? You're the last person on the planet they'd ever suspect of laying in bed with the mob," Sonny snorted.

"Damn it to hell. Do not tell me how to react! I'm telling you we have a problem and if they tie me to these hits, your ass is going down right along with me."

"I thought you said you covered your tracks," Sonny said, unable to keep the agitation from his voice.

"I did cover my tracks."

"Then how the hell they gonna trace it back to you?"

"They're not just looking at Scala's murder, they're looking at Vinci and Pisano and a few others, too."

"Vinci and Pisano?" Sonny asked, not understanding the meaning.

"Did I fucking stutter?"

Sonny leaned back against the doorframe, trying to place the names. After a few seconds, it dawned on him.

"Vinci and Pisano. Jesus, that was over ten years ago," he said, taking a long drag on his cigarette. "Vinci and Pisano were killed in car accidents. Why are they looking at them now?" he asked.

"I don't know and I really don't give a rat's ass. All I care about is me not being linked to them in any way, shape, or form."

"Can't you do something on your end to derail the program?"

"No, it would only make it look more suspicious. I'm too close to the investigation as it is."

Sonny dropped the cigarette butt and stomped it out with his shoe. He nodded as he looked at the shadowy figure. "Well, you're right. We have to do something. You have any ideas?"

"Yeah, I do. I have one that just might work, but you'll have to move fast."

Sonny smiled and lit another cigarette. "I'm all ears," he said, exhaling the smoke.

Rheyna hit the speed dial again and waited for Laura to answer. It rang seven times and then went into her voice mail. "Damn it," she said, pressing the speed dial again. Once again, it rang seven times and then went into her voice mail. She decided to leave a message this time. "Hey, Laura, it's me again. I left you a voice mail earlier and I hope you're getting these messages. You know I wouldn't normally do this without any backup or a safety net, but I don't have much choice. This might be the only chance I get to check out Bayshore. If you've listened to my earlier message, you'll know the details. Also, if you don't hear from me within two hours, send re-enforcements."

She hung up the phone and then made sure it was on

vibrate, just to be on the safe side. She definitely couldn't afford for it to ring if Castrucci or his goons were around. She also knew that Laura wouldn't call until the two-hour window had passed.

She tucked the phone inside her side pocket and then reached over to open the glove box. She pulled out a four-by-four-inch black case. She flipped the lid open, removed the wireless ear bud, and inserted it into her ear. She blew into the tiny microphone to test the receiver and cringed at the highly amplified sound that echoed straight through her brain. She wasn't sure if she would need these items tonight, but had packed them just in case.

What she was about to do was the riskiest move she had made so far in the investigation, next to planting the pen in Castrucci's office. Earlier in the week, she had gotten the chance to affix a quarter-sized radio transmitter under the edge of the table by the pool where Castrucci conducted business. The downside to the device was that it had a battery life of about eight days.

She had thought her time had all but run out when she caught a break. Castrucci, Sonny, and Henry were having lunch when Sonny received a phone call. It was difficult to put it all together, since Caroline was talking in one ear while she was trying to listen in on the conversation at the table with the other.

The phone call was from someone named Charlie. She hadn't heard his name mentioned before and couldn't remember him being listed on any of her briefing reports. Castrucci had referred to him as *Tuna*. From what she could gather, Charlie had a package for them at Bayshore, as well as a gift for Roberto. Those names she did recognize. Roberto was Massino's right-hand man and Bayshore was one of Castrucci's exporting warehouses down at the docks.

After consulting with Castrucci, Sonny confirmed that they would stop in at the warehouse later that evening. He told Charlie they had a previous engagement and would stop by around eight or nine. After Sonny hung up, she had said her goodbyes a few minutes later, leaving under the pretense of a photo shoot appointment. The only appointment she had was with Bayshore, and she was hoping Castrucci showed up closer to nine. The later the better and nine o'clock meant that it would be dark enough for her to move around more easily. It would also lessen her chances of being discovered.

She went home and prepped her gear, grabbed a bite to eat and took Annie for a walk along the beach. Afterward, she slipped on a pair of black cargo pants and a matching hooded jacket with a drawstring and headed out the door. She arrived around seven-thirty and parked her Jeep in a crowded parking lot behind a warehouse located a little way from Bayshore. She parked there because she couldn't risk Castrucci or his men recognizing her Jeep.

She glanced at her watch and then opened the car door. Her plan was to get there before they arrived and get inside the building to look around. She wasn't sure if the building had an alarm system, so she came prepared, bringing along a bypass switch and clip to override the alarm inside the main box. After seeing how the Castrucci estate was wired, she had no doubt that Bayshore would be protected just as well. She made her way across the parking lot and through a field of tall grass that led to several more parking lots.

She heard voices and ducked down in the weeds. She watched several people from the warehouse closest to her file out the back door and head to their cars.

"Come on, damn it. Not now," she swore under her breath. Two of the women from the warehouse stopped next to a red truck. They were having a heated discussion. The shorter of the two was upset and flailing her hands wildly in the air. The other woman nodded her head and patted the shorter woman on the shoulder.

"There's no way I can move. They'll see me" she whispered as she watched the women. Whatever the other woman said, it must have calmed the shorter one down. It was only a few minutes but it felt like forever before they finally got in their cars and backed out of the parking lot.

Bent in a half-crouched position, she quickly made her way across the parking lot. She pressed her back against the side of the building to avoid an approaching set of headlights. She dropped down behind a set of boxes, just as the car turned into the parking lot. The car slowed to a crawl, its searchlight moving up and down the back of the buildings. She held her breath and leaned forward so she could see around the boxes.

She watched the patrol car drive slowly by, and used the back of her arm to wipe off the perspiration beading on her forehead. From her position, she could see the corner of Bayshore. She figured it was approximately fifty to seventy-five yards away. She waited for the patrol car brake lights to disappear around the corner and stood up. She waited a few more minutes to make sure he turned back on the main road before continuing toward the building.

The sun had set and it was getting extremely dark. She glanced at her watch and silently cursed herself. She had wasted more than thirty minutes getting across the parking lots. She couldn't believe how quickly the sun had disappeared, making it almost impossible for her to see her hand in front of her face.

She slowly made her way across the back of the building and thought she was doing pretty good to keep quiet, considering the stabs of pain shooting through her legs each time she bumped into a wooden skid, or whatever else was stacked on the ground. *I'll be covered in bruises this time tomorrow,* she thought when she finally reached the edge of the building. She peered around the corner and looked into the small alley that stood between her and Bayshore.

She listened to make sure she didn't hear anything and then quickly made her way over to a tractor-trailer backed against Bayshore's dock door. She ducked under the trailer and walked toward what vaguely resembled a set of steps that she assumed led into the back of the warehouse. She missed the first step and stretched her arms out to break the fall. She swore under her breath as pain shot through both kneecaps. She stood up, dug the small pebbles out of her palms, and then continued up the steps.

As she ran her hands up the side of the door, she found the bundle of wires. She traced the wires up the long edge of the door, finding that they terminated at the top.

The building had an alarm system and not just any alarm. It was an elaborate, state-of-the-art setup. She looked back at the dark parking lot, finding it odd that there were no lights affixed to the outside of the building, considering the length that Castrucci had went to with the alarm system. She was grateful for his lack of insight, but it made her job a hell of a lot harder. She felt like a blind person stumbling around in the dark.

Carefully, she descended the steps and used her hand to trace the wires along the bottom edge of the building. It was imperative that she find the main box in order to disarm the alarm system. She had brought a penlight with her, had it in her pocket, and didn't want to risk using it, but the lack of lighting gave her no choice. She could tell by the amount of wires in the bundle that she would have no room for error when it came time to clip them. If she screwed up on the termination, she would set off the alarm instead of disarming it.

She was about to turn on the penlight when the sound of gravel crunching stopped her dead in her tracks. The minute she saw the headlights, she dropped to the ground with a thud. She scooted across the ground on her stomach, ignoring the pain as various objects dug into her skin. She slid behind something solid and took a deep breath to quiet her nerves. She looked up in time to see a pair of glowing red taillights pass by. The car came to a stop just a few feet away from the back steps.

The driver, no doubt Tommy, turned the headlights on bright, illuminating the back of the parking lot. Rheyna glanced around and realized that she was crouched next to a large trash compactor and a bunch of wooden crates. She wedged herself between the compactor and the crates, figuring that if she couldn't see the men in the car, they couldn't see her. She heard two car doors open and shut and peeked around the edge of the crates.

Sonny rapped his knuckles on the passenger side window and Tommy rolled it down. "Leave the lights on a minute so we can see what the hell we're doing here," Sonny said before turning to follow Big Tony and Henry up the steps.

"I'm gonna run up and fill the tank. Be back in a few," Tommy yelled before rolling up the window. Sonny shrugged him off with a wave of his hand.

Big Tony flipped the alarm code box open and punched in the code.

"We really need to do something about the lighting back here," Sonny said as he and Henry followed Big Tony inside.

"Have Charlie take care of it tomorrow," Big Tony said, flipping on the light switch.

Rheyna waited for the limo to disappear out of the parking lot before coming out from behind the crates. She looked up at the row of windows located across the back of the building. There was no way she could get in the building using the door, even if it was unlocked. With her luck, it would squeak.

She glanced up at the windows again and decided that was her best option. She was glad to see they had turned on a few of the lights inside the building. If Castrucci, or whoever, had turned all of them on, she would have had to scrap the whole mission. It would have been too risky for her. She also counted her blessings that one of the windows was located directly above the trash compactor. She needed to move and move fast. She had to get inside the building before the limo returned. Otherwise, it would be nearly impossible for her to do so without being seen.

She used the stack of crates to climb onto the compactor and peered through the window. She could see all three men. They were standing on the other side of the warehouse near a row of tables stacked with boxes. She tried to lift the window but it didn't budge. A close look at window revealed an old slide-type lock. She pulled out her pocketknife and wedged it between the panels. Using both hands, she slid the knife sideways, pushing the locking lever to the side. She crammed the tip of the blade between the sill and the window and pushed down on the handle, raising the window just high enough to get her fingers under it. She closed the knife and dropped it into her pants pocket.

She clenched her teeth as she slowly raised the window, silently praying that it wouldn't squeak. *So far, so good*, she thought as she continued to raise the window high enough for her to fit through it.

She took out the small microphone boom, and clipped it to the front of her jacket and then hoisted herself up on the ledge. As she crawled through the window, she heard the men talking. She adjusted the ear bud but was unable to hear their conversation clearly—she needed to get closer. With a deep breath, she slowly lowered herself down onto a four-by-four foot stack of skids. She sat there for several seconds, looking around to get her bearings.

The warehouse was larger than she had imagined. She noticed that the skids, like the one she was on, were stacked every two or so feet apart and that she could reach almost any place in the building by hopping from one stack to another.

Along the back wall, she saw three sets of double overhead doors and to the right were two more sets that opened into the side parking lot. She looked down and felt her stomach do a flip-flop—she was standing a good thirty feet off the floor. She hated heights.

She looked up and instantly regretted it when her head began to swim. She grabbed the windowsill to steady herself. She closed her eyes for a moment and then forced herself to look up again.

Approximately five-feet above her head was a metal, corrugated catwalk that stretched across the entire warehouse. *Just like the Castrucci house*, she thought as she noticed several offshoot passages leading off the walkway, which led to large platforms that were used as storage space for spare equipment and boxes. She noticed a ladder, surrounded by a protection cage, attached to the catwalk in the middle of the warehouse. It stretched all the way to the floor. It reminded her of the ladders on the outside of giant water towers. It made her hands sweat just looking at it.

She could hear bits and pieces of the conversation as the men continued to talk. She decided that now was the time to move. Not only did she need to hear what they were saying, she wanted to see what they were doing. She kept reminding herself not to look down as she stepped across the gap and onto the next stack. She repeated the process several times and with each step, her legs shook and she continued to remind herself not to look down.

One wrong move and she would end up a bloody pile on the concrete floor below—or worse, if she survived the fall, there was no doubt in her mind that Castrucci would finish the job. She wondered if Laura heard her messages as she stepped onto the next set of crates. She felt an instant rush of adrenaline as the stack began to rock violently. Dropping to a crouching position, she tried to steady herself in the middle of the stack. *I can't cross the entire warehouse on these*, she thought, wiping the sweat off her face. She glanced up at the catwalk and made her decision.

She was vaguely aware of the men talking below as she slowly stood up. *I can't believe I'm about to do this*, she thought as she wiped her hands on the front of her pants to get the sweat off. She looked up at the catwalk again and decided that it was her best option. She reached up, wrapping her fingers around the side rail, hoping that it was strong enough to support her full weight. She took a deep breath, clamped her jaws tight to keep from grunting, and then pulled herself up with as much strength as she could muster. She could feel her muscles scream under the full weight of her body.

She let out a silent sigh when she finally felt her knees touch the metal platform. She fell forward, lying on her stomach for several seconds in order to catch her breath. *I really need to start working out again*, she thought as she slowly pushed herself up on her knees. She glanced out across the warehouse. From her position, she could see the top of Castrucci's head and she could clearly hear their conversation.

Sonny lit a cigarette.

"What was that?" Henry asked.

"What was what?" Sonny asked.

Henry held his hand up. "Shh … listen. I thought I heard something."

Big Tony shook his head. "You're hearing shit again. Why don'tcha try cleaning your ears out?"

Henry ignored him and walked toward the stack of skids.

"Get back over here, Henry. I don't have time for this shit. I haven't had dinner yet and want to get this done," Big Tony yelled.

Henry reluctantly did as he was told.

Sonny picked up a small figurine from the table and

handed it to Big Tony.

"Where are her eyes?" Henry asked, looking at a ceramic figure of a little girl in a dress.

"She's getting' new ones," Sonny said.

Henry frowned. "Why?"

Big Tony set the figurine back down on the table.

"Why don't you make yourself useful and go get the bag from Charlie's office?" Sonny said, turning his attention back to the figurines on the table.

Rheyna moved in a little closer so she could see both Castrucci and Sonny. She was hoping they would say a little more about the figurines on the table. She was a little smarter than Henry, and she had a sneaky suspicion that they were being used to smuggle the gems. She thought about the conversation she overhead a few days ago. Although she only heard bits and pieces, she remembered Sonny talking about a shipment of diamonds. When she told Laura about it during their nightly chat, Laura informed her that one of the dead informants had claimed Castrucci was trying to get into the gem market, mainly diamonds. In a crazy sort of way, it was all starting to make sense.

Sonny waited for Henry to leave and slid out a chair. "We may have a small problem but I've already taken steps to fix it."

Big Tony turned to look at him. "What kinda problem?"

"Our *friend's* a little worried about the feds. They brought in some sort of computer hack and he's created a software program to try and link the deaths."

Big Tony frowned. "What deaths?"

"Scala's, for one and our friend says they're diggin' back several years."

Big Tony clicked his tongue against the back of his teeth. "So what, they can't tie us to Scala or any of the others. Otherwise, they'd have done something by now."

"We're not the ones our friend is worried about. The computer program is looking for leaks."

"You say you took care of it?"

Sonny nodded.

"Then that's all I need to know."

Rheyna felt the hair stand up on the back of her neck. Sonny and Castrucci had just confirmed their suspicions. There was no longer any doubt—they had a leak in the bureau and not just a small one. Whomever it was had to be high up the food chain to have obtained the information about Ron and his newly created program.

For the first time since arriving in California, she felt an overwhelming amount of fear. Her mind began to race with the implications and what this all meant. If this person knew about Ron and his program, they had to know about Pandora's Box and if they knew about Pandora's Box, they had to know about her. If Castrucci knew, she didn't understand what he was waiting for. Why had he not come after her? Her mind was racing.

Shit, shit, shit, she kept repeating in her head. We have a major problem, or better yet, I have a major problem. Her mind continued to process the implications. Sonny said he fixed the problem, and depending on how he decided to do that, Ron's life could be in danger. She had to get in touch with Laura as soon as possible. She had heard enough and needed to get out of there.

She slowly inched her way back toward the way she had come and stopped in mid-step—Henry was standing directly beneath her.

"Jesus, Henry, what took you so damn long?" She heard Big Tony yell.

"Jeesh, can't a man take a shit without getting the fourth degree?" Henry yelled back.

Rheyna watched Henry walk over and hand Big Tony a large green bag. Castrucci snatched the bag from his hand, unzipped it, and removed a small, red pouch. He untied the drawstring and dumped the contents out in his hand. The diamonds shimmered like glass.

He put them back in the pouch and tossed it to Henry. "Make sure you get these to Roberto first thing in the morning, along with my apologies for the botched shipment in L.A."

"You got it," Henry said, cramming the pouch into the front pocket of his jeans.

She felt something run over the top of her foot and looked back to see a small tabby cat running along the catwalk.

"What the hell was that?" Henry asked. "Did you hear that?" he asked again, when the two men didn't answer.

Rheyna quickly made her way onto one of the offshoots and ducked down behind some boxes.

"Up there," Henry said.

Rheyna knew they were all looking up at the catwalk.

"I saw something."

"Henry, what the hell are you doing now?" Sonny asked.

Rheyna felt her heart skip a beat. She heard someone climbing up the ladder—she was in big trouble. She saw the top of Henry's head pop up over the edge. He dropped his gun down on the metal catwalk floor with a loud clank and then pulled himself up.

She tried to push herself further behind the boxes, to no avail. She prayed that he would walk straight down the catwalk and not come her way. She pulled the 9mm out of the holster and flipped off the safety. If he chose to come down the side she was on, she would be totally exposed and would have no choice other than to shoot him before he shot her. Suddenly, Henry took off running. With each hard step, Rheyna could feel the catwalk vibrate. He fired his gun in rapid succession, sending bullets ricocheting off the metal support beams.

"What the fuck are you trying to do? Kill us all?"

Sonny yelled as he and Big Tony ran for cover down below.

Out of nowhere, the tabby cat bolted from behind a bunch of crates and ran back down the catwalk.

"Damn cat!" Henry yelled, firing at the retreating animal. The bullets tore through the crates, sending pieces of wood raining down on the men below.

Big Tony was furious. "Damn it to hell, Henry! Get down here now, or I'll shoot you myself!" he yelled at the top of his lungs.

Rheyna waited for Henry to descend the ladder before venturing out from behind the boxes. She put her gun back inside the holster. When she first entered the building, she noticed motion sensors mounted along the inside windows, and she needed to get out before the men did.

She had to make it to the window before they reset the alarm system. As she turned the corner to get back on the main catwalk, she cut it too short. Before she could do anything about it, she felt the microphone boom clipped on her sweat jacket rip away. The tiny boom seemed to fall in slow motion. She watched it hit the concrete and cringed as the tiny pieces of plastic shattered. She wanted to scream as the sound amplified through her ear bud like a freight train.

She looked down at the men—their eyes were now on her. Big Tony pointed his finger. "Get him!" he yelled.

Within a split second, she saw the flash of muzzles as a barrage of bullets zipped and zinged past her head. She looked at the end of the runway and made a split-second decision. Fuck—she didn't have a choice. She broke into an all-out run, heading straight for the open end of the catwalk. Her eyes fixated on the pile of skids standing next to the one she had used to gain entry. Her heart thumped wildly in her chest. The skids were at least ten-feet away from the end of the catwalk—if she didn't time it just right, she would fall to the concrete below.

She hit the ledge and pushed off with everything she had. She closed her eyes and then heard a loud crack as the wood gave way under her full weight. She slid across the skid and felt stabbing pain in the palms of her hands and the front of her knees as tiny splinters of wood penetrated her skin. The stack swayed violently, the wood collapsing beneath her weight like dominoes. She scrambled to her feet and without thinking, lunged headfirst through the closed window.

She landed on top of the compactor with a loud thud, and then she felt two pops. One was from the side of her face slamming into the metal and the second was her shoulder separating from its socket. She closed her eyes and then opened them, hoping to get rid of the tiny white specks jumping around in front of her face. She involuntarily moaned as excruciating pain shot up her arm like a white-hot poker.

The sound of the warehouse door opening snapped her out of the funk. She folded her arm across her chest and held it tightly as she slid across the compactor. She stifled a scream as a bone-crunching shock reverberated through the tips of her fingers when her feet met the ground. The pain continued to run up her arm and then down the side of her neck, before settling in the middle of her back. It felt as if someone had stuck a lightening rod inside her skin.

She took off running across the back of the parking lot, toward a row of tractor-trailers.

"He went this way!" she heard Henry yell just before a bullet whizzed past her head. She weaved back and forth, trying to avoid the little flashes of white as bullets ricocheted off the trailers.

"Have Tommy turn the car around and shine the lights over here!" Sonny yelled.

She had to make it to the tall grass adjacent to the lot.

It was her best chance of losing them. She heard the car engine start and then the lights were fully on the trailers.

Just as Henry came around the side of the trailer, she ducked beneath the rear axle. With her good arm, she removed her gun from the holster. She heard gravel crunch under Henry's feet, each step bringing him closer. She held her breath.

"See anything?" Sonny yelled.

"No, you?" Henry yelled back.

"I think he went this way!" Sonny yelled back in response.

She slowly peeked around the side of the tire and breathed a small sigh of relief when she saw Henry walking back toward Sonny. She felt hot tears spill down her cheeks as the throbbing in her shoulder intensified. She crawled across to the other side and looked out toward the row of trailers. She could see the men from the waist down. They were three trailers over. She looked back toward the tall grass and felt dread. Separating the properties was a three-foot-tall fence. She glanced back toward the men. It was her best option—maybe her only option.

She ran toward the fence and knew it was going to hurt like hell. She propelled her body upward, clenching her teeth tightly to keep from screaming. She easily cleared the barbed wire. Her body slammed into the ground with a thud, the impact knocking the air out of her lungs.

She laid her head down across her arms and tried to catch her breath. Fuck, fuck, fuck, she silently swore at the sound of crunching gravel. She crawled through the grass on her belly and froze at the sound of approaching voices.

"I thought I heard something coming from over here," she heard Henry say.

"I don't think so. I told you, I think he went this way," Sonny replied.

She heard a creaking noise and knew they were

standing next to the fence. Please, God, don't let them come over here.

Henry kicked the fence in frustration with his foot. "We need a damn flashlight," he said.

Rheyna heard another set of feet approaching. She could tell by how hard the gravel crunched that it was Castrucci.

"Let's go, boys. Whoever it was, is probably long gone by now. Sonny, you make sure Charlie gets this lot lit first thing tomorrow," Big Tony said.

They turned to head back to the car. "Who do you think he was? You think maybe Carlos had something to do with it?" Sonny asked.

Big Tony shook his head. "I don't know. Let me see that thing again."

Sonny showed him the broken pieces of the microphone boom. "This looks more like something the feds would use."

"How much you think he heard?" Sonny asked.

"Everything," Big Tony said, nodding at the pieces in Sonny's hand. "Get that to Connie and see what he can find. Also check and see if our friend knows anything about this."

"You got it."

Big Tony turned to Henry. "Check the local hospital. Who knows—maybe one of your piss-poor shots got lucky."

Rheyna heard the car doors open and close and the gravel crunch as the car left the parking lot. She laid her head down across her arms, thinking she just needed to rest for a few minutes. Her eyes seemed to close by their own volition—she tried to open them just for a second and then everything went black.

When she finally opened her eyes, it took her several minutes to realize where she was. She had no idea how long she had been unconscious. She slowly got to her knees and stood up—that was when she realized that every single part of her body ached.

She rubbed the side of her temple with her good hand, trying to soothe the throbbing vein. She felt as if she had been run over by a train and was ninety-nine percent sure she looked it, too. She looked around for signs of movement, but all she heard were crickets. She still had to be careful on her way back to the Jeep. It wouldn't surprise her in the least to find Castrucci sitting somewhere, waiting on the off chance of catching her.

Moving at a turtles pace, she made her way back to the parking lot, the place where this little adventure had begun. She was relieved to see the Jeep still sitting where she parked it. "Ah, shit," she muttered under her breath, realizing that she had a bigger problem.

Her Jeep was a stick shift—there was no way she could drive it in her current condition, and going to the hospital was out of the question. She heard what Castrucci said to Henry, and she knew the first thing he would do was check all the emergency rooms. Although she didn't have a gunshot wound, she couldn't take the chance of having her name on a hospital list.

She opened the passenger-side door and rummaged around on the backseat for the old bandanna she had worn to Caroline's earlier in the day. She shut the door and walked over to the side of the warehouse. She crammed the bandanna in her mouth and bit down as hard as she could.

She took a step back and then slammed her shoulder into the corner of the building as hard as she could.

She heard a crunching sound and felt a pop as the bone went back into its socket. She fell to her knees, tears streaming down her cheeks. She took the bandanna out of her mouth and leaned back against the building.

After a few minutes, she pulled herself up and then wiped the sweat off her face with the bandanna. She walked back to the Jeep and got in. A glance at her watch, told her that she had been there for an hour and a half. That gave her a thirty-minute window before Laura went into panic mode. She pulled the Jeep out of the parking lot and hit the speed dial.

"Girl, you're cuttin' it a little close, aren't you?" Laura asked.

Rheyna downshifted, slowing the Jeep to a crawl as she came to a four-way stop, the move sending stabbing pains through her shoulder. "Yeah, I know. I had a few problems," she said through clenched teeth.

"Are you all right?" Laura asked, hearing Rheyna's deep intake of breath.

"Yeah, I'm okay."

"Okay, you concentrate on driving and once you get home and settled, give me a call, so I can properly chew your ass out."

Rheyna chuckled. "Yes, mother," she said and hung up the phone. She had known when she decided to go into Bayshore without a plan in place, that she would get a tongue-lashing from Laura. It was something she was not looking forward to getting. She was hoping that the Intel she got would lessen the beating.

It took Rheyna thirty minutes to get home. She took Annie out for a short walk and then went back inside. Instead of going out on the deck, she plopped down on the couch, filled with dread. She phoned Laura and sure enough, she got the tongue-lashing she expected. She gave her a quick replay of the events. She could tell that Laura was pissed, but she also heard the concern in her voice.

"Are you sure you're all right?" Laura asked again.

"I've been a lot better," Rheyna answered. She tilted her head back and popped a couple of aspirins into her mouth.

"For Christ's sake, Rheyna, you could've been killed. You should have phoned me first, damn it."

Rheyna found herself getting irritated. "I did phone you—twice, to be exact," she said matter-of-factly.

Laura's voice softened. "I know, and I'm sorry. I got your messages and that's partly my fault. My cell died. I keep forgetting to charge the damn thing."

"But you're right. It was a really stupid thing to do and I won't do it again."

"If you do, I just might kill you myself," Laura said, half joking.

"Hey, that's not funny," Rheyna said, pretending to sound hurt.

"I mean it, Rheyna. I don't care how much Intel you got. It was foolish."

"Okay, Laura. I understand. I said it won't happen again."

"I just don't want anything to happen to you."

"I know and you're right. I should have known better."

"Okay, then. Now that we have that settled, let's move on. So Castrucci never mentioned anyone by name?"

Rheyna unconsciously shook her head and realized that Laura couldn't hear her head shake. "No. They just kept referring to this person as their friend. What concerns me most is that they know about Ron. Sonny described the program perfectly."

"As soon as I hang up from you, I'll see how Kyle wants to handle it. We may need to put extra security on Ron, just in case."

"That's probably not a bad idea and while you're at it, have Kyle take a closer look at Bayshore's shipments. They had a bunch of figurines on the table and I'm pretty sure that's how they're moving the diamonds around the country."

"Well, it's nice to know that up to this point, we've had pretty good information. Is there anything else?"

"They have my transmitter, and it's only a matter of

time before they're able to trace it back to the bureau."

"Hopefully, by that time, we'll have enough to arrest him."

"I wouldn't count on it." Rheyna's pessimism caught her a little bit by surprise. She was usually the one who saw the glass as half-full, not half-empty, but she knew how cunning Castrucci was, and it wouldn't surprise her in the least to find that he had a judge or two in his pocket as well—hell, maybe even a senator, for that matter.

"Right now, we have to be concerned with your safety. There's a good chance that Castrucci already knows who you are."

"Believe me, that thought has crossed my mind more than once."

"I'll talk to Kyle, but we may have to pull the plug, Rheyna."

"Yeah, I thought about that, too."

"When are you hooking up with Caroline again?"

"I was supposed to go over in the morning, but I called and cancelled. I need to give myself a little rest and figure out how to cover all these bruises."

"All right, you get some rest and give me a call tomorrow afternoon so we can go over our next step."

"I'll talk with you later, then." Rheyna hung up the phone and leaned back on the couch. She stretched her legs out on the coffee table. They looked as if someone had run a metal rake over them. It had taken her quite awhile to pick the tiny pieces of wood out of her skin.

She grabbed the tube of ointment off the table and spread the cream over her cuts, flinching from the sting. It would be several days before she would be able to wear shorts around Caroline without generating questions. She was thankful that bruises and cuts were all she had ended up with. She would have had one hell of a time trying to explain a broken arm or leg—or worse, a bullet hole. She leaned her head back against the couch and closed her eyes.

Chapter 17

Artie parked his rental car directly in front of the bank. His hand trembled as he removed the key. He pulled a hanky out of his jacket pocket and mopped the sweat from his forehead. He glanced at the manila folder lying on the seat beside him. Surely, it had been more than enough time, he thought as he picked it up. He rubbed his hands together in an attempt to circulate his blood. After a few seconds, he held his hands out, palm down. He breathed a small sigh of relief. The shaking had almost subsided. He smiled as he rifled through the ashtray for some change.

He got out of the car and walked over to the meter. He looked up and down the street and then inserted a quarter into the machine. As he turned to go in the bank, he found himself looking directly into the chest of a young man. The force nearly knocked his glasses from his face.

"I am so sorry," the young man with dark, wavy, slicked backed hair said as he jerked headphones from his ears.

"Why don't you watch where you're going?" Artie yelled. He bent down to pick up the documents that were now strewn all over the sidewalk.

"Here, let me help you," the young man said as he picked up several papers and a white envelope.

Artie snatched the items from the young man's hand. "I can do it myself," he snapped.

"I'm … I'm really sorry," the young man repeated.

Artie's nodded at the MP3 player attached to the young man's waistband. "In the future, maybe you should turn that thing down a notch and not look at the ground when you walk."

The young man smiled, gave Artie a mock salute, and put the headphones back on. "I'll try to remember that. Have a good day."

Artie watched him walk down the sidewalk. *Kids these days just don't listen to anything they're told*, he thought as he walked through the bank door.

Ron looked up at the sound of beeping. He glanced at the large, flashing red letters on the computer monitor for several seconds, and then moved his mouse pointer over the link. He stared at the screen as the form began filling in the blanks. He couldn't believe it—his program had worked.

He pressed the 'enter' key on the keyboard and waited for the printer to spit out the report. He tore off the printout, and laid it on his desk. He pulled out his laptop drawer, grabbed a ruler, and used it to scan down the lines of data. He highlighted several rows and then walked over to the filing cabinet, pulled out the top drawer, and thumbed through the folders until he found the one he was looking for. He took the folder and sat back down at his desk, flipping open the file to compare the numbers.

"This can't be right." He double-checked the numbers again to be sure. He turned back to the monitor and started tapping on the keyboard. He looked at the list of case files, shook his head, and then picked up the phone. "I don't believe this." He started to dial a number when a knock at the door stopped him. He laid the phone back in its cradle. "Come in."

Sarah Avery poked her head around the door. "I have your mail." She handed him a magazine and a large, white envelope. "The envelope was hand-couriered about fifteen minutes ago."

"Thank you, Sarah." He waited for her to leave and then removed the rubber band, tossing the magazine to the side. The envelope had 'Urgent Delivery' stamped across it.

He ripped the top of the envelope off and pulled out the contents. He flipped through the photos and then picked up the phone. "Come on, come on. Pick up, Kyle," he urged as the phone rang repeatedly. "Damn," he said when Edwards' voicemail answered. "Kyle, this is Ron. I need you to call me back as soon as possible. I think I found our leak." He hung up the phone and picked up the top photo. He shook his head in disbelief, not believing what he was seeing.

It had been two days since Rheyna had snuck into Bayshore, and Edwards and Laura were busy doing their own Intel regarding the smuggling operation. She had been able to get out of seeing Caroline on both days, but Caroline was not about to let her get away with a third brush-off. Today was the day they had made plans to have dinner with Phil and Jesse, and Caroline was not taking no for an answer. Regardless of how much her shoulder hurt, she wasn't about to try to get out of it.

She watched Caroline walk across the driveway. Caroline opened the car door and slid in beside her. Rheyna waited for her to clip on her seatbelt before pulling out of the driveway.

"Are you hungry?" Caroline asked.

"I'm starving."

"Good, I think you're really going to like this place."

"Where am I heading, then?"

"University Avenue. We, my dear, are going to the Cheesecake Factory."

Rheyna's look was incredulous. "Cheesecake Factory? I want real food, woman, not dessert."

Caroline patted Rheyna's knee, still fresh with bruises, and it took everything in her not to flinch.

"Oh relax, why don't you? Live a little. Besides, they're only famous for cheesecake. They do sell other food," Caroline said as she opened the glove box. She fumbled through the stack of CDs. "Mind if we listen to some music?" she asked, and then selected one without waiting for Rheyna's answer. She slid the CD in and turned up the volume.

They drove in silence with Sophie B. Hawkins playing in the background. They slowly made their way through downtown and after a few minutes, they came to the main intersection.

"Make a right at the next light and find a spot wherever you can," Caroline said.

Rheyna got lucky and pulled up in front of the restaurant just as a minivan vacated a prime spot.

Jesse was standing in the lobby, waiting for them. He rushed over and then quickly ushered them to a table in the back where Phil was waiting with a very handsome waiter.

"Hello, Ladies. I'm Josh, and I'll be your server tonight. What can I get you to drink?"

Caroline slid into the seat next to Rheyna. "Hello, Josh. I'll have a glass of white Zin, please."

"And I'll have a bottle of Michelob Light," Rheyna said.

He placed the menus on the table. "Okay, I'll be right back with your drinks and give you a chance to look at the menu."

"So, how have you two been since the last time we saw you? Staying out of trouble, I hope?" Phil teased after the waiter walked away.

"Now Phil, you know I'm a good girl," Caroline chided back.

"That's not what I heard," Jesse continued the tease.

Caroline pretended to be hurt. "Ah, come on, Jesse. I thought you were on my side."

Jesse put his arm around her shoulders and squeezed. "You know that you're my best, best, bestest friend in the whole wide world," he said as he planted a big, juicy kiss on her cheek, complete with sound effects.

She playfully pushed him away. "Jesse, you just aren't right."

"You think that's bad, wait until I tell you my latest joke."

"Oh no, Jesse, not that one again," Phil said, rolling his eyes heavenward.

"Come on, Phil, honey. You know it's not that bad," Jesse teased his lover.

Rheyna laughed at the playful banter going back and forth between the two men. They fit together like a pot and lid, and she loved it.

She shook her head at Jesse. "Okay, Jesse, the suspense is killing me. Will you please tell us the joke?"

He waited for Josh to set down their drinks. "Nope, I'm not going to tell you now."

Caroline shook her finger at him. "Jesse, you can't string us along and then not tell us."

He looked at Phil.

"Oh, go ahead and tell them," Phil said in resignation.

Jesse smiled and then leaned in closer to the table. "Okay, here goes. A woman went to see her doctor and said, 'Doctor, I have this terrible rash.' She raised her blouse to reveal a large 'T'-shaped design on her chest. 'Now, that is the strangest rash I've ever seen,' the doctor said as she examined her. 'It's from my boyfriend,' she explained. 'He goes to Tennessee and refuses to remove his letter jacket when we make love.' The doctor took out her pad and wrote out a prescription for a tube of ointment.

The next day, a different woman came in with a very similar rash in the shape of an 'O'. 'How did you get that?' the doctor asked. 'My boyfriend goes to Ohio State and won't take his letter jacket off when we make love.' The doctor smiled and wrote out another prescription for ointment.

The next day, a very beautiful woman came in to see the doctor. She also had a rash on her chest but in the shape of an 'M'. So the doctor took one look at it and said, 'Let me guess: your boyfriend goes to Michigan?' The woman shook her head, smiled, and said, "No, actually, my girlfriend goes to Washington."

Rheyna looked at Caroline and Caroline looked at her and then they looked at Jesse. The look on his face was priceless. He looked as is if his joke was the best thing since the invention of the wheel. Rheyna and Caroline lost it. Rheyna was laughing so hard, that she had to use her napkin to wipe away the tears. Phil's face was dead serious and that made them laugh harder.

"You know, when he first told me that joke, I didn't get it. I couldn't figure out how she got the 'W' to look like an 'M' if she went to Washington," Phil said.

"Please, please, you two have got to stop. I can't take anymore," Caroline begged as tears ran down her cheeks.

"No, he's right," Jesse nodded. "Would you believe that I actually had to draw him a diagram?"

"No, you didn't!" Rheyna managed to get out before another fit of laughter took hold.

Jesse hung his head in a solemn fashion. "I'm afraid so," he said. "Yep, I had to explain that it had to do with numbers, the numbers of six and nine."

If Rheyna laughed any harder, she thought she would break a rib.

They were still laughing when Josh reappeared to take their order. "I must have missed a really good conversation," he said as he replaced their drinks with fresh ones.

Rheyna nodded her head. "You sure did," she said, trying to pull it together.

"Well, in that case, I'm sorry I missed it."

"Oh no, be glad you did," Phil said with a grin.

Josh pulled out a pen and paper pad. "Okay, then. Have you folks decided what you'd like to order?" he asked.

The four of them looked at each other and busted out laughing.

Jesse was the first to recover. "I think you might have to give us a few more minutes."

"All right, but next time, you have to let me in on the joke." He looked directly at Rheyna and winked before turning away.

Phil slowly peered over his menu. "Ooh, Rheyna. I think he likes you," he teased.

She found the mere thought disturbing. "I think not," she said, and then turned to Jesse. "So Jesse, have you been working out?" she asked.

"Oh no, Rheyna, of all the things you could have asked him and you had to ask that!" Phil said, shaking his head. He and Caroline both buried their face in their hands.

Rheyna looked at them. "What? What did I say?"

Caroline busted out laughing.

Jesse ignored them both, turned to look at Rheyna, and said, "As a matter of fact, I have. Did I ever mention that physical fitness runs in my family?" He ignored the laughter coming from Phil and Caroline. "I mean it. It runs all the way back to my great grandfather. He started jogging ten-miles a day five-years ago when he was eighty-five and we haven't seen him since."

Caroline was practically rolling out of her seat from laughing so hard.

Rheyna tried to look at him with her most serious expression. "Jesse, I can honestly say that I have never met anyone like you in my life."

"Is that a good thing or a bad thing?" he asked.

"It's definitely a good thing," Rheyna laughed.

Phil cleared his throat and held up the menu. "I guess we better order before they decide to kick us out."

The rest of the evening went smoothly. They ate their dinner and chitchatted about Phil and Jesse's party. Before Rheyna knew it, they said their goodbyes and made plans to take a trip together up the coast on Phil and Jesse's boat.

The drive back to Caroline's house had gone by too quickly. She watched Caroline disappear inside the house. The only redeeming feature was the knowledge that she would be seeing her again tomorrow.

Edwards spread the stack of surveillance photos out in front of Laura and Stevens. He picked up the ones that had a large red 'X' marked across the face and slung them across the table. He looked back and forth at the two agents. He slammed his fist down on the table, causing Laura to jump. She reached out to grab the cup of coffee, but not in time to keep it from spilling on the photos.

"This son-of-a-bitch has killed at least four people since we began, and we don't have shit. We can't tie him to any of them." He turned and directed his anger at Stevens. "What are we getting from the restaurant?"

"Nothing we can use. It's all babble. They never talk about business and if they do, it's pretty well coded."

"This is bullshit. That's what this is." Edwards was just plain pissed off. He looked at Stevens and shook his head in disbelief. "Pretty well coded? Are you fucking kidding me? A rookie could have figured out that they ordered a hit on Paul and George, and you should have known that!" he yelled.

It was totally out of character for Edwards to dress down one of his agents in front of another agent, but he had reached his limit. He pointed his finger at Stevens. "You're the Sr. agent on this goddamn operation and it was your responsibility to warn the agents in L.A."

Stevens' face flushed red as his own temper flared. "How the hell was I supposed to know that having dinner meant that it was a fucking hit order? We've never had a case like that before."

"Okay, you guys," Laura intervened. "This isn't solving anything. All of us are stressed, but you two fighting doesn't get us answers."

Edwards paced back and forth in front of the window. He stopped to look out across the street at Pal Joey's. "You're right, Laura, it doesn't. Castrucci knows we're onto him." He turned and looked at Laura and Stevens. "He's been too careful and I know he's not that smart."

Stevens massaged the side of his temples with his index fingers. "Maybe we can rattle his cage," he said.

Laura leaned back in her chair. "Let's go after Bayshore. We know for a fact that they're funneling money through the Cayman's and Rheyna's pretty confident that he's using the computer in his office to make the transactions."

Stevens nodded his head in agreement. "It would make sense to use the one operation that appears to be the cleanest and we all know from past experience that they're usually the ones that turn out to be the dirtiest. Unfortunately, we've failed at all attempts to get any information from his office. He doesn't do much talking in there. In the past, we've tried to upload a remote tracker, but failed. It's obvious that he has some sort of security measure on his end that runs interference."

Edwards considered the information and nodded his head. "Okay then, well, I guess it's up to Rheyna. Since we need to get around his security devices, she'll have to do the upload directly at his computer," he said, turning to Laura. "Laura, you find out what Rheyna needs and get it to her."

Laura nodded, absentmindedly tapping her pencil on the edge of the table. "I think Rheyna's right about this one. We know that Castrucci's into gems and he's getting them from Sierra Leone. I'd be willing to bet that he's using Bayshore as the main front company."

Edwards took a cigarette out of his pocket and lit it. "Okay, I'm convinced. Let's apply some heat and go after Bayshore. I'll set it up and get the warrant." He blew a puff of smoke in the air. "Carl, you'll lead on the raid."

Stevens got out of the chair and grabbed a set of keys from the table. "I'm gonna go grab us something to eat, you guys want anything in particular?"

Edwards shook his head.

Laura pulled a couple bucks from her pocket and handed it to him. "I'll have whatever you're having," she said.

Edwards walked over to the window and leaned his hands against the sill. He watched Stevens get in the car and pull away from the curb. His cell beeped, indicating he had a voicemail waiting. He dialed in and listened to the message, and then immediately called Ron.

"I was just about to call you again," Ron said through the phone.

"I just got your message. Have you talked to the bank manager yet?" Edwards asked.

"Yeah, he was very cooperative. He said it would take a couple of days, but he'd get the info together and give me a call as soon as he's done."

"Okay, Ron. As soon as you hear back from him, let

me know and I'll have someone swing by and pick it up."

"You got it."

"Where is he now?" Edwards asked.

"I told him to meet you down at the L.A. bureau office."

"Did you fax the documents?"

"Yeah, you should be getting them any minute now."

"All right, I'll give you a call later." Edwards hung up the phone and walked over to the fax machine. Within seconds, it started humming and then beeped as it spit out the fax. Edwards pulled the document off the tray. He looked at it and then handed it to Laura. She glanced at the circled areas and shook her head.

Edwards picked up the next sheet and looked at the grainy photo. He still couldn't believe it. He waited for the fax machine to spit out the last document and pulled out a chair next to Laura. He laid the photos on the table. If he hadn't just seen the pictures himself, he still wouldn't have believed it. He was not shocked easily, but this downright surprised the hell out of him.

Laura picked up the photo of Artie standing outside the bank with a dark-haired young man. She looked at the next photo, showing the young man handing documents to Artie. She instantly recognized the man. She flipped through the rest of the photos and tossed them back on the table.

She was the first to break the silence. "You know who that is, don't you?" she asked.

Edwards nodded. "Marco Mancini, one of Castrucci's foot soldiers."

Laura shook her head. "I still can't believe this—Artie, of all people."

"It just goes to show that when you think you know someone, you realize that you really don't know them at all."

"But Artie?" Laura was dumbfounded. She picked up

the bank document and looked at it again. "This shows a deposit of fifteen grand. Surely he's received a lot more than that."

"My thoughts exactly, and that's one of the questions I'm going to ask him."

"It doesn't make sense, Kyle. If he's the mole, why would he get so careless after all these years?"

"I've been asking myself the same question, and the only thing I can come up with is that he didn't know about Ron's program until it was too late."

"But Rheyna said Sonny specifically mentioned the program. Is there any way he could have figured it out?"

Kyle shrugged. "I guess anything's possible. Hell, he's gone undetected for more than ten years, so he's obviously resourceful."

"What about Rheyna?"

He shook his head. "I don't think Castrucci knows about her."

"What makes you so sure?"

"For two reasons—If Castrucci knew, he would've already taken steps to eliminate her, and Artie, if he is the mole, would've known that outing Rheyna ..." he stopped and smiled, "pardon the pun, but outing Rheyna would've pointed directly to someone on the team and he knows this."

"Do you think we should go ahead with the plan?"

He stood up and grabbed his jacket off the back of the chair. "Yeah, he doesn't know that we've decided to have Rheyna try and access Castrucci's system, but run it by Rheyna first. If she's okay with it, then we'll proceed. If not, we'll pull the plug ASAP."

"All right, I'll give her a call and fill her in on what we got so far."

"I'll call you as soon as I'm done talking to Artie." Edwards gathered up the photos and went out the door.

Laura turned at the sound of voices and reached over

to turn the volume up on the receiver. She was listening in to the conversation going on inside Castrucci's office. A few minutes later, she glanced up as the door opened.

"I just saw Kyle drive away. Where's he going?" Stevens asked as he set the bag on the table.

She held up her hand to silence him. "Hold on, I'll tell you in a minute."

Big Tony glared at Sonny and Henry.

Sonny tried to calm him down. "They haven't got shit, Tony and that's why they're doing this. Trying to shake us up, that's all."

Big Tony wasn't buying it. He vehemently shook his head at Sonny. "Carlos is behind this. He has to be."

"It don't make no sense, Tony."

"Paulie and Georgie, that's why!" he yelled.

Sonny shook his head. "Carlos don't know shit, either."

Henry's cell phone rang, interrupting their conversation. "Yeah? How long ago ... He down there now ... Yeah ... Okay ... Call me when they're released." Henry flipped the phone shut.

Big Tony looked at him.

"That was Louie. Marco and Connie just got pinched in front of Pal Joey's."

"What the hell for?" Big Tony asked.

"Some bullshit about consorting with known criminals and Connie was packing."

Big Tony looked as if his head was going to explode. "See? What'd I tell you, Sonny? Last week, they got Richie for no reason."

Sonny sat calmly, taking it all in as he lit a cigarette. "Has Ramono been called?" he asked Henry.

Henry nodded. "He was there waitin' when they brought 'em in."

Laura smiled as she and Stevens listened in on the conversation. She could only imagine the look on Castrucci's face. *If he's pissed now, wait until we go into Bayshore,* she thought. Better yet, wait until he finds out that we got Artie. She wished she could be there to see the look on his face.

Chapter 18

Rheyna had no idea of what took place inside the house, but she knew it was bad and she figured it had to be from the pressure Edwards was instigating. Big Tony looked like a volcano about to erupt.

He jerked the chair back away from the table and sat down. Sonny and Henry took a seat at the table next to him. The patio table next to the pool had turned out to be Big Tony's preferred place to discuss business and it had paid off highly for her. She grabbed the towel off the table and wiped her face and arms while glancing over at the table.

Today was a real scorcher. The thermometer outside the pool hut put the temperature at ninety-eight degrees. She looked down at her legs and was grateful for cosmetic makeup—namely, waterproof concealer. It had done a good job of hiding her scratches. Of course, Caroline had noticed, just as she had suspected she would. She felt bad for blaming it on Annie, but the explanation seemed to satisfy Caroline.

She watched Big Tony reach inside his breast pocket, take out a handkerchief, and use it to mop the sweat off his forehead. What he did next shocked her.

Henry had been leering at Caroline almost from the instant he saw her. With a movement quicker than Rheyna thought possible, Bog Tony slapped Henry upside the head so hard that he nearly knocked him out of the chair. "Put your goddamn tongue back in your mouth before I cut it off," he snarled.

She tried not to laugh and actually felt a little bit sorry for the man. She knew how he felt. Her tongue fell out when she looked at Caroline, too.

"I think he likes you," she said just loud enough for Caroline to hear.

Caroline frowned and playfully slapped her with the magazine she was reading. "Yuck. He can like all he wants."

"He's not that bad-looking," Rheyna teased.

"You think so? Maybe you should take him for yourself."

Rheyna glanced over at Henry and shook her head. "Nah. Not my type."

A look of amusement crossed Caroline's face. "And ... what exactly is your type?" she asked.

Rheyna wanted to say, you are, but held her tongue. "I prefer blondes."

"That figures."

Rheyna turned over on her side to look at her. "What's that supposed to mean?"

Caroline shrugged. "Nothing. Just that most people like the opposite of what they look like."

"Is that true for you, too?"

"Yep," she answered and then ducked her face back behind the magazine.

Rheyna sighed. *She's flirting with me again*, she thought. Come to think of it, she did that a lot these days. She heard a phone ring and looked up to see

Henry talking into his cell again. She heard him say, "Yeah and okay" before hanging up. Her ear bud was useless. She hadn't had the opportunity to get the receiver from under the table to replace the batteries, and she was not about to test fate by being careless. A few minutes later, she heard the door slide open and turned to see Terasa walk out onto the patio.

"Where's Rosa?" Big Tony asked.

Terasa placed a tray of sandwiches down on the table. "She has the afternoon off," she said.

"Thanks, Mrs. Castrucci," Henry said, biting into the club sandwich.

"Thanks, Mrs. C," Sonny said, taking a sandwich for himself.

"You're welcome, boys," she replied with a smile.

She's always smiling, Rheyna thought as she watched Big Tony half stand to kiss Terasa on the cheek.

"Is she great, or what?" he asked the two men.

Terasa picked up the tray and came over to her and Caroline. Caroline sat up and pulled one of the loungers over.

"I thought you two might be hungry," Terasa said, placing the tray on the table between them.

Caroline nodded at the lounger. "Thanks, Mom. Have a seat and join us," she said.

Terasa sat down in the lounger. "Maybe for a few minutes," she said. "I can't stay long. I have my hair appointment today."

"Thank you, Terasa. I didn't realize how hungry I was," Rheyna said as she sunk her teeth into the sandwich.

"Well, if you ask me, the both of you could stand to put on a few extra pounds here and there," she teased.

Rheyna and Caroline looked at each other and then at Terasa. They both answered with a resounding, "No."

Terasa shook her head and laughed. "I think you two girls are incorrigible and an equally bad influence on each other."

"Ah, Mom, that's not fair," Caroline pretended to be hurt.

"So, do you two incorrigible girls have any plans tonight?"

"As a matter of fact, we do. I think I've pretty much talked Rheyna into staying for an all-night movie marathon—unless she decides she's not up to the challenge. She'll probably be asleep by ten anyhow."

Why does everyone who wants me to do what they want, always have a tendency to do it in a challenging manner? First, it was Laura, then Edwards and now Caroline. Rheyna shook her head at Caroline. "You'll definitely go down before I do, especially after a few glasses of wine," she teased back.

"Hey, that was a low blow," Caroline said.

Rheyna smiled. "Well, it serves you right. You're the one who started this. Besides, I already told you that I was up for this marathon of yours," Rheyna said. "And I knew you wouldn't have taken no for an answer, anyway."

Caroline nodded her head. "This is true. I usually get what I want." For emphasis, she ran her tongue over her lower lip, and it worked. Rheyna's eyes were glued to her mouth.

Caroline cleared her voice to get Rheyna's attention. When she looked up, she saw Caroline laughing at her. She has no shame. Caroline was flirting with her and she was doing it in front of her mother. Rheyna felt her face flush and quickly looked away. She was saved when Terasa stood up.

"Well, I need to get going. I don't want to be late," Terasa said.

Rheyna saw Vincent out of the corner of her eye, get up from the table where he and Joey had been playing cards. He followed Terasa into the house.

It was time for her to leave, too. She swung her legs off the lounger and stood to put on her robe. "I'm gonna take off. I need to get Annie and prepare myself for this movie marathon of yours."

"Okay. I'll see you in a couple hours," she said.

Rheyna said her goodbyes to Big Tony and the men at the table.

Edwards crammed his hands in his pockets and looked through the two-way window. He turned to Agent Bill Wilks. "How long's he been in there?" he asked as Artie got up from the chair to start pacing back and forth.

"Almost two hours."

"Did he say anything?"

Agent Wilks laughed. "He was fine until we took him to the interrogation room. He became a little hysterical and started yelling at us. For a minute or two, I thought he was gonna cry."

Edwards picked up the folder. "Well, I might as well get this over with," he said and then opened the door.

Artie stopped pacing and turned toward Edwards. "Oh, Kyle, thank God. I don't understand what's happening. Ron called and said to meet you here and then when I got here, they put me in this room."

"Sit down, Artie," Edwards said sternly, motioning toward the chair.

Artie reluctantly did as he was told.

Edwards sat down across from him and laid the folder on the table. "You have no idea why you're here?" he asked.

Artie nervously fidgeted in the chair and started picking at his nails. He shook his head. "No, I don't."

Edwards opened the file and pulled out the bank document. "Cut the shit, Artie. You know damn well why you're here," he said calmly and then pushed the sheet across the table.

Artie picked up the paper. Edwards watched the color drain from Artie's face as he read the document.

"I, I can explain," he said, his voice shaking.

Edwards pushed his chair back and stood up. He rested his hands on the table and leaned forward. "Oh, yeah? Can you also explain these?" He threw the photos down on the table in front of Artie.

Artie's hand shook as he picked up the photos. He

frowned. "How … where did you get these?"

"It doesn't matter where I got them. I want you to explain to me why you were talking with Marco Mancini."

"Who?" Artie asked, frowning.

"Come on, Artie. Stop bullshitting me. It's over. Do you understand me? It's over."

"But, but I don't know who this man is. I swear. He ran into me on my way into the bank. He knocked the papers out of my hand and stopped to help me pick them up. I swear, Kyle. You have to believe me," he insisted.

Edwards raised his eyebrows. "Believe you? You must be fucking joking." He jabbed his finger at Artie's face. "You're the fucking leak. You've been on Castrucci's payroll for years. You're the reason several people have lost their lives and you want me to believe you. What about Rheyna, Artie, did you fucking tell Castrucci about her, too?"

On the verge of tears, Artie shook his head vehemently. "I swear to God, Kyle, I have nothing to do with Castrucci. I don't even know who Marco Mancini is."

Edwards couldn't believe this. Even with the proof in front of his face, Artie continued to deny his involvement. Edwards slammed his fist down on the table. "Mancini is a foot soldier for the Massino crime family and this proves you took a payoff!" Edwards yelled. He picked up the bank document and slung it at Artie. "You also had direct access to the Vinci and Pisano files."

Artie frowned. "Who's Vinci and Pisano?" he asked, his mind moving a mile a minute as he tried to place the names.

"Yes, Vinci and Pisano. You were one of the case agents assigned to them."

"But that was over ten years ago," Artie said as his mind finally registered the names.

Edwards nodded. "And that shows just how damn long you've been at this, doesn't it?"

Artie shook his head. "They died."

Edwards' eyebrows shot up. "So you admit that you had a hand in their deaths?"

"No, no. I mean they both died in accidents. One in a car crash and the other was a botched burglary."

"Bullshit, Artie. You passed the information to Castrucci and he had them killed."

Artie was becoming hysterical. "I swear ... I swear with God as my witness, Kyle—"

"Just shut up, Artie. Just shut the hell up and how dare you bring God into this!"

Artie shrunk back in his chair. "I, I ... I only stole the money," he said finally.

The statement stopped Edwards cold. "You what?"

"I stole the money. I stole the money from the evidence room." Artie laid his head down across his arms on the table and cried. He looked up at Edwards with puffy cheeks and bloodshot eyes.

"But why, Artie?"

Artie took his glasses off and laid them on the table. "I didn't know what else to do. I'm $250,000 in debt. Alice maxed out our credit cards and the bank was foreclosing on our house."

Edwards was in shock. He expected to get a confession, but not this.

"I went down to the evidence room after our meeting. You can check with Cecil. He'll confirm that I was there."

Edwards sighed as he tried to digest the information. He looked at Artie and shook his head. "I have no choice but to place you under arrest."

"You have to believe me, Kyle," Artie begged.

"I need time to verify what you've told me, and right now, I don't know what to believe," Edwards said honestly. As he picked up the folder and turned to leave. He stopped and looked back at Artie. "You should have come to me first. If you were in trouble, you should have come to me first."

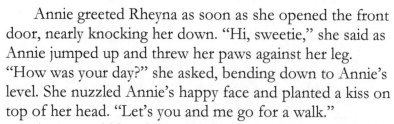

Annie greeted Rheyna as soon as she opened the front door, nearly knocking her down. "Hi, sweetie," she said as Annie jumped up and threw her paws against her leg. "How was your day?" she asked, bending down to Annie's level. She nuzzled Annie's happy face and planted a kiss on top of her head. "Let's you and me go for a walk."

Annie could barely contain herself as Rheyna slipped the leash on her harness and slid open the patio door. She pulled Rheyna down the steps two at a time, and there wasn't much Rheyna could do about it. Annie had grown so big, that she no longer walked her—Annie was the one who walked Rheyna. She had never known what people meant by the term, being walked by your dog, until recently. It was an everyday occurrence for Annie to take Rheyna for a walk. She loved having Annie around—it was good for her sanity.

After a few minutes, she let Annie off her leash and laughed. Without fail, Annie headed straight for the white caps and bit at them. It had become a game to her. She would growl, then bite at them, and then jump back when the water hit her paws.

An hour later, she and Annie arrived back at the house. After feeding Annie her supper, she made her call to Laura. She was caught by surprise when Laura told her that Artie had been arrested. She filled Rheyna in on the details, and Laura was as shocked as she was. Never in a million years would she have suspected Artie. He just didn't seem the type. Laura and Edwards had left the decision up to her as to whether she felt comfortable enough to go forward with her mission. After discussing it at great length with Laura, she had made her mind up—

she would go through with it.

After Rheyna made her decision, Laura's persona immediately turned to business. She and Laura both knew what was at stake. It would be a big night for all of them if Rheyna gained access to Castrucci's office—or more importantly, his computer.

"Do you need anything else?" Laura asked.

"No, it looks like you have everything covered."

Rheyna had picked up the package marked 'photo supplies' from the post office earlier in the week. She now had the contents spread out across the counter.

"How's the rest of the surveillance going?" she asked.

Laura let out a dejected sigh. "Not too good. We have hundreds and hundreds of hours of tapes, but nothing to link Castrucci to the killings."

Rheyna listened as Laura continued to brief her.

"The closest we've come so far, is hearing his regrets for not taking out Massino when he wanted to."

"Well, whatever you guys are doing, it's working. He was so pissed off today, he could have spit nails."

"If you think that's bad, he's really gonna love what's going down in a couple hours. Edwards and Stevens are going after Bayshore."

Rheyna couldn't help but laugh. Seeing Castrucci squirm would be a sight in and of itself. "Couldn't happen to a nicer person, but you're right, he'll be in rare form tomorrow," she said.

"I think Edwards is right. He's much smarter than we gave him credit for," Laura said in response.

Rheyna was beginning to agree with her. "He had a sweeper go through the house yesterday and I thought for sure he'd find the pen."

"Must not been too good of a sweeper. An idiot wouldn't miss the signal coming from that baby."

"No shit," Rheyna agreed.

"I want you to be real careful tonight, Rheyna. Don't

take any unnecessary risks.."

"I promise I'll be very careful and I'll be sure to check in with you later." Rheyna hung up the phone and went back inside.

She pulled out the chair and slid the laptop over in front of her. She waited for it to power up and unpacked the small, handheld Image Master Solo III Forensic unit, also known as IMS. She took one end of the USB cable and plugged it into the IMS port and the other into the laptop. Just like her photo equipment, the bureau hadn't spared any expense on her new gadgets.

The equipment was top of the line and the best that money could buy. She flipped on the power switch and watched the screen come to life. She had used this machine before on other undercover operations, but never in a case like this. She hoped it would work. Annie's ears twitched in time with the beeping. She stood up on her hind legs with her front paws on the counter and leaned in to sniff the machines.

The IMS made a loud beep. Annie jumped back and knelt down with her rear end sticking up in the air. She growled at the machine.

"It's okay, girl. See? It won't hurt you." Rheyna held the IMS up so Annie could smell it. Each time it beeped, she cocked her head. As quickly as her interest began, it was over, and Annie took her usual position down at Rheyna's feet.

The screen on the IMS popped up and asked for a fingerprint authorization. Rheyna touched her index finger to the screen and waited for it to log her in. It took her several minutes to type in the commands to prepare the machines for wireless transmissions. It was imperative that she set everything up right; otherwise, the computer on Laura's end would be useless if it couldn't read Castrucci's files.

Within seconds, the machines beeped simultaneously,

affording her a huge sigh of relief. The two desktop menus were identical and that meant she had done everything right. The IMS was ready to go and so was she. She shut the machines down and went back to the bedroom to pack an overnight bag. She buried the IMS in between her clothes and slid the tracking CD into the outside zipper pocket.

A glance at the clock confirmed that she still had plenty of time to get to Caroline's. She could feel her pulse rate quickening, a definite sign that she was psyched for the job at hand. This was what she lived for and this was one of the main reasons she had joined the FBI. This would be, by far, the largest risk yet. If she got caught, especially inside his house, Anthony Castrucci would kill her. She had no doubt about that whatsoever. She downed a glass of wine and then poured another. She was definitely pumped. She didn't know if she was more scared of what she was about to do, or more scared of spending the night alone with Caroline. She decided it was a little of both.

Charlie stood in the doorway with a shit-eating grin on his face. He watched in amusement as federal agents rounded up his warehouse workers. Several of them now stood up against the wall with their hands spread out above their heads, being searched. Agents were everywhere and he was helpless to stop them from carrying the computer equipment out of his office. He really didn't care one way or the other. He knew something they didn't, and he also knew he had better make a good show of it to be convincing.

"Who the hell do yous' think you are? Yous' can't take those!" he yelled as the boxes on the tables were being opened one by one.

Edwards shoved a set of papers in his face. "These say we can, and in case you can't read, it's a search warrant for this facility, Mr. DeAmotto."

Charlie snatched the papers from Edwards' hand. "This is fuckin' harassment, that's what this is." He pretended to read them and smiled as Edwards walked over to the table where several ceramic owls sat. "I don't know what you're lookin' for. We run a legitimate business here!" he yelled to make sure his voice was loud enough for everyone to hear.

Stevens walked over to Charlie and leaned forward, bringing his face mere inches from his. "And I've got some swampland in Ohio to sell you, Charlie," Stevens said with a grin.

Charlie threw his hands up in the air in resignation. "Fine. Be my guest, 'cause yous' ain't findin' shit."

Edwards picked up one of the owls and tossed it over to Stevens. He turned it over in his hand to inspect it. It looked every bit the tacky knickknack it was, complete with glass-colored eyes—the diamonds were gone. Edwards shook his head in disgust. He slammed the owl into the concrete, shattering it to pieces. "Tear this fucking place apart!" he yelled at the agents near the table.

Charlie laughed a deep belly laugh. "Hey, that'll be three-fifty plus tax, Mr. FBI agent, sir," Charlie chuckled as Edwards leaned against the wall and crossed his arms over his chest.

"What the fuck is this?" Big Tony yelled, stepping through the doorway.

Edwards quickly crossed the floor. At roughly the same size, Edwards stood eye to eye with the big man. He grinned at Big Tony. "We have a warrant to search the premises, and Tony, if you interfere, I'll arrest you for obstruction."

Big Tony took a menacing step toward Edwards, but

Sonny jumped in between them. He placed his hands on Big Tony's chest and pushed him backward.

Edwards continued to bait him. "What, Tony? What'cha gonna do? Huh? You wanna piece of me? Go ahead." Edwards winked at him. He couldn't resist egging him on. "Give me one good reason!"

Big Tony eyed him curiously. Edwards could tell that he was weighing his options.

Sonny grabbed Big Tony by the arm and pulled him toward the door. "Come on, Tony, let's get outta here. We're clean, nothing to worry about."

"You'll be hearing from my attorney!" Big Tony yelled over his shoulder.

"And you'll be hearing from me again real soon. I promise!" Edwards yelled back as he watched the two men get in the limo. Edwards turned to Stevens.

Stevens shook his head. "Nothing, it's clean."

Edwards clenched his fists in frustration. Something in his gut was telling him that Castrucci knew they were coming.

Stevens raised his eyebrows questioningly. "What'ya wanna do?"

"I don't know. I need to think," Edwards said. He walked out the door and climbed into his sedan. "Have Laura go over the tapes," he said to Stevens through the open window. He put the car in drive and started to pull out of the parking lot and stopped. "Tell her to look for anything that might indicate they were tipped."

Rheyna pushed the pieces of grilled salmon around on her plate. Her nerves were too jumpy to eat. She thought about Bayshore and silently prayed that Edwards and Stevens were finding what they needed, but somehow, she knew they wouldn't. Laura was right. They had a big, big problem from the internal side of the bureau. The mole in the department had been feeding Castrucci information—information that might jeopardize her life. She had a gut feeling that it was only a matter of time before things would come to a head. It was inevitable.

Terasa jarred Rheyna back to reality. "So have you girls decided what movies you're going to watch?"

"Well, if I leave it to Caroline, it will be a marathon of chick flicks," Rheyna teased.

"And what's wrong with chick flicks?" Terasa asked, stopping in mid-bite.

"Yeah, Rheyna, what's wrong with chick flicks?" Caroline piped in, a smile forming on her lips.

Rheyna laid her fork down on the plate, feigning disappointment. "Oh no, Terasa, please don't tell me you, too?"

Terasa shrugged. "I'll have you know, *Sweet Home Alabama* is my very favorite movie."

They laughed as Rheyna pretended to beat her head on the table. The scraping of a chair on the other side of the pool caused them to look up.

Vincent stood up and threw his cards down on the table. "You're cheating," he spat at Joey.

"No, I'm not. I won fair and square."

Vincent walked over to where the women were sitting. He looked at Terasa. "Ma'am, if you don't need anything else, I'm going to turn in now."

She dismissed him with a wave of her hand. "No, Vincent. I'll see you tomorrow."

"I'll turn in, too." Joey said, looking at Caroline.

"Good night, Joey," Caroline said.

They watched the two men turn to go inside the house.

Rheyna smiled when Joey playfully pushed Vincent through the door. "You're just a poor sport, Vincent."

"Am not," he replied and shoved Joey back.

Edwards was silent as he watched Laura heave the aluminum case on the table. At first glance, it looked like an ordinary propane tabletop grill. She snapped open the lock and raised the lid. Taking up the entire inside of the case was the ICS RoadMASSter II Portable Forensic Evidence Analysis System. It was the counterpart to the one that Rheyna had programmed earlier, except on a larger scale.

She pressed a switch on the side and waited as the machine went through its power-up cycling modes. The machine beeped and the bright blue screen lit up like a Christmas tree. After a few seconds, the menu for the biometrics security option popped up and asked her for a fingerprint authorization. She pressed her index finger to the screen, just as Rheyna had done.

"How long before we receive the data?" Edwards asked.

"If everything goes as planned, we should see it within a few seconds." She typed in several more commands. "It also depends on the size of the hard drive," she added and then turned in her seat to look at him. "Once Rheyna has access, she'll upload our disk. After that, we'll be able to watch in real time any transactions he makes without detection."

Edwards laughed as she took a drink of coffee and then spit the cold liquid back into the cup.

"That's not funny," she said, turning back to the machine. "The best part about this little doohickey is that I'll be able to see everything on his computer, just as if I was sitting there." She made a few adjustments to the machine and turned her chair around to look at him. She thought that he looked as if he had aged ten years since they began the operation.

"If she gets caught, they'll kill her," he said, frowning as the reality of his words sunk in.

Laura had those same thoughts herself more times than she wanted to admit. "She knows the risks, and she will be extra careful." She said the words as a way to help reassure him, but she said them more to calm her own nerves and the unease that had begun to settle in her stomach.

He walked over to the window. "I know Rheyna will do her job. Castrucci's unpredictability is what worries me, and if by chance he knows about Rheyna, she could be walking into a trap. If that's the case, he'll kill her. I also know that if she can pull this off, we might find enough evidence to bring him down. The way I see it, we have a fifty-fifty shot and I think I increased our odds greatly by limiting those with knowledge of tonight's operation."

"Who else knows?" she asked.

"Just you, me and Stevens," he said, lighting a cigarette.

"So Artie doesn't know about tonight?" she asked.

He shook his head. "Not unless Carl said something to him, and under the circumstances, I don't see him doing that."

"Where is he, anyway?"

"He went for coffee," he said, glancing over toward Pal Joey's restaurant. "If Rheyna's cover's blown tonight, we have a very serious problem," he said as he walked over and pulled out a chair next to Laura. He sat down, stubbed his cigarette out in the ashtray, and buried his face in the palms of his hands. When he lifted his head, she could see that he was troubled. She could see it in his eyes. She had known him too long to mistake the look.

He raised his head to look at her. "They knew we were coming today," he said matter-of-factly.

"How can you be so sure?" she asked.

He leaned back in his chair and crossed his legs at the ankle. "You should have seen him, Laura; he was so smug, so sure that we wouldn't find anything." He laced his hands behind his head. "I could tell by the look on their faces. I knew we wouldn't find anything."

"Who else knew about the raid?"

"You, me, Stevens, two Sr. field office agents from L.A, and the Deputy Director," he answered as he chewed on a piece of skin at the edge of his lower lip.

"Did Artie know?"

He shook his head. "And that's what bothers me."

She looked over at him. "I'm glad to hear you say that. I have an uneasy feeling that I just can't seem to shake."

She had been wracking her brains about the mole for quite awhile and it just didn't add up. Something was wrong, but she couldn't put her finger on what that 'it' was. Deep down, she knew that Edwards was also thinking along the same lines. She had tried to talk herself out of it, but the nagging in her gut was persistent, and she was starting to regret their decision to allow Rheyna to continue with her mission.

No matter how hard she tried, she just couldn't make herself believe that Artie was the leak. It just didn't fit his personality, and it was all too clean—the way it had all been tied up in a nice little bundle and talk about timing—how perfect was that? Ron had verified with Cecil about the missing money from the evidence room. Exactly fifteen thousand dollars was missing from an evidence bag that had been recovered in a drug raid six months ago. For the first time in her career, she was unsure of herself, unsure of how to approach the subject with Kyle. She needed to say something.

"When will Ron get the surveillance tapes from the bank?" she asked.

"He's supposed to get it sometime in the morning and

give me a call as soon as he's had a chance to review it."

"You do know that Aldrich Ames was a thirty-year man." She finally said what she had been thinking all along.

"What's that supposed to mean?"

She knew that he understood what she was getting at.

He shook his head vehemently. "No way, I don't believe that for a moment."

Even if he didn't like her implication, she was glad that she had spoken her mind. It needed to be said, if for nothing else than to lay everything out on the table.

"I don't like the idea, either, but a good agent once told me to always expect the unexpected, even if it leads you down a road you'd rather not take. That same agent also taught me that instead of looking at the big picture, as most suggest, that I should try concentrating on what's going on inside the frame, because nine times out of ten, the real answer can be found in the details. He also said that those small, little, minute facts tend to be the ones dismissed first, because they seem to go nowhere, but in the grand scheme of things, can be tied together relatively easily."

His features softened as he looked at her. "Let me guess, I'm the guy who said those things."

"You got it. You told me that not long after I became an agent." She smiled at him and focused her attention back on the IMS.

The guesthouse was as nice as Rheyna thought it would be. It was roughly the size and layout of her beach house. The only difference was the amount of bedrooms. Hers had three and this had two. She sat on the couch, staring at the white snow on the TV screen. A glance at her watch told her that Caroline had been asleep for about an hour. She moved Annie's front paw off of the overnight bag lying at her feet, took a deep breath, reached in, and rifled through the clothes for the IMS device.

She took the CD out and tucked it in the front pocket of her sweat jacket. She walked over to the bedroom where Caroline was sleeping. She put her finger to her mouth to tell Annie to be quiet. She could hear Caroline snoring softly and quietly pulled the bedroom door closed.

She quietly made her way over to the front window and peered out from behind the curtain. Everything looked quiet. She waited for the last light to go out in the main house. She was breathing heavy, a roaring sensation echoing in her ears as adrenaline rushed through her veins.

She watched the crisscrossing pattern of a flashlight scoot back and forth across the pavement. The guard was near the kitchen and slowly making his way toward the front of the house. As soon as he disappeared from sight, she slid the patio door open and stepped outside.

She ducked behind a large hedge bush near the edge of the sidewalk that led directly to the back of the house. Her senses were reeling with nervous energy. Every nerve ending in her body felt as if it were standing on end. She inhaled deeply through her nose and exhaled slowly through her mouth. She had to try to get her heart rate down. She was a little too pumped up and felt lightheaded. It never changed. It was always the same. She often wondered if it was anything like how a junkie felt when the rush of drugs hit their system.

A low growling sound from somewhere over her shoulder caused her to jerk her head. She felt the muscles constrict in her neck and felt a rush of heat. A very large Doberman was standing behind the fence. He snarled and bared his teeth at her. Damn—she hadn't counted on the neighbor's dog being out. What if he woke up Caroline? What if she got up and found that Rheyna wasn't there, or what if the guard heard the dog? There was no doubt that he would.

In a matter of seconds, a million what if's raced through her mind. She had to make a decision and make one fast. She knew she only had a few seconds before the guard returned to see what was upsetting the dog.

She looked out across the yard. It was now or never. She took off like a banshee and quickly made her way across the grass toward the house, while mentally reciting the alarm code she saw Caroline enter three days earlier. She flipped up the security box, quickly punched in the code to turn off the alarm, and waited for the lock on the door to slide. When it clicked, she slid open the door and entered the kitchen.

Leaning against the wall, she took a few minutes to catch her breath. Her heart was throbbing painfully in her chest. She rubbed her hand against it while she waited for her eyes to adjust to the dark. She replayed the house layout in her head. She knew exactly how many steps it would take for her to get to Castrucci's office.

As she made her way over to the doorway, she counted each step in her head. When she reached the doorway that led out into the hallway, she stopped to listen for any sounds that might indicate someone was still up. She continued to count steps—twenty-six, twenty-seven, twenty-eight—she was almost there. Twenty-nine, thirty, she was just a couple steps from the dining room, and then she hit it. She had forgotten about the little table. In an instant, she saw her life flash before her eyes as the angelic figurine toppled from the table.

Fueled by adrenaline and pure instinct, she dove downward and stretched her hands out, catching the figurine just before it shattered across the floor into a thousand pieces. Her hand trembled as she set the little statue back on the table.

She crouched down in a sitting position and leaned back against the wall. Slowly, she began to regain the feeling in her legs. Her nerves were already frayed to the point that she was not sure she could stand upright.

After a few seconds, she stood and quickly made her way toward the target room. She counted the steps in her head again, until her hand was firmly on the doorknob. She said a silent prayer as she turned the knob, hoping that the door hinges wouldn't squeak.

Total relief was what she felt as closed the door behind her. She didn't waste any time, going straight for the desk, being extra careful not to knock into anything. She ran her hand along the edge of the desk until she found the computer and then felt for the ON button.

While the computer powered up, she knelt down beside the desk and fished the penlight out of her jacket pocket. She held the end firmly in place by clenching it between her teeth. She pulled out the IMS unit and turned it on. It made a loud 'beep' as the screen popped up.

"Shit," she swore under her breath and quickly hit the mute button. She cursed herself for not setting the mute feature ahead of time. *That's the second slip up tonight*, she thought. Forgetting about the dog was bad enough.

A noise from out in the hallway caused her to jerk her head up. She quickly turned off her flashlight and reached up to hit the power button to the computer screen, putting the room in total darkness. There was nowhere for her to go but under the desk. She held her breath as the office door opened. Within seconds, the room was awash in light.

"I forgot something. I'll be right back!" Big Tony yelled from the doorway. He walked over to the desk and stood on the opposite side. From beneath the desk, she could see the tops of his slippers, and if he looked down, there was a good chance that he would see her.

He moved to the side and pulled out the lap drawer. His foot came within an inch of touching her leg. She was afraid to breathe, let alone move, out of fear that he would hear her. She held her breath and waited. She thought about what she would do if he caught her. What would she do? What was the plan? She didn't have an answer.

Her free hand instinctively felt for the 9mm tucked beneath her jacket. She would have no qualms at all about shooting Castrucci if it came to that. She listened as he rifled through the papers on top of the desk.

It felt like forever before he finally found what he wanted. She heard him walk away from the desk and then flip off the light before shutting the door behind him.

She let out the biggest sigh of her life. That was just too damn close. She had a death grip on the IMS unit. She relaxed her hand and felt the blood start to circulate through her fingers. She rubbed her hands together to restore the feeling. She wiped the sweat off her face with the back of her sleeve and crawled out from beneath the desk.

It took her a few seconds to turn on the computer and plug the USB cable into the computer port. This time, she checked beforehand and made sure that the volume was off before pressing the enter button. The menu popped up almost immediately with a 'download in progress' icon. She waited for it to complete the download cycle and inserted the CD into the computer disk drive. She typed in the upload command to run the program on the disk and waited for it to finish.

After doing a check to make sure everything was exactly as she had found it, she crammed the disk in her pocket, removed the USB cable, and made her way over to the door. She leaned her head up against the door to make sure there were no sounds coming from the hallway.

Okay, the easy part's over and now the hard part begins, she thought to herself. She had to get back to the guesthouse undetected. She took a deep breath, opened the door, and waited a few seconds before making her way to the kitchen.

She took special care in avoiding the little figurine on the table and glanced down at her watch. Not bad, she thought. It had taken her less than twenty minutes from the time she left the guesthouse to complete her mission. Oddly enough, it felt like hours.

She ducked away from the sliding door just in time as the guard's flashlight made contact. Jesus, can this be any more nerve wracking?

She waited a couple minutes to give him time to reach the front of the house and then slid the door open. With her back against the wall, she quickly made her way over to the corner of the house. She checked to make sure the guard was nowhere in sight.

She had to make her move now. From her deductions, she figured he was probably coming down the other side of the house and that meant she didn't have much time left. In her current position, she would be the first thing he saw when he came around the corner, and she didn't want that to happen.

She broke out into a sprint across the yard toward the guesthouse. She didn't have much further to go—almost there. She could hear whistling from over her shoulder.

Just a couple more feet and she would be at the large hedge bush.

Laura's head jerked up as the machine beeped to life. She looked over and saw that Edwards had nodded off as well. "Kyle," she said his name to awaken him. "She did it, she got in."

He got up from his chair and took a position directly over her shoulder. They watched as the 'download in progress' icon popped up on the screen. Moments later, the machine beeped, and the 'download in progress' was replaced with the 'download complete' icon.

Laura rubbed her hands together. "Okay, let's see what we got," she said as she began typing in commands.

Rheyna had just ducked behind the hedge when the guard came around the back of the house. She waited for him to disappear and quickly ran over to the patio door and slid it open. She had no more kicked off her shoes and sat down on the couch when the bedroom door opened.

Caroline walked out, yawning. She stretched her arms over her head. "Were you outside? I thought I heard the door."

"I needed some air. I'm not feeling too well," Rheyna said as she slowly slid the IMS into her overnight bag.

Caroline sat down on the couch beside her and put her hand on Rheyna's forehead. Her eyes opened wide with concern. "You're soaking wet."

Rheyna pretended to rub her temples. "I have a very bad headache."

Caroline got up from the couch. "I'll grab a couple aspirins and fix you a cup of tea."

Rheyna watched her trot off to the bathroom and desperately tried to fight off the guilt that was threatening to overtake her. She waited until Caroline went in the kitchen and pulled the CD from her pocket and tossed it, along with her gun, into the overnight bag.

Laura squinted at the screen, leaning in closer. Her fingers tapped rhythmically against the keyboard. She stopped and turned to look at Edwards, a huge smile on her face.

"I think we hit pay dirt. Take a look at this," she said, opening a folder titled 'Hong Kong Services International.' She scrolled down page after page of jpg files. She clicked on one of the thumbnail shots, and her face went ashen with shock. "There has to be thousands of them," she said, shaking her head in disbelief.

Edwards cocked his head to get a better look at the image. "What is that?"

"Child porn," Laura answered. She brought up another photo that showed a small room decorated with cartoon characters. A pink-canopied bed sat up against one wall. A young girl, wearing a lacy pink, flowery dress was kneeling between the legs of a very large man, who was in the process of unzipping his pants—it was Billy Smith's little girl.

Laura knew what the sounds were before she even turned her head. Edwards was heaving in the trashcan next to the door. She gave him a minute to collect himself. She have any children, but Edwards did.

She could feel the anger raging through her veins as she looked through the pictures. She could only imagine what was going through his mind. When he looked up, she saw hate and contempt in his eyes, hate for one man—Anthony Castrucci. Men like Castrucci were monsters—they represented the vilest things in the world.

"Are you okay?" she asked before turning back to the open file.

He nodded, took out his handkerchief, and wiped his mouth.

"That file was hidden in a sector that couldn't be viewed through the normal operating system."

He shook his head with utter disgust. If he didn't hate Castrucci before, he damn sure did now. "That sick son-of-a-bitch," he spat angrily.

Laura opened up several more pictures, each one worse than the previous. The more she saw, the angrier she got. She wiped at the tears spilling down her cheeks. "They can't be more than ten years old."

Edwards squeezed her shoulder in a comforting gesture as the two of them stared at the screen.

"It's no wonder he wants Massino out of the way. They would kill him over this if they knew."

Laura nodded in agreement. "There's no doubt about that."

He grabbed his jacket off the back of the chair and grinned slyly. "It's kinda ironic, when you think about it. The Mafia commits some of the most brutal murders, but they still maintain a code of honor amongst themselves. I know they have certain guidelines and rules you never break under any circumstance. Child pornography is at the top of that list." He lit a cigarette and took a deep drag. "See what else you can find and get it faxed to Washington."

"Where are you going?" she asked.

"To see a federal prosecutor. We need to get a Grand Jury convened so we can bring Rheyna home. With the evidence we have, it shouldn't take long to get an indictment."

Laura stopped typing to look at him. "She's not due to call in for another forty-eight hours."

"That's okay. Just tell her that it's almost over. One way or the other, Castrucci's finished."

She looked at the screen and frowned.

"What? What is it?" he asked, coming back over to see what she was looking at.

"It looks like a dinner menu with a list of names," she said. Her face went blank when she realized what it was. "Oh shit, it's a hit list." She swung her hand against the cup of coffee, knocking it across the table.

Edwards took out his hanky and started blotting up the liquid.

"I knew it, damn it. I told Stevens."

The list showed the names and dates of the various Mafia members that had been killed. The last entry was Georgie and Paulie, the two men that had been shot outside of Lil Vic's Delicatessen.

"Who's next?" Edwards asked.

She slid her index finger down the list and stopped at the last entry scheduled. She read his name aloud. "Carlos Massino, seven, tomorrow night at Barecci's."

Edwards turned to open the door and ran into Stevens.

He looked back at Laura. "Contact L.A. and let them know." He brushed past Stevens, nearly causing him to spill the contents from the tray in his hands. Stevens set the tray on the table.

"I thought you might like a fresh cup," he said and handed Laura a cup of coffee. He took one for himself and sat down in the chair next to her. "Where's he going in such a hurry?" he asked.

"He's going to try and turn the slow wheels of justice, and thanks for the coffee. I really needed it," she answered. She turned the screen toward him so he could get a better view of the photos that she and Edwards had been looking at. "Here, take a look for yourself."

He looked at the screen and shrugged. "Nothing surprises me anymore. Hell, look at Artie. Who would've ever thought he'd be in bed with the mob."

Chapter 19

Edwards was filing paperwork against Castrucci and his cohorts when he received a call from Agent Wilks down at the L.A. Bureau. Wilks asked Edwards to meet him over at an apartment building located in the skid row district of Los Angeles.

The neighborhood looked every bit the part that its name implied. Laura followed Edwards up the steps that led to the top floor apartment and ducked under the police tape draped across the doorway.

She looked around the expansive loft apartment. "Wow, I didn't expect this," she said.

"Yeah, he used to have expensive taste," Edwards said as they walked into the middle of the family room. They looked up at Marco Mancini. His lifeless body was hanging from the end of a rope that had been thrown over the upstairs loft bedroom rail.

"Makes you wonder why he'd commit suicide," Agent Wilks said from behind them.

Edwards turned and held his hand out to shake his hand. "Agent Wilks, I'd like you to meet Agent Forrest," he said as he introduced the two. Wilks nodded at Laura.

"You think it's suicide?" Edwards asked.

"It looks that way right now. From what I'm guessing, he put the rope around his neck and just stepped over the rail. So far, we've found no evidence to suggest otherwise."

The three of them stepped back to allow the Medical Examiner Technicians into the room.

"Was there a note or any indication that he might have

been depressed?" Laura asked as she watched the technicians set a ladder up in preparation of cutting the body down.

Wilks flipped through his notepad. "Nope, nothing at all. I talked to a couple of his neighbors, and they seemed genuinely shocked. The Super downstairs actually referred to Mancini as a very nice young man, if you can believe that one."

"We got a T.O.D. yet?" Edwards asked.

"The ME put time of death around twenty four hours ago."

Edwards looked around the room "Who found him?"

Wilks glanced at his notes. "His sister."

Laura shook her head. "That must have been awful for her."

Wilks nodded. "Yeah, she's taking it pretty hard. Said she dropped by when he didn't show up to meet her for breakfast this morning. She tried calling, but kept getting his answering machine. She said it wasn't like him not to call and decided to check in on him." He turned to Edwards. "This isn't the only reason I called you. Seeing that Mancini here is tied to Anthony Castrucci, I thought you'd also be interested to know that we pulled a badly decomposed body out of the bay a couple months ago." He flipped back through his note pad. "The woman had been strangled. Her name was Charlene Sommers."

Edwards and Laura both shook their head. The name meant nothing to them.

Wilks smiled. "Ms. Sommers was … had been Castrucci's mistress."

Edwards' eyebrows shot up. "I didn't know he had one."

"Oh yeah, and something about this one just plain pissed me off. Yeah, what some people do is beyond comprehension."

Edwards shifted irritably from one foot to the other as

Wilks continued to drag it out.

"Ms. Sommers was two months pregnant," Wilks said finally.

"Think it was Castrucci's?" Edwards asked.

"Who else's could it be? From what I gathered from her neighbors, he was the only one they ever saw coming and going from her apartment, and Sonny Valachi's name was on the lease agreement. I'm guessing that she and the baby were too much baggage for him."

"Can we prove the baby was his?" Laura asked.

Wilks nodded. "The ME ran a DNA test on the fetus and the mother. We just need a sample from Castrucci to confirm one way or the other."

"I'll see what I can do about getting that for you," Edwards said as his cell rang. "Excuse me," he said, turning to answer it. "Yeah, Ron ... Are you sure?" The color drained from his face. "Oh, Ron. I'm so sorry. Is there anything I can do ... All right, you take all the time you need." He hung up and turned to Laura. "Lynn passed away this morning."

Laura's breath caught in her throat. "Oh no," she said, half choking on the words.

Edwards put his arm around her shoulders. "Let's get out of here."

They started down the steps, and Edwards stopped to look at her. "I think you were right about Artie, Laura. Ron said the surveillance video clearly shows that Artie definitely had a chance encounter with Mancini. I think he was setup to throw us off the trail."

Chapter 20

Rheyna was about to open the closet door when the phone rang. She ran down the hall to answer it.

"When are you leaving for Phil and Jesse's?" Caroline asked.

"Probably around eight. What about you?"

"Somewhere between eight and eight thirty, I think."

"Okay, I guess I'll see you later, then, and don't forget to have your dancing shoes ready."

"We'll have to see about that," Caroline laughed and then hung up the phone.

Tonight was the big party. Rheyna couldn't believe how quickly the time had flown by. It seemed like only yesterday when she had first met Caroline and her family. She hadn't spoken with Laura since she installed the software and wondered how it was going. She pushed the thought aside and went back to her bedroom closet to figure out what she would wear.

She tried on several outfits before settling on a black, ankle-length gown with a slit up the side and plunging neckline. She had the perfect pair of two-inch pumps to set it off. She wondered what Caroline would wear, and knew she would like it, no matter what it was. "Caroline could wear a nap sack and still look ravenous," she said to herself as she tried to think of what to do next.

She had several hours to kill, and decided to fix some lunch. Afterward, she would have Annie take her for a long walk on the beach.

Caroline held the gold gown up in front of the full-length mirror. She wondered if Rheyna would like the dress and then wondered why her opinion was so important to her. She knew why it mattered. Because deep down, she wanted Rheyna to like it, but more importantly, she wanted Rheyna to like what would be in it. The thought was shocking. She would be lying if she said she didn't find Rheyna attractive, but after all, who wouldn't? Not only was she gorgeous, she had a great personality as well. She justified the thought by thinking that it was normal for women to check each other out.

After all, most women dress for each other and not for the men in their lives. She had never thought of herself as gay and had never been into women. She didn't know why she didn't have a boyfriend, or why she hadn't been on a date since high school. Those were the million dollar questions, and she didn't have answers. God knows her father had tried to answer it for her by fixing her up with several men in his employ. He finally gave up when he saw that his attempts were fruitless.

If the truth were told, all he really wanted was a grandson. Her thoughts drifted back to Rheyna. She thought about how her life had changed for the better, and that it all started when she met Rheyna. She looked forward to the time they spent together, even when it was something as trivial as taking a walk along the beach with Annie.

She smiled as she thought about Annie. She really loved the dog. What about Rheyna, the little voice inside her head asked. She wasn't sure exactly how she felt about Rheyna. When she did take the time to think about it, she always came to the same conclusion. Her feelings, whatever they might be, were a moot point. Rheyna was a gorgeous woman and could have any man she wanted. There was no way that she would want Caroline with all her baggage.

"This is ridiculous," she said aloud, trying to shake herself out of her daydream. Why could she not just admit that she liked her as more than a friend and that deep down, she wished that Rheyna liked her the same way? She thought about how she found herself basking in the slightest of touches when Rheyna would lay her hand on her shoulder or her leg when she was trying to make a point or explain something to her. She felt her face flush and the heat rise in her feet before working its way up her body. She was attracted to Rheyna, and the thought shocked her—not the thought of being with Rheyna, but the thought of actually being attracted to another woman.

She pushed the thoughts out of her head and decided that what she needed right now was a shower—a very cold one, at that.

The party was in full swing by the time Rheyna arrived at Phil and Jesse's place. At the front door, she grabbed a glass of wine offered by a waiter and made her way to the party room. She took a position against the wall near the stage and surveyed the room to look for Caroline, in case she had arrived early.

She recognized several faces from the local newspaper's business section and could see that anyone who was anyone in Half Moon Bay and Palo Alto was there. She spotted Jesse and Phil across the room. They were engaged in an animated conversation with the mayor and four of the five members of the city council. She thought they made a handsome couple in their matching tuxedos.

Jesse looked up and smiled at her. He held up his glass in a mock salute and then made his way over to her. He threw his arms around her shoulders and hugged her.

"You look fabulous. Girl, I swear if I wasn't gay, I'd go after you in a heartbeat."

Rheyna laughed and hugged him back. "You're too kind and thank you, I think," she said.

"Where's Caroline? I thought the two of you would come together," he asked, and then proceeded to pull her onto the dance floor.

"She should be here anytime."

They hadn't been dancing long when Rheyna felt a tap on her shoulder. She turned to see Phil standing next to them.

"You look ravishing," he said, grinning from ear to ear.

Rheyna felt the color rise in her cheeks. "I have to say, you look rather handsome yourself."

Jesse smiled and winked at her, and then wrapped his arms around Phil's shoulders. "Down, girl ... he's all mine."

"Where's Caroline?" Phil asked.

"She's on her way," Rheyna answered as the band started up with a new song.

Caroline fidgeted in the backseat, tearing a paper napkin to shreds without realizing it. She wadded it up and stuffed it in the ashtray. Joey pulled into the driveway and stopped the limo in front of the entryway.

Caroline waited for him to come around and open the rear car door. She swung her legs gracefully out the side and stepped out of the car. She smiled at the sound of cat whistles coming from a group of young men huddled near the doorway.

Several tendrils had escaped from her upswept hair and hung down around her neck. Her make-up was flawless. She had gone all out and the result was breathtaking. She had chosen to wear a gold, low-cut lame' gown with slits up the sides. It hung seductively across her breasts, revealing the lush curves of her body, leaving very little to the imagination.

Her thoughts immediately turned to Rheyna, hoping that she liked how she looked, too. She passed through the door and smiled at the waiter. She took the drink he offered and stopped in the entryway. She needed to calm her nerves. She downed the drink and quickly selected another from a different waiter's tray. She could hear the music coming from the adjoining room and slowly made her way toward the large crowd.

She scanned the throngs of people dancing. It didn't take her long to spot Rheyna. She was up by the stage, sandwiched between Phil and Jesse, dancing seductively. She was seeing a new side to Rheyna and smiled. She liked what she saw.

Rheyna knew Caroline was there before she saw her. She felt her presence. *I have died and gone to heaven, surely I have*, she thought as their eyes met. Jesse turned to see where Rheyna was looking and nudged his lover.

Phil grinned and wrapped his arm tight around Jesse's waist. He bent to whisper in his ear. "Do you think they'll ever admit to having feelings for each other?"

Jesse nodded and took Phil's hand in his. "Yeah, in their own time and in their own way," he said, turning to Rheyna. "Will you excuse us for a few minutes, Rheyna, while we address our guests?" he asked, pulling Phil up on the stage.

The crowd erupted in loud cheers and whistles as Jesse and Phil stood beside the gorgeous lead singer, dressed in tight ripped up jeans. Phil bowed toward her and then took the microphone.

"Let's hear it for Sienna and Evening Shade, ladies and gentleman."

Rheyna took the opportunity to make her way through the crowd over to where Caroline was standing.

Caroline smiled at her. "You sure looked like you were enjoying yourself."

"I was thank you very much," Rheyna said as she hugged her a little longer than she probably should have. "You look fabulous," she whispered in Caroline's ear, not one bit ashamed to admit that she had noticed. Rheyna leaned back to look at her. She was powerless to stop her eyes from slowly traveling the full length of Caroline's body and felt an all-too-familiar ache as she looked at Caroline's mouth. When she moved to Caroline's eyes, she could have sworn they were laughing.

Caroline leaned over and whispered in her ear. "In case you didn't know it, you are the most beautiful woman here tonight."

Rheyna felt her heart skip a beat. She started to respond, but thought better of it. She was grateful when the crowd started cheering again. She and Caroline turned to look at the stage.

"Thank you for helping us tonight and for joining our fight to find a cure for AIDS," Jesse yelled into the microphone. He turned and handed the microphone to Phil.

"As everyone knows, we hold this benefit party every year to raise research money for the Pediatric Aids wing at Children's Hospital. Although Jesse and I are both resident Physicians, we still rely on your funding to cover the cost of the research, in hopes of one day finding a cure."

The crowd let out a huge cheer. Phil held up his hand to quiet them. "Last year, all of you, our generous friends and colleagues, donated over two and a half million dollars."

The crowd cheered so loud, Rheyna was sure it could be heard in the next city.

Jesse held a green envelope over his head and waved it in the air. "We have donation envelopes like this located on the table in the entryway, or you can get one from any of our gracious servers walking around," he said, handing the envelope to a young man in front of the stage. "And without further ado, I will now turn things back over to Ms. Sienna and Evening Shade." He smiled and then yelled, "Let's party!" as he and Phil jumped from the stage and immediately started gyrating to the beat as the band broke into a raucous pop song.

It didn't take long for the dance floor to fill up. Rheyna turned to Caroline. "Dance with me," she yelled over the music, pulling Caroline onto the dance floor.

"Do I have a choice?" Caroline asked, raising her voice loud enough for Rheyna to hear.

Rheyna grinned at her, shook her head, and mouthed the word, "No."

They danced for several minutes and then the lights began to dim.

"What'ya say we slow things down a bit?" Sienna purred into the microphone.

Caroline turned to leave the floor as a slow, melodic number began.

Rheyna grabbed her by the hand. "Where are you going?" she asked.

"It's a slow song," Caroline answered.

"So what?" Rheyna said, pulling Caroline into her arms.

Caroline laced her fingers around Rheyna's neck and looked up at her. "Do I lead or follow?"

"Neither," Rheyna answered, wrapping her arms tightly around Caroline's waist. Their bodies brushed sensuously against each other in time with the rhythm of the music.

She feels so good, Rheyna thought as she pulled Caroline closer. She could feel her own body trembling and wondered if Caroline was feeling it, too. She looked into Caroline's eyes and she felt more want and desire than she could have ever imagined possible.

Her body ached for Caroline's, and every single fiber in her being wanted her. All she could think about was how right it felt, how it was where she was meant to be. It was just her and Caroline. No one else existed at that moment but them. For the first time in a long time, she felt at peace.

Caroline raised her eyes to meet Rheyna's, her lips slightly parted.

Rheyna lowered her head to kiss Caroline as if it were the most natural thing in the world to do. With Rheyna's mouth less than an inch from hers, Caroline pulled away. Rheyna saw the confusion in her eyes.

She pulled out of Rheyna's grasp. "I ... I can't."

Rheyna put her hand on Caroline's hand and felt a stabbing pain in her chest when Caroline jerked her arm away. Rheyna looked questioningly at the blue eyes staring back at her.

"I have to leave ... I have to leave now," Caroline stammered.

In shock, Rheyna watched Caroline turn and run from the dance floor. "Caroline, wait!" she yelled as she weaved her way through the crowd toward the front door, her progress greatly slowed by the crowd.

She stepped out on the driveway just in time to see the limo's taillights turn out of the gate.

"Damn it," she yelled at the top of her lungs. *I'm an idiot, a complete and total fucking idiot*, she thought to herself as she ran her fingers through her hair out of pure frustration. "Damn it to hell, Rheyna, what have you done?" she yelled, getting the attention of a couple standing near the door. She hoped that she hadn't completely blown things with Caroline. Her lapse in judgment was unforgivable.

Chapter 21

Rheyna was distraught. She couldn't eat, couldn't sleep, and was just downright having a hard time with basic functions. It had been twenty-four hours since Phil and Jesse's party, and Caroline hadn't returned any of her phone calls. She dialed Caroline's number again for the umpteenth time, and once again waited for the answering machine to pick up.

"Caroline, if you're there, please pick up," she practically begged. "I've left countless messages. Why won't you return my calls? I need to talk to you. I need to explain. I'm so sorry; please don't do this."

Rheyna wasn't sure if she was more afraid of losing Caroline, or more afraid that she had blown their operation. What she did was wrong, and she had risked everything without giving it a second thought.

Caroline sat on the edge of her bed, listening to Rheyna's message. Why had she run like that? Was that not what she wanted? She grabbed her car keys off the dresser and left the room.

Joey looked up from his magazine and started to walk around to the rear of the car. She stopped him with a shake of her head and smiled.

"Not this time, Joey. I want to drive myself," she said

as she slid behind the wheel of her Jaguar.

Rheyna was surprised to open her front door and see Laura standing there. She hadn't spoken to her since she had broken into Castrucci's office, but she knew this could mean only one thing—they finally had enough to bring down Castrucci and the Pandora's Box Operation was over.

Laura followed Rheyna inside, her grin quickly turning to a scowl. She pulled out one of the stools and took a seat at the counter. Rheyna instantly sensed something was wrong. Without fail, her mind churned out several worst-case scenarios.

"What is it, Laura? What's wrong? Did something happen with Castrucci?"

Laura shook her head, her eyes watering. "No, no, nothing like that. I didn't want to tell you over the phone, but Lynn passed away."

Rheyna felt a lump form in the base of her throat. "When?" she asked. It took everything in her to keep the tears from falling down her cheeks.

"Yesterday morning. Complications from pneumonia. Ron said his immune system just wasn't strong enough to fight off the infection."

Rheyna thought about the pain she went through when Jenny died. "How's he holding up?" she asked.

"He seems to be doing okay under the circumstances, I guess. His parents arrived this morning, along with Lynn's family."

"When's the funeral?"

"Tomorrow afternoon. He said Lynn wanted to be cremated and made him promise not to have anything too fancy, so they're just having a small memorial service for the family and a couple of friends."

"I wish I could be there."

Laura sighed heavily. "He knows you'd be there if you could, and I hope you don't mind, but I went ahead and ordered flowers and added your name."

"Thank you. I appreciate that."

"Well, besides being the bearer of bad news, I thought you'd be a little happier to see me."

Rheyna leaned over and hugged her. "I'm sorry," she said, pulling out a stool.

"Once we get the indictment, Kyle's pulling you. Your work is done here. Because of you, Castrucci will be spending the rest of his miserable life behind bars. You did a good job, Rheyna."

Her words did nothing to lighten Rheyna's mood or make her feel better as her thoughts turned to Caroline.

"You really like her, don't you?" Laura asked, though it was more of a statement.

"Yes, I do."

Laura continued to watch her. "Are you in love with her?" Her question only half surprised Rheyna. For as long as she could remember, Laura seemed to have a second sense when it came to Rheyna's feelings. Laura affectionately shoved her, nearly pushing her off the stool. "You are! You fell for her, didn't you?"

Rheyna decided to play dumb, knowing that Laura knew her better than she sometimes knew herself. "I don't know what you're talking about," she lied. She had known for some time that she was in love with Caroline. She just didn't want to admit it. She didn't want to accept that she was in love with a woman she could never have—it hurt too much.

Laura ignored Rheyna's halfhearted attempt at denial. "Sure you do. You're in love with her. I can see it on your face."

Rheyna got up and poured herself a cup of coffee.

"Is it mutual?" Laura asked.

"I don't know," Rheyna, answered honestly. She felt a small twinge of pain in her heart. It was a physical pain that ached in her chest. She tried to swallow the lump that had formed in her throat as she thought about the party. "She won't return any of my phone calls. I think I blew it."

"What'd you do? Try to kiss her?" Laura asked jokingly.

Rheyna jerked her head up in surprise and then slowly nodded, causing Laura's eyebrows to shoot up. "Yeah, that's exactly what I did."

"Oh, Rheyna, you still need to be careful. This thing isn't over yet."

"I thought you said that we had enough to put Castrucci away for years."

"As far as Castrucci's concerned, we have enough to send him away for life. But he's still free until we get the indictment."

Rheyna looked at Laura. She could sense that something was troubling her and she had an idea of what it was. "And Artie?" she asked.

Laura shook her head. "Something doesn't feel right."

"What do you mean?"

"Ron sent over a copy of the bank surveillance tape, and it's obvious that Artie was set up."

"Are you sure?"

Laura nodded again.

Rheyna swallowed hard as she thought about the implication.

"And if he was set up, then that means—"

"The informant is still out there," Rheyna finished the sentence for her. "Why hasn't Castrucci come after me, then?"

"I honestly don't know. Unless, by some small chance, he really doesn't know about you. Regardless, you still need to be careful. Your life could still be at stake."

Rheyna could see the concern on Laura's face. It was not just concern—it was downright fear. "Don't you think that some things in life are worth dying for?" Rheyna regretted the question the minute it came out of her mouth.

Laura looked at her as if she was crazy. "I can't believe you just said that."

"I know it was a dumb thing to say, but if you really think about it, isn't that what La Cosa Nostra is all about? They are a family that lives by their own values. They swear their allegiance to each other, to La Cosa Nostra, to this 'thing of ours'. They're willing to risk their lives for their beliefs." Rheyna held her hand up to stop Laura from saying what she knew would be coming next. "I know. It was a stupid thing to say and I promise I'll be careful."

Laura slid off the stool and leaned against the counter. "I haven't had a shower in two days and feel pretty grungy. If you don't mind, I'm gonna jump in the shower and then get out of here."

"What's wrong the shower at your hotel?"

"I can't stand taking another cold one and I'm praying yours will at least be warm."

"Yeah right—your idea of warm is scalding to everyone else."

Rheyna laughed when Laura stuck her tongue out at her. She nodded toward the hallway. "Second door on the right, towels are in the bottom drawer."

Laura gave Rheyna a big hug and trotted off toward the bathroom.

Rheyna heard the water in the shower start and absentmindedly leafed through the pile of mail stacked on the counter. She had no idea of what her next move was, and depending on how fast the indictment came down, she might not have to worry about it. For all she knew, she could be back in Washington by this time next week.

The thought absolutely depressed her and she knew

why. Her thoughts turned to Ron. She would give him a call later to see how he was doing. If she couldn't be there, she could at least let him know he was in her thoughts and prayers.

The doorbell rang, and Rheyna felt her heart skip several beats and then catch in her throat. *Oh no, not now*, she thought. Now is definitely not a good time. She reluctantly scooted off the stool and went to the door. "Please don't let it be her," she muttered under her breath.

She put her hand on the doorknob and thought about not answering it. Then she realized that wouldn't work, since her Jeep, along with Laura's rental car, was parked in the driveway.

She knew when she opened the door that Caroline would be standing on the other side. She swore under her breath and opened it. Caroline stood there with a blank look on her face; one that told Rheyna that the last twenty-four hours had been just as hard on her.

"Hi," she said with a nervous laugh.

"Hi," Rheyna said back. She was completely lost for words.

Caroline shifted from one foot to the other. "I know I should have called first, but—" She didn't finish the sentence. Rheyna watched her eyes move and then come to a stop at some point just behind her shoulder. Rheyna heard her take in a deep breath and then felt the air leave her own lungs. She could tell by the look on Caroline's face what she was looking at.

She slowly turned around. Laura was standing in the hallway, dripping wet, with her mouth hanging open in shock. Rheyna heard Caroline gasp and then she heard a guttural sound come from somewhere deep inside her own throat as Laura's towel dropped to the floor.

Laura shrieked, quickly picked up the towel, and wrapped it tightly around her body.

Caroline turned and practically ran back to her car.

"Caroline, wait! It's not what you think," Rheyna pleaded as she ran after her.

Caroline whirled around, gesturing with her hands toward the house. "You don't need to explain anything to me, Rheyna," she spat back at her.

"It's not what you think," Rheyna said as she tried to get some semblance of control over the situation.

"You're an adult, you can do whatever you want with whomever you want and from what I can tell, that's exactly what you're doing!" Caroline yelled as she got in her car. She slammed the door shut, started the engine, and backed out of the driveway so fast; she sent gravel flying in all directions.

With a sinking feeling in her stomach, Rheyna watched the car disappear from view. *Can this get any fucking worse*, she thought as she went back inside the house.

Laura was still standing in the hall with a horrible look on her face. "Oh, Rheyna, I am so sorry. Talk about shitty timing."

Rheyna smiled at her dear friend. "Maybe it was for the best." She said the words knowing she didn't mean them. She felt her heart breaking into a thousand pieces.

"Can't you just tell her that I'm an old friend, a stewardess, or something and that I just dropped by for a shower in between stops?" Laura asked, coming over to wrap her arms around Rheyna's shoulders.

Rheyna hugged her back. Her brain was already in overdrive as she quickly tried to figure out a way to fix this. "It's okay, Laura. I'll think of something."

Even if the indictment came back today, there was no way she could leave Caroline under these conditions. It was bad enough to think how she would react when she learned that Rheyna was a FBI agent, but it was a completely different matter for her to think that she was sleeping with Laura. She couldn't imagine the thoughts going through Caroline's mind right then, especially after her screw-up at Jesse and Phil's party. She thought about a past sting they had a few years ago on a lengthy fraud case.

"Do we still have the safe house in Palo Alto?" she asked.

Laura frowned, unsure of where Rheyna was going with this. "As far as I know, but why would you want to go there when you have this wonderful house on the beach?" she asked as she re-tucked the towel over her breasts. She looked at Rheyna, smiled, and then wagged her index finger at her. "I know that look in your eyes, Rheyna. What do you have up your sleeve?"

Rheyna ignored the question. "Can you do me a favor and watch Annie for a couple of days? Please?"

Laura shrugged her shoulders. "I guess that's the least I can do for you, seeing how bad I just screwed up your life."

Rheyna threw her arms around Laura's shoulders. "You didn't screw up my life. Meeting you was one of the best things that could've ever happened to me and don't you forget it."

Laura held her at arm's length to look her in the eyes. "I have one condition though—actually, I have two."

Rheyna sighed. "And dare I ask what those conditions would be?"

Laura grinned. "One, that you be extra careful and two, you invite me and Stacie to the wedding."

Rheyna laughed. "Aren't you jumping the gun a bit? Hell, I'll be lucky if I can get her to talk to me again as it is. It's gonna be real hard trying to explain why I had a naked woman, dripping wet from a nice hot shower, I might add, standing in the middle of my hallway."

"Nah, I have faith in you. If anyone can come up with a way to explain me away, it'll be you. You'll just have to use all that charm of yours on her." Laura turned to go back to the bathroom. "She won't be able to resist," she said just before ducking through the doorway.

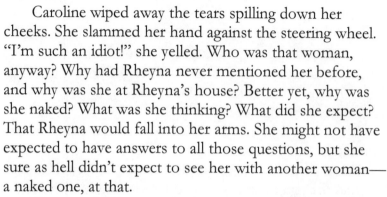

Caroline wiped away the tears spilling down her cheeks. She slammed her hand against the steering wheel. "I'm such an idiot!" she yelled. Who was that woman, anyway? Why had Rheyna never mentioned her before, and why was she at Rheyna's house? Better yet, why was she naked? What was she thinking? What did she expect? That Rheyna would fall into her arms. She might not have expected to have answers to all those questions, but she sure as hell didn't expect to see her with another woman—a naked one, at that.

She was oblivious to the houses and cars passing by her window in a blur. The next thing she knew, she was pulling into her driveway. She was like a zombie, moving on autopilot. She had gotten out of the car, opened the front door, and stepped into the foyer before it dawned on her that she was home. She headed toward the stairs and stopped. It was unusually quiet. It was odd that she didn't hear anything, not even the staff. She listened for voices, but there were none. She turned toward the kitchen, and then she remembered it was Sunday. *That explains it*, she thought, looking at her watch. On Sundays, the staff doesn't work past five.

She didn't feel like talking to anyone, and was doubly glad to see that her mother was not home, either. She was probably playing bridge with a couple of her girlfriends at the country club as she did every Sunday. It was a good thing, too, because Terasa would have taken one look at her and known immediately that something was wrong, and Caroline wouldn't have had any idea how to explain it.

How do you tell your mom that you have the hots for another woman and that you just caught that woman with another woman? She wanted answers to the question herself, but was terrified of the answer. She pushed the door open to her bedroom, closed it behind her, and flipped the lock. She wanted to be alone.

Obviously, Rheyna had been getting out and making a lot more friends than she let on. Where did she meet her she wondered as she tossed her keys and purse on the dresser. The loud ringing of the phone caused her to jump. She debated on picking it up and then decided to let the answering machine get it. She felt an ache in her heart when she heard Rheyna's voice.

"Caroline, Laura is just a friend of mine and nothing more. I swear it's not what it looked like. I owe you several answers. Please give me the chance to explain myself. I'm sorry. I don't know what else to say right now to make you believe me. I need to see you face to face. I'm spending the weekend at a rental cabin in Palo Alto. Please come see me. I will leave a key and directions with your mom in case you decide to come. I hope you can find it in your heart to at least hear my side of things."

Caroline sat down on the edge of the bed. *I am so confused*, she thought. I want to go to her, but—but what, what are you so afraid of the little voice inside her head asked. She knew the answer. She was afraid that Rheyna did have someone else in her life but what if she doesn't, and what if she doesn't like me that way? What if she does and what are you so afraid of? Her mind continued to torture her with worst-case scenarios. I'm afraid that I just might like it and that if I liked it, I'd want more, she finally admitted to herself.

Jesus Christ, what is wrong with me? *This is nuts*, she thought as she walked into the bathroom and leaned against the sink. She looked at her reflection in the mirror. Her eyes were bloodshot, and her cheeks were tear-stained.

"I've really got to stop talking to myself," she said as she reached over and turned on the jets in the hot tub full force.

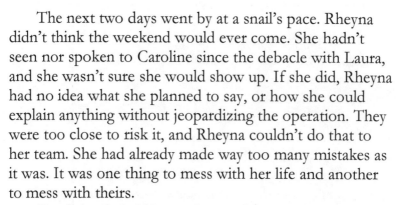

The next two days went by at a snail's pace. Rheyna didn't think the weekend would ever come. She hadn't seen nor spoken to Caroline since the debacle with Laura, and she wasn't sure she would show up. If she did, Rheyna had no idea what she planned to say, or how she could explain anything without jeopardizing the operation. They were too close to risk it, and Rheyna couldn't do that to her team. She had already made way too many mistakes as it was. It was one thing to mess with her life and another to mess with theirs.

She figured she'd have plenty of time to think about it on the drive up to the cabin. She left Laura a note with instructions for Annie and then tossed her bag on the back seat of the Jeep.

She drove the short distance to Caroline's house and was somewhat relieved when Terasa told her that Caroline was at Haven and wouldn't be home for a couple hours. She didn't know what she would have done if Caroline had been home and flat out refused to see her. She had a feeling that she would have just shriveled up and died right there on the spot.

She gave Terasa a key and the directions to give to Caroline and set off on her way to the cabin. The directions were easy, and the cabin was only about thirty-five minutes away. She found it with no problem.

It was tucked back away from the road on a tree-covered lot, and the nearest neighbor was at least a mile or two away. She got settled in first and then she unpacked the bags of food she had stopped to pick up earlier. She walked out onto the back deck and leaned against the rail, looking out toward the far end of the property, thinking how beautiful and serene it was.

A large lake, surrounded by a split-rail fence covered in ivy, stretched from one side of the property to the other. Large rows of Douglas fir trees ran across the back and along both sides, providing extra privacy from the neighbors. To the right and closest to her, a weather-beaten wood platform served as a dock for a small boat. It was tranquil and quiet and just what she needed. It was hard to believe that a thriving town existed only five minutes away.

She unconsciously shivered as the wind began to pick up, sending a pair of wind chimes hanging from the roof into a melodic dance. She glanced up at the sky and the fast-moving grey clouds. It was amazing how quickly the weather had changed. Two minutes ago, it had been warm with not a cloud in the sky. She figured the temperature had dropped fifteen degrees.

She shivered again and went back inside the cabin. She walked over to the fireplace and hit the switch to ignite it. She opened a bottle of wine and poured herself a glass, and searched around for a radio. She found one next to the coffee maker and turned the dial several times before settling on an easy listening station. She turned up the volume, took her glass of wine, and went back out onto the deck.

As dark ominous clouds raced across the sky, she felt light drops of rain hit her skin. In the distance, looking out toward Palo Alto, she could see sporadic bursts of lightening.

Out of nowhere, she felt her pulse rate quicken. She knew Caroline was standing behind her. Something in her sensed it. She slowly turned around.

Caroline stood in the doorway with tears running down her face. She wiped them away with the back of her hand. "I love you, Rheyna. I love you so much that my heart hurts. I don't know if it's wrong or if it's right, but I love you with every part of my being," she said, half choking.

Rheyna closed the distance between them in less than a second. She cupped Caroline's face between her hands. She wiped away fresh tears with her thumb.

"And I … have loved you from the first moment I saw you. My sweet, sweet Caroline," she said, her voice just above a whisper. She lowered her head and this time, Caroline didn't pull away. Their mouths met with the sweetest abandon, gentle, tender, and lingering.

Rheyna raised her head slightly. She kissed Caroline's eyes, her cheeks, and then softly traced the outline of her throat with her fingertips. Caroline yielded to her embrace, pressing her breasts against Rheyna as she slid her hands under Rheyna's shirt.

Oh so soft, and so, so gentle, Rheyna thought as she felt Caroline's warmth permeate every pore of her body. Rheyna ran her hands through Caroline's hair, gently tilting her head back. She brushed her lips tenderly over Caroline's and then they kissed deeply, slowly, passionately. She was shaken by her own excitement.

They kissed as if nothing else mattered, and for Rheyna, the world stood still as she let herself get lost in the velvety sweetness of Caroline's mouth. She felt Caroline shiver and realized they were getting drenched. She had been completely unaware of the sky unleashing a torrent of rain.

Without taking her lips from Caroline's, she maneuvered them back through the open doorway. Rheyna moaned as Caroline pulled away. Her head began to swim as Caroline's lips did a dance up the sides of her neck, leaving love bites as she went.

Caroline ran her tongue over Rheyna's ear, sending a sweet tingling sensation up Rheyna's thighs. Caroline was making it difficult for her to concentrate. Her legs seemed to have a will of their own and were on the verge of giving out beneath her.

"I don't think I can stand much longer," Rheyna whispered into Caroline's ear as she fell back against the wall, taking Caroline with her.

Rheyna's hands instinctively found their way inside Caroline's shirt. She heard Caroline's sharp intake of breath and felt her own excitement as she cupped Caroline's breast in her hands.

She ran her fingers slowly over Caroline's nipples and felt them harden through the thin material. She wanted Caroline out of her clothes.

She removed her hands and slowly unbuttoned Caroline's blouse, reaching around to unhook her bra. Her breath caught in her throat as she slid the garments over Caroline's shoulders.

"Oh, God ...You are so beautiful," she groaned as she bent her head, gently taking Caroline's nipple in her mouth. She kissed the soft spot between Caroline's breasts before taking the other nipple in her mouth.

Caroline moaned; with her hands in Rheyna's hair, she pushed against Rheyna's mouth, her own excitement growing as Rheyna's tongue made circular motions around her nipple.

Rheyna was vaguely aware of leaning back and letting Caroline pull her shirt over her head. She dropped her hands down to Caroline's hips, her fingers resting just inside the waistband of her shorts. She traced a line around Caroline's lips with her tongue as she slid her shorts and panties off.

She took Caroline by the hand and led her over to the area rug in front of the fireplace. Her hands trembled as she held Caroline's face between them. She softly brushed her face against Caroline's cheek.

"Do you have any idea how long I've wanted to do this?" Rheyna whispered hoarsely against Caroline's skin.

"About as long as I've wanted you too," Caroline answered. She lightly caressed the side of Rheyna's face with her hand.

Rheyna closed her eyes, inhaling the fragrance that was Caroline. She gently lifted Caroline's chin to look directly in her eyes.

"You are the most beautiful woman I've ever seen and I do believe that I could get lost in you forever." Her voice was so thick with desire, it sounded foreign to her ears. She needed to know that Caroline was feeling it, too, that Caroline wanted her as much as she wanted Caroline. She studied Caroline's face. She watched her eyes as she traced the curve of Caroline's lower lip with her index finger.

"Are you sure this is what you want, Caroline? Are you absolutely sure?" she asked, silently praying that Caroline's answer would be yes. "Because once I start, I don't think I can stop."

Caroline's eyes were pleading, telling her everything she needed to know, but Rheyna wanted to hear her say it. "I've never been surer of anything in my life," Caroline said seductively, leaning in to run her tongue slowly over Rheyna's bottom lip.

"Please make love to me, Rheyna," Caroline whispered against Rheyna's mouth, her eyes watching Rheyna's reaction as her fingers sensuously danced across her stomach. She shyly moved her hands to Rheyna's jeans and unfastened the button, pulling the zipper down. "You need to take these off," she said, pushing Rheyna's jeans and panties over her hips.

Rheyna kicked the clothes out of the way. She took Caroline's hands in hers; dropping to her knees, she pulled Caroline down on top of her so that Caroline's legs straddled hers.

She sighed as her leg slid against Caroline's wetness. She wrapped her arms around Caroline's waist, rolling over so that she was now on top.

"Caroline," she groaned as her mouth hungrily sought Caroline's. Their tongues met in a fiery search, their passion for each other mounting. Rheyna shivered as Caroline's nails raked across her back and then her hands pulled Rheyna closer, their bodies melting into each other as if they were one.

Rheyna kissed the base of Caroline's neck and then her lips moved over Caroline's skin as if they had a mind of their own. She pushed herself up on her knees, her hands resting on either side of Caroline's head. She gazed into Caroline's eyes. The reflection from the fire made them a deeper blue. Her eyes moved to Caroline's mouth. Her lips were swollen. They parted slightly, as if begging to be possessed. Rheyna leaned forward and took Caroline's bottom lip in her mouth.

Caroline groaned as Rheyna gently sucked on it, tracing the outline with her tongue.

"You're driving me crazy," Caroline panted as Rheyna did the same thing with her top lip. Rheyna tried to calm the throbbing in her groin, squeezed her legs tightly against Caroline's leg. She continued to tease Caroline with little kisses as she worked her way down to Caroline's breasts. She encircled each breast in her hands, taking one nipple in her mouth, and then the other. She felt Caroline squirm as her tongue made circular motions.

She groaned as she felt it grow harder with each lick. Caroline's hands in her hair guided her downward. She caressed Caroline's skin, her mouth following a trail where her hands had been. She ran her hand up the inside of Caroline's thigh, almost collapsing as her hand brushed against a mound of soft, wet curls. She was on the verge of going completely insane with desire. She couldn't take much more. She had to touch Caroline now. She laid her head against Caroline's belly and gently parted Caroline's lips. She felt her breath catch in her throat, her fingers covered in a pool of wetness beyond her wildest imagination.

Caroline moaned as Rheyna slid her fingers slowly

back and forth across her clit.

"Rheyna, please," Caroline begged. She grabbed her knees, raising them slightly off the floor, opening wider. Caroline closed her eyes and pushed her hips against Rheyna's fingers. She cried out, her pain mixed with pleasure as Rheyna's fingers broke through.

Rheyna heard a groan and then realized that the sound had come from somewhere deep inside of her. Her senses were reeling, so hot, so wet, and velvety, she thought as she slowly thrust her fingers inside Caroline. With each rise and fall of her hips, Caroline urged Rheyna on.

With her fingers resting inside, Rheyna used her free hand to hold Caroline open. She lowered her head, rubbing her tongue along the sides of Caroline's lips, luxuriating in the taste of salt and sweat and the smell that was Caroline. She pressed her face into the soft tufts of hair and then took Caroline fully in her mouth. Her tongue began a steady rhythm, matched by the thrusts of her fingers. She loved the taste, loved knowing that she was making her swell, knowing that Caroline was ready to explode.

Rheyna felt excitement course through her body as Caroline's nails raked up and down her back.

"Oh, God, Rheyna!" Caroline cried out, her hips rising slightly off the floor.

Rheyna felt wetness spreading between her own legs as Caroline's passion mounted, her body shaking with spasms. Caroline shuddered as the orgasm rippled through her body.

Rheyna collapsed in a pool of wetness against Caroline's belly, finally resting. *I love this woman. I truly love this woman more than I thought humanly possible*, she thought as Caroline ran her hands through her hair. She closed her eyes as Caroline's fingers slowly traced the lines of her face, gently caressing Rheyna's eyes, her lips, her cheeks.

Caroline pulled Rheyna up to lie beside her. She took

Rheyna in her arms and kissed her softly on the mouth, smelling her own essence on Rheyna's lips, she felt her own vitality returning. *I can't believe this is happening to me,* Caroline thought as she laced Rheyna's fingers with her own. She brought Rheyna's hand to her mouth and groaned against Rheyna's finger as she took it inside her mouth.

She watched the reaction on Rheyna's face as she slowly pulled it out and then sucked it back in. She felt Rheyna shiver, and then heard her deep intake of breath as she ran her tongue between Rheyna's fingers, slowly sucking on one before moving to the others. Without taking her eyes off Rheyna's, she trailed a row of kisses down her arm before moving to her breast. She kissed the soft area around Rheyna's nipple and felt it harden against her mouth.

Caroline leaned back to look at her, "Do you realize how beautiful you are?" she asked huskily.

"Only if you tell me," Rheyna whispered, her grey eyes clouded with desire.

Caroline wanted to please her, to give her the same amount of pleasure that Rheyna had given her. She looked at Rheyna, lowering her head almost shyly. "I want to please you, but I don't have much experience at this," she said apologetically.

Rheyna reached down, brushed Caroline's hair back from her face, and smiled. "Sweetheart, I can promise you that right now, you wouldn't have to do much more than look at me."

"But I want it to be as good for you as it was for me."

"Please touch me," Rheyna whispered.

Caroline was disoriented as she ran her hand over and down Rheyna's stomach. She felt her head spin, heard Rheyna's gasp as her fingers were covered with moistness. *So wet,* she thought as her hands seemed to take on a mind of their own. She explored the warm wetness with her fingers, yielding from the slight pressure and then she penetrated her lover's core. She was stunned by the softness. She felt Rheyna's hands in her hair and then on her shoulders.

Rheyna pulled her up, holding her close against her breasts. Caroline felt Rheyna's legs clamp against her hand and then Rheyna's hands were on her shoulders, her fingers tightening. Caroline found her own hips moving in an urgent rhythm against Rheyna's and then she felt Rheyna stiffen. Her own breathing coming in ragged gasps, she held Rheyna tightly. She covered Rheyna's mouth with her lips, her tongue searching deeply.

"I love you so much!" she cried out against Caroline's mouth, her back arching, pressing hard against Caroline's fingers. Her body shook and then stilled as she collapsed on the floor, her chest heaving.

"Please, not yet, baby," Rheyna said as she reached down to stop Caroline from removing her fingers. "I just want to lay here, hold you, feel you," she said, wrapping her arm around Caroline's waist.

Caroline laid her head against Rheyna's chest. They lay like that for several minutes before Rheyna finally let Caroline remove her hand.

Caroline looked up. Rheyna's eyes were closed, a grin playing at the corners of her mouth. Her eyes fluttered open to look at Caroline.

"See ... what you do to me?" she asked.

"You made it very easy for me," Caroline answered as her fingertips traced the outline of Rheyna's lips and then followed it up with a kiss.

Rheyna grabbed a blanket off the back of the couch, and covered their bodies. Caroline lay back down and draped her leg over Rheyna's leg. She wrapped her arm tightly around Rheyna's waist.

Rheyna played with Caroline's hair as she watched the multicolored flames dancing inside the fireplace. She felt a lump growing in her throat and was powerless to stop the tears flowing down her cheeks. She had to ask the question. She needed to know.

"Caroline?"

"Yes, sweetheart?" Caroline murmured against her skin.

"Have you ever made love with anyone else?"

Caroline raised her head to look at Rheyna. After a few seconds, she shook her head.

"Why not?" Rheyna asked.

Caroline lay her head back down against Rheyna's chest. "I was waiting for you."

Rheyna felt as if her heart were going to burst. She kissed the top of Caroline's head.

"And I am so glad you did," she whispered.

After a few minutes, Rheyna heard soft snoring sounds and realized that Caroline had fallen asleep. She lay there for quite awhile, looking at Caroline and loving her with every ounce of her being. She wanted the night to last forever. As she smoothed Caroline's hair back from her face, her thoughts turned to Jenny, and for the second time that night, she cried. She had kept her promise.

Rheyna woke around midnight. She gently shook Caroline awake and led her to bed, where they made love again. This time, their lovemaking was slow, gentle, loving, unhurried as they took their time exploring each other's bodies.

Around seven, Rheyna slid out of bed. Staying in bed after she was awake was not her style, and today would be no different from any other. Caroline was still asleep when she came in an hour later.

Rheyna set the tray of coffee down on the nightstand. She looked at the woman who had stolen her heart. She was beautiful, even when she was sleeping. Caroline's eyes slowly opened, her mouth curved into a lazy grin.

"Good morning, sleepyhead," Rheyna said as she bent

to kiss her.

Caroline reached up, pulled Rheyna down on top of her, and nibbled on the soft part of her ear.

"That was the best night of my life," she said.

"Mine, too," Rheyna said, leaning back to look at her.

Caroline's eyes twinkled, and Rheyna felt an all-too-familiar ache start to grow in her groin.

"I want more," Caroline said huskily.

Rheyna pulled back the blanket and slid under the covers beside her. She didn't need a second invitation. "Your wish is my command."

Big Tony glanced up from his paper. He watched Terasa pull out the chair across from him and sit down. She picked up a piece of toast and spread jam on it.

"Where's Caroline?"

"She and Rheyna went away for the weekend," Terasa answered as she poured herself a cup of coffee and then refilled his.

A frown furrowed his brow, his eyes narrowing to little more than slits. "I think she spends way too much time with her."

Terasa took another bite of toast and met his gaze. "I thought you liked Rheyna."

He carefully folded the paper and laid it down on the table. "Has nothing to do with it. Doesn't it bother you that she's a dyke?"

Terasa looked up at the ceiling and sighed. "Oh, Anthony, you know I hate it when you talk like that and besides, you don't know that Rheyna's—"

"A queer, she's a queer, Terasa. Just say it," he interrupted. His lips curved into a snide smirk as he emphasized each letter, "Q-u-e-e-r."

Terasa looked at him. She shook her head in disgust.

Big Tony continued to grin at her. "You can call it what'cha want, Terasa, I don't really give a damn. Those two spend way too much time together and you can argue all you want, but that girl is a dyke."

Terasa pushed her chair away from the table and stood up. She threw her napkin down on the table and left the room.

Rheyna and Caroline finally crawled out of bed around noon and took showers before eating lunch. Rheyna handed Caroline a plate to dry.

"What would you like to do today?" she asked.

She looked at Rheyna with a lustful gleam in her eye. It was a gleam that Rheyna was coming to love and fear equally in a very short amount of time. She was so sore; she could hardly walk as it was.

Rheyna kissed the tip of Caroline's nose. "We have to get out of the house sometime today," she teased.

Caroline pretended to act hurt. "Why do we have to get out of the house?"

Rheyna ignored her question. "Do you like to fish?" She didn't realize the humor in her question until she saw the look on Caroline's face.

"Is there a joke in this somewhere?" Caroline chuckled.

"I'm serious. I love to fish."

Caroline's eyebrows rose a good half inch.

"Out ... in ... the ... water," Rheyna said, emphasizing each word and trying like hell to be serious.

"Okay, okay. I get the point," Caroline laughed. "I don't know how to fish, but I'm willing to learn."

"Then I guess I'll just have to teach you." Rheyna

opened the fridge and took out a container of Canadian Night Crawlers.

Caroline scrunched her nose in disgust. "Gross, you have live worms in there?"

Rheyna set the worms on the counter. "How else are you supposed to catch a fish?"

Caroline smiled at her. "The local fish market works for me," she said nonchalantly.

Rheyna couldn't help but laugh. Caroline was killing her. She slid her arms around Caroline's waist and kissed the soft skin behind her ear. She took a deep breath, inhaling the fresh scent of her hair. "Ah, come on, I promise it'll be fun," she whispered.

Caroline turned around and laced her arms around Rheyna's neck. She stood up on her tiptoes to kiss Rheyna.

I love kissing her, Rheyna thought as she tilted Caroline's chin up with her fingers. "How about you get the wine and sandwiches while I round up some poles and a blanket?"

Caroline turned and opened a cabinet door. "I think I can handle that."

Sonny laid the manila folder in Big Tony's outstretched hand. He leaned back in the chair and crossed his feet at the ankles. "It cost us a small fortune, but you were right, Tony."

Big Tony lit his cigar, blew the smoke up in the air, and opened the folder. He looked at the top photo of FBI Special Agent Rheyna Sorento, also known as Rheyna Moretti, meeting with FBI Agent Kyle Edwards. He moved it aside and glanced at the others. "Our friend ... deserves a very large bonus. Explains a lot, don't it now? Explains why they always seemed a step ahead." Big Tony stared at a spot on the wall over Sonny's shoulder. He clicked his tongue against his teeth as he contemplated his next move.

Sonny knew that with each click, a volcano bubbling from deep inside Big Tony grew closer to erupting. He was now in his most dangerous state of mind. Johnny Scala had heard the clicking sound and probably Charlene, too. "How you wanna handle it?" Sonny asked, although he knew what the answer would be.

Big Tony looked back at the folder on his desk and picked up a photo showing Rheyna with her graduating class at the academy. With a flick of his wrist, he flung it across the room. He pushed his seat back and stood, tugging down on his suit jacket. "Let's you and me take a walk."

Rheyna watched with amusement while Caroline fought with the blanket. She would spread it out on one side and then the breeze would catch the edge and blow it back over.

Caroline finally set the picnic basket on one corner and the bottle of wine on the other. She turned and saw Rheyna laughing at her. She placed her hands on her hips. "Why are you laughing at me?" she asked.

"I'm not laughing at you, I'm laughing with you," Rheyna said as she flipped the lid open on the cooler.

Caroline made a pouting look and stuck her tongue out. "That's funny but I don't think I was laughing."

Rheyna grabbed the container of night crawlers from the cooler and walked down to the edge of the water. Caroline came over, stood above her, and watched as she threaded a fat worm onto the end of the hook.

"That is the most disgusting thing I've ever seen," she said.

"Really?" Rheyna asked with amusement.

"Yes, really," Caroline said, and then took two steps back to keep the swinging worm from hitting her.

Rheyna held the pole out to her. "Come over here, please."

Caroline took the pole and stood there with a blank look on her face. She didn't have the slightest idea of what to do with it. Rheyna knew she would like this part of teaching. She came up behind Caroline and put her arms around her waist.

She placed Caroline's hands in the proper position on the pole and reel. "Now, you bring the pole back like this," she instructed as she pulled the pole back over their heads. She pushed Caroline's finger down on the button to unlock the line. "And then you fling it forward like this to release the line."

They watched the bobber and worm sail through the air and then hit the water with a plop. Within seconds, the red and white bobber bounced back up to the surface. Rheyna personally preferred to fish on the bottom without a float, but figured it would be much easier for Caroline, since it was her first time and all. She could teach her how to fish on the bottom on their next fishing trip. She smiled at the thought of having another first with Caroline.

"Okay, now what?" Caroline asked when Rheyna finished setting the line and laid the pole on the ground beside her.

"Now we wait for the fish to bite. You see that little red and white ball out there?" Rheyna pointed at the bobber. Caroline nodded. "When that goes completely under the water, you jerk it real hard, and—"

Before Rheyna could finish her sentence, Caroline pulled her down on top of her and began kissing the sides of her neck.

"I think I could really like this fishing stuff," she whispered in Rheyna's ear between kisses.

Rheyna turned and kissed her. "I could like anything as long as it's with you."

A movement out the corner of Rheyna's eye got her attention. She turned her head in time to see the bobber disappear completely under the water.

"You've got a bite!" Rheyna yelled and jumped up. She grabbed the pole and handed it to Caroline, just as the bobber went down again.

"Oh crap! What do I do? Help me!" Sheer fright was the only way to describe the look on Caroline's face.

Rheyna shook her head, refusing to take the pole. "You can do it … wait … wait…" Rheyna watched as the bobber went down again. "Now, jerk it!" she yelled.

Caroline did just as Rheyna said, and jerked the pole with everything she had. Rheyna wasn't prepared for what happened next. The line and the bobber, with a bluegill fish attached to it, shot out of the water like a slingshot, heading straight for them. They ducked just in time as the bobber, line, fish, and all sailed over their heads and landed on the ground behind them.

Rheyna fell to the ground. She was laughing so hard, she was crying. "I think you ripped its lips off," she managed to say while holding her stomach. She could hear the fish flopping around on the ground. She looked at Caroline. Her face was ashen white—ghost-like.

"It has lips?" Caroline asked seriously and then she lost it. She fell to the ground in a fit of laughter.

"Not anymore," Rheyna said, between laughing and wiping the tears from her eyes.

"Stop laughing at me and help it, please," Caroline said as she tried to get herself under control.

Rheyna struggled to her feet. "Okay, okay," she said as she walked over to where the fish lay flopping. She was still laughing as she gently removed the hook from the bluegill's mouth.

Caroline came over and stood beside her. With

Caroline's hand in hers, they walked down to the edge of the water. Rheyna knelt down and gently put the fish in the water and watched the traumatized little guy swim away.

Caroline ran her fingers through her hair. "I need a drink,"she said.

Rheyna didn't know who was in worse shape, Caroline, or the fish. Caroline fell on the blanket in an unceremonious heap and grabbed the bottle of wine. She poured herself a very large glass and then poured another for Rheyna.

"Are you hungry?" Rheyna asked, and opened the basket. Caroline set her glass of wine down, reached up, and grabbed Rheyna's hand.

"I thought you'd never ask," she said huskily, pulling Rheyna down on the blanket next to her.

Big Tony looked at Sonny. "What time did he say he'd be here?"

Sonny glanced at his watch. "Should be anytime now. He was having lunch at Pal Joey's with Henry."

Big Tony wiped his handkerchief across his forehead. "Damn, it's hot out here," he said as he watched the pool boy methodically run the skimmer across the water and scoop out several leaves. His thoughts turned back to his problem at hand. He had come too far and had paid dearly to get where he was. He'd be damned if he was going to sit back and let some FBI dyke ruin it.

Who the hell did she think she was? Didn't she know who he was and what he was capable of? Scala found out, as did all the others who had crossed him. If she didn't know, she would real soon. He thought about Caroline and shook his head. How was she ever going to find a husband when she spent all of her time with a dyke? He had several men to choose from in the family that would make fine son-in-laws, but none ever seemed to be good enough. He shook his head again in disgust. Nah, she couldn't be, he said to himself as he tried to shake the images from his mind.

Jay Farino walked over to the table, snapping him out of his thoughts. He pulled out a chair and sat down next to Sonny. Big Tony drained the last remnants of scotch in his glass.

He pushed the folder over to Jay. "I want to send a message and I don't care about the details, just take care of it," he said.

Jay opened the folder. He looked at the photo of Rheyna and then tucked it inside his jacket pocket. He stood and left without saying a word. He didn't need to. He knew what his role was in the family. He was the end-all and eventually, everything ended with him. He smiled as he thought about his newest assignment and how much fun he was going to have with this one.

Caroline helped Rheyna load her bags into her Jeep. The weekend had flown by too fast, and Rheyna didn't want to leave. Caroline wrapped her arms around Rheyna's waist. "I don't want to leave. Can't we stay here forever?" Caroline asked, resting her forehead against Rheyna's chest.

Rheyna tilted her head back and gently kissed her on the mouth. "We have a whole lifetime, sweetheart." Rheyna said the words, wanting to believe that it would somehow be possible.

"When can I see you again?" Caroline asked, squeezing Rheyna's waist tighter.

"I have to take care of a few things when I get back

and then I would like to sit down with you sometime tomorrow and talk." Rheyna kissed the top of her head. "I have some things I need to tell you," she said hesitantly.

Caroline must have sensed something in Rheyna's voice. She leaned back to look at her. "Oh no, don't tell me you're married."

Rheyna shook her head.

"You have a string of girlfriends?"

Rheyna laughed and hugged her tightly. "No, baby, nothing like that." Rheyna wished it were that simple. She looked into Caroline's eyes and saw the concern.

"You're starting to worry me," Caroline said half-smiling.

Rheyna cupped Caroline's face between her hands. "Please trust me and know that I love you more than anything in this world," she said, meaning every word.

"I love you, too," she said, and kissed Rheyna softly.

It was hard to say goodbye, and it took everything Rheyna had to get in her Jeep without Caroline at her side. She watched Caroline's taillights disappear and then backed the Jeep out of the driveway. She put it in drive and headed back toward Half Moon Bay. Her emotions were a mess, and she tried to sort them out as she drove home. Home—what a funny thought.

She hadn't felt at home anywhere in a long, long time, but she felt at home with Caroline. She thought about what she would say to her and knew that whatever she said, it wouldn't be the total truth. Caroline didn't really know anything about her, and everything she did know was a lie. Hell, she didn't even know Rheyna's real name. She was worried about how Caroline would react when she learned the truth, how she would feel about the true reason for Rheyna being in her life, and how none of this had happened by chance, except for Rheyna falling in love with her—the one thing Rheyna hadn't planned.

Her stomach did a flip-flop, and she realized she was

terrified. She was terrified that Caroline would hate her, hate her for what she had done to her family. She would rather face ten Castrucci's than deal with the look of disappointment on Caroline's face that was sure to come when she learned the whole truth. Rheyna slapped a CD in and headed for the highway.

Jay Farino shoved Henry, nearly knocking him off the step. "Why don't you watch what the hell you're doing?" he hissed through clenched teeth.

"Jeez, I'm sorry. It's just that I can't see a damn thing," Henry said as reached his hand out to regain his balance.

"Here, hold this," Farino snapped, and shoved the penlight at Henry.

Henry took the flashlight and held it in place while Farino picked the front door lock. "Where are those fancy night goggles of yours that you seem to be so proud of?" Farino asked as the tumbler clicked into place.

"I left 'em home."

"Figures," Farino said as he flung the front door open and stepped through the doorway of Rheyna's house. He reached back and jerked Henry through the doorway by his arm. "Come on, we don't have much time."

"I don't understand why we're here, anyway. We have all the information we need," Henry said, stumbling around in the dark.

Farino snatched Henry up by the front of his jacket, jerking so hard, Henry left his feet. He pulled Henry so that their chests were practically touching. "Are you questioning my judgment?" he asked.

"No, no, it's just that it doesn't make sense why we would risk getting caught," Henry stammered.

Farino let go of Henry's shirt and pushed him away. "I

decide what we do and don't do. Capische?"

"Fine, fine. What do you want me to do?"

"I want you to stand there and keep your freaking mouth shut. Do you think you can do that?"

Before Henry could answer, a low growl came from somewhere across the room. Henry aimed his flashlight in the direction of the growl. Annie was standing near the patio door, baring her teeth at them. Henry pulled his gun out of his waistband and aimed it at her.

Farino grabbed him by the wrist. "What the fuck do you think you're doing?" he asked.

"What'ya mean? I'm gonna shoot it."

"Like hell you are."

"Why do you care?" Henry asked, not understanding Farino's sudden affection for the dog. Farino didn't care about anything, especially a mangy mutt.

"Because the damn dog didn't do anything wrong!" he yelled. "You wait right here and don't move until I come back, and if you hurt the dog, I'll kill you myself."

"All right, just hurry up and do what you came here to do." Henry stood there, not daring to move as Farino made his way down the hallway.

After a few minutes, Farino reappeared. "Okay, let's get the hell out of here," he said.

Henry followed him to the door, careful not to take his eyes off Annie, who was slowly inching closer. Farino took a piece of paper from his pocket, dropped it on the floor, and then shut the door behind them.

Before Rheyna knew it, she was turning onto Ramada. Except for the car she just passed, traffic had been relatively scarce.

She opened the front door, and Annie immediately

greeted her by jumping up on the front of her legs with enough force to knock her down to the ground. There was not a spot on Rheyna's face that Annie's tongue didn't touch. Rheyna grabbed her and kissed the top of her nose. "Hi, sweetie, did you miss me?" Annie answered by soundly throwing her body up against Rheyna's chest. She refused to let Rheyna up until she had given her a proper greeting, along with rubbings.

Rheyna finally got off the floor and flicked on the light switch. She tossed her bag on the couch and walked over to the counter. The answering machine light blinked rapidly. She pushed the button and smiled when she heard Caroline's voice.

"I miss you already. Is it tomorrow yet? I'll be counting down the hours. I love you, baby."

She is positively glowing, Terasa thought as Caroline practically floated into the sitting room. She bent to give Terasa a kiss on the cheek.

"How was your weekend, honey?" Terasa asked.

Caroline smiled from ear to ear. "I had the best time of my life and I learned to fish."

"*You* fish?"

Caroline laughed at her mother's expression. Caroline spread her arms out as wide as they would go. "I caught a fish this big," she said, bringing her arms in until her hands were five inches apart.

Terasa laughed at Caroline's theatrics. Terasa had no idea what had transpired over the weekend, but it was obvious that whatever it was, it had made her daughter very happy and that was all that mattered to her.

Rheyna grabbed her bag off the couch, headed toward the laundry room, and stopped when something by the front door caught her eye. She walked over and picked up the white paper lying on the floor. The house had been dark when she first got home, and she had missed seeing it. She opened it and felt her heart catch in her throat as she read the words. She read it again to be sure. "I know who you are, Special Agent Sorento. Meet me tonight at 11:00 p.m. outside the Lexington Club on 19TH street. Don't be late!" It had been typed in bold letters.

She went directly to her bedroom with Annie on her heels and grabbed the 9mm from her nightstand. She slapped the clip in and slid a bullet into the chamber. She did a quick search of each room and the closets. She came to an abrupt stop when she flipped on the light switch in the bathroom. Written in red lipstick across the mirror were the words: "A dead lesbian is the best lesbian."

Think, think, she told herself as Annie followed her to the kitchen. Her adrenaline was in overdrive. She tucked the gun into the back of her waistband and tried to slow her breathing down. She looked down at Annie's happy face and said a silent prayer, thanking God for keeping her safe. By the placement of the note and writing on the bathroom mirror, someone had been inside her house, and that pissed her off. If they had hurt Annie, she didn't know what she would have done. *Yes, I do*, she thought. I would have killed Castrucci and anyone else responsible.

The realization and the gravity of her situation slowly begun to sink in. It had to be the mole inside the bureau. He or she was the only one who knew who Rheyna was. Someone inside the bureau was a rat and that rat had betrayed her and the Pandora's Box team. She also knew in her gut that it was not Artie. She had a big, big problem and right now, that problem was putting her life in grave danger.

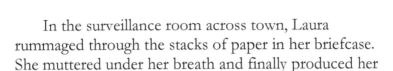

In the surveillance room across town, Laura rummaged through the stacks of paper in her briefcase. She muttered under her breath and finally produced her cell phone. She flipped it open and frowned.

"Damn it, my cell's dead again. I swear I need a new freaking battery."

Stevens looked up from his paper as she dumped everything out of her purse onto the table. Her charger was nowhere to be found. She grabbed her car keys out of the pile.

"I'll be right back. I must have left my charger in the car again."

Rheyna glanced up at the clock and grabbed her jacket off the chair. Annie walked up and shyly nudged her leg.

"I'll be back later, girl. I promise," she said as she knelt down to give Annie a hug.

She grabbed her keys and left the house. She did a quick scan around the yard and then climbed into her Jeep.

Her senses were on high alert, and the adrenaline was flowing. She figured it would take about thirty to thirty-five minutes to drive down to the Lexington Club. Unless she wanted to get her ass chewed off by Laura, she was not about to make the same mistake she did with Bayshore. She picked her cell up off the seat and hit speed dial. She placed it on speaker and waited for Laura to answer. Oh no, not again, she thought, feeling her heart sink when Laura's voice mail picked up.

"Laura, it's me. I wanted to let you and Edwards know that my cover's been blown. I'm on my way to the Lexington Club over on 19th; meet me there as soon as you get this message."

She hung up and turned off the exit that would take her downtown through the Mission District. It was an area she new fairly well. She was grateful that one of the first things she did when she arrived in Half Moon Bay was to check out the bar scene on the internet.

The person or persons who left the note knew she was FBI, and it was obvious that they also knew she was a lesbian. She figured that was why they had chosen The Lexington Club as a place to meet.

She continually checked her mirror out of habit as she turned up and down the streets. She turned onto Lexington and saw the bar up on the corner. She made a right on 19th, and to her dismay, the one-way street was lined with cars on both sides. It was also pitch black, making it all-too-easy for an ambush. The lack of street lamps was not a good thing around a Lesbian bar.

She continued to drive, checking for anything that might seem out of place and then circled back around the block. She finally saw a spot on the right side next to an alley about a half block down from the bar.

She turned the engine off and sat in total darkness for several minutes while she allowed her eyes to adjust. She checked her mirrors and opened the driver's door. She heard a click and instantly knew what it was and then she felt the muzzle ram against her temple. She started to reach for her gun.

"Don't even think about it, bitch, unless you want your fucking brains all over the car," Farino growled into her ear. He was so close; she could smell the alcohol on his breath. He reached in and jerked her out of the car. She then realized he was not alone. Henry Venutti was with him.

This was bad, real bad. Farino reached inside her jacket and pulled her gun from inside her waistband. He handed the gun to Henry. Without warning, he whirled around and hit her in the face with his fist. She heard, and then felt her jaw crack. She choked, and then spit out a mouthful of blood. She involuntary groaned as Henry and Farino grabbed her by the arms and slammed her against the side of the Jeep.

"I oughta slit your fucking throat right now, you queer bitch," Farino whispered in her ear. He leaned back and then she felt his fist slam into her face repeatedly. She lost count after the fifth blow. She glanced down at her chest and felt a sticky wetness.

Farino jerked her head back and hit her again with enough force to knock her backward. She was vaguely aware of the arms that grabbed her by the shoulders. She felt her body flip over and then felt the hood of the Jeep beneath her hands and face. She was blacking out, starting to lose consciousness as her body's defense mechanisms started kicking in. She tried to fight, but was powerless against the men's strength.

Farino leaned over her shoulder. She could feel his warm breath on her skin. "Big Tony sent me to teach you a nice, permanent lesson, cunt, but I have my own for you, first," he whispered in her ear.

She heard the blade of a knife snap open and felt Farino pull at her jeans. With a flick of his wrist, he cut the material away from her skin. She heard the sound of his zipper and opened her mouth. Please, no, her mind screamed, but no words came out. She knew what was coming and then everything went black.

Farino laughed sinisterly as he pulled down his pants. He was thoroughly enjoying this assignment. It sure beat the hell out of just putting a slug in some poor, defenseless schmuck. "Ah, shit," he said, the sound of voices causing him to stop what he was doing.

Two women had come out of the bar up on the corner. They were having an animated conversation, their laughter cut through the quiet night as they stepped off the curb. The women crossed the street. They were walking straight toward the men. With less than fifty-feet to go, they were silent. They were looking straight at Farino, Henry, and Rheyna.

"Hey, what are you guys doing?" the shorter of the two women yelled.

As Farino stopped to zip his pants, Rheyna's body slid to the ground. He knelt down beside her and with pure hatred, plunged the knife blade into her chest. He looked down at the lifeless body lying at his feet and pulled a marble from his pocket. With an evil grin, he wiped off his prints and tossed it on her chest. He grabbed his gun off the hood of the car and turned to Henry. "Let's get outta here."

They took off running up the alley and were out of sight just as the women reached the Jeep. The shortest woman knelt down on the ground beside Rheyna and cradled her head in her lap. She looked up at her girlfriend. "Call an ambulance!"

She shrugged off her jacket and laid it across Rheyna's chest. She pushed several strands of blood-soaked hair from Rheyna's face.

"Hang in there, sweetie. An ambulance is on the way," she said soothingly. *This isn't good*, she thought as she heard gurgling sounds coming from Rheyna's throat. Rheyna turned her head slightly, blood pouring out from the sides of her mouth. The woman silently thanked God as she heard the wailing of a siren in the distance. She looked down at the badly beaten face cradled in her lap. "What's your name, hon? Can you tell me what your name is?" she asked.

Rheyna tried to speak. "Rhey ... Rhey ... Rheyna Sorento." She struggled to get the words out. "FBI Agent Kyle—" she gasped and choked. She coughed and spit blood all over the woman's shirt. "Kyle Edwards," she whispered. "270 ... 421 ... 1," she gasped, took a deep breath and then collapsed in the woman's arms.

"Oh no, oh no, no, no, don't do this to me, please!" the woman screamed as she frantically searched for a pulse. She laid Rheyna's head gently on the ground and started CPR.

Up on the corner, the bar patrons were slowly emptying into the street as the ambulance with siren blaring and lights flashing followed by police cars turned onto 19th Street. The ambulance driver came to a stop next to Rheyna and the two women.

The medics jumped out and ran over to them. The taller woman grabbed her girlfriend and pulled her out of the way. They watched as the medics took over and then the woman pulled out her cell phone. She dialed the number that Rheyna had given her. It rang several times before it was answered.

"Hello, Agent Edwards?" she asked, hoping that she got the number right.

"Yes, this is he."

"Do you know Rheyna Sorento?"

"How did you get this number? Who are you?" he asked abruptly.

"My name is Molly, Molly Armstrong. Rheyna gave me your number a few minutes ago. She's been hurt really bad outside The Lexington Club on 19th street," she said as she heard the sound of tires locking up. "The medics are performing CPR on her now."

"Oh my God," she heard him say before the line went dead. She turned back around and watched the medics lift Rheyna onto the stretcher. One medic had started chest compressions while the other held a bag over Rheyna's mouth and nose, squeezing repeatedly to force air into her lungs.

Molly felt her girlfriend's arm around her waist. She wiped angrily at the tears running down her cheeks.

Laura plugged the charger in her phone. It beeped immediately. She flipped it open and looked at the menu. She had missed a call and had a voice mail waiting. She punched in her password. As she listened, her face drained of all color.

"Oh, shit," she said as she dialed Edwards' cell and immediately got his voice mail.

Stevens looked up from his newspaper. "What's wrong?" he asked.

"It's Rheyna, her cover's been blown. I gotta go, keep trying to get a hold of Edwards. Tell him to meet me at 19th and Lexington," she said and grabbed her keys and jacket off the table. She jerked the door open and ran down the steps, taking them two at a time.

Edwards brought his car to a screeching halt at the corner of Lexington and 19th Street and nearly hit one of the officers cordoning off the area with yellow police tape.

The place was a madhouse. Police cars and people were everywhere. He flashed his badge and ducked under the tape. He saw the medics preparing to lift Rheyna into the ambulance and ran over to her. Taking her hand in his, he leaned over and looked at her badly beaten face. He felt tears sting his eyes.

"I'm here, Rheyna. You hang in there, now. You hear me?" he said as he rubbed his hand gently across her cheek. He felt anger boiling up inside. *This is the final straw,* he thought to himself. I'm going to kill that son-of-a-bitch myself. He looked at Rheyna and shook his head. "Don't you die on me, damn it, you hear me, Rheyna?" He dropped his head, tears running down his cheeks.

Rheyna struggled to speak. "Car, Caroline."

"I'll call her, I promise," he said, jerking his head up to look at her.

The medic nudged him. "We really need to get her out of here."

Edwards took a few steps back so they could get the stretcher into the ambulance.

"Where are you taking her?" he asked the medic climbing into the ambulance.

"San Francisco General," the medic said, and then hit his hand against the wall to signal the driver to get going. Feeling helpless, he watched the ambulance pull away.

"She one of yours?"

"Yes," he answered numbly, turning to see a very large man standing in front of him with a notepad and pen in his hand.

The large man held out his hand. "I'm Detective Robert Sloan, Homicide."

Edwards shook his outstretched hand. "I'm Assistant Deputy Director Kyle Edwards, FBI."

"Pleased to meet you, Director, I only wish it was under better circumstances."

"Likewise, Detective. How did you get here so fast?"

Detective Sloan nodded toward one of the officers standing over by Rheyna's Jeep.

"They found this when they lifted up her body and called me first thing," he said, pulling out a baggie containing a single marble. He handed it to Edwards.

"This look familiar to you?"

Edwards looked at the marble. "Yes, unfortunately," he said as he glanced around, looking at the people crowded behind the police tape. He turned to the detective. "Where's the girl who found her?" he asked.

Detective Sloan pointed at Molly and her girlfriend. They were talking with a uniformed officer on the other side of the street. Edwards crossed the street and walked up to the women.

"Which one of you is Molly?" he asked.

"I'm Molly and this is Tracy," the shorter of the two answered. He recognized her voice. "Is she going to be okay?" she asked.

"I don't know, but I sure hope so," he answered honestly. He looked at the various news crews, now on scene setting up their equipment behind the police tape. *So much for containment,* he thought wryly. He turned back to the women and placed his hand under Molly's elbow. "Let's go over here, where we can talk," he said, leading them over to the edge of the alley where they would be well out of earshot. He looked at Molly. "Can you tell me what you saw?"

"Tracy and I had just left the bar when we saw a couple of men standing over by the Jeep. They were laughing and to tell you the truth, they looked a little out of place. We figured they might be up to something."

"How many were there?"

"Two," she answered without hesitation.

"Did you get a good look at them?" She shook her head. "Not good enough, I'm afraid. Without the lights, it's pretty dark out here. They took off running toward the alley when we yelled at them."

"They were wearing suits," Tracy volunteered.

Castrucci's men, he thought as he took a card out of his pocket and handed it to Molly. "If you think of anything else, please call me." He nodded toward the detective. "I'd appreciate it if you would give Detective Sloan your names and a number where we can reach you."

He thanked the women and turned to go back to his car. He had no doubt that Castrucci was behind this. He had sent his hit man to take care of Rheyna. He opened the car door and heard his cell ringing. He looked at the caller ID and saw that it was Laura.

"It's not good, Laura," he said into the phone. "Castrucci got to her, and she's in real bad shape. I'll meet you over at San Francisco General—and make sure you call Caroline."

He hung up the phone and pulled the sedan away from the curb. It took him less than five minutes to get to the hospital. He parked his car in the emergency room parking lot and shut off the engine, leaning his head against the steering wheel as he tried to pull himself together.

Everything had happened so fast, and he had so many unanswered questions. He knew the doctors were inside doing everything they could to save Rheyna, but she was in such bad shape.

His thoughts turned to Caroline and the conversation he had with Laura earlier in the day regarding Rheyna. Since Laura was Rheyna's case agent, it was her job to keep him updated on everything concerning Rheyna and the Pandora's Box Operation. He knew Rheyna had fallen in love with Caroline and he was okay with it, as long as it didn't jeopardize the operation. His gut was telling him otherwise, that more likely than not, their love for each other had been the real catalyst for this attack.

He no longer had doubt about an internal leak. He knew the leak was responsible for this. The realization troubled him deeply. He thought about Artie. Was it possible that he had been snowballed by Artie's persistent pleas of innocence? Although they had proof that Artie had taken the money from the evidence room and proof that the meeting with Mancini was indeed an accident, was it possible that Artie had planned all of it in order to hide his true deception?

Could Artie have leaked Rheyna's identity before they arrested him? And what about the money—where was all the money that Artie would have received over the years? If he had that much money, why would he be in such dire straits? They knew he was in debt as bad as he claimed. Ron had verified everything. These were questions he just didn't have the answer to. He looked out the window toward the hospital. The leak he thought was contained was the very reason that his agent was in the hospital, fighting for her life.

He wracked his brain, thinking about the countless documents that Ron, the Deputy Director, and he had reviewed. They had spent hours searching for the one common link between all of the deaths, coming up empty every time. The closest they had come was tying Artie to two of the deaths.

He knew it was in front of his face, but he couldn't see it or maybe you don't want to see it, a little voice inside his head said as he opened the car door. He needed to make some phone calls. He needed to call Rheyna's parents. It was only a matter of time before the local and then national news stations learned Rheyna was an undercover FBI agent.

He was sure Laura had phoned Caroline by now. It was bad enough she would learn the truth, but they couldn't let her find out through a newscast. Rheyna wouldn't want that, and it was the least he could do after everything she had risked for this operation.

He took a deep breath and forced himself to go inside the building. He stopped at the nurse's station and showed the nurse behind the desk his badge. "A young woman was brought in earlier from over on Lexington. Can you tell me what room she's in?" he asked.

She picked up the clipboard in front of her and scanned the pages. "She's in surgery right now and then she'll be moved to the ICU. We have her in room twenty-three, twenty-two," she said, writing the room number on a card. She handed it to him and then pointed to a row of elevators at the end of the hall. "Take the one on the right up to the second floor and turn left."

"Thank you," he said, and turned to walk away. He stopped and looked back at her. "Can you tell me where her surgeon's office is located?"

She glanced at the page. "His office is just to the left of the nurse's station on the same floor."

"Thank you," he said as he headed toward the elevator. He rode the elevator up to the second floor and found the doctor's office. He let himself in and took a seat just inside the door, where he sat for a good forty-five minutes, lost in his thoughts. He looked up when the door opened. "How's my agent doing?" he asked after the doctor took a seat behind his desk.

"I have to be honest with you. Right now, it doesn't look good. We were fortunate to get the bleeding stopped, but her injuries are more extensive than just a knife wound. She took a severe beating to the head, which caused intracranial pressure on her brain. In addition to that, she has a broken jaw and an orbital fracture to the right eye socket. We currently have her in a medically induced coma to try and relieve the pressure."

Edwards looked at the doctor with a stunned expression. "Okay, doc. In laymen's terms, what does all that mean, exactly?"

"It means that she's in very serious condition and if she does survive, there's a significant chance she'll have brain damage."

"Is she going to die?" Edwards reluctantly asked the question he was thinking.

"Unfortunately, that's a real possibility," he said, coming from around the desk to take a seat next to Edwards.

"This can't be happening. This just can't be happening," Edwards said, shaking his head. He looked at the doctor. "Okay, what's next?"

"For now, we can only wait and see, and hope that your agent is one helluva a fighter."

Laura quietly closed the door to Rheyna's room and stepped out into the hallway. She wiped the tears from her eyes. *This is all my fault,* she thought as she sat down on one of the chairs a few doors down from Rheyna's room. If she hadn't let her cell die, if she had replaced the battery, none of this would have happened. She looked at the two FBI agents posted outside Rheyna's room and leaned forward, burying her face in her hands. She thought about Caroline.

Calling the Castrucci house was one of the hardest things she ever had to do. She had spoken with Caroline's mother and told her that Rheyna had been in an accident and was badly injured. Caroline's mother was very upset and that was to be expected. She had thanked Laura for calling and said she would bring Caroline to the hospital as soon as possible.

It was only a matter of time before they arrived. She shook her head, not having the foggiest idea of what to say to them. She couldn't very well tell them that her bastard of a husband and father had done this to Rheyna.

She heard footsteps and raised her head. Edwards knelt down in front of her and rested his hands on her knees. "Did you call Caroline?" he asked.

She nodded. "I spoke with her mother. They're on the way." She took a deep breath and stood up.

Edwards took her hand in his, and they walked back to Rheyna's room.

Stevens was standing near the bed, staring blankly out the window. Edwards' heart caught in his throat when he saw Rheyna. He sat down on the chair next to her bed and picked up her hand, holding it gently between his. Her face was so severely beaten that if he didn't know it was Rheyna, he wouldn't have recognized her. She had numerous tubes coming from her body, and he wondered how on earth she had survived to this point.

He knew if it had been any other agent, by now, they would be dead. He also knew that if anyone could make it through this, it was Rheyna. He looked at the bandage surrounding her head. He could see where several strands of her hair, soaked with blood, hung thickly on her shoulders. At the head of her bed, an artificial ventilating machine had been set up, its tubes connected to Rheyna's mouth. It beeped loudly, pulsing, and then hissing each time the ventilator breathed for her. He glanced up at the heart monitor—its beeping sound gave him an eerie feeling.

"This is my fault," Laura said as she blew her nose in a tissue.

He got up and walked over to her, placing his hands on her shoulders. "No, it's not. You didn't do this to her." He tilted her chin and forced her to look at him. "You can't blame yourself for this. Rheyna wouldn't want that."

She shook her head, unable to contain the tears streaming down her face. "Her nurse … her nurse was in earlier," she struggled to get the words out. "They think the bastard raped her."

Before Edwards could reply, the door opened and a nurse walked in. She checked the lines running from the IV bottles hanging at the end of the bed.

Without warning, the alarm on the heart monitor went off, and Rheyna's body lifted off the bed, jerking with convulsions. The nurse pressed a button on the wall as the monitor flat-lined.

"You three need to leave now!" she yelled.

They left the room as a speaker above Rheyna's bed began repeating, "Code blue room two-three, two-two, code blue room two-three, two-two."

They stood helpless in the hall and watched as a flurry of hospital staff ran into the room, followed by an orderly pushing a crash cart. Rheyna's surgeon came running down the hall and went into the room. Edwards saw the doctor place a set of paddles on Rheyna's chest. He heard the doctor say, "Clear," just before a nurse pulled the door shut.

At the end of the hall, the elevator buzzer dinged, and the door opened. They all turned to see Caroline, followed by Terasa, and Vincent, step into the hallway. Caroline saw Laura and ran toward her. It took everything she and Edwards had to prevent Caroline from going into Rheyna's room. They held onto her as the flurry of movement in and out of Rheyna's room continued.

After several minutes, the door opened and one by one, the room emptied. The doctor that Edwards had been talking with earlier came out. He removed the surgical cap from his head. His face was solemn. He looked at them and shook his head. "I'm sorry, we did everything we could," he said softly.

Caroline's legs gave out and she sank to the floor. "Oh God, no, please no … please, please, dear God, no!" she cried out.

With tears streaming down her face, Terasa knelt down beside Caroline and pulled her in her arms. She held her tightly as gut-wrenching sobs wracked Caroline's body.

Chapter 22

The sky was overcast and grey as Rheyna's parents and the last mourners got into their cars and pulled away. The brown casket lay beneath a large tent at San Francisco National Cemetery.

Laura, Stevens, Ron, and Edwards stood at the edge of the drive and watched as a black limousine came to a stop several feet away.

Vincent got out and came around to hold the door open while Terasa and Caroline got out of the backseat. Vincent held an umbrella over Caroline's head and walked with her to the tent. Caroline laid a single yellow rose at the head of Rheyna's casket.

Caroline had been in a fuzzy haze since the night at the hospital, and although she knew the truth, a part of her was in denial. She kept replaying everything in her mind over and over again. How could this have happened? How could this have happened so fast? This can't possibly be real. They were together only a few days ago. Their weekend together had been the happiest moments of her life. She had let herself dream about a future together, a future she wanted to spend only with Rheyna.

She kissed the tip of her fingers and laid her hand on the casket. Her grief was unbearable. She no longer wanted to live. What was the point? She wanted to be wherever Rheyna was. She began to cry and Vincent came over. He handed her a tissue and then wrapped his arms around her shoulders. He held her as she sobbed.

After a few minutes, she leaned back to look at him.

"Thank you, Vincent. I think I'm okay now."

"Are you sure?" he asked with genuine concern.

Vincent took a tissue and wiped the tears from Caroline's cheeks. He held her close against him as he led her back to the car where her mother was waiting.

Caroline was oblivious to the drive home. She barely remembered Vincent pulling into their driveway, or Terasa kissing her on the cheek. All she wanted was to go to her room and be alone.

Caroline sat curled up on the bed with her legs tucked beneath her and stared out the bedroom window. She angrily wiped at the tears spilling down her cheeks. She thought about the times she and Rheyna had spent together. No matter how many times she told herself that Rheyna was gone, she just couldn't believe it. It just wasn't possible. She had waited her entire life for someone like Rheyna to come along. Now she was gone, and it wasn't fair. She reached over the nightstand and turned the radio on.

The tears were automatic as Gloria Estefan's soft melodic voice filled the air. She thought about how many times Rheyna had made her listen to this CD and smiled. She thought back about their trip at the cabin and her first attempt at fishing. She laughed and then she cried. The pain and emptiness in her heart was more than she could take. She didn't want to spend the rest of her life without Rheyna, and fate wasn't giving her a choice.

Terasa knocked lightly on the door and pushed it open. She sat down on the bed, pulled Caroline into her arms, and held her tightly as she cried.

Caroline laid her head against Terasa's chest. "I hurt so bad, Mom. My heart feels like it died, too," she said through tears.

Terasa smoothed Caroline's hair back from her face. "I know you do, baby. I know it hurts and right now, I would give anything to be able to take your pain away."

"I loved her so much. More than anyone I've ever known."

Terasa looked lovingly at her daughter. "And she loved you, too."

Caroline pulled away. She shook her head. "How can you say that? Everything about her was a lie."

Terasa held Caroline's face in her hands. "I saw how she looked at you, baby. She loved you as much as anyone possibly could, and that was something even she couldn't fake."

"She used me. She was playing a role to get to Dad and I was part of it."

Terasa nodded. "In the beginning, I suspect she was. She had a job to do. But somewhere along the way, that all changed for her, just as it did for you."

Caroline started to cry again, and Terasa pulled her closer, rocking Caroline in her arms. "Shh, everything's going to be okay. You try and rest now."

Terasa was worried about Caroline. It had been three weeks since she left her room. She looked down at her daughter's gaunt features and felt a stabbing pain in her heart.

Big Tony leaned smugly back in his chair and laced his fingers behind his head. Sonny tossed a newspaper on his desk.

Big Tony grinned as he leaned forward to pick it up. He read the headline out loud and laughed. *"Authorities no closer to solving the brutal death of FBI Agent Rheyna Sorento."*

He tossed the paper onto the open folder with Rheyna's FBI pictures. Sonny watched his boss revel in the glory of his latest endeavor and then jumped as Big Tony slammed his fist down on the desk. "Nessuno me lo ficca in culo, nessuno!" he yelled in Italian and then repeated it. "Nobody fucks me up the ass, nobody!"

Sonny looked at him. "There will be big repercussions. Carlos won't take kindly to the extra heat coming from the Feds. Informants are one thing, but a FBI Agent comes with a lot of extra baggage."

Big Tony blew a smoke ring in the air and waved his hand. "Fuck Carlos. He doesn't deserve his position. He's a weak old man who refuses to get with the times. He thinks that we can still run things like the old days. Well, I've got news for him, times have changed, and his ten minutes are up."

Stevens looked up as Edwards walked through the door. He removed his headphones and laid them down on the table.

Edwards walked over, pulled out a chair, and sat down next to him. "Anything?" he asked, nodding toward the recorder.

Stevens shook his head. "Did we get the indictment yet?"

"No. Should be any day now," Edwards said as he lit a cigarette. He looked at Stevens and shook his head. "I don't understand why it's taking so long. We have more than enough evidence, especially with what happened to Rheyna." Edwards nodded toward the recording equipment. "I'll take over here for awhile. Why don't you go get something to eat?"

"You sure?" Stevens asked as Edwards picked up the headphones.

"Yeah, I'm sure."

He waited for Stevens to grab his car keys and leave the room before putting the headphones on. He turned up the volume and directed his attention to the conversation going on in Castrucci's office.

Vincent, carrying a pitcher of coffee, followed Terasa into Big Tony's office. Terasa repositioned the covered serving tray in her arms and nodded to Vincent. He walked over, placed the pitcher on the edge of the desk, and then took a position opposite Sonny. He leaned up against the wall, and folded his arms across his chest.

Big Tony glanced up at her, his brow furrowing in agitation. "You forget how to knock?" he asked rudely.

Terasa ignored the question. "Have I been a good wife to you, Anthony?"

He frowned at her. "What kinda stupid question is that?" he asked.

She ignored his question again. "Anthony, I have always done what you wanted and I've always been obedient." He opened his mouth to speak and she held her hand up to stop him. "I've never asked questions and I've never questioned your actions, even when I should have."

He clicked his tongue against his teeth. "And now is not the time to start, Terasa," he said in a low voice, his eyes narrowing to slits.

"You had Rheyna killed," she accused.

Big Tony smiled smugly, puffing out his chest. "So what if I did?" he asked.

The look on Terasa's face was incredulous. She shook her head. "Did you think for one minute about what it would do to Caroline?"

"I was thinking of her!" he yelled, his voice shaking

with anger. "I was right about that bitch, and no daughter of mine is going to lay down with a dyke, a fucking dyke who was dead set on destroying me, destroying our family."

She looked at him, this man who was her husband, and felt nothing but pity and disgust. She leaned forward and looked him straight in the eye. "No, Anthony, you've done that all by yourself."

Big Tony had heard enough. "I won't listen to this. I think you've forgotten your place, Terasa. Now get the hell outta here before I forget that you're my wife," he said, dismissing her with a flick of his hand.

Terasa didn't budge. When she spoke, her voice was eerily calm and controlled. "You can do whatever you want with me but no one and I mean no one, fucks with my child, not even you, Anthony."

Before he could respond, Terasa reached beneath the serving lid and pulled out a gun. The bullet made a swooshing sound as it found its mark, hitting Big Tony between the eyes. His body slumped forward across the desk.

Terasa saw Sonny push away from the wall, his hand reaching inside his jacket and then she heard two popping sounds. She turned to see Sonny's body slide down the wall. Vincent had shot him in the middle of his chest.

Edwards jumped straight up. The back of his legs hit the front of the chair with so much force; it sent it careening across the room and into the wall before slamming to the floor with a loud clang.

"Holy shit!" he yelled, slinging the headphones down on the desk. Although silencers were used, there was no mistaking the sounds he just heard. Terasa had just killed her husband.

Terasa went over to the desk. She grabbed Big Tony by the hair and jerked his head back. She reached down and grabbed Rheyna's folder along with the newspaper. She let go of Big Tony's hair, and his head dropped back down on the desk with a thud. She turned back to Vincent and nodded toward the wall now stained with streaks of blood. "Have Joey help you. I want them gone and this mess cleaned up before Caroline wakes up from her nap." She glanced down at the newspaper in her hand. "Once the bodies are found, I want you to set up a meeting for me with Carlos. In the meantime, I want you to check on something else..."

Edwards paced back and forth. He still couldn't believe what he just heard. Think, think, he told himself as he lit another cigarette although he had one burning in the ashtray. Without hesitation, he went over to the recorder and took out the tape. He grabbed a blank tape and stuck it in the slot just as the door opened. Stevens looked at him questioningly.

Edwards shook his head. "I got nothing. Just the same ole same ole," he said, and grabbed his jacket off the chair and left the room.

Chapter 23

Edwards parked his car a few feet from the Los Angeles Coroner's wagon on pier 38. He looked out the driver's side window. It was taking quite a few police officers to keep the growing group of onlookers back. Judging by the size of the crowd it was apparent that they knew it was somebody important.

He flashed his badge at the officer and ducked under the police tape. When he received the call to come down to the pier, he had known what he would find, but he wanted to see it firsthand for himself. He walked over to the black body bag, pulled back the zipper, and looked down at Sonny Valachi. He noticed two circular, red stains in the middle of his chest.

He could hear excited mumbling from the crowd. No doubt, they were learning that the bodies were that of Mafia Boss Anthony Castrucci and his right hand man. He glanced up at a news helicopter circling overhead. He could see a reporter sitting in the door with his feet dangling out over the side, a camera mounted on his shoulder. He watched the helicopter swoop in low as the camera operator shifted his camera to his other shoulder.

He turned his attention back to the scene playing out approximately fifty-feet away. Several men were pulling on ropes. After several hard tugs, they heaved the massively large body of Anthony Castrucci up over the side and onto the concrete. He walked over to have a look. The body was badly bloated, and there was no mistake about how he died. Directly in the middle of his forehead, almost between his eyes, was a bullet hole.

He had seen enough and headed back to his car. He couldn't help but think how ironic it was that their bodies were found today of all days. Only a short few hours ago, he was sitting in a diner, drinking a cup of coffee and reading the morning paper, when he received the phone call he had been waiting for. Only minutes earlier, the grand jury had handed down the indictment, and the charges had been endless. Overall, he felt that Castrucci had gotten off way too easy, but looking on the bright side, Castrucci wouldn't get another chance to hurt anyone else.

Vincent held the door open for Terasa and followed her inside Barecci's Restaurant. He took a seat at the bar and watched her walk toward the back room.

Carlos and Roberto stood up to greet her. Carlos smiled and bent to kiss the top of her hand.

"Terasa, please join me," he said, motioning toward the opposite chair. "Can I get you something to drink?"

"Seven, seven please," she said, taking the seat he offered.

"Terasa, I must admit that I wasn't surprised to hear from you," Carlos said.

"And I have to admit that doesn't surprise me, either, Carlos," she said, smiling warmly at the older man. She had always liked Carlos, in spite of what her husband thought, and without Anthony's knowledge, she and Carlos had developed a warm friendship that now spanned more than twenty years.

"I kinda figured that, too. How have you been, Terasa? Are you doing okay with all of this?" he asked.

"I'm well, Carlos, and thank you for asking."

Carlos waited for Roberto to set the drinks down

before continuing. "It's really good to see you, even under such dower conditions."

She took a drink and then set the glass down on the table. She covered his hands with hers. "I do appreciate your help more than you could possibly know."

"It's okay, Terasa, and with that all said, I'd like to offer my condolences in the passing of your husband," he said with sincerity. He looked at her and shook his head. He thought about Castrucci and what an idiot he had been. Castrucci had everything, including a very beautiful wife, and he blew it. "I assure you, you and Caroline will be taken care of."

"Thank you, Carlos, for everything," she said, and then waited for him to continue.

Never one to mince words, he got right to the point. "I knew Anthony wanted me dead, Terasa, and I've known it for quite some time now. Believe it or not, you did the family a great service. Not all of us are like the monsters portrayed on TV, but men like Anthony give us all a bad name. Don't get me wrong, I'm not saying that we're angels, either—a far cry from it—but Anthony and Sal were just plain evil. They enjoyed inflicting pain on others. I, on the other hand, only choose that path after all options have been explored, and that's the way it should be."

He stopped talking long enough to motion for Roberto to get him another drink. He looked at her and smiled. "Normally, your actions would be unforgivable, but I think I'll make an exception in this case. Anthony was out of control. He let his position go to his head and in doing so, put the entire family at risk without a second thought. I knew about the girl, and yes, she was a problem, but she was Anthony's problem. A problem that should have never become mine, as it now stands. He did everything for personal reasons and his own morbid satisfaction."

Taking the drink from Roberto, he drank half the

contents before sitting it on the table. He thought about the FBI agent and the despicable act committed against her by Castrucci's hired gun. He could feel the anger boiling in his veins. His thoughts turned to his granddaughter. He shook his head. "What was done to that girl was unconscionable and pure evil. They violated what was sacred and everything that the family stands for, and for that, we will take care of all loose ends and I do mean all loose ends."

The anguish in his voice was evident, and Terasa felt compassion for her friend. She could see the hurt in his eyes. She had known for quite some time about his granddaughter. He had confided in her shortly after he found out. Although Rheyna hadn't been related to her, she still felt the horrific ache of knowing how she had suffered. She was grateful to this man, but there was one more thing bothering her. She had a question that needed an answer.

"I know you've done a lot for me already, Carlos, but I have one more favor to ask of you…"

Chapter 24

Edwards sat in his car outside the Catholic Church and watched the small crowd of people who came to pay their respects to Anthony Castrucci. It had been three days since they pulled his body from the bay, and they were not wasting any time putting it in the ground.

Visibly missing were his wife and daughter, as well as the high-profile members of his crime family. Not one single member had come to the church, and it served Castrucci right.

His cell phone rang, jarring him from his thoughts. "Are you sure, Laura ... Okay ... Yeah ... I'll be there as soon as I can." He shook his head in disbelief as he started the car. Things just kept getting more and more interesting.

It took him less than ten minutes to drive down to The Lexington Club over on 19th street. The usual people were already on scene. Once again, a crime scene was declared as police tape cordoned off part of the street. He glanced across the street where uniformed officers were busy keeping onlookers back, and there was no shortage of reporters, either.

Laura walked over to him shaking her head. "Single bullet to the side of the head," she said as she lifted the police tape up for him to duck under.

They walked over to a green Chevy Caprice that was parked in the exact spot where Rheyna's Jeep had been weeks earlier. Edwards followed her around to the back of the car. Laura nodded at the uniformed officer. The hinges squeaked shrilly as he raised the trunk lid to a fully opened position.

Edwards looked down at Jay Farino's dead body, curled up in a fetal position, his hands bound tightly behind his back, his pants pulled down around his knees, exposing blood-covered legs.

"What's in his mouth?" he asked, leaning over to get a better view.

Laura grinned. "They cut his dick off."

"Couldn't happen to a nicer guy," Edwards laughed as he slammed the trunk lid shut.

Terasa pressed the remote and turned up the volume on the TV. Several news crews were live on the scene down at the Lexington Club. A picture of Jay Farino flashed on the screen and then the camera cut back to a live, close-up shot. She recognized Agents Forrest and Edwards standing near the rear end of a car. They moved out of the way as two of the coroner's assistants prepared to remove the body from the trunk.

The camera switched to a close-up shot of James Styles standing behind the police tape. He smiled broadly, showing a full set of teeth as he spoke into the microphone. "Citing anonymity, an unidentified source with the FBI has confirmed that the dead man in the trunk of the car behind me is Jay Marbles Farino. As some of you may already know, Farino was reported to be a hit man for reputed Mob Boss Anthony Castrucci."

A split picture of Big Tony and Sonny Valachi flashed across the screen before the camera cut back to a wide shot of the reporter, and the crime scene behind him.

"Castrucci, along with his trusted Lieutenant, Sonny Valachi, were found several days ago floating in the San Francisco Bay." He continued to speak as another picture flashed on the screen, showing the bodies being pulled from the water. "According to the same FBI source, Castrucci died just days before a secret grand jury indictment for child pornography and several federal racketeering charges were handed down. It was also reported that Farino was the main suspect in the brutal death of undercover FBI Agent Rheyna Sorento. Her badly beaten body was discovered in this same location earlier this month."

The camera switched back to a close up of the reporter. He smiled at the camera. "This is James Styles, reporting for Channel 2 news."

Chapter 25

It had taken Edwards a good sixty minutes to drive up the coast to Benicia, and he still couldn't believe what he was about to do. It should have been against his better judgment, but it wasn't.

He drove the sedan slowly through the entrance to the park. For once, he was doing what was right, and this was the right thing to do, even if the law didn't agree. He knew he was taking a big risk and that if discovered, it would cost him his job, and more likely than not, he would also be arrested.

There was no doubt in his mind that all parties involved would keep this secret. He laughed as he thought about Omerta, the Mafia's vow of silence, their sacred oath, and how he was now about to take part in it. He had taken an oath of his own and he had sworn his allegiance to the bureau, but the bureau had let down one of its own when they failed to protect Rheyna, and that just plain pissed him off.

He followed the signs leading to Dillon's Point and pulled the sedan into one of the empty parking spots. A glance at his watch showed he was early, and that was fine by him. He could use the time to stretch his legs and shake off some of the nervous energy he was feeling. He walked around to the front of the car and leaned back against the grill.

Lighting a cigarette, he inhaled the smoke deep into his lungs. He needed to quit this nasty habit and he knew his wife would appreciate it. He took another drag, flicked the cigarette across the pavement, and then hoisted himself up on the hood of the car. With his hand raised in front of his face to shield his eyes from the sun, he glanced around the park. It was larger than he had imagined. He looked to his right and saw a couple of hikers enter a trailhead.

His thoughts turned back to the event that had brought him here today. The phone call he received earlier in the week had surprised him. Actually, it had surprised the hell out of him, catching him totally off guard, and that was something that didn't happen very often.

Over the years, he had seen and heard just about everything humanly possible. Sometimes, he got to see the best in people, but more often than not, it was mostly the worst. It was a wonder that he had been able to keep his sanity over the years.

He turned to see an approaching car's headlight and watched as the black limousine pulled into the spot next to his sedan. Vincent got out and came around to hold the rear door open. *She's definitely more attractive in person,* he thought as Terasa Castrucci slid out of the backseat. He hadn't seen her since Rheyna's funeral, but could tell from the look on her face that the events of the last month and a half had taken their toll on her, too.

She smiled warmly and walked over to him. To his surprise, she put her arms around his shoulders and hugged him. He could see the gentleness in her. She was genuine and obviously loved her daughter more than anything on earth. Her actions and intentions had made that perfectly clear when she phoned him. If Caroline was anything like her mother—and he suspected she was—Rheyna hadn't stood a chance. He understood how she had fallen in love with her.

Terasa turned to Vincent and took the manila envelope from his hand. She handed it to Edwards. She looked at him thoughtfully. "I can't thank you enough for what you have done for me and my daughter, Agent

Edwards."

He looked at the envelope, turning it over repeatedly in his hands. He raised his head to meet her gaze. "I hope you understand that we were only doing our jobs, and Rheyna never meant to hurt you or Caroline."

She nodded and smiled. "I do understand, and I also understand that Rheyna was the best thing to ever happen to my daughter, and I think the reverse was true for her as well. When the two of them were together, it was like the sun and sky. I've never been one to believe in soul mates, but I truly believe that's exactly what the two of them were to each other."

She leaned against the side of the car and sighed deeply. "As for Anthony, I guess deep down, I always knew it was only a matter of time before it came to this," she said, looking out over the bluff. She absentmindedly fumbled with the top button on her blouse as she collected her thoughts. She struggled with the words now caught in her throat, and Edwards could see the pain in her eyes.

"I did care for my husband, Agent Edwards, but even I have a breaking point. I'd had enough. I just couldn't take it anymore. I made a decision to no longer stand idly by and watch him destroy yet another life. It makes me sick to my stomach to think of all the decent people he's ruined— or worse yet, killed. Some of those people meant the world to me."

Edwards felt for this woman. She was a good person, and through unforeseen circumstances, and no fault of her own, she had been thrown into the Mafia way of life—a life fueled by greed, power, and crime so brutal, it usually resulted in death. It was inevitable. It was the La Cosa Nostra way and always would be.

"You know I could lose my job and possibly my freedom for what I'm about to do," he said, sliding his hand inside his jacket pocket. He pulled out the cassette tape from the surveillance room and handed it to her along with a small, white envelope. "But I don't really care. I think you and Caroline have suffered enough and it's the least I can do to repay you."

She watched him take out his pocketknife and cut a slit in the envelope. He pulled out several sheets of paper. He looked at the offshore bank account numbers used to launder the money from Bayshore. He quickly scanned the sheet containing the names of several high profile officials on the mob's payroll and their payoff schedules. It also included the amounts they had already been paid.

He felt his stomach knot up as he removed the photos paper-clipped to the top of the page. He shook his head in disbelief as he looked at the photo showing Special Agent Carl Stevens accepting an envelope while shaking the outstretched hand of Sonny Valachi. He thumbed through the photos, each one showing Stevens at a different time and place as he met up with Big Tony's right hand man. He stuffed the items back into the envelope and took out a cigarette.

"Thank you, Terasa," he said, opening the car door.

Terasa and Vincent got back in the limo, and Edwards watched them leave as quietly as they had arrived. He waited until the limousine's taillights disappeared over the hill and out of sight before getting into his car. He took a drag from his cigarette and blew the smoke out the window.

How could Stevens have done this? They were supposed to be best friends. Their wives shopped together, their kids attended the same schools. Hell, they even went on family camping trips together. How could he have been so heartless to do this to Rheyna—and for what, a few extra thousand dollars?

From the beginning, he knew this didn't feel right; he felt it in his gut sitting in his office the night the team had their first meeting, and somewhere deep inside, he had suspected Stevens could be the leak. There were just too many coincidences. He had discovered that in some way or another, Stevens had direct access to the information coming from the bureau's relationship with the informants. Each time he found an inconsistency, he excused it away with some sort of rationalization.

He just didn't want to believe it, and although the hard truth was staring him in the face—along with the documents and pictures to prove it, he still had a hard time accepting it. He should have known to trust his gut and because he didn't, his agent paid a very high price. He felt responsible for what happened to Rheyna. He broke his own rule—he forgot to practice what he preached.

Laura had reminded him not too long ago to look at the little details inside the big picture. She gave him a taste of his own medicine, and he hadn't heeded his own advice. All along, the details pointing to Stevens were there, and he ignored them.

He let his mind drift back to when he first entertained the idea it could be Stevens. It was the conversation with Laura after Paulie and Georgie were killed in front of the delicatessen. Stevens blatantly ignored the notion a hit was going to take place, and he ignored Laura's suggestion to contact the L.A. field office.

However, it was when Laura commented on Aldrich Ames that he seriously considered the idea. Ames had also been a thirty-year man in the bureau. It was obvious by Laura's comment that she had also entertained the idea of it being Stevens. What Stevens had done was comparable to the heinous acts perpetrated by Aldrich Ames' betrayal to America.

At the time of his arrest in 1994, Ames had been spying for the Soviet U.S.S.R. for nine years, having received nearly two-million dollars. His betrayal turned out to be one of the deadliest in U.S. history, costing several Russian informants their lives. Ames had sold the identities of those informants to the KGB and once the KGB had the informants' names, the men were rounded up, arrested, and then executed.

Edwards started the engine and backed the car out of the parking lot. He glanced down at his watch. His flight back to Washington was not due to leave for another three hours. That would give him plenty of time to hang out in the airport bar for several much-needed drinks. Laura and Stevens had left the day before and would already be there when he arrived. He picked up his phone and dialed Laura's cell number.

Five hours later, Edwards pushed through the double doors of the J. Edgar Hoover building. He noticed Laura sitting on one of the sofas with two armed guards standing a few feet away. She stood up, walked over to him, and waited as he flashed his badge to the security guard behind the desk. Then the two of them, along with the guards, stepped inside the elevator. They rode up to the fifth floor in silence, both knowing that nothing was worse than arresting one of your own for a crime. What made this especially bad was the crime hadn't only been against a fellow agent, but a minimum of seven informants had lost their lives in the process.

When Edwards had phoned Laura on the way to the airport and confirmed that Stevens was the mole, she was not the least bit surprised, and like Edwards, she felt guilty. She felt guilty for not being able to answer her cell phone and for not pushing the issue harder with him regarding her suspicions. She listened as he filled her in on the details.

Afterward, he was grateful that she was professional enough not to say, "I told you so." It wasn't her style, and he knew it. She was too classy for such pettiness, and he appreciated it.

Although it took only seconds to reach the fifth floor, it felt like forever. Normally, Edwards dreaded moments like these, but all he felt right now was anger—blood-boiling anger. He stepped through the open doors and felt an immediate rush of adrenaline.

Stevens was standing at the end of the hallway near the conference room. A puzzled look crossed his face as he looked at Laura and then at Edwards, and then at the two guards walking beside them.

Edwards walked up to him and stopped. He leaned forward and brought his face within an inch of Stevens'.

Edwards glared at him, feeling nothing but rage. He looked Stevens squarely in the eyes. "You're under arrest, you son-of-a-bitch," he said through clenched teeth.

Stevens held his hand up to protest, and without giving it a second thought, Edwards drew his arm back and hit Stevens squarely in the mouth with his fist. The impact sent Stevens reeling backward into the wall. He instinctively put his arms up in front of his face as Edwards drew his arm back to strike him again.

"No, Kyle, he's not worth it," Laura said, grabbing Edwards by the arm, pulling him back.

Stevens slowly got to his feet. He used the back of his sleeve to wipe the blood from his mouth. He started to say something and stopped when Edwards and Laura both turned their backs to him.

Edwards nodded at the guards, who proceeded to slam Stevens up against the wall. They pulled his arms behind his back and as they cuffed him, doors began opening along the hallway. Several agents came out of the adjoining offices and watched with a look of dismay as one of their own was led away in handcuffs.

Terasa stood at the door for several minutes looking at Caroline. She was glad to see Caroline had gained some of her weight back, and she was equally thrilled to see that she had finally left her bedroom, even if she was only standing on the outside balcony.

The past month and a half had been so hard on her. She thought about Edwards and the risk she herself had taken. What she had done would have been unfathomable if her husband were still alive. In fact, she would have paid the highest price for her betrayal. She would have paid with her own life.

Terasa went outside. She leaned against the rail next to her daughter. Caroline smiled as Terasa wrapped her arm around her waist.

"I love the view from up here," Caroline said as she looked out across the bay.

Terasa looked around the expansive property and nodded in agreement. She sighed heavily. "The view is what first sold me on the property when we decided to build the house."

It felt like a lifetime ago. She turned to Caroline and reached up to brush a few stray hairs back from her face. "You know, I have truly loved only one person in my life," she said, and then paused to collect her thoughts. "I met her in Sicily while attending college. I was twenty-two at the time, she was twenty-four." She laughed at the surprised look on Caroline's face as the realization of what her words meant sank in.

"Oh—wow, Mom, I had no idea," Caroline said,

unable to keep the surprise from her voice.

Terasa smiled and looked back out at the bay. "When my father found out, he forbade me from ever seeing her again." She laughed again at the shocked expression on Caroline's face.

"What did you do?"

Terasa chuckled. "We sneaked around until we got caught, and when your grandfather found out, he sent me to America. He arranged for me to marry your father and told me that if I cared about Serena, I would do as he asked, or she would pay the price for my disobedience."

Caroline turned to look directly at her mom. She reached up and wiped the tears from Terasa's cheek. After all these years, she could clearly see the pain in her mother's eyes.

"She was the most beautiful woman I'd ever seen, with hair like black silk and piercing grey eyes. In a lot of ways, Rheyna reminded me of her."

Terasa smiled as she thought about how much Serena and Rheyna resembled each other. There were times when she thought if Serena ever had a child, she would look just like Rheyna. "I wanted to die. Just knowing that Serena was out there somewhere without me was unbearable," she said, her voice shaking with emotion. She turned to look at Caroline. "But I loved her enough to let her go."

Terasa tried unsuccessfully to keep the tears from spilling down her cheeks. She placed her hands on Caroline's face so she could look her in the eye. "No person on the face of this earth should ever be forced to pretend to be something they're not, or to live life as a lie."

Caroline's heart was breaking for her mother. "Maybe you can still find Serena. There's no one to stop you now."

"Maybe," Terasa said, taking Caroline by the hand. "Come with me, there's someplace I want to take you."

"And where might that be?" Caroline asked as she let Terasa lead her back into the house.

A sly smile formed on Terasa's mouth. "You'll just have to wait and see," she answered as they stepped outside to the waiting limo and Vincent. He nodded to Caroline and smiled as he held the door open.

Caroline turned to Terasa with a puzzled look on her face. Her mom was up to something and had obviously enlisted Vincent's help in this little adventure. "Can't you at least give me a clue?" she asked after they were settled onto the backseat.

Terasa shook her head and gently squeezed Caroline's hand. "No, I told you it's a surprise." Terasa thought about the strings she had to pull to make this happen and the countless number of favors she now owed. They were big ones, but in a short time, each one would be worth it because Caroline was the only thing that mattered to her. She would do anything to ensure her daughter's happiness, no matter the cost.

Caroline looked out the window and noticed they were heading up the coast. She turned to Terasa. "Mom, what are you up to?"

Terasa feigned ignorance. "I'm not up to anything, dear. What would ever give you that idea?"

"Yes, you are and somehow, you've talked Vincent into helping you."

"Nonsense, you just sit there like a good girl," Terasa said, trying to hide the smile playing at the corners of her mouth. Caroline was too much like her, and she knew she was not about to give up that easily.

Vincent turned onto Topanga Canyon Boulevard and headed south. Caroline looked out the window and turned back to Terasa. She held her thumb and index finger an inch apart. "Can't you at least give me a tiny hint?"

Terasa was not about to give in. She patted Caroline on the knee. "I'm not telling you. I promise we'll be there shortly."

Caroline leaned back in the seat and tried to relax as

Vincent maneuvered the car along the winding road. After fifteen minutes of driving, he turned onto a side road and then into the driveway of a small beach house.

Terasa didn't wait for him to come around and open the door. She pulled Caroline out of the car by the hand.

Caroline looked at her with a confused expression on her face. "I don't understand," she said as Terasa led her around to the back of the house.

"Whose house is this?" Caroline asked, continuing to follow her mom onto the back deck. She heard a radio playing *Inside Your Heaven* by Carrie Underwood and then she heard a dog barking somewhere in the distance.

She turned and looked toward the beach and then stopped dead in her tracks. She looked at the two figures walking near the water. She felt her heart catch in her throat. "Oh my God—How ... Mom—I don't understand." She turned to Terasa and saw tears streaming down her face, and felt her own eyes fill up with tears.

"Go, go to her," Terasa said, waving her hand toward the beach.

Caroline took the deck stairs two at a time. By the time she hit the sand, she was sobbing. She flung off her shoes and ran down the beach where Rheyna stood playing with Annie.

Terasa felt Vincent put his arm around her waist. The two of them watched Caroline run through the sand.

Rheyna turned to look at the figure running toward her. It took less than two seconds for her to realize who it was. The cane in her hand fell to the ground.

"Caroline!" she yelled, and quickly closed the remaining distance between them. She caught Caroline in her arms and lifted her up off the ground, spinning in circles.

Caroline cried as she took Rheyna's face in her hands. She kissed her with so much tenderness and love. "Please, please, don't ever leave me again," she said between kisses.

"I promise I'll never leave you again," Rheyna said, pulling Caroline close and kissing her deeply.

Caroline pulled back to look at her. "I think you have some serious explaining to do."

"I know I do, but can I do it later?" Rheyna asked sheepishly.

"I guess so," Caroline said as she cupped Rheyna's face and kissed her softly.

Vincent laughed as Annie playfully jumped around the two women and then proceeded to knock them to the ground. She happily licked Caroline's face and then Rheyna's and then Caroline's again.

Teresa turned to Vincent and smiled. He turned his head to keep her from seeing the tears running down his cheeks.

"Are you getting soft on me, Vincent?" she asked, hugging the big man close.

He puffed out his chest and shook his head, trying to compose himself. "Me, soft? Never!"

Terasa knew better. Deep down, Vincent was one big lovable teddy bear. She saw the little smile form at the edge of his mouth as he turned and looked at Caroline and Rheyna laying on the beach, and Annie who had now turned her attention to biting at the waves.

Chapter 26

Terasa looked at Caroline and felt her heart swell up with pride. "You are positively glowing from head to toe," she said, stepping through the doorway.

"And I have you to thank for it," Caroline said, spreading her arms out. She turned in a complete circle. "So ... What do you think?" she asked, although she could tell by the smile on Terasa's face that she did indeed look every bit the bride that she was. She glanced at herself in the full-length mirror and smiled. Rheyna had chosen her gown, and seeing how the white strapless gown hung seductively over her breasts, she could see why. She turned to face Terasa.

"Oh, Mom," she said, walking over and wiping the tears from Terasa's cheek. "You're going to ruin your makeup."

"I'm sorry, sweetheart. I can't help it," Terasa said, bending to smooth out the small train hanging from the back of Caroline's gown. "I'm so proud of you, and I just want you to be happy," she said between sniffles.

"I am happy. I have never been happier in my life, and I owe it all to you."

Terasa reached over and took Caroline's hand.

Caroline smiled. "I love you, Mom."

"And I love you, too. Are you ready?"

"I'm as ready as I'll ever be," Caroline said with a nervous laugh.

Terasa kissed her on the cheek. "Do you know that I've dreamt about this moment since the day you were born?"

"How did you know I would one day marry a woman?" Caroline teased.

"I knew you would marry the person of your dreams and obviously, I was right," Terasa said smugly and pulled the veil down over Caroline's face before she could respond. Caroline laughed and laced her arm through Terasa's and together, they stepped on the white carpet leading out toward the gazebo in the backyard.

Caroline's heart skipped a beat as Carrie Underwood's melodic voice began singing the song she had chosen, the one she heard at the beach house. All eyes were now on her as the guests turned in their seats to watch Terasa walk Caroline down the aisle.

Caroline looked at her side of the aisle and then over to where Rheyna's family and friends were sitting. *This has to be a first,* she thought. Agent Edwards had to be salivating all over himself, and she wouldn't have been the least bit surprised to see foam coming from the corners of his mouth. On her side of the aisle, sitting in the front row, and dressed in a black tuxedo, was Don Carlos Massino. Next to him, sat Vincent and Joey, and the seats directly behind the three men contained the high-profile members of Massino's crime family.

On Rheyna's side was the FBI. Agent Laura Forrest and her lover Stacie, along with Annie, were sitting in the front row next to Rheyna's parents. Directly behind them were Agent Edwards, his wife Tess, Ron, Phil, Jesse, and several other friends of the family.

She looked at Rheyna, standing next to the minister, and felt her pulse quicken. Rheyna had decided she wanted to wear a white pantsuit, but insisted it be from the exact material as her own gown. Caroline had to admit that the result was stunning.

Terasa placed Caroline's hand in Rheyna's hand and then leaned forward, kissing Rheyna on the cheek before taking her seat next to Carlos.

The minister looked out at the guests and cleared her throat. "I would like to thank all of you for coming here today. We are gathered together to witness the union between Rheyna Sorento and Caroline Castrucci as they celebrate their love for and commitment to each other."

She looked at Rheyna and smiled. "Rheyna, you may now recite your vows."

Rheyna's hand trembled as she raised Caroline's veil. She took both of Caroline's hands in hers. "Caroline, I can't begin to describe how you've touched my heart. You have brought so much joy and happiness to my life. I never thought I would ever be able to love anyone as much as I do you. You have consumed my very being, completing my soul. I feel so much love when I look at you, when I hear your voice."

She paused to wipe tears from Caroline's cheek. "I promise you that from this day forward, I will spend my lifetime loving you, protecting you, and cherishing every single moment that we are together. But most of all, I want to tell you how grateful I am for your love and to thank you for choosing me as the one to spend the rest of your life with."

The minister turned to Caroline. "Caroline, you may recite your vows."

Caroline took a moment to wipe the tears from her eyes. She turned to Rheyna. She laid her hand against Rheyna's cheek, lightly caressing the small bruise still visible beneath her eye.

"Rheyna, there are so many things that I want to say to you." She looked at the guests and laughed nervously. "But I don't think they can hang around that long, so instead I want to tell you how you have changed my life for the better in so many ways. You have shown me that dreams do come true and that there is such a thing as true love, complete with a happy ending. I found that love when you walked into my life. You opened up a part of me I never knew existed. I love you so much at times, it makes my heart hurt. The idea of loving someone to the depths I love you is amazing. I promise you I will never take you or your love for granted and I will spend my lifetime making you happy. I promise to love only you until the day I die."

They turned to face the minister.

"May we have the rings?" she asked.

Rheyna turned to her father and took the gold band from his hand. She lifted Caroline's hand. "I give you this ring as an expression of my love and commitment to you," she said, sliding the band onto Caroline's ring finger.

Caroline turned and took the matching band from Terasa. "And I give you this ring as an expression of my love and commitment to you," she said as she slid the ring onto Rheyna's finger.

The minister looked at Caroline and then at Rheyna and smiled. "You may kiss your bride."

Rheyna leaned over and kissed Caroline softly on the lips. "You ready?" she asked, taking Caroline's hand in hers as the guests stood, cheering them on.

"You better believe it," Caroline answered.

Together, the two of them walked down the steps and then ran up the aisle. They came to a stop at the end of the carpet and tossed their bouquets back over their heads. They turned to see Terasa and Vincent each catch one.

Vincent's lips curled into a shy smile as a handsome young man on Rheyna's side of the aisle winked at him.

Chapter 27

Rheyna watched Caroline as she sipped on a margarita. It had been almost a month since their union ceremony and every once in awhile, she still had to pinch herself to believe it was true.

Terasa had made all the arrangements for their honeymoon and had booked them aboard Olivia's Silver Wind Ship for a South American cruise. After sailing for several days, they flew to Rio de Janeiro and spent the better part of the week shopping, drinking, dancing, eating, and then more shopping, and several sleepless nights making love. They left their hotel and boarded the cruise ship to finish their journey, which brought them to Argentina, where they now lay on the beach, drinking margaritas, and working on their tans.

Rheyna glanced toward her left, where Laura and Stacie were lounging. They had arrived the previous day, after much prodding by Caroline. After everything they had been through, Caroline had insisted that Laura and Stacie needed a vacation as much as she and Rheyna.

Terasa had been adamant about keeping Annie for the first two weeks and then reluctantly agreed to let Vincent keep her for the last two since she had made travel arrangements of her own.

Rheyna turned to Caroline. "Did you ever find out where Terasa was going on her mini-trip?"

"Nope," she said, and continued flipping through her magazine. "She was very secretive about it, but she promised to drop us a postcard when she got there."

Rheyna leaned back in her chair. She let her thoughts drift to Terasa. She was a remarkable woman, courageous, brave, loving, and just like her daughter. Edwards and Laura had filled Rheyna in on all the events that had taken place while she was recuperating from her injuries. She knew what Terasa had done out of love for Caroline. Not only did she love Terasa for what she had done, she gained a newfound respect for Terasa because of it.

Rheyna hated keeping things from Caroline after everything that had happened, but the truth regarding the circumstances of her father's death was something she would never learn from Rheyna. His death had been hard enough on Caroline as it was, and although Rheyna hated the man with every ounce of her being, she truly loved his daughter. There was absolutely nothing to be gained then or ever by telling Caroline that her mother was the person responsible for his death.

She thought about Edwards' the last minute decision to fake her death at the hospital. He told her afterward that he had a strong suspicion that Stevens was the mole inside the bureau and was the one responsible for blowing her cover.

They had to convince everyone that she had died, even if it meant hurting Caroline. Edwards knew that if word got back to Castrucci through Stevens that she was still alive, it would only be a matter of time before he sent someone else to finish the job. The fact that she was a federal agent hadn't fazed him a bit—that was an obvious conclusion, seeing that he didn't hesitate to send Farino after her.

She understood Edwards' reasoning from being involved in similar situations before, which had ended with good results. He had taken the time to meet with her parents to let them know that she was alive and well because he knew they would hear the news reports eventually.

Throughout all the craziness, the one thing Edwards hadn't counted on was Terasa figuring out the truth. He had asked her later, how she knew. She shrugged and laughed. She had been a little suspicious from the beginning when she and Caroline were not allowed to go in the room after the doctor had pronounced Rheyna dead. She never saw Rheyna's body. She had heard about cases where the FBI or CIA faked a person's death in order to protect them, and she had prayed that this had been the case with Rheyna.

She also knew she had information Edwards needed and figured that if her hunch was right, he might be willing to make a trade. The fact that she loved her daughter more than anything had made all her decisions very easy and she had called in a couple of favors from Carlos in order to pull off her plan.

Out of gratitude for her friendship and loyalty, Carlos agreed to forget and forgive. As for tying up the loose ends concerning Jay Farino, Carlos had done that strictly for his own personal reasons. She had learned through Terasa about Massino's granddaughter, and although it didn't change anything, it had offered him a small piece of revenge. He also had Terasa's father as motivation. The two of them had grown up as friends together in a crime-infested Sicilian neighborhood. Her father had been the one responsible for saving Carlos' life when he took a bullet to the chest after being caught in the crossfire between two rival street gangs.

They all knew that Carlos was behind the killing, but had chalked it up to hard knocks. If he could forget, so could they, the FBI. Unfortunately, it was going to take years of therapy in order for her to forget and forgive.

As for Stevens, he currently sits in a Leavenworth jail cell awaiting trial on a slew of charges, including several counts of accessory to murder for the deaths of the informants. She was told that his chances of ever seeing daylight again are zilch.

She felt the most sympathy for Artie. He had been given the choice of resigning in order to avoid jail time on his own charges. Not only did he lose his job and pension, his wife Alice had sought help for her drinking and gambling addiction and had immediately filed for divorce upon being released from the treatment center.

Ron was doing as well as anyone, considering his circumstances, and he had actually been on a date with a friend of Stacie's. She smiled as she thought about Stacie never missing or passing up the chance to play matchmaker.

Caroline got to her feet and stretched. "I think I'm ready to head back to the hotel for lunch, if that's okay with the three of you," she said, jostling Rheyna from her thoughts.

"I could use a bite to eat myself," Stacie said as she stood up and slipped on a terrycloth robe. She picked up Laura's robe and tossed it to her.

Rheyna got up from her lounger, grabbed Caroline, and wrapped her arms around her waist. "I'm a little hungry, too," she whispered in Caroline's ear.

Caroline playfully pushed her away. "I need real food, real nourishment. Besides, I want to see if we got anything from Mom," she said, slapping Rheyna with the magazine.

"Don't you two ever stop?" Laura asked with a mischievous grin.

"Like you have any room to talk," Stacie said as she gathered up their things.

Laura took Stacie's hand in hers. "Are you complaining?" she asked.

"Never," Stacie said, leaning in to kiss Laura on the cheek.

Caroline laced her fingers with Rheyna's, and the four of them strolled slowly along the beach toward the hotel.

"Have you thought about where you'd like to live?"

Rheyna asked.

Caroline smiled. "I don't care, as long as I'm with you. I would live on the moon if I had to."

"I don't think I'm ready for anything that drastic, honey, at least not right now. I was thinking more along the lines of a house in the hills, or maybe on the beach. How about Provincetown?" Rheyna laughed at the expression on Caroline's face, and then added, "But if you really want to go to the moon, I'll see what I can do."

Caroline squeezed Rheyna's hand. "Do you have any idea, any idea at all just how madly and hopelessly in love with you I am?" she asked.

"Maybe just a little," Rheyna answered.

When they reached the hotel, Rheyna held the door open. "How would you like to spend the next fifty years showing me?" she asked.

"I think I can handle that," Caroline said as she went through the door.

Laura and Stacie headed for the elevators. "We'll see you two in a couple of hours," Laura said over her shoulder.

Rheyna glanced at her watch. "How about we meet down here for dinner around six?"

"Sounds good to me," Laura answered just before the elevator door closed.

Caroline and Rheyna walked over to the receptionist's desk. A young dark-haired woman with big brown eyes looked up from her notepad. "May I help you?" she asked with a thick Argentine accent.

"Can you please check to see if you have anything for Caroline Castrucci-Sorento?" Caroline asked.

They waited as the receptionist searched through the stacks of mail. "I don't see anything here. I'll check to see if there is something in back."

After a few minutes, she returned with a postcard and handed it to Caroline. Caroline turned the card over and read the back. She smiled as she handed the postcard to Rheyna.

"Sicily? What's she doing in Sicily?" Rheyna asked, not understanding the meaning.

"Boy, do I have a story for you. You're simply not going to believe it," Caroline said, pulling Rheyna toward the elevators.

The taxicab wound its way slowly up the cobblestone street and through a cluster of citrus trees.

Terasa had forgotten just how beautiful Palermo was until the two-story villa overlooking the blue waters of Mondello Beach came into view. The house itself was breathtaking, nestled between several groups of olive and fig trees and thick, rolling green hills that shot off to the right, and stretched as far as the eye could see.

She waited for the driver to come to a stop and leaned across the seat to pay him. She took a deep breath, trying to calm her racing heartbeat and opened the cab door. She must have been crazy for coming here. When Caroline made the comment that no one was standing in her way now, she had allowed herself to think about the future and the endless possibilities it might hold, but now that she was here, she couldn't help thinking she had completely lost her mind.

She had been second-guessing herself since her plane landed. She had a million 'what if's'. What if she's not home, or what if she doesn't want to see me? Or worse— what if she's with someone else? Surely, after all these years, she has to have someone in her life. The private detective had told her repeatedly that there was not. He also reassured her that his investigators had determined that no one had been in her life for years. Terasa still found it hard to believe.

She walked up to the door, took another deep breath, and pressed the buzzer. She glanced down at her trembling hands and waited for the door to be answered. She heard the lock click. She slowly raised her head and felt her breath catch in her throat—she was every bit as beautiful as she remembered.

Serena let out a gasp, recognition setting in. Without uttering a word, Serena pulled Terasa into her arms and gently kissed her on the mouth.

The End

SHE LEFT ME BREATHLESS

Trin Denise

RAGZ BOOKS

Copyright

Print Edition

ISBN-13: 978-1-908822-21-5

(RAGZ BOOKS)

Cover Art by Claire Chilton

Editor: Margaret Farrell

EBook Structural Editor: Claire Chilton

Print Edition Structural Editor: Trin Denise

She Left Me Breathless

Sydney Welsh is a self-made millionaire. She is successful, confident, and seems to have the world at her feet but something is missing. Her life is a catastrophic mess and the reality of her situation sets in when she arrives home from a business trip and finds her lover in bed with a female executive from her company.

She realizes that the only woman she has ever loved was Rachel Ashburn and that ended thirteen years ago when Rachel made a choice, a life-changing choice that did not include Sydney. Sydney knew she could compete with another woman, or even a man for Rachel's love, but how can anyone compete with God.

Now with more money than she knows what to do with, she puts an elaborate plan in motion to bring Rachel back into her life. She tells herself that she is doing it for revenge, and hiring business wiz-kid Caitlyn—Rachel's nineteen-year-old daughter for an internship with her company is a key part of that plan.

She learns that it's okay to make plans as long as you don't plan the outcome when an embezzler is suspected inside her company. She makes several miscalculations and unknowingly puts Rachel and Caitlyn's lives in danger when Caitlyn is kidnapped.

As with all best laid plans, things can go wrong and once again, Sydney finds herself falling head over heels in love with Rachel, the only woman who had the power to leave her breathless.

Dedication

This novel is for all those ladies who have finally found the woman who left them breathless. For those who haven't found her yet, be patient, she's out there. I promise!

Acknowledgements

I would like to thank Author Claire Chilton for doing such a fantastic job on the book cover. She is by far the Queen of cover design and structural editing in my opinion and I love, love, love the cover you made for SLMB!

I would also like to thank Author Eileen Gormley who in my opinion is the Queen of book blurbs!

I would also like to thank Margaret Farrell for all the help she gave me in bringing SLMB to fruition. Without your hard-core critique's, SLMB wouldn't be as good as it is. You are the Queen Beta Reader LOL.

Elisa, one of my biggest fans in the Netherlands: Thank you, thank you, thank you. Your suggestions and feedback were so fantastic, I had to implement them, and I am so glad I did!

Chapter 1

After taking the red-eye flight, Sydney was happy to be home although she hated Ohio winters. They could be downright brutal and today was no exception. All throughout the week, she had kept a close eye on the weather channel. The forecasters stopped short of calling the snowstorm blanketing Ohio a blizzard. Sydney begged to differ. Four-feet of snow falling in less than thirty-six hours, a thirteen-degree temperature, and winds of 37 mph were definitely a blizzard in her book.

When her assistant first suggested December would be an ideal time for her to wrap up a long overdue business engagement in Florida, she had protested rather strongly. However, once the sweltering heat of Miami hit her in the face, she was glad she was there. After six days of non-stop negotiations, lasting from sunrise to sunset, she had finally accomplished what she set out to do, and she was one day ahead of schedule. She glanced at the briefcase lying on the seat beside her. In it were signed documents, declaring her the new owner of seventy-five acres of prime real estate, which included a fifty-thousand square-foot warehouse.

Driving from the Greater Dayton Airport in Vandalia would be a long, time-consuming adventure. For the first time all year, she used the 4-wheel drive option on her Ford 350 crew cab truck. She expertly maneuvered around a snowplow to keep from having her truck sprayed with a mixture of salt and sand. It was amazing that the roads were as clear as they were considering the amount of snow on the ground.

As was the case every winter in Ohio, slick roads were not the main problem, Ohio drivers were. For some reason, Sydney swore they went brain-dead during the first snowfall. It was as if they had never seen nor driven on snow in their entire life.

A trip that normally took her thirty minutes had now reached the hour and a half mark. She turned off Mad River Road onto Hempridge Drive. Her house was the last on the block and sat at the end of the street. At least her driveway did.

Frankie would be getting an extra nice Christmas bonus this year, Sydney thought as she easily wove her way up and around the winding lane. Frankie had plowed the drive so clean that all you could see was blacktop. If it weren't for the six-foot high snowdrifts on both sides of the drive, a person would have no idea that it had been covered in snow just a short time ago.

As Sydney made her way around the circular drive, she recognized Meredith's green Jaguar parked near the front of the house. What she did not recognize was the red car sitting next to it. From the look of both cars and the amount of snow covering them, they had been there for quite awhile. She circled the large fountain that sat in the middle of the drive, pulled her truck up next to the Jaguar, and shut off the engine. She would take her things in first, unpack, and then put the truck in the garage.

With her briefcase in one hand and a suitcase in the other, she walked over to the red car. She might not know whom it belonged to but she knew damn well what kind of car it was. It was the new German made Mercedes Maybach. She also knew there were only twenty in existence. She had come within a hairs inch of buying one for herself but the price tag stopped her. She didn't care how much money she had, she could not justify spending $350,000.00 on a car that looked more like a Buick sedan than a Mercedes. She glanced at her truck and smiled. She could buy eight new Ford trucks for the cost of one Maybach and be happy as hell.

She fished her keys out of her coat pocket and headed up the steps with her luggage. She glanced back at the cars, finding it slightly odd that Frankie had not cleaned them off when she plowed the driveway. She wedged her briefcase under the same arm that was holding her luggage and unlocked the front door, then pushed it open with her knee.

She let out a sigh of relief as she stepped into the brightly lit two-story foyer. It felt good to be home. She looked down at the freshly polished travertine marble floor. She kicked off her shoes and set them off to the side. Edna would not be too happy with her if she tracked snow and salt everywhere. She might own the house, but anything cleanable, Edna took personal ownership of and that included the floors.

With a smile on her face, she took a running step and then slid across the slick marble in her socks, stopping just before her toes hit the bottom step on the left side of a spiraling dual staircase that framed the entry into the expansive family room. She dropped her luggage on the carpeted step and slid back across the floor to the entryway table. She caught her reflection in the twelve-foot, ornately decorated mirror that hung on the wall above the table. Her cheeks were still a little flushed from the biting cold. She ran her fingers through her hair, brushing the long black tresses back from her face. She laid the briefcase along with her keys on the table and pulled open the top drawer. She glanced toward the family room and wondered where Meredith was.

The house was too quiet. There was always someone around, yet it felt and sounded empty. Thinking that Meredith was probably in her office, she turned her attention back to the huge stack of mail lying in the drawer.

She picked up the tightly bound bundle and removed the rubber band. *Bills, bills, junk mail, and more bills,* she thought as she thumbed through the stack of envelopes. She stopped at the sound of laughter.

She laid the mail on the table and slowly made her way toward the staircase that led to the second floor bedrooms. She hesitated for a second and then climbed the stairs. She stopped approximately ten steps from the top. Her heart pounded in her chest as her brain registered what her eyes were seeing. She bent down and picked up a lacy hot-pink bra. She took several more steps and found the matching panties. She knew immediately that neither one belonged to Meredith. Meredith hated pink. Sydney looked at the lingerie as she continued up the steps. When she reached the landing, she had to wait a few seconds to gain control of herself.

For some reason, she was finding it terribly difficult to contain her emotions. She covered her mouth with her hand to keep from laughing. *What is wrong with me,* she thought as she made her way toward the second floor master bedroom, the room she shared with Meredith.

She stopped in front of the closed door and took a deep breath. *Okay, here goes,* she thought as she placed her hand on the doorknob. "Hi, honey, I'm home," she yelled, flinging the door open with a bang.

"Sydney! What the hell are you doing here?" Meredith shrieked and grabbed the sheet. She quickly pulled it over the head of the naked woman crouched down between her legs.

Sydney smiled as she walked over to the bed. "I finished my meetings a little earlier than expected sweetheart and thought I would surprise you. I can see that I was successful by the look on your face." Before Meredith could reply, Sydney reached down, grabbed the edge of the sheet, and flung it back.

Sydney instantly recognized the close-cropped blonde

head. The woman between Meredith's legs slowly turned her head to look up at Sydney.

"I think these belong to you," Sydney said, tossing the lingerie on top of Meredith's stomach. "It's good to see you, Anne. You come here often?" Sydney laughed at the irony in her question.

"I ... I um, don't know what to say, Sydney. Um, it's not what it looks like," Anne muttered, grabbing her bra and panties. She quickly slipped them on and climbed off the bed.

"Not what it looks like? You are joking, right. Please tell me that was a fucking joke, right, Anne?" Sydney's look was incredulous. She watched with enjoyment as Anne nervously fumbled around for the rest of her clothing.

Meredith leaned back against the headboard and crossed her arms over her breast. She opened her mouth to speak but the warning look from Sydney made her reconsider.

"I think you can show yourself out," Sydney said, after Anne finished dressing.

Anne picked her purse up off the dresser. She ran a trembling hand through her hair. She started through the doorway and stopped. She turned to face Sydney. "I'm sorry, Sydney."

Sydney shook her head in disbelief. "Actually, Anne, what I believe is that you are just like everyone else who gets caught with their proverbial panties down. You aren't sorry you were sleeping with my lover, you're sorry I caught you." Sydney looked first at Meredith and then at Anne. "How long has this little fling been going on? Never mind, don't answer that because I really don't give a damn."

Anne opened her mouth to speak but Sydney held her hand up to stop her. "Out of curiosity, how much do you make in a year?"

Anne's brow furrowed into a frown. "What?" she

asked.

"Come on, it's not a hard question. How much is your yearly salary?"

The color of Meredith's cheeks was nearly the same flaming red color of her hair. "Sydney, what the hell are you doing?" she asked.

Sydney turned and looked at Meredith. "I don't think I was talking to you and if you have any sense whatsoever, you will sit there and keep your mouth shut."

"Around $250,000.00," Anne said, pulling her car keys from her purse.

"If memory serves me correctly, I think your bonus last year was somewhere around a hundred grand." Sydney smiled at Anne. "I guess what I really want to know is, was she worth it? Was fucking my girlfriend's ears off worth more than a quarter million dollars a year?"

Meredith slid off the bed and wrapped the sheet tightly around her body. "Come on, babe, don't do this," she said, coming around the side of the bed to stand next to Sydney. She laid her hand on Sydney's arm.

"Don't touch me!" Sydney said, emphasizing each word as she shrugged Meredith's hand away. She looked at Anne. "As for you, you're fired! Don't bother going to work tomorrow. I will have Maureen pack your stuff and send it by courier. Now get the hell out of my house!"

Without a backward glance, Anne quietly left the room.

Meredith was livid. She stomped her foot on the floor. "You can't do this, Sydney!" she yelled.

Sydney whirled around to face Meredith. Her light brown eyes were almost black as she glared at the woman who had shared a bed with her for the last ten years. Meredith, seeing just how angry Sydney was, took a nervous step back.

Sydney jabbed her finger at Meredith's face. "Now it's your turn, you, you cold, calculating, ungrateful bitch!

You're fired and I want you out of my house, out of my sight, and out of my life."

Meredith began to sob. "Where am I supposed to go?" she asked, her voice cracking with emotion.

Sydney wasn't buying it. "I don't give a shit where you go and you can knock off the fake tears. You forget that I know you better than you know yourself. You have one hour to get your shit packed and get out."

Meredith's whole demeanor changed. Not a single tear ran down her cheek. She looked at Sydney with pure contempt. "I need at least three weeks to find another job. Can you at least give me that?"

"You have one week, Meredith, and that's final."

"Can I stay here tonight? I promise to make other arrangements tomorrow?"

"I want you out of my house today. There are plenty of hotels you can choose from or better yet, have one of your gal pals put you up for the night."

"Fine," Meredith said, grabbing a pair of slacks from the closet. "Would you mind giving me a little privacy?" she asked sarcastically.

"Why? It's not like you have anything I haven't seen before."

"If you paid more attention to me, I wouldn't have to spread my legs for other women."

Sydney couldn't help but laugh. "How stupid do you think I am? Do you think that I don't know you've been spreading your legs for every Tom, Dick, and Harriet that comes along? I know exactly whom you've been sleeping with. I also know when you slept with them and how many times. I didn't get to where I am by sticking my head up my ass."

"If you knew, why didn't you say or do anything about it?"

Sydney shrugged. "Because you just weren't worth the hassle and as long as someone else was servicing you, I no longer had to."

"I can't believe you just said that," Meredith said, shaking her head.

"Do you know what the difference between a whore and a prostitute is, Meredith?" When Meredith didn't answer, Sydney said, "A prostitute is at least smart enough to charge for a piece of ass. Just think about it, if you charged, you'd be a millionaire by now."

"You are one heartless bitch," Meredith said through clenched teeth.

Sydney laughed. "Maybe I am but I'm not your bitch anymore." She stopped in the doorway and turned to look at Meredith. "You have one hour to get your things packed. I want you gone as soon as possible and if you think I'm joking, try me. I won't hesitate to call the police and have you physically removed."

Meredith snorted. "I'm surprised you don't have your goons do it for you."

"That's something you don't need to worry your pretty little head about. What I do or don't do is no longer any of your concern," Sydney said, slamming the door shut so hard that the chandelier hanging in the foyer rocked back and forth.

Sydney stood outside the door for several minutes while she gained some semblance of control over her frayed nerves. She was relieved that it was finally over between her and Meredith and she was grateful to Anne for giving her an excuse to do what she had wanted to do for a long, long time, what she should have done years ago.

Her thoughts turned to Frankie, Maureen, and Caitlyn. They were the only ones who knew she would be coming home a day early. She also knew Frankie well enough to know that the big bear of a woman had intentionally left the snow on the two cars for Sydney to see.

Sydney took the steps two at a time in an almost giddy sort of manner. She practically floated over the family room floor. She went behind the wet bar, grabbed a beer from the fridge, and then retrieved the stack of mail from the foyer table. A glance at her watch told her it was almost 9:00 A.M. and Jackie wouldn't be there for another hour. Sydney hoped that Meredith would be gone by the time she arrived. She was eager to see what new information Jackie had for her and whatever it was, it had to be good, otherwise Jackie would have waited until their usual appointment on Friday to come over.

She dropped into an oversized recliner and kicked the footrest up. She tossed the stack of mail on the coffee table, took a long swig from the bottle, and glanced up at the ceiling. The sound of slamming drawers and stomping feet made her smile. Meredith was thoroughly pissed and Sydney couldn't be happier.

Meredith glanced at her reflection in the mirror. *I'm an attractive woman. I have a fantastic body for a woman in her forties,* she thought as she tucked several, long strands of red hair behind her ears. Her green eyes flashed with anger. "Who the hell does she think she is?" she asked herself. She grabbed a handful of clothes and slung them into the suitcase sitting on the edge of the bed. It took everything inside of her to fight back the tears that threatened to spill onto her cheeks. She would not give Sydney the satisfaction by shedding one tear.

"No one dumps me and gets away with it," she muttered under her breath. She stomped over to the closet and yanked several suits from their hangers. She looked around the room. Sydney was crazy if she thought she could take everything she owned right now. She would have to send someone to fetch the rest of her things and Sydney would just have to deal with it. There was just no way to pack ten years worth of stuff in less than an hour.

I can't believe she's doing this to me, she thought as she flung several pairs of panties and a handful of silk bras into the case. So what if she had a fling or two or three or fifty over the course of their relationship. Personally, she thought it helped to keep things fresh, at least on her part and if Sydney had tried to spruce things up a little more, maybe she would not have been so apt to look at anything wearing a skirt. *Ah, who the hell am I kidding,* she laughed at her own thoughts. Of all the relationships she had been in, not one single woman had been able to keep her eyes and most importantly, her hands from wandering.

Meredith tossed the smaller of two jewelry boxes into the suitcase and zipped the lid shut. She grabbed the luggage handle and turned toward the door. She caught a glimpse of her reflection in the mirror and smiled. If Sydney thought she could just kick her to the curb with no repercussions, she had another think coming. No one dumps Meredith Lansing and gets away with it. Not even the great, Sydney Welsh.

Sydney looked up at the sound of the door opening. She watched Meredith come down the stairs.

Meredith sat the suitcase on the floor next to the couch. "Are you sure about this, Sydney?" she asked. "Once I walk out of here, I'm not coming back."

"Yes, Meredith, I'm sure. You and I have known for awhile that this was coming."

"How can you just end it like this? Do all the years we spent together mean nothing to you?"

"You have got to be kidding me. I just caught you in bed with one of my executives and you have the nerve to turn this around on me," Sidney said calmly.

"Well, I'm not giving up that easily. If you think you can just toss me out like yesterday's garbage I've got news for you and—"

"That's why I'm giving you this," Sydney interrupted. She reached down and picked her checkbook up off the coffee table. "I want you out of my life for good, Meredith. No more games." She ripped off the check and shoved it in Meredith's hand.

Meredith looked at the check and frowned. "$500,000.00? What in the hell am I supposed to do with this? How can you expect me to live on such a measly amount?" she asked sarcastically.

"If you don't want it, I'll take it back," Sydney said, reaching for the check.

Meredith pulled it back and crammed it in her pocket. "I guess I'll just have to make do. I wouldn't want to put you out or anything."

Sydney resisted the urge to shoot another dinger at Meredith regarding who's doing all the putting out. She felt her temper flare again. "You're lucky I'm giving you that much. If you remember correctly, the good citizens of Ohio voted down the gay marriage proposal, so by law, I don't have to give you a penny and—" Sydney stopped in mid-sentence and stood up from the chair. She threw her hands up in the air. "You know what, Meredith? I am so over this. I just want you gone."

"Come on, Sydney. Please don't do this," Meredith practically begged as she followed Sydney into the foyer.

Sydney jerked the front door open and stood off to the side.

Meredith, dragging her luggage behind her, stomped unceremoniously through the doorway. She turned to look at Sydney, her eyes full of contempt. "I meant what I said. If you think I'm just going to go away quietly without a fight, you're sadly mistaken, Sydney."

"Goodbye, Meredith."

"I'll send someone over tomorrow to collect the rest of my things," Meredith yelled over her shoulder just before Sydney slammed the door shut in her face.

Sydney closed her eyes and fell back against the door. Feeling the coolness of the wood permeate through her blouse, she took a deep breath, and forced herself to relax. After a few minutes, she opened her eyes. She glanced at her watch. *Jackie would be ...*

The doorbell rang before she had a chance to finish her thought. "Damn it, Meredith," she swore as she jerked the door open.

Jackie Christopher, a behemoth of a woman with short sandy brown hair, smiled sheepishly. "Sorry, Syd, it's just me."

"I'm sorry, Jackie, please come in," Sydney said, stepping back to allow her through the doorway.

Jackie walked into the family room and took a seat on the couch. She took off her sunglasses and laid them on the coffee table next to the file folder she had brought with her. She was silent as she watched Sydney go over to the wet bar.

"Kinda early to be hitting the sauce, huh?" Jackie asked, her eyebrow rising slightly as she looked at Sydney.

"You know what they say, it's five o'clock somewhere. Care to join me?"

"Oh what the hell, you only live once, right?" Jackie laughed.

"So they say," Sydney said, grabbing two bottles of beer from the fridge.

Jackie took the beer Sydney offered and twisted off the cap. She took a long swig from the bottle. "So, you wanna tell me what's going on or do you want me to guess?" she asked.

"Meredith and I broke up," Sydney sighed.

Jackie snorted. "There's a real shocker."

"You aren't the least bit surprised?" Sydney asked,

cocking her head to look at Jackie.

"As far as I'm concerned the two of you should have split a long time ago," Jackie answered, shaking her head.

"You aren't the first person in my life to point that out," Sydney laughed.

Jackie looked down at the bottle of beer in her hands. She tore a piece of the label off the bottle. She studied Sydney for several seconds. "Are you okay?" she asked thoughtfully.

"Yeah, actually I am," Sydney said, answering honestly.

"If you don't mind my asking, what happened?"

"I just caught her in bed with Anne."

"You're shitn' me," Jackie said, barely managing to choke out the words as she spit a mouthful of beer on the coffee table. She quickly wiped the liquid off the file folder and turned to look at Sydney.

"I shit you not," Sydney said with a shake of her head.

"Anne Burbank?"

Sydney nodded.

"Wow just damn wow," Jackie said with a completely dumbfounded look on her face.

"And I caught them in my bed." Sydney glanced at her watch and added, "About an hour ago."

"And Meredith just left?"

Sydney shook her head. "Not without giving me a little crap."

"Just a little? I would have thought she'd go ballistic," Jackie said.

Jackie picked up the file folder. She pulled out several documents and laid them on her lap.

"I think Meredith may look for a way to cause me trouble," Sydney said.

"Well, whatever she does, I'm sure you'll be able to handle it."

Sydney nodded at the papers on Jackie's lap. "What do you have for me?"

"Before I give these to you, are you one-hundred percent sure this is what you want to do?"

Sydney nodded. "I think right now, this is the only thing in my life that I am sure about," she said, reaching for the documents. She looked at Jackie. "How's she doing at EMCOR?"

"Very well actually and as a matter of fact, two days ago she was promoted to Senior Designer."

"That doesn't surprise me a bit. She always wanted to be an architect," Sydney said as she looked at the documents.

They were both silent for several minutes as Sydney digested the information and with each passing minute, the color in her cheeks grew redder. Finally, she raised her head to look at Jackie. "How long has this been going on?" she asked.

"From what I can tell, it seems to have started right after they were married," Jackie answered. She had been dreading Sydney's reaction from the minute she discovered these new details. She pushed several pictures across the table toward Sydney.

"Why didn't we know about this before now?" Sydney asked, trying hard to keep the irritation out of her voice.

Jackie shrugged. "I never had a reason to check hospital records. I only did so after noticing the small bruise on her cheek when I saw those pictures."

Sydney looked at the attractive blonde-haired woman in the photo. The bright blue eyes sparkled in spite of the large purple and green bruise covering the woman's right cheek. Her eyes were still as beautiful as Sydney remembered yet she looked different. The thirty-seven-year old face staring back at her looked sad, haunted, not the bubbling, happy, "I'm grateful to be alive" woman she used to know.

Jackie pulled out several documents stapled together from the file folder and slid it across the coffee table to

Sydney. "This is a little more detailed and gives the so-called reasons for her injuries."

Sydney looked at the first entry on the paper. "This happened less than a month after they were married."

"Yeah, says she slipped and fell while getting out of the car. She just so happened to break her arm in the process."

Sydney used her finger to scan down the list of entries. "She was treated for a concussion four months later when she accidentally fell down the basement stairs." Sydney shook her head. "She was pregnant when these things happened."

"She's been to the hospital fourteen times in the last eight years but none in the past year, which seems odd since most abusers don't just stop."

"Stitches, concussions, broken bones, cracked ribs, fractured wrist, you name it, and she's had it. Why in the hell would she stay with a man like that?"

"You know as well I do that some women come up with all sorts of reasons to justify the abuse and somehow it's always their fault. His supper was late or she forgot to renew his newspaper subscription. You know the drill."

Sydney shook her head again. "It has to be more than that. He must have something on her. The woman I knew would never put up with this."

"You haven't seen her for almost thirteen years. People change."

Sydney's anger was almost to the boiling point. "That son of a bitch. I'd like to see him do that to me," she said, tossing the photos on the coffee table. Her thoughts turned to Rachel's two daughters. Both girls were technically defined as prodigies and Rachel's youngest, Alyssa, was just eight-years-old, yet she was already in the seventh grade. "What about Caitlyn and Alyssa?" she asked.

"From what I can tell, he doesn't lay a hand on the

girls, just their mother."

"He's not Caitlyn's biological father, he died before she was born but I think if Edward was abusing her I would have seen the signs."

"Not necessarily. There are more ways to inflict abuse on a person besides physical. He's definitely a real piece of work. Take a look at this," Jackie said and handed Sydney two documents.

Sydney scanned the documents. "I don't understand, what is this?" she asked.

"Well, after I found the hospital records, I had a friend of mine in D.C. do a little deep digging for me. Seems that Mr. Eddie Ashburn isn't who he claims to be."

"Do tell," Sydney said with a smile.

"Edward Ashburn, born June 16th, 1964 in Scottsdale, Arizona died at childbirth."

"Are you kidding me?"

"Nope," Jackie said.

Sydney looked at the documents again. One was a copy of a death certificate; the other was the birth certificate for Edward Ashburn, infant son of Martha and Samuel Ashburn. "Then who the hell is he and why is hiding out under an assumed name?"

Jackie shrugged. "Your guess is as good as mine but I intend to find out."

"I want you to make this priority number one and the minute you find out what Mr. Ashburn is hiding, I want to know," Sydney said as she gave the documents back to Jackie and stood up. "Whatever he's hiding has to be pretty damn big."

"My thoughts exactly. Most people who change their identity are on the run. We just need to find out what or whom, he's running from. It would make my job a little easier if I could get my hands on a set of his prints," Jackie said as she put the documents back into the file folder and followed Sydney over to the door.

"I'll see what I can do about getting those for you." Sydney laid her hand on Jackie's shoulder, giving it an affectionate squeeze. "Thank you. I really appreciate everything you've done for me."

"That's why you pay me the big bucks," Jackie laughed.

Sydney playfully pushed Jackie through the open doorway. "You know it's much more than that."

"You're right. I do," Jackie laughed again as she stepped off the porch. She stopped and turned to look at Sydney. "I should know something in the morning and I'll call as soon as I do but before I go any further, I need to ask you one more time. Are you really sure, I mean one hundred percent sure you want to go through with this crazy scheme of yours?"

Now it was Sydney's turn to laugh. "We've been following their lives for almost ten years now. So yes, for the umpteenth time, I am sure and before you say anything else, let me assure you that I know what I'm doing."

Jackie shook her head and grinned. "Famous last words." Jackie looked at her for a moment. "Can I ask you one more thing?"

Sydney laughed. "Sure, not sure I will answer though."

"I've never questioned anything you've asked me to do and I've never asked about Rachel but what is it about this woman? Why her?"

"Out of all the women I've known in my life, she's the only one who ever left me breathless and ... she broke my heart. Crushed it actually," Sydney answered without hesitation. She intentionally left out the part that her actions were now fueled by revenge. Rachel Ashburn had ended their relationship without a second thought. It was bad enough that Rachel had decided she didn't want to share the rest of her life with her. She could have dealt with that but it was the reasons behind Rachel's decision that Sydney just couldn't accept and no matter how hard she tried, she could not get the woman out of her head.

People say that time heals all wounds but it doesn't. Time may lessen the pain but it never goes away, not completely. She wanted Rachel to feel just one iota of the pain she had felt all those years ago. The physical abuse that Edward inflicted wouldn't come close to the emotional havoc she was about to unleash on Rachel Ashburn.

Jackie knew exactly what Sydney meant. "Remind me to never get on your bad side," she chuckled. Although she said it more as a joke, she knew that Sydney Welsh was the last person she would ever want to cross paths with unless they were fighting on the same side. She herself knew that the wrath of a woman scorned didn't compare to a lonely woman with a cold broken heart.

"Now get out of here before you convince me I'm crazy," Sydney said with a wink.

She watched Jackie back out of the driveway and waited until her car disappeared down the drive before turning to go back in the house. She had just closed the door when her cell phone rang. She raced into the family room and snatched the phone off the coffee table. "Hello," she said into the receiver.

"Hey, Syd, it's me. Sorry to bother you at home," Caitlyn said through the phone. "But this is really important," she added before Sydney could respond.

"It's okay, Caitlyn, what's going on?" Sydney asked, sensing that something was wrong.

"You know how I've been working on updating our main computer system?" Caitlyn asked.

Sydney nodded although Caitlyn couldn't see her. "Yes," she answered.

"Well, I've found some major discrepancies. I went over it several times and each time I came to the same conclusion. I should have had some idea that this was going on."

"Spit it out, Caitlyn," Sydney laughed.

"Ninety percent of our client accounts show monetary discrepancies." Caitlyn inhaled deeply and then added, "A substantial amount of money is missing."

"How substantial?" Sydney asked, not completely sure she wanted to know the answer. Caitlyn became so quiet, Sydney thought she was no longer on the line. "You still there, Caitlyn?" she asked just to be sure.

"Um, yeah. I'm still here."

"How much?" Sydney asked.

Caitlyn took a deep and then said, "Close to four and a half million dollars."

Sydney's jaw almost dropped to the floor. There must be a mistake. She cleared her throat. "Did I hear you right?" she asked, wanting Caitlyn to repeat it just to be sure.

"I'm afraid so," Caitlyn answered.

"And you're sure that it should be there?" Sydney asked, still not believing what she was hearing.

"Yes, Syd, I'm sure. I checked, checked it twice, and then crosschecked my checks. The money is missing, gone, vanished, vamoosed, history."

"Am I right to guess that you might have an idea where it went?" Sydney asked, a small grin forming at the corners of her mouth.

"Do you really need to ask me that question?"

"Nah, just testing you," Sydney chuckled.

"I do have a few ideas that I would like to run by you but I don't think we should discuss it over the phone. Will you be coming into the office today?" Caitlyn asked.

"I hadn't planned on it but if this can't wait, I'll be in," Sydney said.

"I don't think one more day will make much difference. So, I guess I will see you in the morning then."

Sydney smiled. "Thank you for taking good care of me."

"You're welcome."

"I'll see you tomorrow," Sydney said.

Chapter 2

Sydney shook her head, tossed the phone on the couch, and headed upstairs. She hoped that Caitlyn was wrong but something in her gut was telling her different. She went into the bathroom and turned on the shower. She stripped off her clothes and grabbed a fresh towel out of the linen closet. *I don't think this day can get much worse,* she thought as she stepped under the hot water.

Fifteen minutes later, she came out of the bathroom wearing a fluffy, light blue, terrycloth robe, and feeling fully refreshed. She pulled open her dresser drawer. A loud thud against the side of the house caused her to jump nearly an inch off the floor. She went over to the window and pulled the curtain back. A blood-curdling scream pierced her ears. It took her mind a good three seconds to realize that the scream came from her throat. A grey-haired old man, perched atop a ladder with a string of Christmas lights in his hand stared at her through the window. His lips curved upward, revealing a toothy smile.

Sydney raised the window and poked her head out.

"I'm sorry, ma'am. I didn't mean ta startle ya," the man said with a southern accent as thick as road tar.

"And I don't mean to be rude but who are you exactly?" Sydney asked, not recognizing the man.

"My name is Jedidiah Saunders," he answered. He let go of the ladder to extend his hand to her and in the process lost his balance.

Sydney reached out and grabbed his arm just in time to keep him from falling to the ground below. "Maybe you should keep both hands on the ladder," she suggested.

"I'm thinkin' the same thing," he said, a flustered look on his face.

"What are you doing out there?" Sydney asked, frowning.

"Replacing this here string of lights, ma'am. When I came by ta check out my handiwork last evenin', I noticed that this'n here string was deader than a doorknob."

Sydney laughed. "A dead doorknob, huh?"

He grinned at her. "Yes, ma'am. I reckon a doorknob is pretty darn dead."

"Yes, I suppose it is," Sydney said, grinning. "Well, Mr. Saunders, it's very cold out there, so why don't you finish hanging the lights and come on inside to warm up for a few minutes. Have a cup of coffee."

"Thank ya, ma'am. I just might'n take ya up on the offer when I'm done."

Sydney looked down at the front yard. Christmas decorations were everywhere. She shut the window and closed the curtain. When she arrived home earlier, she had been so curious about the car sitting next to Meredith's Jag, she hadn't noticed any of the decorations on the house, nor did she notice the ones scattered around the front yard and bushes.

The sound of voices caught her attention. She tossed her robe on the bed, grabbed an old pair of grey sweats and a t-shirt, and quickly got dressed. She made her way over to the upstairs rail and looked down into the family room. Her house was a flurry of activity with moving bodies. Everywhere she looked there seemed to be a person. Several were in the process of hanging decorations around the windows, while others were busy wrapping garland and lights around the oak rails that surrounded both staircases in the foyer.

A young man and woman carefully slid a fifteen-foot blue spruce tree across the floor. They positioned it so that it sat directly in the middle of the large oval picture windows that overlooked the large lake near the back of the property. Two men dressed in overalls brought several boxes over to the couple. While the young man began wrapping the tree with lights, the young woman began the tedious task of sorting ornaments.

Sydney couldn't believe it. In the short time it took her to take a shower and talk with Mr. Saunders, her house had become organized chaos. The front door opened and a line of men and women dressed in white caterer uniforms marched through the foyer and down the main hallway toward the kitchen.

She slowly walked over to the spiral staircase that ran down into the family room. She took the steps two at a time and stepped onto the landing.

"You're home," Edna shrieked, her voice full of excitement. Before Sydney could respond, the older woman rambled over and threw her arms around Sydney's waist, wrapping her in a big bear hug. "Let me look at you," Edna said, holding Sydney at arm's length.

Edna, I've only been gone six days," Sydney laughed.

"I know, I know, but six days is an awful long time."

Sydney leaned forward and kissed Edna on the cheek. "Well, it's good to see you, too," she said and meant it. Edna had been her housekeeper for the past eight years but she was more than that to Sydney. She was like a second mother. In fact, she was more of a mother to Sydney than her own was. Sydney smiled at the way Edna looked. She was wearing a white apron over a red velvet dress that hung just above her knees. The sleeves and hemline of the dress were trimmed with white fur. She laughed at Edna's red booties, complete with two furry red balls where they laced up. Edna had pulled her grey hair up in a bun and pinned it to the top of her head. Sydney thought the short, rotund woman looked like Mrs. Claus and she was unable to control the giggles that escaped her throat.

Edna placed her hands on her hips, pretending to pout. "Are you making fun of me?" she asked.

"Um, no, I think you look adorable, Mrs. Claus."

"Well, thank you, that means I'm in good company," Edna grinned, making her blue eyes twinkle.

Sydney made a sweeping gesture toward the family room with her hands. "What's with all the decorations?"

Edna placed her hands on her hips again. "Sydney Welsh, I swear I don't know about you sometimes," she said with a shake of her head.

"What?" Sydney asked, frowning.

"Do you know what today is?"

"Thursday the sixteenth," Sydney answered.

"And what is tomorrow?"

Sydney's right eyebrow shot upward. "Uh, Friday."

"And what are we doing on Friday?" Edna patiently prodded.

"I'm going to work, coming home, having dinner, same as any other Friday."

"I'm talking about tomorrow night," Edna said, stomping her foot.

Sydney thought about it for a moment and then it dawned on her. "Crap, I forgot all about it."

"I don't know how. It's only the biggest and best Christmas party ever," Edna teased.

"Aw, you're too kind, Mrs. Claus," Sydney teased back.

"Yes I am. I'd love to stand here and chat but I have a house to get decorated and I need to check on Fred Rick," Edna said, turning toward the kitchen.

"Say hi to Mr. Claus for me," Sydney laughed.

Edna stopped and looked over her shoulder. "I sure will," she said with a wink before disappearing behind the closed door.

Sydney dodged several workers as she cut across the floor to grab the stack of mail from the coffee table.

Tomorrow was the seventeenth, the day she chose for her annual Christmas party. With everything that had been going on, it had completely slipped her mind. A glance around the expansive family room made it clear that Edna and the rest of the staff had everything under control.

Jedidiah Saunders walked into the family room. Sydney threw the mail down on the table and walked over to him. "All done, Mr. Saunders?" she asked.

He took off his hat and gloves. "Why yes, ma'am I am," he answered.

"Please call me Sydney."

"Well then, call me Jed and I'm pleased to meet'cha," he said, holding out his hand.

"It's nice to meet you, too, Jed. I don't think I've ever seen you before," Sydney said, taking the man's large hand in hers. He gave it a rigorous shake before releasing it.

"That petite little red-head hired me." Jed scratched his head. "Ya know, I been decorating outside yer house fer the last five years and I never been invited in before."

Damn Meredith, Sydney thought. She was not in the least bit surprised that Meredith had not invited Jed in. One look at his bibbed overalls would have turned Meredith off instantly. Jedidiah Saunders would be deemed a peasant to Meredith and a peasant was way below her standards.

She and Meredith had way too many conversations or better yet, arguments regarding the staff and the way Sydney interacted with them. Meredith thought the hired staff should be treated like lower class servants, not people with actual feelings. Sydney didn't agree and the more Meredith protested, the more Sydney did just the opposite of what Meredith wanted. Sydney never regarded anyone on her payroll as servants. She believed that Edna was just as important and valuable as the Vice President of Marketing at Welsh who handled multimillion-dollar accounts and as such, Edna deserved to be treated with the same amount of respect, and sometimes more than her company execs.

"Ya have a beautiful house, Sydney. My better half's eyes would plum bug outta her head if she were here," Jed said, interrupting Sydney's thoughts.

"Thank you, Jed. I kinda like it."

"Well, I best be goin' now. Thanks fer lettin' me warm up my fingers and toes. That was awful nice of ya."

Sydney walked Jed to the door. "Do you have any plans tomorrow night?"

Jed turned to look at her. "Gerty, that's my better half, she has some shoppin' at the Krogers and that's about it, I'm thinkin'. Is there somethin' more you'd like me ta do?"

Sydney grinned. Meredith would have a field day with the way Jed pronounced his words. His diction would drive her crazy. Sydney liked it. She thought the older man standing in front of her was quite charming. "No, Jed. I have nothing else that needs done. I was asking because I would like to invite you and your better half to my Christmas party tomorrow night. That is, if you don't already have plans."

Jed's eyes lit up. "Yer not pullin' my leg?"

Sydney smiled and shook her head. "Nope, I'm not pulling your leg. Party starts at seven and there will be plenty of food and drinks. All you need to bring is yourself and Gerty."

"Well, thank ya, Sydney. Gerty'll just be beside herself when she sees yer beautiful home. I'll see ya tomorrow then."

Sydney closed the door behind him and decided to go to the kitchen to see what Fred Rick had planned for tomorrow night's menu. Knowing her flamboyant chef, she had no doubt that a few of the menu items would be hard to pronounce. As long as he had lobster, stuffed mushrooms, and the wonderful chocolate mousse concoction he made, he could fix whatever his heart desired.

After Jed left, Sydney had gone to the kitchen to talk with Fred Rick. She had wanted to make sure he as well as everyone else in the house had what they needed for the Christmas party. Satisfied that everything was under control, she had gone up to the bedroom she had once shared with Meredith. In less than an hour's time, she had moved all of her belongings to the first floor master bedroom.

Meredith couldn't understand why Sydney had designed a house where the master bedroom was located at the front of the house and to make matters worse, Meredith had argued that no one in their right mind would have the entrance to the bedroom directly off the foyer. Sydney had countered by saying that it was not directly off the foyer because you had to walk through a small hallway to get to it.

To prove her point further, Sydney had asked Meredith what was the very first thing she did when she came home from work. Meredith made Sydney's case for her by saying that when she got home, she wanted out of her work clothes. Exactly, Sydney had said triumphantly. Her decisions in the design were based on logic.
After a tiring day at work, she did not want to walk all the way across the house and up the stairs to change her clothes, so it made perfect sense to have her bedroom next to the office because she usually had a briefcase and laptop in tow. Meredith however, refused to see reason and after much arguing, Sydney had finally given in and moved to the upstairs master bedroom.

Chapter 3

Sydney got up at 6:00 A.M. on the dot, it was the first time she had ever slept in the downstairs master bedroom, and not once had she woken in the middle of the night. When she finally opened her eyes, she had felt completely rested. It had been the best night of sleep she'd had in years. She had showered, dressed and went down to the kitchen to have her breakfast with the rest of the staff. Today was omelet, sausage, biscuits, and gravy day. Once breakfast was over, she had gone to the office, grabbed her briefcase, and headed out the door to her waiting truck.

Her drive had been non-eventful and in no time, she turned onto Monarch Lane and drove the short distance to the Welsh Enterprise driveway.

Situated on the outskirts of Miamisburg on Route 725, Welsh's Corporate Headquarters building sat just a stone's throw away from the Avery Dennison building, formerly known as the Paxar Corporation. Avery, a multibillion dollar a year company, which is known worldwide for their office and self-adhesive products, pulled off quite a coup in 2007 when they acquired one of their biggest competitors along with its merchandise security tagging divisions for a mere $1.3 billion dollars. If you ever wondered where those fancy little security alarm tags affixed to the clothing you buy at a department store come from, chances are they were purchased from Avery's Paxar Group.

Welsh also did business with the company, using their self-adhesive labels on the Laptop and Desktop computers manufactured under the Welsh logo. Welsh wasn't as big as Avery but the company was on its way. With sales hitting an all time high of $2.8 billion last year, projections for this year were doubled and as of last week, they were on pace to beat that projection as well.

Sydney waved to one of the security guards as she pulled into her reserved parking space. She shut off the engine and grabbed her briefcase. *Oh great*, she thought as she climbed down out of the cab.

Allen Carmichael, Assistant Vice President of Computer Logistics swaggered over to her. "Welcome back, Sydney," he smiled, showing a mouthful of teeth that were too perfect and too white to be his own.

"Thanks, Allen. It's good to be back," Sydney said.

"Everything is running as smooth as when you left. I took extra care to make sure there were no hitches," he said, falling into step beside her on the sidewalk.

"That's good to know. I have no doubt that Welsh was in capable hands," she said. The man reeked of arrogance. Everything about him was perfect. From his grey custom tailored pinstriped suit, to his $800 chiseled haircut. He was more suited to be on the cover of GQ and she would have preferred that to having him in her boardroom.

"I also took the liberty and had the main conference room set up for your meeting with Bill Amos at 9:00."

"Thank you, Allen, that wasn't necessary but I appreciate it," Sydney said, sliding her badge in front of the security door reader. "Karen would have taken care of everything."

"Here, let me get that for you," he said, holding the door open. "I know it's not my job and I'm sure that Karen is very capable but I didn't want to take the chance of anything going wrong. I know how important this meeting is to you," he said with a smug look of satisfaction on his face.

He was right about that. This meeting was important to her. In fact, this meeting was the catalyst that would set the stage in order for her to carry out a much larger plan. The plan she had been working on for the last two years now. The same plan that centered on the work Jackie had privately been doing for her.

Allen followed Sydney across the lobby to Karen's desk. Sydney couldn't help but smile when she saw Karen. The woman's state of dress never ceased to amaze her. Today, the twenty-seven year-old redhead was wearing a black studded dog collar around her neck with matching studded earrings. Her face was paler than usual, making her ruby red lipstick stand out against her white complexion. Sydney noticed immediately that Karen had recently cut her hair. The red two-inch strands of hair stuck up all over Karen's head and Sydney liked it. It was so Karen. Based on the black fishnet top covering Karen's white checked blouse, Sydney guessed that Karen was back to her Goth kick. She would have also been willing to bet that Karen was wearing a leather miniskirt and six-inch high-heeled boots that stopped just below the knee.

Sydney watched Karen as she spoke animatedly into her headset. Her hands were flailing around in the air as she tried to make a point to whoever was on the other end of the phone. Finally satisfied that the caller understood what she was saying, she disconnected the line. Karen glanced up. Her eyes went wide and a big smile crossed her face when she saw Sydney.

"Well, would'ya look at what the vampire's drug in," Karen said, standing to lean over the desk to hug Sydney.

"I swear you people act like I've been gone for months. It was less than a week."

Karen's facial expression turned serious. "Oh glorious one who holds domain over this wonderful establishment we call Welsh, we missed you so, so much."

Sydney laughed. "I swear you're not right."

"I think she looks as beautiful as ever. The Florida sun did wonders for her tan, don't you agree, Karen," Allen said, from behind Sydney.

"She always looks great, Allen," Karen said, with a tinge of annoyance in her voice. The smart retort was not surprisingly, lost on Allen.

"I will see you two ladies later. I have reports to run and we all know those little sheets of paper will not run without my help and guidance."

Karen and Sydney watched Allen disappear inside the elevator.

"Pardon me while I puke," Karen said, putting her finger in her mouth and pretending to make gagging sounds.

"Oh he's not that bad, Karen," Sydney chided although she felt like puking herself.

"Not that bad? Surely, you jest wonderful employer of mine. If he bent his head down any further to kiss your ass, his neck would have snapped."

"Yeah, I guess he *was* pretty bad," Sydney chuckled.

"Be it far from me to ever question authority but—"

"Since when?" Sydney teasingly interrupted.

Karen ignored her. "As I was saying … I still can't understand how such a pompous ass like him was ever hired to begin with."

"I'm not the one who hired him, Meredith did."

"That explains it, 'nough said." Karen twisted her red lips into a smirk. "The Florida sun did wonders for her tan," she sarcastically mimicked what Allen had said. "How could he not know that you have dark skin all year round? In fact I think you are the only person I know who can get a tan sitting in the shade unlike my white albino ass."

"Maybe he's not as perceptive as you are and maybe he was just trying to make small talk."

Karen cleared her throat. "I bet that's not the only small thing about him."

Sydney lost it. She was laughing so hard that tears were in her eyes. Out of all the employees she had personally hired, Karen was one of the best. No matter what was going on in her life, Karen always had a way of making her laugh.

"Seriously though, I am so glad to see you. Have you spoken with Caitlyn yet this morning?"

"No, I was planning on going to see her next."

"Here, I want to show you something." Karen came out from behind her desk to stand beside Sydney. She pointed at the carpet in front of the desk. "See that spot right there?"

Sydney nodded and Karen kneeled down on her knees. She made a sweeping gesture with her hand over a two-foot section of carpet. "Can you see how the carpet is worn down in this here area?" She stood up and pulled down the edges of her skirt.

"Those marks are from your protégé. She has driven me absolutely freaking bonkers this morning. Since six A.M., she has shown up at my desk every fifteen minutes asking if you have arrived yet. Those indentations you see, they're from her pacing. For the love of God woman, will you please go see her before I have to get new carpet installed?"

Sydney laughed. "I promise as soon as I drop off my briefcase, the first thing I will do is go to her office."

"Thank you sweet Jesus of vast mother earth," Karen said with a mock salute.

"By the way, I love the new haircut. The skull and crossbones on your boots are a nice touch," Sydney said over her shoulder as she stepped into the elevator and punched the button for the fifth floor.

"Oh great payer of paychecks, that compliment means more to me than you'll ever know," Karen yelled just as the elevator door closed.

Sydney laughed at Karen's over the top theatrics. She had been right about the leather miniskirt and boots. Karen Lauder was something else. She had been the main receptionist at Welsh for the last seven years and attended college in the evenings. She had one semester left before she received her B.A.S. in Computer Programming with a minor in Business Management. Sydney's gift to her would be a promotion to high-level management on the day she graduated.

The elevator door opened and Sydney stepped out onto plush burgundy colored carpet. She glanced up and down the empty hallway that Karen had so lovingly nicknamed Executive Boulevard. She called it that because the fifth floor was filled with spacious conference rooms and offices that housed all of the Welsh Executives and their assistants.

Her office sat at the far end with a conference room on one side and Maureen, her assistant's office on the other. With luck, she would make it to her office without being accosted by an executive who thought their problems required her immediate attention. Her first order of business of the day would be with Caitlyn, followed by her meeting with Bill Amos. Depending on how her meetings went, she just might take the rest of the day off.

She walked into her office and kicked the door shut with her foot. She let out a sigh of relief and tossed her briefcase on the desk. She took off her black leather jacket, slung it over the back of her chair, and pushed the sleeves up on her sweater.

The smell of freshly brewed coffee hung in the air. She silently thanked Maureen for having the coffee ready. She poured herself a cup, added four packs of sugar, some cream, and took it back to her desk. She dropped down onto her chair with a thud. She glanced at the stack of messages piled up near the phone and decided to look at them later. They couldn't be too important or Maureen would have said something when Sydney had called to have her pack Anne's things.

She glanced around the festive looking room. Maureen

always decorated her office for the holidays. It didn't matter whether it was Halloween or Easter and Christmas was no different. Maureen had placed Poinsettia plants on either side of the gas fireplace at the far corner of the room. Christmas lights were strung around the floor to ceiling bookcases and lighted candles had been placed on all four windowsills.

Sydney took a sip of coffee and leaned back in her chair. Her thoughts turned to Caitlyn Ashburn, her protégé as Karen had called her. Caitlyn was only nineteen-years-old and made almost as much money as her executives. Sydney knew that it had ticked off certain employees when Caitlyn came to work at Welsh but she didn't care. Caitlyn was a prodigy and had more intelligence than all of her executives combined.

When Caitlyn walked into Welsh Enterprises, it was the first time Sydney had seen her in thirteen years. The last time was when Caitlyn was just six-years-old. She had been a little concerned given Caitlyn's level of intelligence that she might have remembered her. When it was apparent that she hadn't, Sydney was more than relieved.

Since the age of eight, Sydney had kept an eye on Caitlyn and received weekly updates on the girl's progress. By the age of ten, it was obvious that Caitlyn possessed the intelligence of a graduate student. By the age of fifteen, she had graduated from high school and by the age of seventeen, she had completed her Masters degree in Computer Science as well as a Masters degree in Business Management. In less than three months, she would have her Doctorate.

It was at the age of seventeen that Sydney had sent two of her top executives to approach Caitlyn and her parents with a job offer. She would be assigned to work in the IT department and would be reporting directly to Welsh's CEO.

Caitlyn of course was thrilled, as was her adopted

stepfather, Edward who Sydney suspected only saw dollar signs. Caitlyn's mother however, had some reservations.

Although Caitlyn was above intelligence, to her mother, she was still her little girl. In the end, Rachel had conceded and Caitlyn had joined Welsh much to Sydney's relief. Having Caitlyn work at Welsh was an integral part to the success of Sydney's grand plan. Without Caitlyn, there would have been no plan at all.

Sydney pushed away from the desk. She refilled her coffee, grabbed a pen and notebook, and left the office. She didn't have to go far. Caitlyn's office sat directly across the hall from hers. She rapped lightly on the door with her knuckles, pushed it open, and poked her head in.

Caitlyn had been oblivious to the knock on the door and Sydney watched for several minutes as the young woman continued to tap away on her keyboard. No matter how many times Sydney saw Caitlyn; she was taken aback by the young woman's beauty. To say she looked like her mother would be an understatement. Caitlyn was the spitting image of Rachel. The two women looked more like sisters than mother and daughter. Rachel was slightly taller and Caitlyn wore her hair a little longer but they had the same strong jaw line, same shaped face, and bright blue penetrating eyes that sparkled when they laughed.

Caitlyn looked up. Her face instantly lit up at seeing Sydney.

"Good morning. Hope I'm not interrupting anything," Sydney smiled.

"And good morning to you also," Caitlyn grinned. "You have no idea how glad I am to see you."

Sydney stepped into the office and shut the door. "I think I do," she laughed.

Caitlyn frowned. "How long were you standing there?"

Sydney grabbed a chair and slid it over next to the desk by Caitlyn. "Not long," she answered, dropping down into the chair. She laid the pen and notebook on the edge of the desk. "You looked so intent. I didn't wanna bother you."

"You are the only person besides my mom who I would never classify as a bother."

"I think that may have been a compliment," Sydney said with a chuckle.

"It was."

For the first time since Sydney came into Caitlyn's office, she took notice of the young woman's attire. The Bob Marley t-shirt, faded jeans, and sneakers were in stark contrast to Caitlyn's normally ultra conservative three-piece suit and heels. On rare occasions, Sydney would see her in pleated slacks and a blazer. "Uh, Caitlyn … how long have you been here?"

"It will be two years in February. Why do you ask?"

Sydney laughed. "I don't mean your hire date. I meant the last twenty-four hours," Sydney said, nodding at Caitlyn's clothes.

"Oh," Caitlyn said, glancing down at her t-shirt and jeans. It was obvious that Caitlyn had been so preoccupied with what she was working on that she hadn't realized how she was dressed. "Since nine … um, yesterday evening," she said almost apologetically. "I went home but I couldn't stop thinking about the software code so I decided to come back in. I guess I didn't realize how long I had been here. I can go change. I keep extra clothes in the closet."

"That's not necessary. You look fine dressed the way you are and besides, I like Bob Marley," Sydney laughed.

"It used to be my mom's."

Visions of Rachel's firm breasts straining against the t-shirt flashed through Sydney's mind. She shook her head to dispel the image. "Okay, tell me what's going on."

"This missing money has got me stumped," Caitlyn sighed. "Well, actually that's not true. I'm not stumped. I know how they did it but I'm having trouble figuring out who did it and it's making me a little more than nuts."

Sydney knew by the furrowing of Caitlyn's brows that she was frustrated and that was something that did not happen often, actually, it never happened. She couldn't think of one instance where she had seen Caitlyn unnerved or upset. It just did not happen. "Okay, why don't you start from the beginning and tell me exactly what you've found, how you found it, and then we can go from there."

"What do you know about the Salami Technique?"

Sydney didn't know what she expected Caitlyn to say first but salami fit nowhere in the equation. She pretended to think about it for a few seconds and then said, "I like mine on a hoagie bun with provolone, tomatoes, lettuce, mayonnaise, and lightly baked."

Caitlyn laughed a deep belly laugh, showing straight white teeth. "That's not the salami I'm talking about."

"I kinda figured that," Sydney said with a wink.

"Okay, how about I give you a little history first and then I will explain how it's being used to embezzle money from our client accounts."

Sydney leaned back in her chair, crossed her legs at the ankle, and smiled. "I'm all ears," she said, lacing her fingers behind her head.

"It all started with the banking industry and the advent of computers. When the banks went from manual bookkeeping and converted to computerized systems they unwittingly opened a very large door to a form of embezzlement that beforehand had been impossible to pull off, which is now known as the *Salami Technique*."

Caitlyn got up from her chair and walked over to the coffee maker sitting on a small table in the corner. She poured herself a cup and turned to Sydney. "Would you like a warm up?" she asked.

"Since when did you start drinking coffee, and yes I would like a warm up, thank you."

Caitlyn glanced at her wristwatch. "Almost six days ago," she said as she poured coffee into Sydney's mug.

"See what happens? I go out of town for six days, everything falls apart, and you become a java junkie," Sydney said, grinning as she took a sip of the steaming liquid.

"Just means you are too valuable to leave us," Caitlyn laughed as she sat back down in her chair. "So the Salami Technique got its name after a bank employee who also happened to be a computer programmer accumulated a large amount of money. He averted any suspicion by not taking large amounts of money at one time; instead, he sliced off thin quantities of cash from thousands of customer accounts. He then redirected that cash into an account that he had full control over. The analogy is that he shaved money from customer accounts like a butcher would shave pieces of salami to make a sandwich."

"Okay, I'm with you so far. How did he do it?"

"He wrote a program that would randomly transfer thirty to forty cents from several thousand customers' checking accounts into the account he controlled. Over a couple of years, you can imagine how much money he had stockpiled. I think by the time he was caught it was estimated that he had stolen over three-million dollars.

"Why did it take so long to catch him?" Sydney asked.

"No one complained. The amounts he took were so small that most customers never bothered to report that they had thirty to forty cent discrepancies on their statements. He was also smart enough to never take money out of a customer's account more than three times a year."

"That's unbelievable," Sydney said, shaking her head.

"Well think about it. Would you go into your bank and make a fuss if you were missing thirty cents?"

"No, I wouldn't," Sydney admitted.

"And that's what made him successful. He was banking on that exact assumption."

"So, how did he get caught then?"

Caitlyn smiled. "Well it seems there was one old man

who had grown up during the great depression and he was not happy that the bank had cheated him out of seventy cents over the course of one year. He went into the bank and threw what one would describe as a temper tantrum until the bank was forced to look at it."

"And that's how they caught the guy?"

"Yep and the old man got his seventy cents back as well as free checking for the rest of his life."

Sydney chuckled. "How common is this problem?" she asked.

"More common than you would think. Several movies have been made about it. You've probably heard of them, *Superman III*, *Hackers*, and *Office Space* just to name a few."

Sydney nodded. "I have seen all of those movies but I had no idea that what they were doing actually had a name for it."

"I will give you an example of how easy it is to pull something off like this if you know what you are doing. Between 2007 and 2008, a 22 year-old Plumas Lake, California man named Michael Largent used the Salami Technique to accrue $50,000 in funds from the two brokering houses, E-trade and Charles Schwab and Co. He then used it to get another $8,000 from Google checkout.

"How is that possible?"

"When you open an account with any of those companies, you have to provide your checking account number as well as the banks routing number. The companies then make a small monetary deposit into your account. It can be as little as one penny and as high as two-dollars. You the customer, then have to go back to the company's web site and enter the amount deposited into your account in order to verify yourself and open an account with them. PayPal is another company who has the same verification process.

Sydney got up from her chair and refilled her coffee cup. She brought the pot over and topped off Caitlyn's cup.

"Thank you," Caitlyn said, taking a sip. "So, in order to pull it off, Largent took advantage of a logic flaw in the computer programming. He designed an automated script program that set up 58,000 fake accounts and when the companies like E-trade deposited the funds, Largent then transferred the money into his own account."

"How'd he get caught?" Sydney asked.

"The brokerage houses discovered it and contacted the authorities and that's when the United States Secret Service and the FBI got involved. Now the kicker here is that Largent did not do anything illegal, at least not in theory by setting up the accounts. None of the companies involved specified any limitations on how many accounts a customer could open but the Department of Justice ended up charging him with fraud."

Sydney frowned. "Okay, if what he did wasn't illegal then how could they charge him for a crime?"

"The Assistant United States Attorney, Matthew D. Segal, who is a prosecutor in the office's Computer Hacking and Intellectual Property unit or what's known as C.H.I.P., claimed Largent used false names, driver's license, etc. and that constituted fraud. I personally think his arrogance was his undoing. You see, some of the names he used were cartoon characters and comic book heroes."

"Bugs Bunny opening an account would definitely raise a red flag," Sydney laughed.

"In 2009 he pleaded guilty to two counts of fraud and was sentenced to fifteen months in prison and ordered to pay $200,000 in restitution."

"Did he say why he did it?"

"He wanted to pay off his credit card debt and he didn't think he was doing anything wrong and legally he wasn't, but morally and ethically he was."

Sydney shook her head. "If he was that talented why would he waste his time doing something illegal?"

"That is the same question the judge asked before sentencing him. My guess is that it was an adrenaline rush, like pulling one over on big brother. If he had used real names, it's hard to say how long he could have gotten away with it. Probably years, maybe forever."

Sydney sat up in her chair, resting her elbows on her knees. "Okay, I think I have a pretty good idea now of what and how the Salami Technique works, so how does it all pertain to us?"

"I found the problem when I ran a beta test on the upgraded billing system program. When I loaded the programs, I created a mirror image of both systems so I could run them simultaneously for a step-by-step comparison. What I found was a discrepancy between the amount billed to our customer's invoice and the amount our customer's actually paid to Welsh."

"If you're telling me that our customer's were charged more than they should have been due to embezzlement, this could be a public relations nightmare. Our stock will go into the toilet," Sydney said, shaking her head. This is the last thing she needed to deal with right now.

"The invoices that our customers received showed the correct amount they owed."

"I don't understand," Sydney said, her brows furrowing.

"Someone with highly sophisticated programming skills accessed our billing system software and used a backdoor in the program to rewrite several lines of code. They set up several logic algorithms so that when a customer sent in their payment for the invoice and our customer service representative marked it as paid in the system, the program would kick in and round down to the nearest dollar. The change that was left over was then transferred into a separate account and the invoice billed in the system was automatically changed to reflect that amount. What they did, I mean the way they rewrote the program, is quite ingenious actually. I've never seen logic used in this fashion."

"Probably because you don't think like a thief," Sydney teased. "Okay, just so I understand what you're saying, let me give you an example and you tell me if I'm on the same page as you."

"Shoot," Caitlyn said, leaning back in her chair.

Sydney stood up from the chair. She paced slowly back and forth in front of Caitlyn's desk. It was something she did whenever she was deep in thought. She stopped to look at Caitlyn. "I know we have different ways for customers to pay their invoices. Some do it over the phone and some have terms, and some send in checks, etcetera. For this example let's say I'm Joe Blow and I get an invoice in the mail for $2,921.26. I call up Welsh to pay my bill over the phone with a credit card. Once the customer rep takes the payment and marks the invoice as paid, this rewritten program code kicks in and removes the twenty-six cents, changes the invoice in the system to reflect the amount as if the twenty-six cents never existed. The missing twenty-six cents is then rerouted into an unknown bank account. Is that correct?"

"You got it. That's exactly how it works. Slicing off pennies like you slice salami to make a sandwich," Caitlyn smiled. "That's also why this doesn't have to be a public relations nightmare for us as you say. Our customers don't need to know anything about it because they were invoiced the correct amount and they paid the correct amount. The money is being stolen from Welsh, not our customers."

"How did you figure this out?"

"I told you that I made a mirror image of the system. On one side, I had our old system records and on the other was the new program. It just so happened that several customers happened to pay their invoices in between the time it took me to load up the new software."

Sydney grinned from ear to ear. "You compared the

same invoices from the old and new software?"

Caitlyn smiled with satisfaction. "That is exactly what I did. I had to make sure that all the data fields on the invoices were the same and they were except for the invoice amount. Do you know why that is?" Caitlyn asked.

"Testing me again, aren't you?" Sydney chuckled.

"Just want to see how your logic is doing, that's all," Caitlyn teased.

"It wasn't the same because the new software you loaded does not have the same logic code to change the values," Sydney answered triumphantly.

Caitlyn clapped her hands together and smiled at Sydney. "Bravo, bravo. You are correct and you just won a new Dirt Devil vacuum cleaner."

"Why a Dirt Devil?" Sydney asked, frowning.

"Because they suck better," Caitlyn said, her expression serious.

"I'm gonna ask although I probably shouldn't. How do you know they suck better?"

"It's a matter of creating the correct formula in order to make calculations based on the pull of gravity, how quickly what's being sucked in is pulled into the hose, and how many inches it travels over time once it's entered into—"

Sydney held her hand up to stop Caitlyn's explanation. She shook her head and smiled. "I knew I was gonna regret asking."

Caitlyn laughed. "What's the problem? I was explaining it in very simple terms."

"Okay then ... how about we forget I asked and in that case, I would like one in candy-apple red please," Sydney said with a laugh.

Caitlyn chuckled. "I'll get right on that."

"Now that we've got the vacuum settled, do you have an estimate on how long this code has been active in our system?"

"Around seven years."

"Holy shit. You have any thoughts on the person or persons who would be able to do this?" Sydney asked.

"Yes ... but you're not going to like it," Caitlyn said, shaking her head.

"Try me."

"It has to be someone here at Welsh and I say that because whoever has done this had to have access to our system, our password protected system."

"Executives are the only ones with that type of authorization," Sydney said, thinking of the implications.

"Exactly, and to narrow it down further, this person has to have programming abilities, which means it could be anyone on the executive floor." Caitlyn smiled. "I took the liberty to pull all of the executive's résumés and eighty percent of them have programming experience although that is not their primary job function here at Welsh. Most have secondary Computer Science degrees, even the Marketing VP."

"Eighty percent, huh? That leaves us with what, six, seven people?"

Caitlyn nodded in agreement.

"How many people know about this?" Sydney asked.

"No one except for you and me," Caitlyn said with a shake of her head.

"Good. For two reasons I would like to keep it that way. The first is that if it is someone here, we don't want them to know we are onto what they've been doing, otherwise they may stop, and we'll never catch them. The second reason is that this is dangerous as hell. We're talking millions of dollars and people have killed for much less."

"And since no one but the two of us know I've been testing out this new system billing program, I think we should keep that to ourselves as well."

"I agree. Do you have any idea where the money is

going or how we can catch whoever is doing this?"

"I'm working on that. I have spent the last twenty-four hours trying to find the account where the funds have been dumped but it's too tedious to do by hand seeing that we have over two million customers worldwide," Caitlyn said, massaging the sides of her temples with her fingertips. "I decided to write a new logic program where I can input the monies that have been rounded down from several invoices and have the system search for an account or accounts that match a deposit for those amounts. It shouldn't take long once I finish writing the code."

Sydney leaned against the corner of the desk. "What about catching them?"

Caitlyn smiled. "I have in my possession several pages of code written by all the programmers at Welsh. I will compare those samples with the code in our system. Programmer codes can be like fingerprints and all programmers have their own nuances, kind of like their own signatures in the way they write the code."

"Interesting, I didn't know that," Sydney said, thinking that every time she was around Caitlyn, she learned something new.

Caitlyn shrugged. "It's a long shot considering that the person may not directly be in a position where they have written code for Welsh. There is also a chance that they have changed their programming fingerprint to throw anyone off the trail just in case the code is discovered."

"It's better than nothing at this point," Sydney said.

"I did something else as well. Last night when no one else was in the building, I loaded spyware as well as keystroke logging software on all of the executive's desktops. I need to get my hands on their laptops as well."

"Very sneaky! I like it," Sydney laughed. "I have a meeting to attend when I'm done here. Several of the execs on your list will be in that meeting and it might be a good time for you to try to load your software onto their laptops."

"I'm not sure they would be happy if they knew. I hate doing those kinds of things but I'm also not keen on knowing that someone I work with has a problem with ethics," Caitlyn said, frowning.

"I agree but when you use company equipment, you're fair game and it clearly states that in fine print on the application for employment. Will they have any idea that the software is running?"

"No, only you and I will know and I will be able to see and track everything they do from my computer, Caitlyn said, shaking her head."

Sydney glanced at her watch and stood up. "I need to get ready for the meeting. Please keep me updated on your progress."

Caitlyn nodded. "You will be the first to know."

"Are you coming to my Christmas party tonight?"

Caitlyn shrugged and said, "I don't know. I really haven't given it much thought."

"Ah, come on. It'll do you some good. You spend too many hours here as it is," Sydney said and it was true. Next to her, Caitlyn put in almost as many hours as she did.

"I don't have a date," Caitlyn frowned.

"You don't need one." Sydney saw the hesitation on Caitlyn's face and said, "Why don't you bring your parents along."

Caitlyn thought about it for a second or two. "I don't think you've ever met my mom," she said.

"I don't believe I have either," Sydney agreed with a shake of her head as butterflies began to dance around in her stomach.

Caitlyn snorted. "You're not missing much with my stepdad."

"You two don't get along?" Sydney asked.

"He's a class-A jerk," Caitlyn said and did not elaborate and Sydney did not ask.

"I insist you take the time off and come to my party tonight. I'm sure my house is big enough that you might only see your stepfather once or twice in passing," Sydney said with a smile.

Caitlyn sighed. "Is that an order?

Sydney grinned at her. "Yes it is."

"Dress or casual?" Caitlyn asked in resignation.

"Dress or casual, whatever feels most comfortable to you. You can come in jeans if you like," Sydney smiled. "By the way, after I'm done with my meeting, I will be taking the rest of the day off. Party starts at seven. Maureen can give you the address if you don't have it. I'll chat with you later tonight."

Caitlyn smiled. "I'll see you later then."

Sydney went back to her office and closed the door behind her. She had a few minutes until the big meeting. She pulled open her desk drawer and grabbed the file folder marked William Amos. She didn't bother to look up at the knock on her door. "Come in," she said, pulling out several sheets from the folder.

"Good morning," Meredith said.

Sydney looked at Meredith and wondered how she could have ever been in love with the woman. "Good morning, Meredith. How are you?" she asked, then realized that maybe the feelings she'd had for Meredith bordered more on lust than love.

Meredith was definitely pulling out all the stops. She was wearing a fiery red skirt suit, black silk stockings, and a sexy pair of black stilettos. The ensemble just so happened to be one of Sydney's favorites and Meredith knew it. She looked fantastic.

Meredith sashayed over to Sydney's desk. "I was

scheduled to be in the meeting with Bill Amos this morning and in lieu of what has happened between us, I wanted to know if you still required my attendance?"

"Yes, Meredith," Sydney sighed. "I haven't told anyone about our breakup and I would appreciate it if you did the same. We don't need any more gossip floating around here than what already does," Sydney said, trying like hell to keep the annoyance out of her voice.

Meredith's cheeks flushed red. "Don't you think they will fucking know when I'm no longer working here? Don't you think people will start talking as soon as they see me packing up my office?"

Sydney shot Meredith a look that said she had just about had enough of her attitude. "Keep your voice down for crying out loud. I thought by doing it this way, you could at least save some face when you left and you can pack your things in the evening when everyone else is gone," Sydney said through clenched teeth.

"I'm sorry, babe, I didn't mean to snap at you," Meredith said, her voice softening.

Just like *Jekyll and Hyde*, Sydney thought as she picked up the file folder. "Since you will only be here for one more week, I want you to tie up all your loose ends. That means I want a list on my desk by end of day detailing all the projects you've been working on."

Meredith put her hands on her hips. "Fine. You'll have the list. What about the Computer Logistics Vice President position that's still open in the IT department?"

"What about it?" Sydney asked, thinking it really wasn't any of Meredith's business.

"Thomas Sosia has been gone for almost three weeks now, Sydney. I've been interviewing personnel for it but I assume you will take over that job now. Do you have any idea who you're going to hire for the position?"

She brushed past Meredith. "Not that it's any of your concern, but yes I do. I've already interviewed several people and have a candidate in mind for the job. I will be making the announcement soon. We have a meeting to attend," she said over her shoulder and went out the door. Meredith, with her mouth gaping open stared at Sydney's back. After a few seconds, she regained her composure and followed suit.

Sydney walked the short distance to the conference room. She could hear the buzzing sound of multiple conversations coming through the door. She pushed the door open and the room went silent. "Can you close the door, please?" she asked Meredith who came in a few seconds behind her.

She waited for Meredith to close the door then took her place at the end of the long table. Bill Amos sat in a chair to her right. He looked considerably older than Sydney remembered. His hair seemed whiter, his eyes were not as lively, and it was obvious that he had lost a considerable amount of weight based on the way his suit jacket hung loosely around his shoulders. The stress of his fledgling company had taken its toll on him. Andrew Amos, Bill's grandson sat on her left, directly across from his grandfather.

"Ms. Welsh," the older Amos said as he stood. His hand shook as he took her hand in his.

"Mr. Amos," Sydney nodded then turned to shake Andrews's hand. "Please be seated," she said as she laid the file folder on the table. She picked up a carafe, and poured herself a cup of coffee. "Mr. Amos, can I get you something to drink?" she asked, offering the carafe.

"I'm good, thank you," he said, shaking his head.

She looked at his grandson, who declined her offer with a shake of his head as well. Sydney pulled out the chair and sat down. She glanced around the table. Allen Carmichael, the Assistant VP of Computer Logistics sat at the far end of the table, Virgil Parsons, VP of Acquisitions sat directly to his left, Kenneth Worthington, the Computer Design Manufacturing Manager sat on his right. Robert VanDersmote, the Sr. Manager over Computer Manufacturing sat next to Andrew with Meredith directly on his left.

The conference room door opened. "Good morning, sorry I'm late," Bev Andrews, VP of Marketing, said apologetically as she took the empty seat next to Meredith.

"Good morning, Bev, no biggie, we're just getting started," Sydney said, flipping open the file folder. "If everyone's ready, let's begin," she said, looking at Bill Amos and then his grandson.

Bill Amos cleared his throat. "With all due respect, Ms. Welsh, I think your behavior is reprehensible concerning my company."

He certainly doesn't beat around the bush, Sydney thought as she met the older man's steely gaze. "With all due respect, Mr. Amos, I find it just as appalling that your company has basically been run into the ground."

Andrew Amos stood up from his chair. He glared at Sydney. "How dare you speak to my grandfather with such disrespect? He built that company from the ground up with his own two hands."

"It's okay, Andrew," Bill said soothingly to his grandson.

"I do not owe either of you an explanation. I only called this meeting out of courtesy. Welsh Enterprises has done nothing wrong. Your shareholders sold their stock freely."

Andrew's look was incredulous. "What did you expect they would do when you offered them twice as much as the stock was worth?"

"Greed can make the most honest person think

irrationally," Sydney said with a shrug of her shoulders.

"If your actions were above board, then why did you use separate Welsh holding companies to secure the stock?" Bill Amos asked.

Sydney looked at Virgil Parsons. "I'll let our VP of acquisitions answer that question for you."

The grey-headed older man pushed his glasses up on his nose. His voice shook slightly as he spoke. "Um, well yes, it's true. We did use three of our smaller holding companies to purchase the stock but that is a regular practice of ours. Depending on where the company we are interested in acquiring is located, we decide which of our holding companies offer the best tax incentives in those areas."

Bill Amos shook his head. "I don't care how you try to justify it, Ms. Welsh. You went beneath the radar to secure the majority share of my company's stock."

"We're not even sure that buying up your stock is in the best interest of Welsh. At least I'm not," Allen said from the end of the table.

"I tend to agree with Allen," Robert offered, adding his two cents.

Sydney looked at Robert and then at Allen. She could not believe what she was hearing. She would put both of them in their place later. How dare they undermine her decisions. She looked at Bev. "Have you had time to review the financials I sent you?" she asked.

"I sure have," Bev said with a smile and pulled out several documents.

"What do you think about it, Bev? Your honest opinion," Sydney said, knowing that Bev would support whatever decisions she made. If she had a problem, she would talk to Sydney privately about her concerns. She would never undermine Sydney's decisions as Allen and Robert had just done.

"I think it's a wise investment. Coupled with our

manufacturing division, a computer oriented design firm that specializes in office renovations and custom architecture design offers Welsh a large market share that we would never have been able to get otherwise. We will be a one-stop shopping avenue for our business customer division."

"Thanks, Bev. I understand that you have an important meeting yourself so if you have nothing else to add, you're free to go."

Bev stood and gathered her things. "No, I'm good," she said and left the room.

Sydney looked at Kenneth, who had been quiet the whole time. "What are your thoughts, Kenneth?" Sydney knew what his answer would be before she even asked. Kenneth was a follower, a man who could not think on his own, and a man who had never had an original thought in his life.

Kenneth looked at Allen before turning to look at Sydney. "I hate to say it, Sydney, but I'm not sure how I will fit office design into our business model," Kenneth answered, confirming Sydney's opinion about him.

Sydney looked at Meredith who immediately averted her eyes. Sydney had told Meredith that she thought she was making a mistake when she had hired Allen, Robert, and Kenneth. Their comments today only cemented what Sydney already knew. "You can be excused," she said finally, when Meredith looked at her. "I want the documents we discussed earlier on my desk before you leave for the day."

Without a word, Meredith gathered her things and left the room.

Sydney felt the heat rise up her neck all the way to her ears. "Can someone please explain to me how I can be in a room that's overflowing with male testosterone, yet I'm the only one who has any Goddamn balls?" she asked, her voice rising several octaves.

She glanced at her executives and then turned in her seat to look Bill Amos directly in the eye. "Here's the deal, Bill. I own Welsh Enterprises and the buck always stops with me. As the majority owner of Welsh, I also control ninety-five percent of your company. I don't give a rat's ass if you built EMCOR from the ground up. If you had done your job, I would have never been able to get my foot in your door. Therefore, I'm now going to give you two options. Number one, you will sell your remaining stock to me at three times what it's worth or number two, I will slowly and systematically disassemble your entire company down to the nuts and bolts, and then I will fire every single employee." She looked at Andrew Amos. "And I'll start with your grandson first." She turned back to Bill and looked at him with eyes so dark they looked black. She smiled and shrugged. "It's just business, Bill, nothing personal."

Bill Amos looked as if he were going to have a heart attack. He slammed his fist down on the table so hard that it knocked the carafe over. "How dare you threaten me, you ruthless, heartless bitch," he yelled, sending spittle across the table.

Sydney leaned back in her chair and laughed. "It's not a threat. It's a promise." She opened her file folder and pulled out a piece of paper. She slid it across the table.

Bill Amos picked it up. His eyes quickly scanned the document. He tossed it back down on the table.

"You know what the real kicker is? If I had been a man and just pulled off this deal, all of you," she looked at each man in the room, "would have been patting me on the back for pulling off such a coup. Instead, I'm relegated to the title of heartless bitch and for that, I thank you. I will wear it proud." She stood up and pushed the chair back with her legs, sending it into the wall behind her with a loud bang. "I expect to have that document signed and on my desk by the end of business today. I trust the two of you can show yourselves out and the rest of you have work to do," she said and with that, she took her file folder and left the room.

Sydney was still fuming two hours later when Maureen tapped lightly on the door. "Come in," she said a little too gruffly.

"Hey, Syd, rough morning?" Maureen, Sydney's trusted assistant hesitantly asked.

Sydney shook her head. "Nah, sorry, just some rough moments."

"Well, I have something that might cheer you up."

Sydney finally noticed that the giddy green-eyed blonde was bouncing on the balls of her feet and that her hands were hidden behind her back.

"I could definitely use a pick me up right about now."

Maureen handed her the document. Sydney looked at the paper. "All right, yes," she said, adding a fist pump in the air. Her day just got better and another piece of the puzzle just fell into place.

"It arrived a few minutes ago by courier."

"You just made my day," Sydney said with a grin as she looked at Bill Amos's signature.

"I need your signature on these two documents as well so I can add my Jane Hancock and get them mailed," Maureen said, handing Sydney the papers and a pen. Sydney signed them and handed them back to her.

She watched Maureen as she added her signature. "That looks so uncomfortable," she said.

"What does?" Maureen asked, as she picked the papers up.

"Writing with your left hand because I swear it looks like you write upside down."

Maureen shrugged. "You know what they say about us southpaw's."

"What's that?" Sydney asked.

"We're the only ones in our right mind and the rest of you are left out," Maureen laughed.

"Whatever," Sydney chuckled.

With red painted manicured fingers, Maureen smoothed the front of her suit jacket.

Sydney could tell that her assistant wanted to say something. "Spit it out, Maureen."

"Um, I heard about you and Meredith and I wanted to say I'm sorry. Is there anything I can do?"

Sydney frowned. "Who told you?" she asked, thinking *damn it Meredith.* She specifically told her not to say anything. She should have known that Meredith couldn't keep her mouth shut.

"You know how it is around here, Syd. Nothing stays secret for very long."

"Especially when you're head of the gossip machine, huh," Sydney grinned.

"Hey, I can't help it if we have a lot of little birdies flying around."

Sydney stood up and grabbed her jacket. "Whatever," she said, shrugging her arms into the sleeves. "Can you do me one more favor?"

"Sure."

"Please call Bill Amos. I want him to arrange a company meeting at EMCOR with all of his people for 9:00 a.m. on Monday morning. Can you also order pastries and have a caterer set up a breakfast buffet in the main conference room at EMCOR prior to the meeting?"

"You got it."

"I'm taking the rest of the day off but if you need to get ahold of me, call me at home."

"I think I'm gonna take off a little early too if you don't mind."

"Not at all, you are coming to my party tonight, right?" Sydney asked although it was more of a statement.

"Are you kidding? I wouldn't miss it for the world."

"See you tonight then."

Chapter 4

When Sydney left Welsh, she had decided to do some Christmas shopping. She usually spent the holiday at her mother's house and enjoyed the day playing around with her twin twelve-year-old niece and nephew, Sara and Seth. For hours, they would sit and test out the latest and greatest new toys on the market because that is what Sydney usually bought them. The two kids had everything, her sister saw to that, so it was a challenge at Christmas and birthdays to find something they did not have. Last year, she had bought them the Wii game system along with twenty to thirty games and all the external gadgets that went along with the system. Seth loved the Wii skateboard while Sara was partial to the boxing gloves. Her sister, Liz was none too happy when Sara announced that she wanted to be a boxer like Mohammed Ali's daughter, Alia.

After several trips up and down the aisles of Toys "R" Us, Sydney had settled on two electric rocket motorcycles. The twins would love them; she wasn't so sure about Liz. Aunts were supposed to buy a toy that the parents hated, that was one of the fun things about being an aunt. It was almost like a golden rule with Sydney.

The one thing she was not looking forward to on Christmas day was spending six continuous hours with her mother, Deidre. It wasn't that she disliked her mother or anything like that. It had to do with the endless badgering and constant barrage of negative comments that came from her mother. No matter what Sydney did, it never seemed to be good enough in her mother's eyes. If her hair was short, her mother claimed it needed to be longer. If her hair was long then her mother said she needed a haircut.

Over the years, Sydney had become accustomed to her mother's criticisms. The baffling part was that her mother treated Liz as if the sun rose and set in Sydney's baby sister and because of that, Liz usually ended up becoming the referee when the discussions became a little too heated. Sydney swore to Liz that her mother hated her because she looked just like her father whereas Liz, with blonde hair and blue eyes looked like their mother. Liz told her she was imagining things but later changed her mind when she overheard their mother tell Sydney that she was stubborn as a mule and took after her father unlike Liz who was levelheaded and laid back like her. From that day on Liz always came to Sydney's defense whenever Deidre started in on her eldest daughter.

Sydney had just finished wrapping gifts when the first slew of guests began to arrive. By the time she took a shower and changed her clothes, the party was already in full swing. She stepped into the family room and glanced around. The live band that Edna hired was singing the chorus line of *Jingle Bells*. Her stomach twisted in knots as she scanned the crowd for Caitlyn and her parents and when she didn't see them, she was somewhat relieved, yet disappointed at the same time.

She grabbed a glass of champagne from a passing waiter. She scanned the crowd again looking for her staff. One of her rules was that if she had any type of party, the staff was to hire temporary replacements and the staff was to join in the festivities. At first, some of them had protested but when they saw that she would not budge on the rule, they had finally caved in. It was now to the point that her staff looked forward to the parties more than she did.

Edna came racing across the floor. She threw her arms around Sydney's neck and hugged her.

"The house looks fantastic, Edna. You've really outdone yourself this year. Thank you for everything."

Edna smiled warmly. "Thank you and you are most welcome."

"Oh, there you are love," Fred Rick yelled as he made his way across the floor toward the two women. He leaned in and planted fake kisses on Sydney's cheeks.

Sydney smiled and shook her head. "Fred Rick, the food selection this year is over the top. You are definitely the best chef in the world."

"I do try, my dear," Fred Rick said, flipping his hand flamboyantly in the air. He pretended to brush his hair back away from his face. "Now, if you'll excuse me, I see a handsome young man across the room and I can tell that he is just dying to meet me."

Sydney couldn't help but shake her head as Fred Rick disappeared amongst a crowd of bodies who were dancing near the band's stage. Sydney excused herself from Edna when she saw Jackie come in.

On the far side of the room near the Christmas tree, Allen, Kenneth, and Robert stood huddled together with their wives. The women were a bit overdressed for a Christmas party and were more suited to be at the president's inauguration. The three men extricated themselves and headed off toward the dining room.

"Where do you suppose they are going?" Danielle VanDersmote, Robert's wife asked.

"I'm sure their talking business, you know how dedicated our husbands are, Danielle dear," Victoria Carmichael cooed.

"By the way, I love your dress, Victoria. Is it Vera?" Carmen Worthington, Kenneth's wife asked.

"Heavens no, darling, It's Versace'. I would not be caught dead in a Wang dress," Victoria corrected as if Carmen had insulted her. "Look at her," Victoria said with a nod of her head.

The two women looked in the direction Victoria had indicated. Sydney and Jackie stood next to the doorway that led into the foyer, talking.

"What about her?" Carmen asked.

"I just cannot believe she flaunts her lesbian sexuality around in the open for all to see. What do two women do together anyway? For the life of me, I cannot understand how they have sex. Do you think she straps one on or what?"

Carmen and Danielle laughed.

"If you don't know how two women can have sex with each other, Victoria, that tells me one thing. You've never had an orgasm in your entire miserable life and when Allen's dry humping your ass like a dog, you become nothing more than a human waste disposal, you know, like a fuck dump for all of his deformed little swimmers," Karen said from behind the women.

The three women whirled around, their faces registering shock as they stared at Karen. It was obvious that they could not believe anyone, let alone someone like Karen would speak to them in such a manner. Victoria's eyes took in Karen's red, green, and black Goth outfit. She made no attempt to hide the smirk on her face as she looked Karen up and down from head to toe.

"Like anyone would ever take anything you had to say seriously," Victoria said with as much dignity as she could muster.

"Like anyone in their right mind would ever wanna fuck you," Karen said and then laughed as the women's mouths dropped open. "By the way, I'm orgasmically endowed, how about you?" Karen said with a wink before walking away from the women.

Sydney smiled as Karen approached. She grabbed two glasses of champagne from a passing waiter and handed one to Karen. "I saw you talking with the triplets, learn anything interesting?" she asked.

"More like the *Hounds of Baskerville*," Karen laughed. "Those bleach blonde-haired hoity toity bitches don't have an interesting bone in their bodies. They don't understand that without their "husbands" so called upper status at Welsh they wouldn't be shit," Karen said, making a finger quote her with hand.

Jackie looked at Karen and laughed.

"I think you may be right. Hear, hear," Sydney said, laughingly as the two of them clinked their glasses together. "Oh great," Sydney sighed.

"What?" Karen asked, turning to see what Sydney was talking about.

Meredith walked in with a hot little petite blonde by her side. She ignored Sydney and crossed the room.

"I'm not even going to ask," Karen said with a shake of her head.

This is a really nice party, Syd," Jackie said and then took a sip of her champagne.

"So this is where we're congregating," Maureen smiled as she walked up to the group of women.

"I was beginning to think you weren't going to make it," Sydney teased.

Maureen shook her head. "I told you I wouldn't miss it for the world."

Sydney looked at Jackie and then at Maureen. "I don't think you two have met."

The two women looked at each other and shook their heads.

"Well then, Jackie Christopher, I'd like you to meet Maureen Olsen. Maureen I'd like you to meet Jackie."

"It's nice to meet you, Maureen," Jackie said. "Have you worked at Welsh for long?" she asked, taking Maureen's hand in hers. *Damn this woman is hot,* Jackie thought as her eyes unabashedly took in the luscious curves of Maureen's body.

"It's nice to meet you, too and it will be ten years next month," Maureen grinned.

"If you'll excuse me, I see someone I'd like to say hello, too," Sydney said, turning toward the foyer. She felt instant butterflies as she watched Caitlyn step into the foyer, followed by her stepfather and Rachel.

Caitlyn's eyes lit up when she saw Sydney.

"Hi, Caitlyn, I'm glad you could make it, Merry Christmas," Sydney said.

"Merry Christmas to you also," Caitlyn said as she took her parents jackets and gave them to the young woman doing coat checks. "Thank you," she said to the woman before turning back to Sydney. "I would like you to meet my mom and stepdad."

Sydney looked first at Edward Ashburn and then at Rachel. Her heart thumped wildly in her chest, the sound echoing so loud in her ears that she was convinced the others could hear it. She swallowed a lump that had suddenly formed in her throat.

Rachel was far more beautiful than she remembered. The photos didn't do her justice at all. She wore a midnight blue ankle length gown that fit snuggly against the curve of her hips. On each side of the gown, a three-inch wide, thigh high slit ran down to her ankles, exposing long, and tan, shapely legs. Sydney's eyes continued to travel up the length of Rachel's body. Her eyes stopped at the plunging neckline and ample cleavage. The figure-hugging gown left little to the imagination. When her eyes locked with Rachel's, she saw a cloud of confusion behind the long blonde lashes.

She forced herself to look at Edward. He looked exactly like she had pictured. Dressed in a black tuxedo, he stood approximately six-foot-tall and was ruggedly handsome with dark chestnut colored hair and blue eyes. Sydney thought she could describe him in two words—conceited bastard.

"Mom, I would like for you to meet my boss, Sydney Welsh," Caitlyn said, pulling Sydney from her thoughts.

Sydney held out her hand. "I'm pleased to meet you," she said, looking Rachel in the eye.

To say Rachel was shocked would be the understatement of the year. Rachel's eyes were full of questions as she held out her hand. "It's nice to meet you, Ms. Welsh," she said, taking Sydney's outstretched hand. "Caitlyn talks about you non-stop."

Sydney smiled. "It's all good I hope and please call me Sydney."

"Of course it's all good," Caitlyn beamed and then said, "This is my stepdad, Edward."

"I'm pleased to meet you as well," Sydney said, taking the man's hand in hers.

"Caitlyn never said a word about how beautiful you are. You're quite the looker and I swear to God if I didn't have a wife—"

"But you do," Sydney said, cutting him off before he could finish the sentence.

Edward whistled loudly as he looked around the foyer. "This is some place you got here. What is it, six, seven thousand square feet?"

"Twenty-five-hundred, sixty feet," Sydney said, thinking that the man reeked of arrogance and alcohol.

"Only two-thousand, five-hundred, and sixty feet, huh, that's not as big as I thought. Sure looks a lot bigger. My house is just a little under five thousand. That's definitely bigger than yours," he said, smugly.

His house? What a total jackass, Sydney thought. The only thing he owned was his 1996 Toyota Camry. Everything else was in Rachel's name and that included the house. His name isn't on the deed and she hadn't given it a second thought when she had seen a copy of the loan papers. Now she understood why, because his name wasn't really Edward Ashburn. A loan would have raised all sorts of questions, like credit scores, past job experience, references, etcetera, but why wouldn't Rachel have questioned him on this? Did she know that her husband wasn't who he claimed to be? Even if she did, she couldn't see Rachel involved in anything shady.

He had to have told her one helluva story and the plot continues to thicken, she thought as she looked at Edward and shook her head. "I think you misunderstood me. It's not twenty-five hundred, it's twenty-five thousand, six-hundred square feet," she said, grinning with satisfaction at the shocked expression on his face as the figures finally sunk into his tiny little brain.

"You're not supposed to ask questions like that. It's rude, Edward," Rachel said, looking apologetically at Sydney.

"What's something like this cost, three, four million?" he asked, undeterred by his wife's admonishment.

Caitlyn and Rachel looked as if they wanted the floor to open up and swallow them. Sydney glanced at Caitlyn. She winked at her protégé before turning back to Edward. "Eighteen-million dollars," she said and then added, "Cash."

Sydney had caught Edward off-guard. If she had any reservations about the man before now, he had quickly solidified her opinion of him and her opinion was lower than she had initially thought.

"You got anything stronger than sissy-ass champagne?" he asked as a server passed by.

Sydney nodded toward the foyer doorway that led into

the family room. "There's a wet bar through there. Help yourself."

Edward didn't wait for a second invitation. Without a word to Rachel or Caitlyn, he left the foyer. *No doubt on his way to get a drink, as if he needed one,* Sydney thought as she turned to Caitlyn. "I need to go speak with someone. Why don't you show your mother around? Get something to eat and drink. Have a little fun."

Caitlyn looked at Sydney and mouthed a silent thank you. Sydney gave her a "you're welcome" smile before turning to look at Rachel. "It was nice meeting you, Mrs. Ashburn, please excuse me," she said and left the foyer. She had to put some distance between herself and Rachel. She had been waiting for this moment for so long that she had not given a second thought on how it would affect her when the time finally came. Her emotions were in overdrive. She grabbed a glass of champagne from a server's tray and was not surprised to see that her hand was shaking.

She walked back into the family room and looked around. This had to be the largest Christmas party yet. The place was jam packed with bodies and from what she could tell; most Welsh employees were in attendance. She waved to the Mayor of Miamisburg who seemed to be having an animated discussion with Edna and Allen. *What a combination,* she thought.

"Well howdy, Sydney. Merry Christmas ta ya," a voice said just over her shoulder.

She didn't need to guess at whom the voice belonged to. She turned to see the smiling face of Jedidiah Saunders. "Hello, Jed. I'm glad to see you could make it and Merry Christmas to you," she said. "This must be your lovely wife, Gerty."

Jed smiled at the portly grey-haired, older woman standing beside him. "Yes it tis."

"I am so pleased to meet you, Ms. Welsh. Thank you

so much for inviting us. You have a very beautiful home," Gerty said as she took Sydney's hand and shook it soundly.

"Please call me Sydney. Ms. Welsh sounds so formal," Sydney said, marveling at the strength of the woman's grip on her hand. "Are you two having a good time?"

"Oh yes," Gerty said, releasing Sydney's hand.

Sydney looked at Jed and smiled. "I've been thinking about you."

"Really? Why you wanna go waste your thoughts on that?" he grinned.

"Yep," Sydney said and nodded. "I was wondering if you had a full-time job?"

"No ma'am, I don't. I been retired from General Motors now goin' on five years I reckon."

"Would you like a job? I need someone who's handy to look after things around here but I don't want you up on any ladders."

Jed scratched his head as he thought about the offer. "Well, Gerty here's been tryin' to get me outta her hair for some time now, says I'm always under foot."

"Cause you are," Gerty said, playfully shoving her husband.

Sydney couldn't help but smile at them. They made a cute couple. "Why don't you come by Monday evening and we can discuss the particulars."

"I sure will," he said, his mouth curving into a smile.

"Now that we've got that out of the way, why don't you go ahead and show Gerty the rest of the house, after all, starting Monday, you'll need to know the lay of the land too, and don't forget to check out the dining room. We have a full buffet set up. Make sure you try the stuffed lobster, it's to die for," Sydney said to Gerty.

"I love seafood," Gerty chuckled.

"I love seafood, too. When I see food, I eat it," Jed said over his shoulder as he and Gerty headed off toward the dining room.

Sydney laughed and shook her head. She couldn't help but like Jed. Her gut told her that he was a good man and in many ways, he reminded her of her own dad. Her eyes systematically searched the room looking for Rachel. She found her standing next to Edward, who was standing next to the wet bar with a drink in both hands. Their eyes met and Sydney felt heat rise from the bottoms of her feet and settle in her groin. She forced herself to look away.

Well now is as good a time as any, she thought as she made her way to the stage. She leaned over and said something to the lead singer who promptly directed the band to stop playing.

Sydney took the microphone and walked over to the staircase. She climbed high enough that she could look out over the entire family room.

"May I have everyone's attention please," she said into the microphone. When the crowd quieted, she continued. "First of all, I would like to thank everyone for coming and I hope that you are all having a good time." She smiled at the *whistles and oh yeahs* coming from the crowd.

"As all of you who work at Welsh know, we have had an awesome year." The crowd erupted with a clap of hands. She held her hand up to quiet them. "And since we have had such a fantastic year, everyone's Christmas bonus will be doubled to thirty-percent your salary instead of the usual fifteen." The crowd went nuts at the announcement. "In addition to the bonus, which by the way will be reflected in next week's checks, just in time for some last minute shopping, I have also decided to give everyone two additional days off before Christmas and none of you are to return to work until the third of January. I also know that some of you are workaholics and will still show up to work on those extra days I've given you off so you will be paid double-time."

She scanned the crowd looking for the few people she was specifically talking about. "Karen, Allen, Virgil, you all are hearing this right?" Sydney laughed.

"Those extra days are with pay?" someone yelled from the back of the room.

"Yes, that's with pay," Sydney laughed again as the crowd erupted in applause. She again held her hand up to quiet them. "I have one more announcement to make," she said as her eyes scanned the crowd for Meredith. She found her and the clingy blonde standing near the triplets.

"Some of you know that I have been in the process of interviewing candidates for the position vacated by our former VP of Computer Logistics, Tom Sosia. Well I'm happy to say that I have found the right person for the job. I would like for all of you to help me in congratulating our newest VP, Caitlyn Ashburn."

For several seconds, you could have heard a pin drop. Sydney looked at Meredith, whose mouth was hanging open. Sydney grinned with satisfaction as she watched Meredith grab her date by the arm and storm out of the room.

"Way to go, Caitlyn, that's my girl," a drunken Edward yelled out from the back of the room. That's all it took to get the rest of the crowd on board as claps and cheers rang out. At least some of them were clapping. Sydney's eyes searched the crowd. She found Caitlyn standing next to Rachel. Both women had shocked expressions on their face. She then scanned the room for Allen. She found him huddled together with Robert, Kenneth, and their wives. The look on Allen's face told Sydney that she had made the right decision. Allen said something to Victoria, then turned and left the room with Robert and Kenneth on his heels.

Sydney handed the microphone back to the bandleader who then promptly directed his band to start playing.

"I have to hand it to you, Sydney, I didn't see that one coming," Karen chuckled over Sydney's shoulder.

Sydney turned and smiled. "Yeah, I'd say it caught

more than a few people off guard."

"Brilliant, absolutely fucking brilliant," Karen laughed. "Did you see the look on the *Hounds of Baskerville's* face and their husbands? It was priceless, absolutely fucking priceless! You don't need to give me a Christmas bonus, what you just did was payment enough."

"Girl, you are so not right," Sydney laughed. She looked around the room, her eyes scanning the crowd. "Have you seen Jackie?"

"Nah, but I really haven't been looking for her."

"Damn, I was hoping to talk to her before she left."

"I'm sure she's around here somewhere." Karen grinned. "You check the buffet table?"

Sydney put her hands on her hips. "And what exactly is that supposed to mean?"

"I have no idea what you're talking about, my sweetest, dearest employer," Karen said, feigning complete ignorance with a smile. She winked at Sydney. "I just thought maybe she might be a little hungry."

"Uh huh, I'm sure that's exactly what you thought."

"Maybe she's at the chocolate fondue table," Karen snorted.

Sydney shook her finger at Karen. "You need to behave yourself missy."

Karen frowned. "Now where's the fun in that?" she asked and grabbed two glasses of champagne from a server. She offered one to Sydney.

Sydney shook her head. "I'm kinda champagned out and I need to visit the little girl's room."

"Suit yourself," Karen said as she moseyed across the room. She snuck up behind the triplets and leaned in so she could eavesdrop on their conversation.

Danielle laid a hand on Victoria's shoulder. "I am so sorry, Victoria, I know how much Allen wanted that promotion," she said, sympathetically.

"I cannot believe that woman gave a snotty little

nineteen-year-old know-it-all, a position of such importance," Carmen chimed in.

"She has no business making more money than our husbands," Danielle said, shaking her head.

"Just look at them over there," Victoria snorted. "I cannot believe Sydney fraternizes with her servants the way she does." She made a sweeping gesture with her hand toward the staircase where Fred Rick, his part-time boyfriend Carlos and Edna, along with Jed and his wife were talking with the Mayor of Miamisburg.

"They mingle with the guests as if they were our equals," Carmen said in agreement.

Karen had heard enough. She came around to stand directly in front of the three women. "Sydney treats everyone the same, Carmen, whether she employs them or not. It's called being human, you should try it sometime." She looked at Victoria. "As for your husband getting the promotion, that'll be the day. Caitlyn might only be nineteen but she has more brains in her little pinky than the three of your sorry ass husbands put together. You three miserable uptight hags need to take your bigoted asses back to high society Centerville."

Karen emptied the contents of her champagne glass in one gulp. "And while you're at it, take your husband's with you. Sydney Welsh and Caitlyn Ashburn are soooo out of your league."

"I, I don't think I was talking to you," Carmen stammered.

Victoria stomped her foot on the ground. "How dare you speak to us that way, you white trash bitch," she hissed.

Karen took a menacing step closer. She brought her face within an inch of Victoria's. Her voice was eerily calm as she spoke. "How dare I? How dare you! If you three bitches didn't spend most of your time stuck on stupid, you would see that Sydney and Caitlyn are two of the best people on this planet and they're my friends. If I hear one more derogatory word come out of your mouth, this white trash bitch from Dayton, is going to kick your snooty ass all over this room."

Danielle grabbed Victoria by the arm. "Come on, hon, let's find our husbands, and get out of here."

"Smartest thing you've said all night," Karen said. She grinned, a look of satisfaction on her face as she watched the three women go off in a huff in search of their husbands. A few minutes later she saw them leave.

The desk light inside Caitlyn's office flicked on. A mysterious figure covered in black from head to toe and wearing a ski mask, used a gloved hand to turn on the computer. While the computer booted, the gloved hand pulled out a piece of paper and laid it on the desk. The arrow pointer zipped around the screen as the mouse slid over its pad. The fingers moved to the enter button and pressed it, instantly changing the display. Rows and rows of computer code appeared on the monitor. The mask covered head leaned forward to look at the paper. Both gloved hands reached for the keyboard and began typing.

Somehow, Rachel had found her way into the kitchen. She looked around the large room, thankful that she was alone. She had needed to get out of there. It was too much. She needed to be by herself. She needed time to think. *How could I have been so stupid? I should have known*, she thought as she systematically began a search of the cabinets.

Syd Welsh, Sydney Welsh. Formerly Sydney Baxter, Welsh was her mother's maiden name. She should have known, she told herself again. *I should have been able to put two and two together*, she thought as she opened one door, slammed it shut, and then repeated the process over again.

For two years, Caitlyn had been working for Sydney, yet Rachel had no idea that the Syd who Caitlyn constantly talked about was the former love of her life, Sydney Baxter. When she saw Sydney in the foyer, she could not believe her eyes. It took everything in her to maintain her composure. Everything in her brain screamed at her to run—she should have.

She flashed back in time and found herself drawn to those warm light brown eyes all over again. Sydney was just one year older than she was and Rachel had never believed the saying, 'you get better looking with age', but she believed it now. Sydney's hair was longer than she remembered and hung in waves, reaching just above her bra line. The color was a little different too. Her normally black hair had traces of brown streaked through it. A small area just about her left eyebrow showed the slightest trace of white. If you were standing more than a few feet away, it would be unnoticeable. The black pleated slacks Sydney was wearing had hung seductively on her hips. Her dark green silk blouse, open at the neck revealed darkly tanned skin and enough cleavage to suggest the promise of ample breasts beneath the shirt. She had looked older, more distinguished, and sexy as hell.

What am I thinking, she chastised herself for having such thoughts. Never in her wildest dreams did she ever expect to see Sydney again, at least not in this lifetime. It was obvious that Caitlyn knew nothing about their past relationship. I wonder why—

"If you tell me what you're looking for, I may be able to help," Sydney said, her voice jolting Rachel from her thoughts.

Rachel's cheeks flushed pink as she turned around to face Sydney. "I'm, uh, I'm looking for something to drink. Something strong," she said, turning to resume her search of the cabinets.

"I don't think you will find anything in there," Sydney said. "I suggest the wet bar or the fridge."

Rachel stopped what she was doing. For the first time since entering the kitchen, she took the time and actually looked at the room. It was huge. She had never seen a kitchen this size in her life. "Exactly how many cabinets are in this kitchen?" she asked.

"I don't know, I'd say around thirty, maybe forty but that's just a guess," Sydney said as she walked over to the stainless steel refrigerator and pulled open the double doors. "All I have is some white Zin. Will that do?" she asked, looking at Rachel.

Rachel leaned back against the bar, which ran the full length of the kitchen. She brushed her hair back from her face with her hand. "Anything will do right now," she said.

Sydney grabbed two wine glasses and brought them over to the bar. She poured each of them a glass and handed one to Rachel.

"What the hell is going on, Sydney?" Rachel asked.

Sydney shrugged. "You and I are about to have a drink together," she answered nonchalantly.

"That's not what I mean and you know it. How long have you known that Caitlyn was my daughter? Did you know it when you hired her? Why haven't you told Caitlyn that you and I know each other? You had to have known that I would be here tonight. Did you think about what a shock this would be for me?" Rachel asked, firing question after question at Sydney.

"I knew what you meant, Rache," Sydney said. She watched the emotions play out on Rachel's face at her use of the familiar nickname. "No, I didn't know she was your daughter when I hired her," she lied. "I found out after she came to work at Welsh," she lied again. "She had a photo of you and Alyssa on her desk. I recognized you immediately, which of course I didn't mention to Caitlyn. She then filled in the blanks for me. She informed me that Alyssa was her half-sister. That you had remarried when she was eleven, and Alyssa was a result of that marriage nine months later. She doesn't have any pictures of your husband in her office, though. I thought that kinda odd."

Sydney took a sip of wine. "As for knowing you would be here tonight, that's not a true statement. I told Caitlyn to invite you and your husband but I wasn't sure she would and I wasn't sure you would come even if she did. By the way, I thought you handled yourself very well during the introductions. I don't think Caitlyn or Edward suspected a thing."

"Why didn't you tell her that you and I knew each other?" Rachel asked again as she pulled out a barstool, grateful to have something to support her shaking legs before she fell to the floor.

"What would you have liked me to say? *Oh, by the way Caitlyn, I knew your mom almost in the biblical sense way back when.* No, Rache, I decided that if you wanted that part of your life known, then you should be the one to tell her. It wasn't my place."

Sydney watched Rachel as she eyed her suspiciously. It was as if she were debating with herself as to whether Sydney was telling her the truth or not.

"I'm not sure I believe you," she said finally, confirming Sydney's thoughts.

"That's your choice," Sydney said with a shrug, and then added, "I'm not the same person I was thirteen years ago, regardless of what you think or believe about me."

Rachel continued to stare at Sydney. "Why didn't you terminate Caitlyn's position after you realized she was my daughter?"

Sydney's look was incredulous. "You can't be serious, terminate her? Her job abilities have absolutely nothing to do with you and I. She is one of the best and most intelligent employees I've ever had. I would promote her before I would ever consider firing her."

"I can see that." Rachel smiled as she thought about her oldest daughter. "She is pretty special and she definitely loves her job.

"Are you going to tell her?" Sydney asked, coming around the bar. She pulled out a stool and sat down next to Rachel.

"I don't know. I'm not sure what can be gained by telling her about us. If anything, it would lead to more questions that I'm not sure I want to answer. I don't have to tell you how inquisitive Caitlyn is or can be."

"No, you don't," Sydney agreed. She looked at Rachel's eyes. They were the most fascinating shade of blue she had ever seen. The only person Sydney knew of who had eyes similar in color was Elizabeth Taylor. It was only natural that Sydney's gaze fell to Rachel's mouth. Some old habits are hard to break. "You're even more beautiful than I remember, Rache, and I like the way you're wearing your hair, it suits you," Sydney said the words aloud without realizing it.

Rachel's throat felt like it was constricting. She struggled to swallow. She unconsciously ran her fingers through her hair. "Thank you. It's a little shorter than I normally wear it but it's more manageable."

She looked at Sydney then quickly averted her eyes. She glanced down at her wine glass. *What am I doing here? I should not be sitting here having this conversation, at least not with Sydney Welsh.* She felt an old familiar pain in her heart. Sydney was the last person she ever expected or wanted to see again, yet she couldn't seem to force her legs to get up from the stool. She should leave right now. Go out the door and never look back.

"Does Edward know?" Sydney asked although she already knew what the answer would be.

Rachel shook her head. "Some things are better left in the past and that's a part of my life I would just as soon forget," Rachel answered, her voice barely above a whisper.

Sydney felt as if someone had stabbed her in the chest with a knife. That's not true. It was deeper than that. Her heart literally ached. She still hates me. *After all these years, she absolutely hates me.* Once again, Rachel made it perfectly clear that she regretted the love they had once shared.

Rachel slid her bracelet watch around her wrist. She stood up from the barstool. "It's getting late, almost eleven. I should go and find Caitlyn and see if she's ready to go home."

"Yeah, I guess I should return to my party," Sydney said as she reached for Rachel's wine glass at the exact same time Rachel did. The glass toppled off the counter and crashed to the floor, sending shards of glass in every direction.

"I can be so clumsy sometimes," Rachel said, kneeling down to pick up the glass pieces from the floor.

Sydney knelt down beside her and picked up several large shards of glass. "It's not a big deal, besides I'm the one who knocked it off, not you," Sydney said.

"Ouch! Damn it," Rachel swore under her breath as a slow stream of blood from the tip of her right pinky finger ran down the side of her hand and dripped onto the floor.

"Shit! You cut yourself," Sydney exclaimed, jumping to her feet. She grabbed Rachel's left hand and pulled her to her feet. "We need to get this washed off," she said, pulling Rachel behind her over to the sink.

"It's not that big of a deal," Rachel said with a nervous laugh as Sydney turned on the water faucet and placed the bloody pinky under the cold liquid. "It stings," Rachel said, trying to pull her hand away.

"Keep it right there until the bleeding stops," Sydney said firmly.

Rachel started to comply but the tone of Sydney's voice made her reconsider. Her right eyebrow shot up. "I'm not one of your employees that you can boss around," she snapped.

Sydney felt her temper flare slightly. "You're right. You're not and I probably wouldn't have hired you either," she said, although she didn't mean it. Rachel was a very intelligent woman and would be an asset to any company. Her daughters were perfect examples of that intelligence. They had to have gotten their smarts from Rachel because they sure as hell didn't get them from their fathers.

Sydney didn't look at Rachel because if she had, she would have seen how much her words had stung. She opened the cabinet door just above the sink and pulled out a first aid kit.

"I don't think I need first aid. It's not that bad."

Sydney reached over and turned the faucet off. She grabbed a clean towel off the counter. "It doesn't matter how small the cut is. It still needs to be cleaned or it can become infected and cause more problems." She took Rachel by the hand and led her over to a barstool. "Sit," she instructed. "Will you please sit?" she asked nicely when it was apparent that Rachel had no intention of sitting on the barstool.

"That's better," Rachel said, pulling out the barstool. Sydney used her foot to slide a stool over next to Rachel. She sat the first aid kit on the counter and flipped open the lid. Rachel watched as Sydney took out a tube of antibiotic cream, an alcohol packet, and a band-aid, and laid them on the counter.

Without thinking, Sydney slid her stool over so that her knees were up against Rachel's legs. "Let me see your hand," she said, holding her hand out to Rachel.

Rachel's right eyebrow shot up again and Sydney

smiled. "Please let me see your hand."

"I, I still don't think this is necessary," Rachel said with a nervous laugh as Sydney took the towel and gently patted the water off her pinky finger.

"This is going to sting just a bit," Sydney said, ripping open the alcohol packet.

Rachel flinched as the alcohol hit the open cut. "Jesus, Mary, and Joseph," Rachel grimaced. "I thought you said just a bit."

"I'm sorry," Sydney said as she bent her head and blew softly on the cut to help ease the sting. She felt her heart rate increase as the warmth from Rachel's legs permeated through her slacks. She needed to distance herself from Rachel before she said or did something she would regret. She didn't wait ten years to have her plan blow up in her face in a matter of minutes. Now is not the time, she told herself as she spread a small dab of ointment over the cut. She tore the wrapper open and then wrapped the band-aid loosely around Rachel's finger.

Without thinking, she brought Rachel's hand to her mouth. She heard Rachel's deep intake of breath as she lightly kissed the bandaged finger. "All better?" she asked as Rachel's eyes met hers.

"I ... uh—"

"There you two are," Caitlyn exclaimed as she pushed the kitchen door open.

Rachel jerked her hand away as if she had been burnt by fire.

"I've been looking everywhere for you both," Caitlyn said, looking first at her mom and then Sydney.

Rachel smiled. "Looks like you found us. I ... we ... um—"

"What happened?" Caitlyn interrupted as she moved closer, her voice rising slightly as she took in the first aid kit lying on the counter and the small band-aid on her mom's finger.

"Your mom cut herself on a broken wine glass but she's okay," Sydney answered.

Rachel laughed. "You know how clumsy I can be sometimes."

Caitlyn's just like Rachel, Sydney thought as Caitlyn's right eyebrow shot upward.

"Yeah, Mom, you're about as clumsy as I am and we both know that I'm not clumsy at all."

Sydney knew Caitlyn's words held a hidden meaning that Rachel understood perfectly.

"I'm fine. Really, I am," Rachel said, trying to reassure her daughter. "Sydney and I both tried to grab the glass at the same time and it fell off the counter and broke all over the floor and—"

"That's not what I'm talking about and ..." Caitlyn said and then stopped when she saw the pleading looking in Rachel's eyes.

Sydney was right. She had no doubt that Caitlyn was aware of Rachel's hospital visits. It was obvious by her double talk that she didn't think her mom's clumsiness had anything to do with all the trips to the ER.

Caitlyn turned to Sydney. "With all the goings on in the other room, I didn't get a chance to say thank you. This promotion means more to me than you'll ever know and I promise to be the best employee ever."

Sydney took Caitlyn's hand in hers and gave it an affectionate squeeze. "You're welcome. As for you being the best employee ever, you need to stop trying so hard because you already are. I would not have given you the promotion, Caitlyn, if I didn't think you deserved it or couldn't handle it. So, now tell me what your first order of business is going to be."

Caitlyn grinned like a Cheshire cat. "I would like to order a new phone system for the entire company. The ones we use are so antiquated. What do you think?" she asked, looking at Sydney.

"I think it's up to you to decide and I will agree with whatever you say. I also think it's getting late and I need to go check on my guests and offer the proper goodbyes," Sydney said, sliding off her barstool. "If I don't see either of you before you leave, have a Merry Christmas." She looked at Rachel. "It was nice to meet you, Mrs. Ashburn. Make sure you keep that cut clean and bandaged until it heals," she said and then left the kitchen.

Sydney was not surprised to find Edward Ashburn propped up against the wet bar.

"What would you like ma'am?" the young bartender wearing a nametag that said Ted asked.

"I'll have two of whatever he's having, Ted," Sydney said, motioning toward Edward.

"I'm drinking Kentucky Bourbon on the rocks," Edward said, his speech slurring as if he had a mouth full of food.

"I like Bourbon," Sydney said as she took the glass and offered the second one to Edward.

"You're a really, really beautiful woman, Sydney. May I call you Sydney?" he asked.

"Yes you may, Edward, and thank you," she said, smiling and thinking that she was about to puke as he openly leered at her.

"You and I should get together for a drink sometime and maybe some extracurricular activities if you know what I mean."

Sydney smiled her best smile at him. "I know exactly what you mean and I think that is a wonderful idea."

"I could probably teach you a thing or two," he said as he moved closer. He rubbed his leg against hers and she fought the urge to raise her leg and knee him in the balls.

She batted her eyes dramatically at him. "I bet you can. How can I get ahold of you?" she asked.

"Sweetheart, I know several ways that you can get ahold of me," he said, taking out his wallet. "My cell number's on the back," he said as he pulled out a business card and handed it to her. He leaned in close. "Don't look now, baby, but here comes the old ball and chain," he whispered into her ear.

Thank God, Sydney thought as she turned to see Rachel and Caitlyn approach.

"Are you ready to go home, hon?" Rachel asked her husband.

"Hell no, the parties just getting good," he said, frowning.

"All the guests are leaving and I'm sure Sydney has work to do tomorrow," Caitlyn said.

He shot a warning look at Caitlyn. "I'm not done with my drink."

Sydney smiled at him. "I can take care of that for you," she said and turned to the bartender. "Can you give me a to-go cup with a lid, please?" She took the cup and held out her hand for Edwards drink.

"You're something else and hot as hell to look at on top of it," he said, openly flirting although his wife was standing right next to him.

Sydney smiled as he held his glass of Bourbon out to her. *This piece of shit doesn't have a decent bone in his body*, Sydney thought as she carefully placed her fingers near the bottom of the glass and dumped the Bourbon into the to-go cup. "All set," she said and handed Edward the cup.

He grabbed Sydney's hand and brought it to his lips. "Thank you for a marvelous evening," he said, leaving a wet mark on her skin where his lips had just been.

"You're quite welcome," Sydney said, thinking that she needed to scrub her hand with bleach.

"Goodnight, Sydney. We had a good time," Caitlyn

said as she glanced at her stepdad.

"Thank you for coming and I will see you at work," she said, looking first at Rachel and then at Caitlyn.

Sydney watched the trio leave and then turned to the bartender. "Do you have any bags back there buy chance?" she asked.

"Sure do," Ted said, handing her a brown paper bag.

Sydney picked up a napkin and carefully placed it around the empty Bourbon glass. With a flick of her wrist, she snapped the bag open. "Gotcha," she whispered as she placed the glass inside the bag and folded it shut.

Chapter 5

First thing I need is a strong cup of coffee, Rachel thought as she left her office and headed down the hallway toward the break room. She was surprised to see that most of the tables and chairs were taken and the occupants all seemed to be immersed in deep animated conversations. Usually by this time of the morning, the break room was nearly deserted.

"I wonder who brought these in," she said to herself as she looked at several boxes filled with all sorts of pastries and donuts. She finally settled on a plain glazed donut. She poured herself a cup of coffee and took her donut over to the table where her assistant Lilly, along with Helen and Mary from purchasing were sitting. The three women were leaning over the table, talking in hushed voices.

Rachel pulled out a seat next to Mary and sat down. "What's all the hubbub about?" she asked. She couldn't remember when the last time the atmosphere at EMCOR was filled with this much electricity.

"Didn't you get the email?" Lilly asked excitedly.

Rachel took a bite of the donut. "What email?" she asked after she wiped her mouth off with a napkin.

"The one that said we were having a meeting in the large conference hall at nine on the dot," Helen answered. "Oughta be a real doozy," she said, nodding her head to the point that a normal person would be dizzy.

Rachel found it amazing that no matter how violent

the shake or nod, not one bleached blonde hair on the woman's head ever moved. She had been telling herself for quite awhile now that she really needed to ask Helen what kind of hairspray she used. "Who's meeting in the conference room?" she asked.

"You really should read your emails in the morning, Rachel dear," Helen sighed as she used a bejeweled hand to pat down her bouffant-do.

Mary cupped her mouth with both hands in a conspiratorial fashion and leaned forward. "I heard from Jeff in shipping that he overheard young Amos talking to someone on the phone about a hostile takeover," she whispered.

"That's just nonsense. You of all people should know better than to listen to office gossip," Rachel teasingly scolded the young brown-haired woman who was just one year older than Caitlyn. It wasn't too long ago when the local gossip machine had Mary dating Ernie, the sixty-year-old mail clerk. The idea wouldn't have been so hard to believe if it weren't for the fact that Ernie was actually Mary's great uncle.

"How do you explain the donuts and the fancy smancy breakfast buffet that's set up in the conference room then?" Helen asked.

"It did say that the meeting was mandatory for the whole company," Lily added, shyly.

Mary nodded. "Yeah that makes you wonder all right."

Rachel snapped her fingers to get the women's attention. "Will one of you please tell me exactly what the email said?"

"It said that everyone was to meet in the main conference hall at nine for an important announcement," Helen volunteered.

"You three are a mess. Maybe the breakfast was Bill's way of saying Merry Christmas and maybe the meeting is so he can announce the wonderful Christmas bonuses we all get this year," Rachel said, trying to look on the bright side of things.

"Yeah right and I'm Cleopatra," Helen said with a wave of her hand.

Mary glanced at the clock hanging on the wall by the coffee maker. "I guess we'll find out soon enough. It's eight fifty-five, we should be going," she said, pushing her chair back.

Rachel tossed her half-eaten donut in the trashcan and then followed the women out of the break room.

Sydney was unusually nervous. She had checked the bathroom stalls beforehand and finding them empty, she had locked the door. She needed a few minutes to herself without any interruptions. She looked at her reflection in the bathroom mirror. It was important for her to exude confidence and to pull that off she had chosen a black pantsuit with thin white pinstripes, accented by a white silk blouse buttoned at the collar. The two-inch heeled half boots brought her eye level with most men.

Caitlyn referred to this outfit as Sydney's vamping power suit. The name fit the clothes well and when Sydney wore it, she did indeed feel powerful. She wasn't what you would call an extreme femme, yet she wasn't exactly butch either. She liked wearing makeup as long as it consisted of a small amount of blush and black eyeliner, and maybe a little mascara.

She had Rachel to thank for the eyeliner. She had told Sydney that she loved the way it brought out the tiny black specks surrounding her brown eyes. She used her hands to brush her hair back away from her face, not quite tucking the strands behind her ears.

"Time to get this show on the road," she said as she

unlocked the door.

Bill Amos, his grandson Andrew as well as Caitlyn, Allen, Kenneth, Maureen, and Bev were waiting for her in the small room located near the front of the main conference room. "Thank you," she said, taking the file folder from Maureen.

By the time the women from the break room reached the conference hall, all seats except for three in the back row had been taken. Helen and Mary quickly took a seat and when Lily offered Rachel the third one, she shook her head and walked over to the table where the buffet bar had been set up. She refilled her coffee cup and leaned her back up against the wall. The entire room buzzed loudly with jumbled conversations. She caught bits and pieces and could tell that most centered around speculation regarding the meeting.

Just as she took a sip of coffee, the door located at the front of the conference hall opened. She nearly choked, spitting coffee everywhere when Sydney, followed by Caitlyn, Bill Amos, his grandson, and the Welsh executives walked into the room. If she thought the conversations couldn't get any louder, she was mistaken.

Sydney walked up to the podium, which had been placed in the center of the room. She laid the folder down, picked up a wireless microphone, and clipped it to her lapel. She poured herself a glass of water while she waited for her executives to line up behind her. She turned back to the crowd who had suddenly become quiet.

"Good morning and thank you for coming," she said as she surveyed the crowd. "I know this meeting has caught most of you off-guard so I will get right to the point. For those of you who don't know who I am, my name is Sydney Welsh. I am the President and CEO of Welsh Enterprises and these are my executives," she said, turning and motioning with her hand at the people standing behind her. "Less than forty-eight hours ago, Welsh Enterprises became the full owner of EMCOR."

"What does that mean for us?" an older man wearing a ball cap and blue Izod shirt yelled from the back of the room.

Sydney scanned the room to locate the questioner. She lost her train of thought for a moment when she saw Rachel leaning against the back wall. *Focus,* she told herself as she looked for the man behind the voice. She found him standing near the rear entrance. "What is your name, sir?"

"Carl Monroe, ma'am," he said, taking off his hat.

"Well, Mr. Monroe, I'm going to tell you exactly what Welsh owning EMCOR is going to do for you." She stopped to take a drink of water.

"Are we going to lose our jobs?" asked a matronly looking woman sitting in the front row. "Oh, and my name is Edith," she added with a smile.

Sydney could not help but smile back at the woman. "You won't lose your job unless you want to, Edith." Sydney made a sweeping gesture toward the crowd with her hand. "And that goes for the rest of you as well."

Another man in the front row started to say something but Sydney held up her hand to stop him. "I have several things to tell you and when I'm finished, I will open up the floor and try to the best of my ability to answer all of your questions."

She came out from behind the podium and walked to the left side of the room. She stopped within two feet of the people in the front row. "I understand how change can be a scary thing for some people but I want to tell you that not all change is bad. In most cases, it's for the best even if we don't believe so at the time. Without the constant of change, things will stagnate and die. Take a fishing pond for example. Without the movement of ripples in the water, everything in the pond will die. It starts with the microorganisms that feed the algae. Without them the algae dies and once the algae dies, the fish have no food and they die and the cycle goes on and on until nothing is left. The same can be true for a business. EMCOR is the pond and Welsh Enterprises is now the ripple."

She turned and walked back to the podium. She took another sip of water and looked out at the faces of her new employees. She could tell by their expressions that they understood what she was saying. She was in her element. The one thing she knew how to do was work a room and in the process, hopefully her enthusiasm became contagious and it had nothing to do with being a good con-artist, it was because she believed in what she was saying.

She refilled her glass and walked over to the right side of the room. "For the next month or two, it will be business as usual while several of my executives evaluate the business plan and processes here at EMCOR. They will also be evaluating specific job functions and the employees who fill those roles. No one ... and I repeat, no one will be terminated or laid off if after the evaluations, it is determined that they are not the best candidate for that particular job. All of you are important to the success of EMCOR and you may or may not be utilizing your full potential and that is what we want to find out."

She paused for a few seconds to allow her comments to sink in before continuing. "I know some of you are still skeptical and that's okay. You wouldn't be human if you weren't. Believe me when I say I want this transition to go as smoothly as possible for all of our sakes. My philosophy has always been that if you respect and take care of your employees, they will take care of you. I would not be where I am today without hardworking, loyal employees. Without you, my businesses wouldn't exist and I also believe that my employees should share in the wealth they help to create."

She stopped to clear her throat. "Since EMCOR is now part of the Welsh family, you will be receiving the same courtesy's and benefits that all Welsh employees get and that starts with your Christmas bonuses. I've had the opportunity to review the standard bonuses here at EMCOR, and by Welsh standards, it's just not acceptable. In this week's paycheck, every single employee will receive a $10,000 bonus." At this news, the entire place went nuts with whooping and hollering and a couple of hell yeahs. Sydney had to smile when she overheard an elderly man ask if he had heard her correctly.

She held her hand in the air to quiet them. "In addition to the bonus, you will also be given the Thursday and Friday off before Christmas and none of you are to return to work until the third of January and before anyone asks, yes it is all with pay."

"Wow, I never expected this in a million years," she overheard a young man in the second row whisper to the woman sitting next to him.

So far, so good, she thought as she turned and went back up to the podium. "Okay, does anyone have a question?"

Several men and women stood up from their chairs. As she pointed to a young woman near the back of the room, she locked eyes with Rachel and felt her heart skip a beat.

Rachel pushed away from the wall and walked over to the doorway. She stopped and turned to look back at Sydney. She shook her head and then slung her coffee cup into the trashcan before storming out of the room.

Sydney looked back at the young woman. "I'm sorry, ma'am. Can you please repeat the question?"

"I can't believe this. What in the hell does she think she's doing?" Rachel mumbled under her breath as she hurried back to her office. "First, she takes my daughter and now the company that I've worked my butt off for. I have to get out of here before I scream or break something." She jerked her jacket off the hook on the back of the door, grabbed her purse and keys, and left the office, slamming the door shut behind her.

"Okay, if no one else has any more questions for me, I'm going to turn it over to our Vice President of Computer Logistics, Caitlyn Ashburn. She's going to explain to you how we will be transitioning EMCOR's information system over to Welsh's proprietary software and how that change will affect each of you."

Sydney looked at Caitlyn and grinned. The young VP looked as if she were about to vomit. She removed the lapel microphone and covered it with her hand. "You'll be fine," she whispered into Caitlyn's ear. "When you're done, have Allen explain how our email system at Welsh works and the process we will use to get all EMCOR employees converted over."

The coloring in Caitlyn's face was several shades paler than what Sydney was accustomed to seeing. "I have the utmost confidence in you, Caitlyn. I promise you'll be fine and I'll see you back at Welsh," Sydney said with a wink and then left the conference hall.

She rushed down the hallway toward Rachel's office. The light was off and the door was closed. She continued down the hall to the front receptionist's desk.

"May I help you?" a cheerful young man who looked to be sixteen-years-old at the most asked. Sydney looked at his nametag badge. "Good morning, Parker. I was wondering if you saw Mrs. Ashburn leave the building."

"Yes ma'am, she did. Not more than two minutes ago," he said, nodding his head.

She pulled her car keys out of her pocket. "Thank you, Parker."

"You're welcome. Have a good day, ma'am."

"I'll try and you do the same," she said over her shoulder as she pushed the entrance door open.

Rachel slammed her purse down on the kitchen counter. "I have to find a new job. That's all there is to it," she said as she pulled out the basket in the coffee maker and put in a new filter. "I won't work for a company she owns." *Why not,* a little voice inside her head asked. "I just won't," she said, continuing to talk to herself as she scooped coffee into the filter. *Can't or won't,* the little voice asked. "Won't, can't, won't, can't. What makes the difference?" *It does make a difference,* the little voice said. "Okay, okay. I can't work for her and I won't because I can't be that close to her," she admitted as she filled the glass pot with water and poured it into the coffee maker.

Since the night of the Christmas party, thoughts of Sydney filled her head constantly. No matter what she did to get her mind off things, her thoughts returned to Sydney. She remembered how warm and gentle Sydney's hands were when she had cleaned her cut. She remembered how her heart skipped a beat when Sydney's legs touched hers when she slid the bar stool over. She remembered the smell of Sydney's cologne and smiled. After all these years, she still wore Calvin Klein's CK1. "You have to stop thinking like that," she admonished herself. "I'm not going through this again. I just can't."

Her hands shook as she poured herself a cup of coffee and took it over to the kitchen table. She shook her head as several thoughts ran through her mind. *I'm a married woman. Things are different. I'm different and she's different. We are not the same people we used to be.* She tried to clear her mind but the image of Sydney's face wouldn't go away. Sydney was the first and last woman she had ever loved, actually the only person she had truly loved.

The kitchen door opened, snapping Rachel from her thoughts. Caitlyn walked in and laid her briefcase on the counter. She opened the cabinet and grabbed a coffee cup. "I was wondering where you went. I saw you leave the conference room," she said, pouring herself a cup of coffee. "You missed my first company speech."

"I'm sorry, honey. I felt the beginnings of a migraine and like a dummy I left my meds in my nightstand," she lied. Rachel frowned as she looked at the cup in Caitlyn's hand. "Since when do you drink coffee?"

Caitlyn eyed her mom suspiciously. "Yeah, I thought that might have been the reason and since about a week ago."

Rachel looked at Caitlyn and shook her head. She fought to keep the anger out of her voice. "You're my daughter, Caitlyn. You could have at least warned me this was coming. Instead I was blindsided like everyone else."

Caitlyn pulled out a chair and sat down. "I think you know me better than that, Mom. I couldn't warn you because I didn't know about it. I found out twenty minutes prior to us arriving at EMCOR."

"Then you should have called me," Rachel snapped.

"I tried but it went straight into your voicemail."

Several seconds passed without either one of them saying anything. "I'm going to start looking for another job," Rachel said, finally.

"What? Why? You love what you do. You told me yourself only three days ago that EMCOR was the best company you had ever worked for," Caitlyn, said, her eyebrows furrowing into a frown.

"That's beside the point. You may think highly of Sydney Welsh but I have no desire or intention of working for her."

Caitlyn rested her elbows on the table and laced her fingers together. "What's going on, Mom?"

"I don't know what you mean."

"Hellooo," Caitlyn said, waving her hands in front of Rachel's face. "This is me you're talking to. Something is going on with you and I know it. I can't
put my finger on it but you've been acting a little strange since Sydney's Christmas party."

"I really don't know what you're talking about," Rachel said, playing dumb. She could tell by the look on Caitlyn's face that she wasn't buying any of it.

"For some reason you have this new hostility and it seems to be directed at Sydney. She's a really good person and Welsh buying EMCOR was the best thing that could have happened to that company."

"If you say so," Rachel said, shrugging her shoulders.

Caitlyn nodded. "I do say so. I saw the paperwork on EMCOR. William Amos ran it into the ground and if Sydney hadn't intervened, the company would have been forced into bankruptcy and everyone, including you, would have lost their job."

"I think EMCOR is nothing but a new feather in Sydney Welsh's cap. Whatever she wants she gets and she doesn't care who she hurts to get it."

"Who exactly is she hurting, Mom?" Caitlyn asked. "I don't think you understand just how good of a person she is. Just look at the bonus she's giving to the EMCOR employees. When all is said and done it will cost Welsh well over a million dollars. I can't see Bill Amos or any employer for that matter putting out that kind of money for a group of employees, especially people who Sydney never laid eyes on until today."

Caitlyn stood up from her chair. She looked at Rachel and frowned. It was so out of character for her mom to be like this. It was obvious she did not like Sydney, which made no sense to her.

She grabbed her briefcase off the counter and turned back to Rachel. "I don't care what you say. I know something is going on with you and my gut tells me it has to do with Sydney. I'm not sure what kind of conversation the two of you had in her kitchen. Maybe she said something you didn't like or maybe someone said something bad to you about her but whatever it is, I hope you can get past it. You can deny it all you want but I know when something's not right."

Rachel sighed. "Can we call a truce for now and let it rest?"

"For now," Caitlyn agreed with a smile. "I just want you to know that you, Alyssa, and Sydney are my three most favorite people in the world and I don't want any of you to be upset for any reason. Speaking of Mini-me, where is Alyssa?"

Rachel chuckled. "She had a sleep over at Christy's but she'll be home this evening."

Caitlyn leaned forward and kissed Rachel on the cheek. "I have to get back to work. I'm already behind on one of mine and Sydney's special projects but I will see you tonight at dinner."

Rachel stood up from her chair and hugged Caitlyn. "Okay sweetie, I'll see you tonight and please don't worry about me."

"Easier said than done," Caitlyn grinned as she pulled the door shut behind her.

Rachel walked over to the counter and refilled her coffee cup. She pulled the curtain back from the window and watched Caitlyn back her car out of the driveway. She felt like such a heel. She could not believe she allowed her hostility toward Sydney to become so apparent that Caitlyn had picked up on it. She would have to be careful and guard her tongue a little more closely, at least for Caitlyn's sake.

She picked the morning paper up off the counter and tossed it over on the table. Just as she was about to sit down, there was a knock at the door. "What did you forget this time?" she asked, jerking the door open. She felt her heart instantly skip a beat. "What are you doing here?" she asked.

Sydney smiled. "Is that how you talk to all of your guests?"

"You're not my guest." Rachel glared at her. She attempted to shut the door but Sydney stuck her foot out to prevent the door from closing.

"Well, I would be if you'd invite me in."

She's laughing at me. I can see it in her eyes. "What are you doing here, Sydney?" she asked again, not bothering to be polite.

"I would like to talk to you." This was going to be harder than she thought and for the second time since she had concocted this crazy scheme, she was beginning to have doubts—serious doubts.

"I don't see where you and I have a damn thing to talk about." Rachel hoped that she sounded angrier than she felt. Her heart was doing flip-flops at seeing Sydney again and she was having a hard time trying to figure out why.

"I assure you, we do. I'll say my piece and then leave."

"Fine," Rachel said, throwing the door back. She turned and went back over to the table.

Sydney shut the door and walked over to the counter. "You have a lovely home," she said, glancing around the large kitchen. "I love the wallpaper. I never realized you could do so many things with the shade of blue."

"I'm sure you didn't come here to discuss my wallpaper," Rachel said, sarcastically.

"You're right, I didn't. Do you mind if I have a cup of coffee?"

Rachel shrugged. "Help yourself, second door on the right above the coffee maker." *She's more fit than I remember,* Rachel thought as the muscles in Sydney's arms flexed as she reached up and opened the cabinet door. When Sydney turned around, she quickly averted her eyes. Staring was the last thing she wanted Sydney to catch her doing.

Sydney took a sip of the steaming liquid, leaned back against the counter, and crossed her legs at the ankle. No matter how many times she saw Rachel, she never tired of her beauty. Today, she wore a tan colored pantsuit and a light blue chemise blouse, which only served to enhance the violet blue of her eyes. Thinking that the house seemed very quiet she asked, "Where's your youngest daughter? If memory serves me correctly, today's the first day of Christmas break."

"She's at a friend's house," Rachel said, crossing her arms over chest. "What's this about, Sydney? I know you're much too busy to be making social calls for the hell of it."

Sydney nodded. "You're right. This isn't what you would call a social call. It's strictly business."

"Speaking of business, did you know that I worked for EMCOR before you plotted out your little hostile takeover in your mega war room?"

Sydney laughed. "I would hardly call it a war room." Did she want to tell Rachel the truth? She debated in her mind for several seconds before answering. "No, not at first," she lied. "I did however, glance at the personnel list after the final papers were signed." She had to choose her words carefully. "When I saw your name, I took a look at your file. Congratulations, by the way on your promotion."

"I would say thank you if I actually believed you meant it."

"I do mean it. You are very talented and I know this

because I took the liberty to tour three buildings where you oversaw the interior design renovations. I'm a little puzzled why someone with your talent wouldn't open her own architecture firm. I know you have the brains for it."

If those words had come from anyone else, Rachel would have been thrilled with the compliment. She watched Sydney refill her coffee cup. "Would you like some?" Sydney asked, holding the pot in the air.

Rachel shook her head and Sydney put the pot back on the warmer. "I want you to oversee the total interior renovations of my house."

"Huh, what did you just say?" Rachel asked, thinking she hadn't heard her right.

"I want you to renovate my house," Sydney repeated.

Rachel shook her head. "You're joking right?"

"If you knew me at all, Rache, which I suspect you don't or ever did for that matter, then you would know that I never joke when it comes to business."

Rachel's look was defiant. "No, Sydney! I'm not going to do it and there's nothing you can do about it," she said, shaking her head.

Sydney had forgotten how stubborn Rachel could be. It was maddening before and even worse now. "You are an employee of EMCOR and seeing that I now own EMCOR, you are my employee as well."

Rachel jumped up from her chair and smiled. "Then I quit! Neither you nor anyone else is going to tell me what I can or cannot do."

"You made that perfectly clear thirteen years ago."

"This ... this, whatever this is..." Rachel shook her hands in the air. "Has nothing to do with us. Hell, I have no idea what this has to do with. You'll have my resignation on your desk first thing in the morning."

Sydney leaned back against the counter and laughed. She looked at Rachel with eyes that had darkened so deeply, they looked black. Her voice was even and controlled as she spoke. "You're going to do this, Rache, and here's why. If you don't agree to do as I ask, I will fire Caitlyn."

Rachel looked at her with a stunned expression on her face. She couldn't believe what she was hearing. She shook her head. "You wouldn't dare. She thinks the world of you and only God knows why, because I sure as hell don't."

Sydney pulled out her cell phone. It was strange to hear Rachel using curse words in the same sentence with God. She smiled at Rachel. "I would dare and you have less than ten seconds to make a decision," she said, pushing the speed dial for Caitlyn's phone. "Nine, eight, seven, six—"

"All right, all right, I'll do it," Rachel said just as Caitlyn's voice came on the line.

"Hey, Caitlyn, it's me. How'd everything go at EMCOR?" Sydney said into the phone. She looked at Rachel who silently mouthed the words, "please don't."

Sydney turned her back to Rachel. "Okay, great. See, you had nothing to worry about." She smiled as she listened to Caitlyn's run down of the meeting. "All right ... yeah, I have a few personal things to wrap up, and then I'm heading back to the office. I'll see you soon." She disconnected the line and said a silent thank you to herself for Rachel giving in. Regardless of what she had just threatened to do, she would never in a million years fire Caitlyn or cause her any type of pain, at least not intentionally. Caitlyn was the main reason she had nearly pulled the plug on her little scheme. Over the last two years she had come to love and care for the young woman as if she were her own daughter and the thought of Caitlyn hating her if she ever found out what Sydney was about to do to her mother was almost too much to handle—almost.

"What's next?" Rachel asked, pulling her from her thoughts.

She turned and faced Rachel. "Be at my house

tomorrow, eight o'clock. That's A.M., not P.M.," she clarified in case Rachel tried to get cute.

"I will do this, Sydney, because of Caitlyn but don't expect me to like it. I will put in my hours just as I would if I were at my office. No weekends and no overtime and when I'm done, I'm done. No strings attached."

"That's all I'm asking."

"I think you mean that's all you're demanding. There was no asking about it." After all these years, just being in the same room with Sydney still had the power to unnerve her. "I mean it, Sydney. It will take me two weeks, maybe less to do what you ask and when it's over, I never want to see you again." She prayed the angry tone of her voice would be enough to keep Sydney from wanting to go through with her threats.

Sydney unabashedly looked Rachel up and down. Her eyes lingered on Rachel's breast, then her lips, before settling on her eyes. "I've spent the last thirteen years without you being in my life. Do you really think it will pain me not to have you there for the next forty?" Sydney asked sarcastically.

Rachel turned her back to Sydney—no way would she let Sydney see just how much her words had hurt. After several seconds, she slowly turned and faced Sydney. "How am I supposed to explain this to Caitlyn or, or my husband?"

"It's just another special project. Trust me, she'll understand. As for your husband, I would be surprised if he's sober long enough to notice, so you can tell him whatever you like. I really don't give a damn," Sydney answered with a shrug.

"Please don't do this, Sydney," Rachel pleaded one last time. When Sydney didn't respond, she walked over to the door and pulled it open. She placed her hands on her hips. "I would like for you to leave now before my husband gets home."

Sydney sat her cup down on the counter and pulled out her car keys. She removed a key from the ring and laid it on the table. Without a backward glance, she walked out of Rachel's house.

Tears welled up in Rachel's eyes. She shook her head as if to clear her thoughts. *Oh God, what am I going to do?* She grabbed her cup from the table and refilled it. "I can do this. I have to for Caitlyn's sake. I will treat Sydney just as I would any other client. Two weeks, that's all the time I need to go through Sydney's house. I will create the new designs, order the materials needed, then hire the contractors to implement the changes, and then Sydney Welsh will be out of my life for good."

"Hey, hon, what are you doing home so early?" Edward asked.

Rachel jerked her head up in surprise. She didn't hear him come in. "How long have you been standing there," she asked, silently praying that he hadn't heard her talking to herself.

Edward, wearing a yellow hard hat, dirty jeans, and a red and black flannel shirt, stood in the doorway that separated the kitchen from the dining room. He leaned against the doorframe, his arms crossed over his chest. She could tell he hadn't shaved for several days based on the stubble covering his jowls and chin. His eyes were bloodshot and she could smell the alcohol clear across the room—he looked like hell.

"Just walked in," he said, half staggering to the refrigerator. He jerked the freezer door open.

"You usually come in the back door."

"It's my goddamn house, I'll come in whatever door I want," he said, slamming the ice cube tray on the counter. Several pieces of ice shot out of the tray and landed on the floor. He turned around to face her. "Now see what you made me do," he snarled through clenched teeth.

"I'm sorry. I know it's your house. I didn't mean to

upset you," Rachel said, her voice shaking as she bent to pick up the melting ice. She started to toss the cubes in the sink but he reached out and grabbed her by the wrists.

"You're hurting me," she cried out as he pulled her roughly against his body, pinning her arms down to her side.

He pushed her painfully against the counter. She could feel his arousal through his jeans as he crammed his crotch against her. He released one of her wrists only to grope her breast, his fingers squeezing like a vice around her nipple. He lowered his head to trail a row of sloppy kisses down the side of neck. She felt a burning sensation as he raked the prickly stubble from his beard against her skin.

Rachel's eyes filled with tears as she pushed against his chest with her free hand. "Please stop, Edward," she pleaded.

Edward grabbed Rachel's forearms and squeezed. "You frigid bitch," he spat, flinging her away from him. "Do you have any idea how many women would trade places with you in a heartbeat?" he laughed, his voice full of conceit. "And you wonder why I pick up hookers on North Dixie," he snorted.

Rachel was silent as she looked down at the floor. She was afraid to say anything, afraid of setting him off again lest he finish what he started. Her insides shook as she thought back about the last time they had sex. It had been at least six months. Edward liked it rough and the more she fought, the more excited he got. She knew that spousal rape existed but in a million years, she would never have thought that she would experience it. It was her duty to honor and obey her husband. It was her duty to satisfy her husband sexually. She thought about her daughter. Alyssa was almost nine-years-old and Rachel counted the days, down to the last minute when her youngest daughter would turn eighteen. She only hoped she would live long enough to see that day.

She thought about the prostitutes that walked the Dixie strip. If it were possible, she would have invited one of them to live in her house. As long as the prostitute was taking care of her husband, she would be safe. She rubbed the area of her arms where his fingers had been and shivered. She would have to wear a long sleeve shirt tomorrow to hide the bruises.

"I'm gonna go watch TV, why don't you make yourself useful for once in your life and fix me a drink," he said, his voice snapping her from her thoughts.

She sighed in relief as he turned and stumbled out of the kitchen. She opened the cabinet door, pulled out a glass, and tossed in several half-melted ice cubes. She grabbed the bottle of Windsor sitting on the counter and filled the glass almost to the rim. She picked up the glass of whiskey, thinking that if she were lucky, Edward would drink until he passed out.

She heard the bubbly voice of Reagan O'Neal announce that it was time for the six o'clock news. What she said next got Rachel's full attention. "At six fifteen, our news crew will take you live to Welsh Enterprises where Danielle Brisbane is reporting on the latest takeover by the entrepreneur extraordinaire, Sydney Welsh."

"Damn," Sydney mumbled as she turned into the Welsh parking lot. News vans and reporters were everywhere. She would have to sneak in through the back entrance. Thank heaven she drove something as non-conspicuous as a pickup truck because she was able to pass right by the reporters without getting a second glance.

She found a spot just to the left of the back door. She grabbed her briefcase and quickly made her way to the building. She slid her ID badge down the reader, slipped inside, and let out a sigh of relief when the door closed quietly behind her.

With briefcase in hand, she made her way down the carpeted hallway. As she turned the corner, she saw Caitlyn leaning against the receptionist's desk.

"Hey, Syd," Caitlyn greeted her with a smile as she approached the desk.

"What's going on?" Sydney asked as she looked at Karen's flustered face.

Karen ripped the headset from her head and laid it on the desk. "I'll tell you what's going on, these damn mother freakin' reporters are driving me nuts."

"That bad, huh?"

"You have no idea," Caitlyn said as the sound of the ringing phone continued to buzz on different lines.

"Yeah, I saw all the news vans out front. That's why I snuck in through the back entrance."

"It's been this way for over an hour," Karen said as she placed the head set back over her ear. She glanced down at the caller ID on the new switchboard phone console that Caitlyn had installed a few short hours earlier. She recognized the number and growled.

"Watch this," Karen said, selecting the line with a touch of a button. She pressed another button to put it on speakerphone. "Hello, you've reached the office of the one and only supreme genius. This is Karen speaking, and how may I help you today?"

"Hello, Karen, I'm Jason Kindle from the *Daily Ledger*. I was wondering if you would like to comment on the rumors regarding Ms. Welsh's sex life?"

Sydney raised her eyebrows as she looked at Karen

and then Caitlyn. Karen shook her head.

"Are they true?" Jason Kindle asked after several seconds went by in silence.

"How the hell would I know about her sex life?" Karen asked the man on the other line.

"I thought you said you were the office of Supreme Genius?" Jason Kindle laughed.

"Yes I did and I am," Karen said, nodding her head in an exaggerated fashion.

Jason Kindle cleared his throat. "The public has a right to know."

Karen's cheeks flushed red, matching the fiery color of her hair. "It's none of your freakin' damn business, Mr. Kindle, and it damn sure isn't the public's business."

"I have repeatedly called you over the last hour and I have better things to do with my time and I demand an answer!" Jason Kindle yelled through the speakerphone.

Sydney and Caitlyn both stifled a laugh at the expression on Karen's face. The man had no idea who he was dealing with.

Karen shook her head, floored by the man's boldness. "Oh, you demand, do you? Well, Mr. Kindle, you've just been redirected to the office of *I don't give a freakin' shit.* You have a great day now," Karen laughed and then promptly disconnected the line.

"What the hell is he talking about?" Sydney asked.

"Come on, I have something to show you," Caitlyn said, motioning for Sydney to follow her. They walked past several offices and stopped in the doorway of the break room where a group of employees sat huddled together watching the TV mounted on the wall. As soon as they saw Sydney and Caitlyn, the room went instantly quiet.

Caitlyn pointed at the TV. "That's what he was talking about."

Sydney watched the TV as several pictures appeared on the screen. The photos showed Sydney along with

Meredith and several other women who were either entering or leaving the downtown Dayton Lesbian bar called Covers. One photo showed Sydney and Meredith with their arms around each other. A caption at the bottom of the screen stated that Meredith and Sydney had split up after ten years together.

Sydney took a deep breath as her eyes fell on the photo of her and Meredith engaged in a kiss and it wasn't the friendly peck on the cheek type of kiss. Another photo clearly showed the tip of Meredith's tongue tracing an outline around Sydney's bottom lip.

"Damn her to hell," Sydney muttered under her breath. Meredith had threatened her but Sydney never thought she would stoop this low. If winning her back was Meredith's goal, she sure was going about it the wrong way.

Sydney glanced at the employees in the break room, their eyes glued to the TV screen. She crossed her arms over her chest and leaned against the doorframe for support. She felt her anger rise to the surface as she made a deliberate show of loudly clearing her voice. When the employees turned to look at her, she said, "I think all of you probably have something better to do with your time."

Chairs scraped on the linoleum, and a pop can tumbled over on the table as the employees, embarrassment written on most of their faces, mumbled apologies as they made a hasty exit from the room.

"Look on the bright side, Syd. Welsh stock shot up six bucks a share when the news broke," Caitlyn said with a nervous laugh.

"I'm sure that's a small consolation to some of our old-school male stockholder's," Sydney said, shaking her head. "To them, reputation is more important than the size of their bank accounts."

"I wouldn't be so sure about that. You've made your major stockholder's very wealthy, besides, if they have a problem with your sex life, I would venture to bet they're just jealous because you can get a better looking woman than they can," Caitlyn chuckled.

Sydney couldn't help but laugh. She wrapped her arm around Caitlyn's shoulders. "Have I told you lately how glad I am that you work for me and not my competitors?"

Caitlyn smiled. "Ah, maybe once or twice but you can tell me again. Do you have time for a quick meeting?" she asked, her expression turning serious.

Sydney glanced at her watch. It was a little after six and Jackie wouldn't be here for another forty-five minutes. "Sure, your office or mine?"

"Mine. I have some news regarding our Salami problem that I think you will be interested in."

Edward glared at the TV screen. His knuckles were white from squeezing the glass in his hand. He looked up as Rachel came over to refill his glass.

"Did you know that she was a fucking dyke?"

"Who?" Rachel played ignorant. She knew exactly what he was talking about and had stopped dead in her tracks when the announcer on the TV mentioned Sydney's name.

"Sydney Welsh. She's a Goddamn dyke," he said between clenched teeth. "I knew something was wrong with her."

"Um, no. I had no idea," Rachel lied. She could see the anger in his eyes and the last thing she needed right now was to say something that would set him off.

"Why didn't you tell me she bought your company? Were you trying to hide it from me?" he asked, accusingly.

"No Edward, I wasn't. It just slipped my mind."

The news reporter began talking about the EMCOR

takeover and how the news about the self-made millionaire's sex life didn't seem to be affecting Welsh stock. If anything, it had risen in value. The reporter went on to describe the woman kissing Sydney in the photo as Meredith Lansing, an executive at Welsh Enterprises who also happened to be Sydney's long-term girlfriend of ten years. Rachel looked at the gorgeous woman in the photo and then something unexpected happened. She felt sick to her stomach as a deep-seated pain settled in her chest. Her face flushed as she realized what the pain was—jealousy.

Edward jumped up from his chair, startling her. He jabbed his finger at her face. "I don't want you around that woman and if that means quitting your job then that's what you'll do."

Rachel sighed. "Fine, Edward. I will look for another job," she said in resignation. She was too tired to argue.

"Women like her are trouble. She'll try to turn you queer. She's probably trying to turn Caitlyn queer, too. Hell, she may already have. That's what her kind do, you know."

Rachel shook her head and had to try hard not to laugh at the absurdity of his statement. "No, Edward, I didn't know that's how they recruited their women."

"I meant what I said. I don't want you anywhere around that perverted woman," he said as he downed half the contents of his glass.

"Whatever you say, Edward," Rachel said as she turned and went back to the kitchen. She had fully planned to tell Edward about her new job assignment but after seeing his reaction toward Sydney, she knew that was no longer the smart thing to do. She would keep to her usual routine in the morning and dress in her business attire as if she were going to her job at EMCOR. She would pack an extra set of clothes and change into jeans once she arrived at Sydney's house. If she was going to do this, she might as well be comfortable, at least as comfortable as she could be around Sydney Welsh. She wondered if Sydney would be there or if she would have free reign to make whatever changes she saw fit. Whatever the case may be, she hoped with any luck, she would be able to go in, get the job done, and be out of there and out of Sydney's life for good. If she could pull this off, she didn't see any point in telling Edward.

She sat down and laid her arms on the table. She felt a lump in her throat and was powerless to stop the tears streaming down her cheeks. She laid her head across her arms. How in the world did she ever let her life get this messed up? This was not even close to the life she had dreamed of for herself. She raised her head and wiped the tears from her face just
as the back door opened.

"Hi, Mom," Alyssa shrieked happily when she saw Rachel. The bubbling eight-year-old was the spitting image of Caitlyn. She came over, wrapped her arms around Rachel's neck, and kissed her on the cheek.

"Hi, baby," Rachel said, forcing a smile on her face as she tucked a strand of Alyssa's hair behind her ear.

Alyssa leaned back to look at her mother's face. Her eyebrows pinched together. "Are you okay? Have you been crying?"

Rachel felt her heart break as she looked at her youngest daughter. She could see the concern in her bright blue eyes. Just like Caitlyn, Alyssa was just too intuitive for her own good.

"I'm okay, babe, I just have a slight head cold," Rachel said with more confidence than she felt. "Did you have a good time at Christy's?"

"We had a blast. Oh, and I made you something," Alyssa said as she reached into her coat pocket. She pulled out a small yellow colored daisy made from felt and handed it to Rachel. "There's a magnet on the back so you can put it on the refrigerator."

"And that's exactly where I will put it. It's beautiful, baby. Thank you. I love it." Rachel wanted to cry.

"Is Daddy home yet?" Alyssa asked.

"He's in the living room honey and I'm sure he will be happy to see you, too." Her heart swelled with love as she watched Alyssa leave the kitchen. *She is the reason why I have to stay and make this marriage work* she told herself for the thousandth time.

Sydney closed the door to Caitlyn's office. She laid her briefcase on the table next to the coffee maker. She grabbed two coffee cups and filled it with hot steaming liquid. She took the cups over to the desk and sat them down.

"Thanks," Caitlyn said without taking her eyes off the computer monitor.

Sydney slid a chair over next to her. "You're most welcome," she said as she watched Caitlyn maneuver the mouse around the screen.

Within a few seconds, several pages of code scrolled down the screen. Caitlyn clicked her mouse and the page stopped. "See this line of code here?" she asked, pointing at the gibberish on the screen.

"Yeah, kinda looks like all the rest," Sydney laughed. Although she knew how to use computers, the intricacies of how these things actually worked still baffled her.

Caitlyn shook her head. "Well, it's not. In fact, it's very different."

"I have no idea how you can tell but I sure am glad you can."

"We had a visitor Friday night," Caitlyn said, turning in her seat to look at Sydney.

Sydney frowned. "How can you tell?"

"Remember the key loggers I installed on the executives desktops and laptops?"

Sydney nodded.

"I also installed them on my desktop as well as yours."

Sydney's eyebrows shot up. "Why ours?" she asked, wondering what could have possessed Caitlyn to do that.

"I figured that if whoever was behind the embezzlement somehow figured out that we were onto their little scheme, maybe they would use mine or your computer to access our system, hoping to throw us off."

Sydney was impressed. "And?" she asked, her lips curving into a smile.

"They did. Actually, they used mine," Caitlyn said.

"You're kidding?"

Caitlyn shook her head. "They accessed it Friday night, Syd."

"Friday night," Sydney repeated the words. They were silent for several seconds. "That was the night of my Christmas party," Sydney said as she sipped her coffee. "Do you have an idea of what time?" she asked.

"Eleven-ten," Caitlyn said then added, "I could kick myself in the ass over this."

Sydney's head shot up. She looked at Caitlyn. As long as she had known the young woman, she couldn't recall ever hearing Caitlyn swear. "Why do you say that?" she asked.

"Because, when I wrote the new code to alert me if our system was accessed I also added code that would forward the information to my Blackberry the second it happened and it just so happens, I locked it in my desk drawer and didn't find it until this morning."

"You are way too hard on yourself, Caitlyn."

"It was irresponsible of me, Syd. If I had taken my Blackberry, we may have been able to catch the perp in the process."

Sydney laughed. "The perp, huh?"

"You like that?" Caitlyn asked, grinning from ear to ear.

Sydney chuckled. "Yeah, I do but I don't want you to even think about confronting anyone by yourself. If and when you get another alert, the first thing I want you to do is call me." When Caitlyn didn't say anything, Sydney nudged her with her shoulder. "You hear me, Caitlyn? I'm dead serious, here."

Caitlyn shook her head. "Trust me, Syd. I have no intention of confronting anyone by myself."

Sydney rubbed the sides of her temples with her fingertips as she thought about her Christmas party and the time regarding the so-called break-in at Welsh. "You said it came in on your Blackberry at eleven-ten?" When Caitlyn nodded, Sydney continued. "It could have been any of the execs seeing that the only ones left at the party at that time were you and me."

"I know. I thought about that already. However, I do have some good news," Caitlyn said, a look of smugness on her face. She paused to a take a drink of coffee. She smiled at Sydney.

"Not funny, Caitlyn," Sydney laughed at Caitlyn's obvious attempt at theatrics.

"I know the owner's name of the Salami account," she said finally.

Sydney's eyebrows shot up in surprise. That is not what she expected Caitlyn to say. "You're serious?"

"Dean & Rodgers Bank and Trust and the account belongs to one Carlos Delgado."

"How in the world did you figure it out?" Sydney asked in amazement.

"It was pretty easy actually. I wrote this simple little logic program that looked at any type of transfer, totaling one dollar or less. I then had it crosscheck those transfers to see if any account received twenty-five or more deposits allocated to the same bank and Mr. Delgado won the prize."

"You are absolutely incredible, Caitlyn. I honestly don't know what I'd do without you," Sydney said and she meant every word.

Caitlyn leaned back in her chair and laughed. "You'd probably go broke."

"You're probably right. What do you—"

The intercom buzzing on Caitlyn's phone stopped Sydney from finishing her question.

Caitlyn looked at the caller ID and pressed the answer button. "Hi, Maureen, what's up?"

"Hey, Caitlyn, I hate to bother you but is Sydney with you by chance?" Maureen asked through the speakerphone.

"Yeah, I'm here, Maureen," Sydney answered.

"I have Ms. Christopher standing at my desk. She says you're expecting her."

Sydney glanced at her watch. It was ten after seven. "Can you direct her to Caitlyn's office please?"

"Will do," Maureen said, then disconnected the line.

Within seconds, there was a knock at the door. Maureen pushed the door open and stood to the side to allow Jackie in. "I'm calling it a day," Maureen said, looking at Sydney.

"Okay, thanks, Maureen, I'll see you tomorrow."

Jackie turned to Maureen and smiled. "It was nice seeing you again, Mo," she said, holding her hand out to Maureen.

"Likewise," Maureen smiled as she took the big woman's hand in hers. "Goodnight, Caitlyn, Sydney," Maureen said and then left the office, closing the door behind her.

"I think she likes you. You should ask her out," Sydney teased.

Jackie's cheeks flushed pink with embarrassment. She crammed her hands in the pocket of her grey hoodie.

"Nah, I don't think so. Being single is so much more fun than lugging around dead weight."

"See, that's exactly what I'm talking about," Sydney laughed. "Maureen says the exact same thing you just did. You two would have a marriage made in heaven." Sydney winked at Jackie. "I'm pretty sure she's not interested in men although I've never seen her with a woman."

"What makes you think that?" Jackie asked, her eyebrows rising.

"For the past few years and just like clockwork, she gets roses monthly from a secret admirer named John and she has no idea who he is. When the flowers come, she just shrugs as if she couldn't care less," Sydney laughed.

"That would drive me crazy not knowing," Caitlyn said.

"Me, too but I guess if you don't care, then it doesn't matter," Sydney said with a shrug.

Caitlyn laughed. "I think it's kinda creepy."

Jackie looked at Sydney and smiled. She then walked over to Caitlyn and offered her hand. "Hello, Caitlyn, I've heard so much about you from Sydney and I didn't get a chance to meet you the other night or offer my congratulations on your new promotion."

"Okay, okay. I get it," Sydney said in response to Jackie changing the subject.

Caitlyn shook Jackie's hand. "Thank you and it's nice to meet you as well."

"You want some coffee?" Sydney asked.

Jackie pulled out a chair on the opposite side of the desk and sat down. "Nah, I'm good," she said, leaning back in the chair.

"How's the research coming?" Sydney asked.

"Not as good as I'd like. Without some proof that I know what I know, they're calling my bluff and keeping their mouths shut tight." Jackie crossed her legs at the ankle.

"I may be able to help you out on that." Sydney got up from her chair and went over to her briefcase. She snapped open the lid, pulled out a brown paper bag, and handed it to Jackie.

Jackie opened the bag and peered inside. "I think this should do it," Jackie said, looking at the glass with a napkin wrapped around it.

"Good. Now how long do you think it will take?" she asked, looking at Jackie.

"I need at least three or four days. May take a little longer depending on how quick my contact at the bureau can move."

"When you find—"

"I will call you immediately," Jackie said before Sydney could finish her sentence.

"Fantastic. Now I have another little matter that we," Sydney looked at Caitlyn and winked, "need your help on."

"I'm all ears."

"Caitlyn, can you write down for Jackie, the name of the bank and holder, and the account number regarding our internal problem."

"Sure." Caitlyn wrote the information down on a post-it-note. She ripped the paper off the pad and handed it to Jackie.

Jackie read the information. She looked at Sydney and frowned. "What would you like me to do with it?"

"We have a major problem. Someone is embezzling money from my company and whoever is doing it accessed our main computer system. They reconfigured the computer programming code in order to pull it off."

Sydney paused to refill her coffee cup. She leaned against the desk. "Caitlyn was able to trace the stolen money to the account written on the paper in your hand. I want to know who Carlos Delgado is, where he's at and I want my money back and I want whoever's behind this in a jail cell."

"How much is missing?"

"Over four million dollars," Caitlyn answered.

"Wow," Jackie said, shaking her head. "Have you called the police?"

"No and I'm only going to do that as a last resort. If this gets out, it could affect the price of our stock and send it to the basement."

"How did you discover it?" Jackie asked, looking at Caitlyn.

Caitlyn looked at Sydney, not sure how much information she should divulge. Sydney nodded for her to go ahead.

"No one except for Sydney knew that I was in the process of adding a whole new computer system and when I ran a beta test I discovered the discrepancies in our accounting numbers. From there, I wrote new code to find the missing funds, which I did."

"Sounds pretty technical to me," Jackie said. She was impressed. She knew Caitlyn was a computer wiz kid based on everything Sydney had told her but she never really had a handle on just how intelligent the young woman was until now.

"You ever hear of the Salami Technique?" Caitlyn asked.

Jackie nodded. "Sure. In my line of work, there's not much I haven't seen or heard of."

"Well whoever did this, hacked into our system on Friday night," Sydney said.

Several seconds went by without any of them saying a word. Jackie folded the paper and put it in her pocket. She looked at Sydney. "Well, I'll be the first to admit that I don't have any answers but if I was a betting person, I'd say it was an inside job."

"We agree," Sydney said as she brushed her hands down the front of her jacket. "There aren't too many people here at Welsh who have the knowledge and access to our computer system, which narrows it down to one of my executives. I will gather all of their information and fax it to your office. Once you trace the bank account, I would like you to take a close look at my execs. Check their bank accounts. See if they are living beyond their means or if they have any unexplained expenditures, etcetera."

Jackie stood up from her chair. "That should be easy enough to do. Most people with that kind of money sitting around will have a hard time not spending it."

"My thoughts exactly," Sydney said as she walked Jackie to the door.

"I'll get started on the bank account first thing in the morning and keep you posted."

"Thanks, Jackie. I appreciate it."

"Not a problem. I'll put a big rush on our other little matter, too," Jackie said and then left the office. Sydney turned to Caitlyn. "Let's get out of here kiddo." She grabbed her briefcase off the table and waited for Caitlyn to close her computer down.

Chapter 6

Rachel, with a duffle bag slung over one shoulder, her laptop over the other, and an armful of swatch books, walked up the porch steps to Sydney's house. She repositioned the books on her hip and used the key Sydney had left on her counter. She unlocked the door, shoved it open with her hip, and stepped into the foyer. Once inside, she kicked the door shut with the back of her foot.

She immediately noticed a white note card leaning up against a candle on the entryway table. With a groan, she dropped the swatch books and duffle bag on the floor.

"I can only imagine what this says," she said as she picked up the card and begun reading it aloud.

"Good morning, Rachel. If you're reading this little note, then it's obvious that you decided to keep up your end of our little deal— wise choice."

Rachel made a growling noise in her throat. "Wise choice my butt. *You* gave me little choice." She slid her laptop bag off of her shoulder and let it slide down onto the floor beside her feet. She leaned back against the table as she continued to read the note.

"Please make yourself at home and feel free to take a look around so you can better familiarize yourself with the layout of the house. I have also taken the liberty to set up a design room for you. Go down the hallway located on the opposite side of the family room, the second door on the right is just for you. I have some things to wrap up at work this morning but once I'm done, I will be home so we can talk about the changes I would like for you to make. If you need anything at all, just ask Edna. If you haven't met her yet, I'm sure you will soon, especially if you're tracking up her clean floors with

your messy shoes." The note was signed, *Sydney.*

"I'm glad to see that somebody is happy," Rachel mumbled as she looked at the small 'Happy Face' Sydney had drawn directly beneath her signature. She then looked at the floor and saw the little puddles from where she had tracked in snow. "Crap, Edna's going to kill me."

"Every morning that I wake up on the right side of the grass makes me happy and I promise not to kill you."

"Oh my gosh," Rachel exclaimed, clutching her hand to her chest. "You must be Edna and I'm so sorry about your floor."

Edna smiled at Rachel. "And I'm sorry for scaring you. Yes, I am Edna and don't worry about the floor, it'll dry." Edna leaned forward in a conspiratorial manner. "Don't tell anyone but I love giving Sydney a hard time about it, so she feels it's her duty to warn anyone who walks through the door," she whispered.

"Your secret is safe with me and I usually don't startle so easily, I just assumed I was the only one here."

Edna shook her head. "In this house, someone is always around."

"Well, in that case, good morning, Edna," Rachel said and smiled.

"And top of the morning to you as well and you must be Rachel," Edna said with a wink. "May I take your coat?"

"Yes I am and thank you," Rachel said, shrugging the coat from her shoulders.

"Can I get you a cup of coffee?" Edna asked as she took the coat and hung it in the closet located next to the elevator.

"I would love a cup but you don't have to wait on me. If you can point me in the right direction, I can get it myself."

"Nonsense, and if you don't mind the company, I think I'll join you," Edna said over her shoulder as she went through the large doorway, separating the two sets of stairs in the entryway foyer.

"I wouldn't mind at all," Rachel said, following Edna across the dining room toward the double doors that led into the kitchen. "This house is simply—"

"Too much," Edna laughed as she grabbed two ceramic cups from the cabinet located above the stove.

"Actually, I was going to say, amazing," Rachel said as she watched Edna pour coffee into the cups.

"It's definitely that," Edna said as she slid a plate that contained sugar and cream over in front of Rachel.

"Thank you," Rachel said as she spooned two sugars and half the contents of the cream into her cup.

"Would you like a little coffee with your cream?" Edna asked and then chuckled at the expression on Rachel's face.

"Oh, I'm so sorry," Rachel said, looking slightly embarrassed. "I will refill it for you," she said, sliding her bar stool back.

"No, no, you just sit right there and enjoy your cream and coffee," Edna grinned, waving Rachel off with her hand.

Rachel laughed and sat back down. "Sydney used to tease me and say that she could save the waitress several trips by just hooking the cow up to the table."

Edna's eyebrow shot upward, a little grin playing at the corners of her mouth. "Did she now?" she asked slyly as she sipped her coffee.

Rachel looked up in surprise, realizing that she just spoke her thoughts aloud.

Edna laughed. "So I take it that you and Sydney know each other?" She said it more as a statement than a question.

Rachel nodded. "Yeah, I guess you could say that." Several seconds went by without Edna saying a word. A look of relief crossed Rachel's face when she realized that Edna wasn't going to pry. Instead, Edna pushed her bar stool back and stood up.

"Would you like a warm up?" she asked as she refilled her own cup.

"Yes, please," Rachel said, sliding her cup across the bar so Edna wouldn't have to stretch.

"I understand from Sydney that you're going to be redecorating the place," Edna said as she placed the pot back on the warmer.

"That I am," Rachel said, nodding her head. "I honestly don't know why though. The place is beautiful just the way it is."

Edna shrugged. "Maybe she just needs a change."

"Maybe," Rachel said in agreement but she doubted a *change* was the reason behind Sydney's decision. She just wasn't sure exactly what the true reason was. It couldn't simply be that she wanted to make Rachel's life miserable. It had to be something else and she was determined to find out the answer.

"If you'd like, I can show you around," Edna volunteered.

"I would love that," Rachel said as she got up from her bar stool.

"I'll use any excuse I can to put off cleaning and if giving you a tour around this big old house can help me do that, I'll take it," Edna laughed.

"Really?" Rachel asked and then chuckled as she slid her fingers over the air vent above the stove. She held her hand up for Edna to see—her fingers were spotless.

"And your point is?" Edna asked with a grin.

Rachel laughed. "No point at all. So ... how about that tour now?" she asked.

Allen Carmichael quietly closed his office door as he

stepped out into the hallway. He walked toward the opposite end of the hall where Sydney and Caitlyn's offices were located. He slowed his pace as he came to Maureen's office and poked his head through the open doorway. He glanced at his wristwatch. The digital readout said that it was 9:32 A.M.

"Just like clock-work," he mumbled under his breath as he looked at Maureen's empty chair. Everyone at Welsh knew that Sydney's assistant made a break-room run at 9:30 and 2:30 every day. Over the years, Maureen had developed an addiction for the strawberry Danish's from the vending machine. She was so predictable that you could set your watch by her food craving and that's exactly what he had been counting on.

He smiled as he crammed his hands into the front pocket of his trousers. With one last glance down the hallway to insure he wouldn't be seen, he walked past the closed door of Sydney's office and stopped at Caitlyn's office. He knocked lightly on the door with his knuckles. When no one answered, he slowly pushed the door open. Seeing that the office was empty, he slipped inside and closed the door behind him. He wasted no time and headed straight for her desk. He pulled her chair out and sat down.

"Okay, let's see if you're as smart as everyone says you are, Caitlyn," he whispered as he pulled open her lap drawer and sifted through the contents. Not finding what he was looking for, he systematically began pulling out every drawer on the left side of the desk and searched through them. He sighed in frustration, running his hands through his hair. "You're fucking crazy if you think I'm gonna let some nineteen-year-old little bitch ruin me," he muttered under his breath as he searched through the drawers on the right side of the desk.

Karen watched Caitlyn walk past her desk for the third time in less than fifteen minutes. "Stop right there!" she yelled.

Caitlyn stopped dead in her tracks and turned to look at Karen. "Are you talking to me?"

With a dramatic look on her face, Karen slowly looked around the lobby. "No, I was talking to that tiny little woman with horns protruding from her forehead. You know, the one sitting on your shoulder. Hell yes, I'm talking to you."

Caitlyn's right eyebrow shot upward as she looked at her shoulder. She smiled as she slowly walked over to Karen's desk.

"You've already worn a bare patch in the floor in front of my desk, are you trying to destroy the hallway carpet as well?"

Caitlyn shrugged. "Maybe."

"Hold that thought," Karen said, picking up a pen and a large white index card. She scrawled something on the card, folded it in half like a tee-pee, and then set it up on the counter for Caitlyn to see.

Caitlyn burst out laughing as she read it aloud. "*The Remarkable and Luscious Dr. K. - Office of Supreme Intelligence. All problems welcome. Payment required at time of service. Will trade smart ass answers for sex.*"

"You like that, huh?"

"You crack me up," Caitlyn said as she looked at Karen's clothing choice for the day, which consisted of a pink leather miniskirt and 'come fuck me' knee high pink boots with lace down the side. "By the way, the new studded pink dog collar is way cooler than the black one."

"Way cooler? Oh young protégé of the all mighty and powerful Welsh employer, you really need to work on your vocabulary, honey."

Caitlyn frowned. "What's wrong with my word choice. I think I speak with very proper diction."

"See right there, that's what I'm talking about," Karen groaned.

"What?" Caitlyn looked completely confused.

"Diction? Who the hell says diction?"

"Hey, I can talk hip and slang with the best of them."

"Uh huh, sure you can and thanks for the compliment on the collar. I have matching furry pink handcuffs to go with it. You wanna come over to my house and try them on sometime?" Karen winked and then laughed at the expression on Caitlyn's face.

"Um ... uh ... I—"

"OMG. Stop the press," Karen yelled. "Why, Ms. Caitlyn, you sure do turn the prettiest shade of red when you're all hot and bothered," Karen teased, speaking in a twangy southern drawl.

Caitlyn grinned and shook her head. "TMI, TMI," she said just as Karen took a sip from her Starbucks cup.

"SCAOMK," Karen choked as she spit coffee out of her mouth.

Caitlyn frowned. "I don't think I know that one."

"Uh freaking duh. Spitting-Coffee-All-Over-My-Keyboard," Karen grinned.

Caitlyn shook her head. "You are just too dang funny."

"Thank you. Lord knows I do try," Karen said as she pulled herself together. She sat straight up in her chair and laced her fingers together in front of her. With as serious of an expression that she could muster, she looked at Caitlyn. "Okay, Young Apprentice, tell me why you're really pacing back and forth in front of my desk ole little one with many problems."

"Since you ask. I have a quagmire," Caitlyn laughed.

"SMFH," Karen laughed.

Caitlyn frowned. "Why are you shaking your f-ing head?"

"You have a quagmire? Do you know what that word

means?" Karen laughed.

Caitlyn smiled at Karen. "Of course I know what it means. It's a soft wet area of low-lying land that sinks underfoot."

"Thank you for that definition, little Webster. Now explain to me why you think you are in an area of soft wet low-lying land." Karen held her hand up in the air. "On second thought, I don't wanna know." She tapped her finger on her wristwatch. "We're on the clock here and time is sex. So what's the problem?" she asked.

Caitlyn looked down at her hands. "I've met someone."

Karen slapped her hand on the counter, causing Caitlyn to jump. "Hot damn. It's about time."

"It is?"

Karen laughed. "Hell yes it is. So when's the big day?"

"The big day?" Caitlyn asked, frowning.

Karen shook her head. "Is there an echo in here or do you always talk like a parrot?"

"I don't understand," Caitlyn said.

"I meant when is your date? You know the big day?" Karen asked, her eyebrows rising.

Caitlyn shook her head. "That's just it. I haven't asked them out yet and I'm not sure how to even do it."

Karen shook her head in disbelief. "Why the hell not?" she asked.

Caitlyn shifted nervously from one foot to the other. "Um ... I ... I've never been on a date before."

Karen's eyebrows shot upward in surprise. "No fucking way."

"I'm serious, Karen," Caitlyn said, almost apologetically.

"Wow," was all Karen could manage to say. For the first time in her life, she was actually speechless. She took a deep breath. "So is this person you like fucktastic or fuckalicious?"

Caitlyn busted out laughing. "And you have the audacity to talk about my word usage. Is fucktastic or fuckalicious even a word?"

Karen laughed. "They are now. Seriously though. Do you really like him?"

"Who says it's a him?" Caitlyn asked, her right eyebrow shooting upward.

"Do you really like her?" Karen asked without missing a beat.

"Yes, I really like this person," Caitlyn answered without confirming one way or the other who or what the person was.

Karen pretended to roll her eyes in a dramatic fashion. "Okay, now that we've got that settled. Does this person like you?"

Caitlyn shrugged. "I'm not really sure. I don't even know if they know I exist."

Karen looked Caitlyn up and down in an appreciative, yet seductive manner. "Trust me when I say this. You're gorgeous and you can bet that not only do the men notice you but the women do as well."

"Thank you for saying that. So what do I do now?"

Karen laughed. "Grow some balls and I don't mean literally. Go up to them and just ask them out. If going out for dinner scares you then start small and ask them to let you buy them a coffee or something."

"It's that simple, huh?" Caitlyn asked.

Karen nodded. "Yeah. It really is."

Caitlyn smiled. "Thanks, I think I can do this."

"You'll be fine," Karen said, patting Caitlyn on the hand.

"You know. I can see why Sydney loves you so much," Caitlyn said, nodding her head.

"Yeah and I can see why she loves you as well." Karen picked up a pen and scribbled something on a post-it-note. She held the paper out to Caitlyn.

"What's this?"

"My number in case you wanna join me for a night of mad, freaky, uninhibited blow your mind kinky ass sex," Karen said with a cheesy grin. She laughed at the shocked expression on Caitlyn's face. "I'm just teasing you, honey."

"I knew that," Caitlyn said as she grabbed the pen and wrote her number down.

"Sure you did," Karen said, nodding her head as she took her cell out and added Caitlyn's number to her list of contacts.

"Thanks for the advice. I guess I better head on back to my office. The work isn't going to get done by itself."

"I hear you. I still have two fingernails left to file," Karen said with a wink.

"You're incorrigible and thank you for this," she said as she looked at the number scrawled on the paper.

"Don't mention it and since I know that you now know text jargon, shoot me one or just give me a call if you need to talk."

"I'll do that," Caitlyn said as she finished programming Karen's number into her Blackberry.

"Hey, Caitlyn?"

"Yeah," Caitlyn answered, turning to look back at Karen.

"You can stop by and chat with me anytime as well."

Caitlyn, with a smile on her face walked toward the elevator. She waited as the door slid open. "I can do this," she whispered to herself as she pressed the button for the executive floor.

"Just what the hell do you think you're doing?" Caitlyn asked. She glared at Allen from her open doorway, her hands on her hips.

Allen shoved the desk drawer closed with a bang. "I ... um ... I was looking for the report on the Dem Project," he stuttered as he got up from her chair.

Caitlyn's right eyebrow shot upward.

"You know, for the new recycling plant," he said after a few seconds passed without Caitlyn saying a word.

"I know what it is but that doesn't explain why you were just rummaging through my desk."

"I ... I just thought that since it's a current project that ... that it would be in your desk drawer."

"Well, you're not going to find it there," Caitlyn said as she walked over to the filing cabinet located against the wall, next to her coffee maker. She pulled out the bottom drawer and flipped through the stack of manila folders. She pulled out a file that had a red tab affixed to the top of it. She kicked the drawer shut with the back of her foot as she turned to face Allen.

"Why do you need this folder anyway? I thought Virgil was handling the logistics behind this project with Sydney having the final say."

"Yeah ... yeah he is. I just thought I would take a look at it in case something got overlooked."

"Really?" Caitlyn asked. *Something just isn't adding up here*, she thought to herself as she held the folder out to him.

"Thanks," Allen said as he took the folder from her. "You know what they say here at Welsh? An extra set of eyes on a project never hurt anything," he said as he walked over to the doorway.

"Hey, Allen?"

"Yeah?" he said, stopping to turn and look at Caitlyn.

"The next time you need something from me, try asking me first. I don't appreciate you or anyone for that matter, searching through my desk or being in my office when I'm not here."

"Sorry. It won't happen again."

Caitlyn smiled at him. "I hope not, otherwise Sydney and I will be having a nice conversation about it."

"Have a good day, Caitlyn," Allen said over his shoulder as he left her office.

"Yeah, you do the same," she said to the empty room. Once she was sure that he was gone, she went over to her desk and pulled out the drawer she caught Allen searching through a few minutes earlier. She shook her head as she looked at the stack of papers. "The Project Dem file my butt. Just what were you doing in my office and what were you really looking for Mr. Carmichael?"

She sat down in her chair and glanced around the office. "What are you up to, Allen? Whatever it is—"

The sound of her desk phone buzzing stopped her from finishing her thoughts. She looked at the caller-ID and seeing that it was Sydney, pressed the answer button. "Hey, Syd, what's up?"

"Are you free at the moment?" Sydney asked.

"Yes, ma'am I am."

"I would like for you to join me and Jackie in my office, please."

"I'll be right there," Caitlyn said and then pressed the button to disconnect the line.

Sydney leaned back and stretched her legs out in front of her. She took a sip of her coffee and looked at Jackie over the rim of the cup. A knock on the door caused her to sit up in her chair.

"It's open," Sydney said as she placed her cup down on the desk.

Caitlyn pushed the door open and poked her head in. "What's up, boss?"

"Come on in and close the door behind you, please,"

Sydney said, motioning to Caitlyn with her hand. "Get yourself a cup of coffee, this could take awhile."

Caitlyn's right eyebrow shot upward. "We having a party?" she asked, looking at Jackie and then Sydney.

Sydney tried not to laugh at the characteristic eyebrow thingy that Caitlyn did. She looked just like Rachel when she did that. "I would never have a party without inviting you," Sydney teased. "But to get to the heart of this pow wow, Jackie has some info regarding *our little problem*," Sydney said, making finger quotes in the air for emphasis.

"I have some news of my own concerning the same thing or at least I think there may be a connection," Caitlyn said as she poured herself a cup of coffee and then sat down in the chair beside Jackie.

"Well, let's get this party started then." Sydney looked directly at Jackie. "So, out of all of the executives, you have two who you think may be the most likely to have pulled this off based on the background checks you ran. Is that correct?"

"That would be correct," Jackie said, nodding her head.

"I guess the floor is all yours."

Jackie flipped open the folder lying on her lap. "I'll start with the reports I just received last night and as you said, two in particular stand out."

"I'm not sure that's good news or bad news. I've been secretly hoping you would come up empty," Sydney said, her brow furrowing into a frown.

"Well, at least this way we may be getting one-step closer to finding out who your embezzler is. Either of you care to take a guess which two it is?" Jackie asked, looking at Sydney first and then at Caitlyn.

"I'll guess. One of them wouldn't happen to be Mr. Allen Carmichael by chance?" Caitlyn asked.

Jackie grinned at her. "Give that girl a prize."

Sydney looked at Caitlyn with a mild expression of

shock on her face. "I'm not even gonna ask but I will say this ... you cannot have the red vacuum. I've already won that fair and square," she said, winking at Caitlyn.

"Dang it and I needed a new vacuum worse than anything," Caitlyn laughed.

"How about a brand new shiny silver blender instead?" Sydney asked, causing Caitlyn to chuckle.

Jackie looked at Sydney and then Caitlyn as if the two of them had completely lost their minds. "Am I missing something here?" she asked.

"Just a private little joke," Caitlyn said as she wiped tears from her eyes. "Seriously though, I told you I had some news of my own," she said, looking at Sydney.

Sydney got up from her chair. "I think I need a warm up. Would you like one?" she asked Caitlyn.

"Sure why not. I've only had two pots already this morning. What's one more cup, right?" Caitlyn answered.

"Would you like some, Jackie?"

"No thanks. I'm all coffee'd out." She looked at Caitlyn. "Two pots by yourself?"

"Probably three but who's counting," Caitlyn laughed as she held her cup up for Sydney.

"Who's the other exec?" Sydney asked as she sat back down in her chair.

"The other is Robert VanDersmote," Jackie answered.

Sydney leaned back in her chair and laced her hands over her head. "Okay fill us in about Allen first. What's going on with him?"

"I'll start by saying he likes to play the stock market and he's not very good at it. Actually, he really sucks and he sucks so bad that his house is one month away from foreclosure."

"Are you serious?" Sydney asked. She couldn't believe it. Allen made over a half-million dollars a year just in salary. That didn't include what he took home in bonuses.

Jackie nodded. "Yes ma'am and that's not all. Last

week he applied for a loan at one of Welsh's credit unions."

Sydney leaned forward in her chair. "Which one and for how much?"

"The East Dayton branch and," Jackie flipped through the papers inside the folder and then said, "four hundred grand."

Sydney shook her head as she digested the information. "You think he's so far in debt that he would embezzle from Welsh?"

Jackie shrugged. "The question is do you think he's capable of it."

Sydney looked at Caitlyn. "What do you think?

"Do I think he's capable or do I think he did it?"

"Both," Sydney answered.

"I certainly think he's capable but I really can't say yet as to whether he did it without seeing the proof in black and white. I can tell you without a doubt that he certainly has the programming skills needed to pull it off and if I recall correctly, he graduated at the top of his class."

"Where did he go to school, Jackie?" Sydney asked.

Jackie used her finger to scan down the top document on her lap. "B.A.S from the University of Dayton, Masters degree from Ohio State. He majored in computer programming at U.D. and as Caitlyn stated, he graduated at the top of his class at both colleges."

"All right. What's going on with Robert?" Sydney asked.

"Not quite as drastic as Allen but his financial problems could still be a red-flag. He has a very sick mother he's been caring for financially. She has a rare blood disease and lung cancer on top of that. He's been paying all of her medical bills in addition to covering several trips to Europe over the last year."

"What's in Europe?" Sydney and Caitlyn both asked at the same time.

"They say great minds think alike," Jackie laughed. "To answer you both, experimental medicine is what's in Europe, more specifically, a clinic just outside of London claims to have made a breakthrough in curing the blood disease. Some sort of multi-drug cocktail that's not available here in the states."

"And his education is in what?" Sydney asked.

Jackie pulled out the sheets from the folder she had written up on Robert. "Same as Allen's except his B.A.S. is from Wright State University."

Sydney leaned forward, lacing her fingers together on top of the desk. She took a deep breath. "Just how much in debt is Allen?"

"Almost a million," Jackie answered.

"And Robert?"

"One point six."

"Holy shit," Sydney said, shaking her head. She looked at Caitlyn. "So which of those two would you put your money on?"

"Allen," Caitlyn answered without hesitation.

"Why?" Sydney asked.

"Remember me saying I had some news of my own?" Sydney nodded.

"A few minutes before you called and asked me to join you and Jackie, I caught Allen in my office. He was going through my desk drawers."

"He was doing what?" Sydney asked, not believing what she was hearing.

"You heard me right. He was going through my drawers."

"What did you say to him?" Sydney asked.

"I asked him what the hell he was doing. He gave me some lame excuse about wanting to see the Dem Project files."

"I take it you didn't believe him?" Jackie asked.

Caitlyn shook her head. "Not for a minute. If you

could have seen the look on his face, you wouldn't have believed him either. He was looking for something specific and it wasn't the Dem Project files. I told him that if he ever did it again, I would talk to Sydney about it."

"Do you have the slightest idea of what he was looking for?" Sydney asked.

Caitlyn shook her head. "Not a clue but I will figure it out."

Sydney looked at Jackie. "Are you any closer to tracking down the owner of the checking account where the funds are being dumped?"

"Not as close as I'd like to be. Whoever he is, he's a lot smarter than I thought. The funds have been funneled through several different accounts, ending in the Cayman's."

Sydney sighed in frustration. "I think until we know who this man truly is, it makes it hard to pin anything on Allen or Robert or anyone for that matter."

"I know you're frustrated but we will get this guy," Jackie said.

Sydney stood up from her chair. "Just keep me updated, please."

"I'll keep at it on my end and hopefully I'll have some concrete answers for you soon."

"I sure hope so," Sydney said.

Jackie got up from her chair. She walked over to the door. She stopped, turned, and smiled at Sydney. "Have I ever failed you?"

Sydney smiled and then shook her head. "No you haven't and believe me when I say, I appreciate everything you're doing now and everything you've helped me with in the past."

"I'll catch you gals later."

"See ya," Caitlyn said with a wave of her hand.

Sydney waited for Jackie to close the door. She came out from behind her desk and leaned against it. She crossed her arms over her chest. "All right, out with it."

Caitlyn laughed. "Out with what?"

"You know what. Tell me what you're really thinking about Allen."

"Honestly, I'm not really sure what to think."

"I can see those little wheels turning in your head."

"Seriously, Syd. This whole thing is kinda crazy but I'm willing to bet a year's salary that Allen was looking for something else."

"And I agree with you, so how do we figure out what that *something* is?"

"I'm going to start by running a key log report on his laptop and desktop. I'm guessing that I will be able to find some kind of trail indicating what he's been searching for. Whatever it is, he's obviously convinced that I have it and if I do, I will find out what it is."

Sydney grinned at her. "I have no doubt about that at all." Sydney glanced at her watch. "I'm going to be working at home for the rest of the day so if you need me, that's where I will be."

"Yeah, I heard that you put Mom on a special project to redecorate your house," Caitlyn said, grinning from ear to ear.

Sydney frowned. "She told you?"

"I didn't give her much choice. The duffle bag with blue jeans and a t-shirt in it kind of gave her away."

Sydney's thoughts automatically took a wrong turn as she imagined Rachel wearing a very tight pair of jeans and an extremely snug t-shirt. The image made her smile and she suddenly had an overwhelming urge to get the hell out of there.

"Uh, hello ... earth calling Sydney," Caitlyn said, waving her hand in front of Sydney's face.

Sydney shook her head as if the motion would somehow clear the thoughts from her mind. "I'm sorry. What did you say?" she asked.

"I asked you if it would be okay if I dropped by later?"

"Caitlyn, you don't need an invitation to come to my house. You're always welcome anytime you feel like it."

Caitlyn stood up from her chair. She ran her hands down her slacks. "Thank you, I appreciate that. Hopefully I will have some info about Allen when I come."

"Sounds good. I will see you later than."

Caitlyn walked over to the door. She stopped and turned to look at Sydney. "Tell Mom I said not to do anything I wouldn't do," she said with a wink and then shut the door behind her, leaving Sydney standing there with her mouth hanging open.

"What the hell?" Sydney smiled as she pulled her jacket off the hanger. "Time to face the firing squad," she laughed as she grabbed her keys and laptop bag off the desk.

Chapter 7

Rachel, having changed into a pair of jeans and a t-shirt in spite of the small bruise on her arm, looked around the home theater room. "This is insane," she said as she counted sixteen movie chair recliners.

"You have to admit that watching movies on a screen bigger than a highway billboard is awfully nice," Edna said.

"It's actually incredible," Rachel said as she continued to look around the large room. If she had to guess, she would say that the room measured at least forty-feet long by thirty-feet wide and the viewing screen was almost as wide as the room itself.

The two sidewalls as well as the back wall were completely covered with red-velvet drapes. Hanging on each wall and evenly spaced two-feet apart were lighted movie boxes that contained full size movie posters of various films. At the back of the room was an oak and glass concession stand filled with every type of candy imaginable. Next to the stand was a floor sized popcorn maker and cotton candy machine. On the opposite side of the concession stand was a full service soft-drink fountain machine and hot dog cooker.

"The floor is even carpeted and ramped just like a theater," Rachel said, shaking her head. "My youngest daughter would fall in love with this room."

Edna laughed. "Trust me, quite a few adults would fall in love with it as well."

"My daughter is a huge movie buff, to the point that she can recite the dialogue right along with the characters."

"Sounds like Sydney," Edna chuckled.

"She does that, too?"

Edna nodded. "Sometimes it's maddening."

"Believe me, I know," Rachel laughed as she glanced up at the ceiling.

"Pretty amazing isn't it?" Edna asked as she followed Rachel's eyes.

"That's an understatement," Rachel answered as she looked at the gold-colored octagon shaped boxes that made up the design on the ceiling, giving it the appearance of a giant honeycomb.

"If you like this room, wait until you see the indoor-outdoor pool," Edna said as she headed toward the door.

"Exactly how many rooms does this house have?" Rachel asked as she followed Edna out into the hallway.

Edna used her fingers to count as she mentally calculated the number in her head. "Twenty-three," she finally answered.

"How many of those are bedrooms?"

Edna smiled. "Eight with nine and half baths and that doesn't count the ones in the guest house."

"Good grief. How do you keep from getting lost?"

"It happened often when she first had the house built. I still have days where I get all twisted around."

Rachel let out a deep breath. "I think I need a map."

"Knowing Sydney, she's probably already laid one out for you," Edna said with a chuckle. "Come on, I wanna show you the pool. If you think the home theater room was something else, you'll probably have a heart attack when you see it."

"Maybe I shouldn't see it then," Rachel laughed.

"I think you're gonna love it," Edna said as she headed down the hallway and through an open archway that led down another long hallway. She stopped next to a marble column and waited for Rachel. "After you," she said, motioning with her hand for Rachel to go first.

Rachel's mouth gaped open as she stepped into the

pool room. In all of her life, she had never seen anything like what she was now looking at.

Edna looked at Rachel and laughed. "I take it I was right?"

"You were more than right. It's beautiful," Rachel said as she continued to look around the room. The back wall surrounding the kidney-shaped pool was rounded and looked like what you would see in a Greek coliseum. Large marble columns, interlaced with tiny flecks of gold leaf overlays were spaced every four feet and were connected to each other by scalloped archways, which sat directly atop the column. Sitting inside the archways were floor to ceiling windows that offered an exquisite view of the back area of the property, which included a huge lake.

The sidewalls were covered with murals of mountains and the ceiling was painted to resemble a crystal blue sky with clouds so white, they looked like cotton candy. The scenes created were so realistic that Rachel felt as if she were standing in the hills of Tennessee.

Her eyes settled on the pool itself. It was recessed into the floor with one-foot high blond-colored Italian pavers circling it. At the small end of the pool were stacks of various types of rock formations that were shaped to resemble the side of a mountain. All throughout the spacing between the rocks, water seeped out, running back down into the pool, giving it the appearance of natural flowing springs. To the right of the rock formations was a spiral slide that ended next to a large glass window that with a push of a button, rose to allow access to the outdoor pool on the other side of the wall.

The outdoor pool was almost as spectacular as the one on the inside and was a continuation of the rock formation theme. The main difference between the two pools was that the one on the outside also included a low and high set of diving boards.

"Simply incredible," Rachel said, shaking her head.

"Just wait until you see it at night when it's all lit up," Edna said as she linked her arm through Rachel's arm.

"I can only imagine," Rachel said as she allowed Edna to lead her out of the room.

"How about we go check out that new design room of yours?" Edna asked.

Rachel smiled at her. "I'd like that very much, thank you."

Sydney stopped at Karen's desk. She waited patiently for her to finish her phone conversation.

Karen disconnected the line and pulled the head set off and laid it on the desk. She smiled at Sydney. "And what can I do for you my wonderful, charming employer who has the sun set and rise in her eyes every morning of her esteemed life?"

Sydney laughed as she shook her head. "Just when I think you can't shock me any further, you—"

"What do you mean further?" Karen asked, interrupting Sydney before she could finish the sentence.

"Have you ever thought about going into the theater?" Sydney asked.

Karen smiled. "Of course, I make it a regular habit of seeing at least one movie per week. As a matter of fact I saw a classic just this week."

Sydney ran her fingers through her hair and then laughed. "You are a classic and you're in a world all of your own."

"Okay now that we've got that all cleared up, my illustrious supreme employer, is there something I can help you with?" Karen asked with a crooked grin on her face.

"You got me so damn flustered that I can't even remember why I stopped here to begin with," Sydney said, shaking her head.

Karen batted her eyes dramatically. "Yeah, I heard that I had that kind of effect on people."

"I swear you are so not right," Sydney said and she believed it to be true. Karen was in another world all by herself but that was a good thing.

Karen looked at the laptop bag slung over Sydney's shoulder and the car keys in her hand. "Um ... are you by chance leaving for the day?" she asked.

"As a matter of fact I am and if you could find the time in your busy schedule, please forward all of my calls to my home office."

"I will try my best to fit you in," Karen said, giving a mock salute with her hand.

"You do that and I'll see you tomorrow," Sydney said with a wave of her hand.

"How did she manage all of this so quickly?" Rachel asked as she looked around the design room that Sydney had set up for her.

"She's very resourceful when she has the right incentive," Edna replied.

"So I've noticed," Rachel said as she pulled out the high-backed stool sitting in front of the drafting table. She looked at the blueprint lying in front of her. It was a complete layout of the entire house.

"What did I tell you?" Edna asked. She was standing next to a large oak desk that had a computer monitor and color laser-jet printer sitting on it. She picked up a piece of paper lying on the keyboard, brought it over, and handed it to Rachel.

Rachel shook her head and laughed as she looked at it. It was a miniature map of the house. "I'd say you know her pretty well."

"Yeah, I guess I do but then again, she's quite predictable when it comes to certain things," Edna said with a wink.

"How long have you worked for Sydney?" Rachel asked. She hated to admit it but her curiosity was starting to get the better of her.

Edna thought about it for a few seconds. "Going on twelve and a half years now, I'd say, give or take a couple months."

Rachel's mind whirled as she calculated the timeframe in her head. *It must have not been long after Sydney and I went our separate ways. Just what have you been doing with yourself all these years Sydney Welsh, other than trying to take over the world and romancing beautiful women,* she thought to herself.

"Well, if you don't need anything else from me for awhile, I'll let you get settled in," Edna said, snapping Rachel from her thoughts.

Rachel smiled. "Thank you for the tour and especially for your company. I really enjoyed it."

"Flattery will get you everywhere," Edna chuckled. "And I enjoyed your company just as much. It was a nice change from Fred Rick's ramblin'. "

Rachel frowned. "Who's Fred Rick?"

"Our flamboyant chef," Edna laughed. "Oh just you wait. You're in for a real treat when you meet that one."

Rachel smiled. "Well, if he's half as nice as you, then I think I will like him very much."

"Like who very much?" Sydney asked as she came into the room.

Rachel looked up in surprise and then felt her breath unexpectedly catch in her throat.

Edna looked at Sydney and grinned. "Your chef, that's who she thinks she's gonna like very much."

Sydney met Rachel's gaze for the first time since walking into the room. For several seconds they just stared at each other, both seemingly unable to break the eye contact.

Edna cleared her throat. "If you two need me, you know where I'll be."

Rachel, feeling slightly embarrassed looked down at her hands.

Sydney glanced at her watch. She smiled as she turned to look at Edna. "Yeah, you'll be kicked back in a recliner getting ready for your soaps."

Edna shrugged. "A girls gotta do what a girl's gotta do when it comes to romance and when you get to be my age, you'll understand."

Sydney shook her head. "I've been telling you for years that stuff's gonna rot your brains out."

"So that's where they went," Edna laughed and Rachel, unable to control herself, laughed too.

"Now look at what you've gone and done? She's only been here for a few hours and you're already corrupting Rachel," Sydney teased.

"Ciao," Edna said as she sashayed out of the room.

"She's really something else," Rachel said.

"She's something else all right. What that something else is, still remains to be seen," Sydney said, trying her best not to laugh.

"You kind of outdid yourself here, didn't you?" Rachel asked, making a sweeping gesture with her hand around the room.

Sydney shrugged. "I just wanted to make sure you had everything you might need."

"Well, you definitely did that," Rachel said, looking Sydney in the eye. If she didn't know any better, she could swear she saw Sydney's eyes sparkle.

"If you can give me a few minutes, I need to go change out of my monkey suit and then we can sit down and discuss the changes I would like done."

"Yeah, that's fine. I'll be right here waiting for you to

get back," Rachel said, her voice tinged with slight sarcasm.

The narrowing of Sydney's eyes as she looked at Rachel indicated that the sarcasm hadn't been lost on her either. Sydney's gaze shifted to look out the window directly over Rachel's right shoulder. She was silent for several seconds. "I'll be right back," she said finally. She glanced at Rachel for a split-second and then left the room.

Rachel hadn't realized that she had been holding her breath until she let it out. "How am I going to do this? How can I possibly be around her on a constant basis for the next few weeks? One minute I want to rip her head off and the next minute my thoughts turn to just how attractive she still is. I had no idea how damn sexy a pinstriped suit could look," she whispered aloud without meaning to. No, no, no she chastised herself. I can't have thoughts like this. "Business, stick to business, Rachel, because that's all this is. That's all it can or ever will be where she's concerned," she mumbled under her breath.

"I see you still have a habit of talking to yourself," Sydney said, startling Rachel.

"Yes, I still talk to myself. Do you have a problem with that?" Rachel asked. Her words came out sounding harsher than she intended because her mind had suddenly taken a wrong turn—a very wrong turn.

Try as she might she couldn't help notice that Sydney had changed into a tight pair of black jeans that did little to hide the curve of her hips and the low cut t-shirt revealed more cleavage than what should be allowed by law.

"Down girl," Sydney laughed as she walked further into the room and stopped less than a foot away from Rachel.

"And would you ... would you please not invade my space," Rachel said, taking a step backward only to have her progress stopped by the drafting table.

"Am I making you uncomfortable?" Sydney asked, her voice sounding husky to her own ears as she moved closer.

Her eyes fell to Rachel's breast, traveling upward to her neck. She watched the pulse point in Rachel's neck as it beat rapidly. Her eyes continued their path up Rachel's neck, stopping on her mouth. She unconsciously licked her lips, her mouth suddenly dry. Right now, the only thing Sydney could think about was kissing Rachel and by the look in Rachel's eyes, she knew she was thinking the same thing.

Rachel tried to move further back but there was nowhere to go. Sydney moved closer, their thighs and breasts touching. Sydney leaned in, her lips just below Rachel's ear. "Mmm, you smell so good," she whispered, her breath caressing Rachel's skin like satin.

Rachel placed her trembling hands on Sydney's chest. She knew that if she didn't move away, she was about to do something she was going to regret. "You know darn well what you're doing," she said, her voice shaking as she pushed Sydney away.

Sydney threw her head back and laughed. The move only served to make Rachel angrier. Sydney had switched gears so fast, it made Rachel's head spin. "I'm glad you think it's so funny," she said in a stern voice.

"Not at all. So let's get down to business then, shall we?" Sydney asked as she moved away and pulled out the extra stool tucked under the drafting table and sat down.

Rachel glanced at Sydney before sliding her own chair over. She sat down, taking extra care to make sure there was enough space between the two chairs so their legs wouldn't touch.

Sydney picked up a red line pencil and proceeded to make circles around the family room, dining room, office, and her bedroom. These are the rooms I want changed first," she said as she laid the pencil down on the table.

Rachel turned slightly in her chair so that she could look directly at Sydney. "May I ask you a question?"

Sydney leaned her head on her hand as she looked at

Rachel. "You can ask but I can't guarantee I will answer."

"Edna gave me a tour of your house and for the life of me, I can't figure out why you want to change it."

"Is there a question somewhere in there?" Sydney asked, the corner of her lips curving into a slight grin.

Rachel's right eyebrow shot upward and Sydney laughed.

"I was getting to the question and why are you laughing at me?" Rachel asked.

Sydney leaned back in her chair and crossed her arms over her chest. "I'm not really laughing at you. I was grinning because after all these years, you still do that quirky little eyebrow thingy when you get annoyed or angry."

Rachel looked at Sydney with what she thought was her best glare. "Well, if I have to be around you for the next several weeks, I suggest you better get used to it," she said.

Sydney clutched the area of her chest where her heart was. "I'm so heartbroken now, Rache. Are you trying to make me cry?"

"Don't you have to have one first in order for it to get broken?" Rachel asked and immediately regretted it. For a brief instant, she thought she saw a flicker of pain flash in Sydney's eyes and then it was gone faster than it had come.

Sydney cleared her throat. "So what was the question you wanted to ask me?"

"I would like to know why you want these design changes."

Sydney thought about it for several seconds. There was no way she could tell Rachel the complete truth. "Because so many things in my life have changed lately and I figure why stop now." She shrugged. "If I have to go through changes, my house should too."

Rachel looked at her through narrow eyes. "Why do I get the feeling there's more to it than that?"

Sydney shrugged. "I don't know why you have that feeling. Maybe it's just indigestion."

"I'm serious, Sydney," Rachel said, an annoyed expression on her face.

"Okay, I'll tell you why. Meredith did all of the decorating and for the most part, I've always hated it, especially what she did to my office and bedroom. She used dark woods, like walnut and cherry and maple and it's just too damn depressing." Although this was a partial truth, she waited, hoping this explanation was enough to satisfy Rachel's curiosity.

She breathed a silent sigh of relief when Rachel turned to look at the blueprint.

"All right, which room would you like for me to tackle first?" Rachel asked.

Sydney shrugged, shaking her head at the same time. "I honestly don't care. You're the designer so you decide what room to do first."

"Can you at least tell me what colors you have in mind?" Rachel asked in exasperation. Sydney was getting on her nerves and the worst part was that she seemed to be enjoying it.

Sydney laughed. "Nothing dark."

"You're not gonna make this easy on me, are you?" Rachel growled as she ran her fingers through her hair in frustration.

Sydney did a double take. *That is one of the sexiest things I've ever seen and heard at the same time,* she thought as she continued to watch Rachel. Without meaning to, her eyes settled on Rachel's lips before moving back up to her eyes.

Rachel slid her stool back away from the table. "I need colors, Sydney, you know, like blue, green, orange, etcetera, etcetera."

"All right but no orange and it's already decorated in blues. I want something different." Sydney was quiet for several seconds as she thought about it. "How about, mauve, burgundy, cream, and maybe forest or hunter green mixed with some tans?"

Rachel smiled and Sydney felt her heart skip a beat. "Now that's something I can work with. I love those color schemes," she said, nodding her head.

"Good. I just don't want any dark browns or blacks though and absolutely no reds. I hate red."

Rachel looked down at the red t-shirt she was wearing and laughed. "I guess I should probably go change my shirt, huh?"

"Or ... you could just take it off," Sydney said in a nonchalant manner. She felt her skin tingle as she pictured what Rachel would look like sitting there, wearing nothing but a pair of jeans.

Rachel leaned back in her chair. She tapped her index finger against her chin. "You know, I don't remember you ever being this um ... what's the word I'm looking for?"

"I have no idea," Sydney laughed.

"Brazen, arrogant, obnoxious, egotistical, maddening, and—"

Sydney held her hand up in the air. "Okay, you can stop anytime. I get the picture and that was more than one word."

"This isn't getting us anywhere," Rachel sighed.

Sydney slammed her hands on the table so hard, it made Rachel jump. "You know what? You're right, absolutely right." She got off her stool, walked over to the desk, and flipped the power ON button to the computer and dropped down in the chair. She turned and looked at Rachel. "Have you seen this little baby yet?" she asked.

"No, I haven't got that far," Rachel said, shaking her head.

"I think you're really gonna love what Caitlyn and her group has done to EMCOR's design software."

"I can only imagine," Rachel said, her expression softening at the mention of her daughter's name.

"Have a seat," Sydney said, motioning to the chair beside her.

Rachel pulled out the chair and sat down. She quickly jerked her leg back when it accidently touched against Sydney's leg.

Sydney laughed. "I won't bite, you know."

"I'm not so sure about that," Rachel said as she folded her hands in her lap.

Once the computer was fully booted, Sydney clicked on an icon that was shaped like a door. She moved the mouse around, making several clicks through various screens. "Check this out," Sydney said as she opened the file titled, *Sydney's House*.

Rachel looked at the computer monitor and smiled. On the screen in 3D was a picture of Sydney's house. "I can't wait to see how it looks on the inside."

"You're gonna love it," Sydney said and clicked an icon on the left that said "Family Room."

"Amazing," Rachel said as a 3D view of Sydney's family room came into view. What made it incredible was that the picture displayed looked like it had been shot from a 35-millimeter camera in real-time.

"See this little directional arrow icon here," Sydney said and tapped the screen with the tip of her fingernail.

Rachel nodded.

"Watch this," Sydney said and clicked the down arrow. As she did, a circle appeared and as she slowly dragged her mouse pointer over it, the view of the room rotated. "Now check this out." She clicked the mouse on the curtains hanging on the window next to the fireplace. A small popup box opened and gave a list of ten different types of curtains. She selected the one called "Crisscross" and as she did, the "Balloon Valance" curtains were replaced with ones that she had selected.

"Oh my," Rachel exclaimed.

Sydney laughed. "And if you want to change the color,

just right click and a whole palette will open up for you."

"Can I try?" Rachel asked and without waiting for an answer, slid her chair closer to Sydney. She was so excited she didn't realize that her leg was fully pressed up against Sydney's but Sydney sure noticed.

"Have at it," Sydney said, sliding the mouse over to Rachel. She watched as Rachel excitedly changed colors and then added stripes to the Crisscross curtains. She then clicked on several of the other rooms, playing around with the software.

Rachel leaned back in her chair and smiled at Sydney. "Do you have any idea how groundbreaking this software is? This will save designers thousands of dollars just in time wasted alone, which will save our customers money in the end."

"Yeah, I think I do realize it and not only will it be used at EMCOR, we will be designing an additional package that we'll market and license to our competitors for a substantial profit."

"I have to admit that I'm impressed. Where did you come up with the idea to do this?" Rachel asked.

Sydney leaned back in her chair and laced her hands behind her head. "Your daughter."

"Caitlyn did this?" Rachel asked as she continued to play with the software.

"Yes, ma'am she did, along with her team of programmers and *you* are our very first user."

"This is really something else, Sydney," Rachel said, shaking her head.

"I would like for you to keep a few things in mind when you're testing it."

Rachel turned in her chair to look at Sydney. "Like what?"

"Like bugs or problems that you see, things that you feel would make it better or if you think we need to offer more choices such as the amount of curtains or fabrics, etcetera."

Rachel grabbed the mouse and clicked on the couch in the family room. She right clicked it again and a popup box opened that listed several fabric types to choose from. "I can change the fabric, the carpet, the wallpaper. You name it and I can change it."

Rachel was like a kid in a candy store and it made Sydney smile. "Anything that is clickable in the picture, you can make changes to it too, even the paintings on the wall."

Rachel looked at her. "Where did you get the idea to create something like this?"

"I told you it was Caitlyn's idea," Sydney said with a grin.

Rachel laughed. "I know that much but where did she get the idea?"

"From her beautician," Sydney chuckled and then waited for Rachel's reaction.

Rachel's right eyebrow shot upward. "Are you serious?"

Sydney nodded. "Yes, ma'am I am."

"Dare I ask why?" Rachel asked.

"Why she goes to the beautician?" Sydney laughed.

"No silly, you know what I mean," she said and playfully shoved Sydney.

Damn she's beautiful when she smiles like that, Sydney thought as she looked at Rachel. Stop thinking like this, she silently scolded herself. "Have you ever seen those fancy programs they use where they take a picture of you and then give you a list of different hairstyles and with a click of the mouse, you can add it to your face to see how it would look on you?"

Rachel thought about it for a second. "Yeah, I've seen them but never used one."

"Well that's how Caitlyn got the idea. She thought that maybe we could take the design software that EMCOR uses, make some major programming changes, and put the Welsh spin on it," Sydney said. The look of pride on her face was evident.

"She really is something else, isn't she?" Rachel asked.

Sydney pushed her chair back and stood up. "I can honestly say I have never met anyone like her. She is more talented than almost all of the people I have working for me put together."

Rachel leaned back in her chair. "You really like her, don't you?"

"Yeah, I do," Sydney said, nodding her head. "Listen, I have a few things I need to do so I'm gonna get out of your hair for awhile and let you get to it."

"Okay, I think I'm going to play around with this a bit if you don't mind."

"Take your time, there's no hurry," Sydney said.

"Once I get comfortable with it, I'll start making changes based on your new color schemes. As for the time it takes, I think you may have just shortened my stay here by several days." Rachel said the words and for reasons she couldn't explain, the thought of shortening her time with Sydney suddenly bothered her.

Sydney walked over to the doorway. She turned and looked back at Rachel. "Maybe I should take the computer away then." She left before Rachel had a chance to respond.

Rachel looked at the empty doorway. After all these years, the woman still had a way of getting under her skin. "Okay, time to get to work," she said as she pushed the chair back away from the desk.

Meredith snapped the lid shut on her compact case and crammed it in the side of her purse. She used her key and unlocked the front door. "Where are you my darling?" she whispered as she stepped into the foyer. She pulled her key out of the door and then pushed it closed. She walked across the foyer toward the family room as if she owned the place.

"If I were you, where would I be right now?" she mumbled under her breath. She smiled as she crossed the family room and headed down the hallway toward the downstairs bedroom.

She stopped in the open doorway. Sydney stood in front of the dresser with her back facing Meredith. "I thought I might find you here," she said, seductively.

Sydney whirled around, her face registering shock as she looked at Meredith. "What are you doing here? How did you get in?" Sydney asked, not bothering to keep the annoyance out of her voice.

Meredith made a pouty face with her mouth. "What? No hi honey, good to see you, I've missed you?"

"I've missed you like I'd miss an extra hole in my head," Sydney said with a straight face.

"Aw, babe, you don't really mean that," Meredith said as she moved stealthily across the room. She was in front of Sydney and had wrapped her arms around Sydney's waist before she even had time to realize what had happened.

"Don't, Meredith," Sydney said, placing her hands on Meredith's shoulders.

"I know you miss me and I know you missed this," Meredith said as her hand slid upward, her fingers closing over Sydney's right breast.

"Stop," Sydney growled as she grabbed Meredith's hand. "I want—"

"Oh, I am so sorry," Rachel said from the doorway, a look of embarrassment on her face.

"Damn it," Sydney swore under her breath as she met Rachel's gaze.

"I didn't mean to interrupt," Rachel said, as she held eye contact with Sydney.

"I don't think we've met. I'm Meredith," Meredith said in a syrupy sweet voice as she walked over to Rachel and held out her hand.

"It's nice to meet you, I'm Rachel Ashburn," Rachel said as she shook Meredith's hand.

"Meredith was just leaving," Sydney said.

"Not on my account, I hope," she said looking at Sydney. "I just came in to see if you had a preference as to how many shades of mauve I used in the family room." She turned and looked at Meredith and then in a sweet voice said, "Have a good day." She looked at Sydney, winked, turned, and left the room.

Sydney stood there, her mouth gaping open. *What the hell was that all about?*

"So that's *thee* Ms. Rachel," Meredith said, interrupting her thoughts.

"Huh? What did you say?" Sydney asked. She was still trying to figure out the little word play thingy that Rachel had just used.

"I see what you're doing, Sydney. So you think you still have a shot with that frigid Catholic bitch after all these years?" Meredith snarled, a snotty look on her face.

Sydney looked at her with mild disbelief. How did she put that together so quickly.

"Don't look so shocked, sweetheart. Yeah, I remember you telling me about Rachel and how she broke your little ole heart."

"I don't know what you're talking about and even if I did, I don't give a damn what you think and it's none of your business anyway," Sydney said, her voice shaking with anger. She held out her hand to Meredith.

"What?" Meredith asked.

"You know what. Give me the key," Sydney said through clenched teeth.

Meredith's expression softened. "Come on, babe. Just give me one more chance. Please?"

"Give me the key," Sydney said, motioning with her outstretched fingers.

Meredith pulled her key ring out of her purse. She removed a gold colored key and handed it to Sydney. "You're going to regret this, Sydney Welsh," she said over her shoulder as she left the room.

"I already do," Sydney whispered as she laid the key on the dresser.

"So that's Meredith," Rachel mumbled to herself as she sat down at the desk. She tapped her nails on the keyboard, staring blankly at the screen. From the look of things, it sure seemed as if she and Sydney weren't quite as split as what the media was leading everyone to believe.

She continued to talk to herself as she used the mouse to open the design software. "She's very beautiful. I can see how Sydney would be attracted to her if trashy was what she was going for." *Why do you care,* a little voice inside of her head asked? "I don't care. Not really." *Sure you don't. Then why is it bothering you so much?* the little voice asked. "I have no idea but I need to get my thoughts off of her and focus on the job that I have to do here so I can be done with it and her once and for all."

"Who are you talking to?"

The sound of Sydney's voice caused Rachel to jump. "I'm sorry. I was just talking to myself again. I guess that's a habit I will probably never break," Rachel said, shrugging her shoulders.

Sydney chuckled. "I do it too and I personally think that sometimes it's the most intelligent conversation I have all day."

Rachel laughed. "Yeah, I guess so."

"I just wanted to stop by and check to see how things were going."

"Just getting started but I think I can get quite a bit of work done today before I leave," Rachel said.

Sydney leaned against the door jam. "As for the mauve's, use whatever combinations you think will look good. I've got some other things I need to work on but if you need anything, Edna can help you out."

"Okay, thank you," Rachel said as she turned away and began making selections on the monitor.

Sydney pulled her truck into the garage, shut off the engine, and popped the hood. She slid out of the driver's seat and walked over to her workbench. She grabbed a toolbox and several packages of spark plugs.

Just as she pushed the hood up on the truck, Jackie walked in carrying a cup of coffee in her hand. Tucked under her other arm was a manila envelope.

Sydney grinned at her. "Well, look what the cat drug in."

"Good to see you, too," Jackie laughed. "Doing a little car repair?"

"Yeah, she needs a tune-up after my last road trip. Some new spark plugs, air filter, oil change, you know, the regular stuff," Sydney said as she took the new spark plugs out of their packages. "You got something for me?" she asked as she rooted around in the toolbox.

"I sure do," Jackie said as she pulled the envelope out from under her arm and opened it.

Sydney pulled out a ratchet and several sockets. "Damn I'm good," she laughed as the first socket she tried slipped easily onto the end of the new sparkplug.

Jackie laughed. "Yeah, right, I know that you knew exactly which socket would fit."

Sydney waggled her eyebrows. "Mayhaps, mayhaps not."

"Exactly what does mayhaps mean?"

Sydney frowned. "How can you not know what that means?"

Jackie shrugged and then laughed. "Just dense, I guess."

"It's a cross between a maybe and perhaps. You know, mayhaps," Sydney said as she took a gapping gauge and set the gap on the sparkplugs.

"Whatever floats your boat," Jackie snickered as she pulled several sheets out of the envelope.

Sydney stopped what she was doing to give Jackie her full attention. She leaned back against the side of the truck and crossed her arms over her chest.

"I got the information back on Ashburn's prints. His real name is Martin Hollis and you're not going to believe this, but he used to be a real estate mogul."

Sydney's look was incredulous. "You're kidding?"

"It gets better, Syd. He was the main money launderer for the Med—" Jackie stopped in mid-sentence, her eyes looking toward the open door.

"Hey, there you are," Caitlyn said as she stepped into the garage. "Edna said I would probably find you out ..." She stopped when she noticed Jackie, her gaze dropped to the papers in Jackie's hand. "I'm sorry to interrupt. I didn't know you had company."

"It's okay. We were just finishing," Sydney laughed.

"Hi, Caitlyn. How are you?" Jackie asked as she slid the papers back inside the envelope.

Caitlyn smiled. "Hi, Jackie. I'm just peachy."

"I will call you later," Jackie said, looking at Sydney.

Sydney glanced at her watch. "I should be free anytime after six if you're available."

"Sounds good. See you ladies later," Jackie said as she left the garage.

Sydney grinned at Caitlyn. "So, what do I owe for the pleasure of your company?"

"A year's pay," Caitlyn laughed.

"Sounds reasonable," Sydney said with a shrug.

"Seriously, I was wondering if we could talk and not as boss and employee."

"Okay, do you mind if I work while we talk?" Sydney asked as she slipped on a pair of latex gloves.

"Not at all," Caitlyn said as she walked over to the front of the truck and looked at the engine.

I'm all ears," Sydney said as she pulled off a spark plug wire and then slipped the socket onto the sparkplug.

"What's going on with you and my mom?" Caitlyn asked.

Sydney stopped what she was doing and looked at Caitlyn. She decided to play dumb. "I don't know what you mean."

Caitlyn's right eyebrow shot upward. "You don't, huh?"

Sydney made several more turns with the ratchet and then pulled out the old spark plug.

"Let me try a different approach then," Caitlyn said as she handed Sydney a new sparkplug. "Do you think I'm stupid?"

Sydney looked up at her in surprise. "Of course not. What kind of a question is that?"

"About as stupid of a question as you telling me that you don't know what I mean."

Sydney laughed. "Touché."

"I may have been young but I remember you, Sydney."

This time Sydney was unable to hide the shock on her face. She should have known that with Caitlyn's intelligence and her near photographic memory, there was a better than good chance that she would remember things that most kids her age wouldn't. "What exactly do you remember?" she asked as she laid the ratchet down on the engine.

"I remember that you were there and then you were suddenly gone and that Mom has never been the same since. She thinks I don't know and that I don't remember but it's hard to forget when you see the light go out of your mom's eyes."

"Wow," was all Sydney could say. She had no idea that Caitlyn was this perceptive and not giving it a second thought had been a major mistake on her part. She shook her head as she looked at Caitlyn. "Are you telling me that when you first met me, that when you joined Welsh, you remembered me then?"

"Of course," Caitlyn said nonchalantly as if it she had just been asked if she liked flowers.

Sydney was still trying to wrap her mind around this information. To say she was shocked was an understatement. "Then why haven't you said anything after all of this time?"

Caitlyn laughed. "Because I was patiently waiting and hoping you or Mom would say something but I have finally come to the conclusion that I will be eighty-years-old before that happens."

Sydney grinned. "You may have been right about that." She shook her head again as she looked at Caitlyn. All these years and Caitlyn had known all along who she was—incredible. "So what made you bring this up now?" she asked.

"Honestly? It was Mom's reaction to you buying out EMCOR, although I did think that the two of you looked a little cozy in your kitchen the night of the Christmas Party."

"I hadn't seen her in thirteen years until that night," Sydney said, her voice just above a whisper.

"What happened? Please tell me what was going on with you and my mom."

Sydney didn't want to answer her. She wanted to tell her that it was none of her business but the look of genuine concern on Caitlyn's face prevented her from doing just that.

"You loved her, didn't you?" Caitlyn asked.

Sydney could only nod her head. She was afraid that if she opened her mouth, the stinging behind her eyes would send tears spilling down her cheeks.

"And she loved you, too." Caitlyn said it as a statement and not a question.

"Yeah, she did," Sydney said with a nod of her head.

"Were you in love with her?"

Sydney smiled. "More than you could ever imagine."

Caitlyn frowned. "Then, I don't understand. If she loved you and you loved her, what happened between you?"

Sydney replaced the spark plug wire and pulled off the next one in line. "I don't think it's my place to tell you that. I think that maybe you should be asking your mom these questions."

"I'm not a child, Sydney, and although you're my boss, I like to think that you're my friend as well."

As Sydney thought about what to say in response, she removed the spark plug and tossed it in the trashcan. "I am your friend and I'm glad you think of me that way, too. I will tell you this much. Your mother and I were very much in love with each other but nothing ever happened between us."

"You mean in the biblical sense?" Caitlyn asked, her eyebrow raising in surprise.

Sydney laughed. "Yes, that's what I mean."

Caitlyn leaned back up against the front of the truck. "Why not?"

"Has anyone ever told you that you ask an awful lot of

questions?" Sydney asked.

"Yeah, you have. So why not?" Caitlyn wasn't going to let up.

"Because your mom made a choice and that choice was her choosing the church and her beliefs over me and us and that's all I'm going to say. If you wanna know more of your mom's reasons behind it, then you're going to have to ask her yourself."

"It was Grandmother and Grandfather. They were behind it, weren't they?" Caitlyn groaned.

"Ah, my two favorite people, Roberta and Lou or as I like to call them, Cruella and Deville. Lovely people," Sydney said in a voice filled with sarcasm and then regretted it. "I'm sorry, Caitlyn. I shouldn't have said that about your grandparents."

"Oh no. I think you know them pretty well. Everyone knows how whacked they are with their activism. I don't know if you saw the big protest up in D.C. two weeks ago. It was all over the news."

"Was that the one where the Catholic Church was protesting contraceptives for women?" Sydney asked, thinking she did see something in the paper about it.

Caitlyn laughed. "Yep. That's the one. Well, Roberta and Lou were both arrested for trespassing."

"So, after all these years, Cruella is still at it, huh?" Sydney asked.

"I think she gets worse the older she gets, if that's even possible. You want to know what I did to her for fun?" Caitlyn asked, a grin on her face.

"Do tell." Sydney smiled. "This should be good."

"Oh, it is. I told grandmother that I was a dyslexic insomniac agnostic and that I lay awake in bed at night wondering if there really is a Dog," Caitlyn said with a straight face but then she busted out laughing.

"No, you didn't," Sydney managed to say between fits of laughter.

"Yes I did and if you could have seen the look on her face," Caitlyn said as she wiped tears off of her cheeks.

Sydney laughed. "I bet it was priceless. I would love to have seen it for myself."

Caitlyn cleared her throat as she pulled herself together. "I do have something else I would like to talk to you about and it has nothing to do with you and mom," she quickly clarified when she saw the worried look on Sydney's face. "This is about me."

"Oh thank Dog," Sydney laughed as she pretended to wipe sweat off of her forehead.

"Thank Dog, huh?" Caitlyn asked as she fought to keep her laughter in check. "It was pretty funny. Okay we have to stop or I will never get this out," she said as she held her sides from laughing so hard. "Seriously though. I've met someone."

"Woo hoo," Sydney yelled, much to Caitlyn's surprise.

Caitlyn frowned. "You act like I never date."

"Um ... cause you don't," Sydney laughed.

Caitlyn looked at Sydney with a mischievous grin. "Then I guess it's time I started."

"So, who's this lucky fellow? What's his name and where did you meet him?" Sydney asked.

"The lucky fellow is Natalie and she works in the shipping department at EMCOR," Caitlyn said and then waited for Sydney's reaction.

Sydney shook her head as if she hadn't heard right. "Um ... uh ..."

"Wow. I left you speechless for a change and yes, you did hear me say her name was Natalie," Caitlyn said as if she could read Sydney's thoughts.

Sydney laid the ratchet down. "Are you telling me that you're a lesbian?"

Caitlyn laughed. "Yes, Sydney, I am a lesbian and I know I've been one all my life."

"I'm sorry. I don't know what to say. I think I'm still

in shock," Sydney said, shaking her head.

"Your gaydar must really suck," Caitlyn laughed as she handed Sydney a new sparkplug.

"It must suck badly," Sydney grinned as she picked up the ratchet and proceeded to remove another sparkplug.

Caitlyn nodded at the engine. "You know, at this rate, it's going to take you ten hours just to change the sparkplugs."

"You're telling me. For some reason, people keep interrupting my progress," Sydney laughed. "So, have you told your mom yet?"

"No, but I plan on it and soon. Like real soon."

"So tell me about Natalie. Are you two dating?" Sydney asked as she tightened the new plug and then replaced the plug wire.

"Um ... we've never been on a date."

Sydney's eyebrows rose in surprise. "Are you planning on going on a date?"

"I'm not sure. I mean I don't know yet," Caitlyn said, grimacing.

Sydney grinned. "You haven't asked her out yet?"

Caitlyn shook her head. "I don't even know if she likes me but I'm planning on asking her out tomorrow."

"You'll be fine. Just take a deep breath and jump in with both feet and be sure to let me know how it goes," Sydney said as she moved over to the opposite side of the engine and jerked off the plug wire.

Caitlyn handed Sydney a new plug. "I think I'm going to talk to Mom tonight."

"Yep, that's pretty soon. I would love to be a fly on the wall just to see her face," Sydney said as she inserted the new plug.

"Yeah, I hope she doesn't react like two of my friend's mom did."

Sydney looked up at Caitlyn. "And what would that be?" she asked.

Caitlyn threw both of her arms up in the air. "Oh God no, why me?" she yelled in a high-pitched voice as she ran around in a circle. "Oh dear God in heaven ... Where did I go wrong ... Oh why, Lord," Caitlyn shrieked as she grabbed her hair with both hands.

Sydney was laughing so hard she thought she might break a rib. "They really did that?" she asked in disbelief.

Caitlyn nodded. "Oh yeah and to hear them tell it, you would have thought the world had come to an end."

"I don't think your mom will be that extreme."

"I sure hope not because I won't be able to keep a straight face, no pun intended," Caitlyn laughed.

"How is your mom really doing?" Sydney asked the question she had been wondering about for a while now.

"Sometimes I think she's okay and at other times, I know she's not. She and Edward fight a lot. I don't think she's had a truly peaceful day in years and that makes me angry. Edward is a drunk. I think you've probably figured that out by now, too.

Sydney nodded. "I figured as much. Is that why you spend so much time at work?"

It was Caitlyn's turn to nod. "I like to be home in the evenings when Alyssa and Mom are home because I know Edward won't hit Mom in front of us."

"Gotta love a man with manners," Sydney said, sarcastically.

"He thinks I'm stupid, like I don't know that he's physically hurt my mom." Caitlyn snorted. "I mean seriously, how many times can a person fall down the steps or run into things?"

Sydney felt the heat rise in her neck and face as she thought about Edward hitting Rachel. She wanted to kill him. She could tell by the look in Caitlyn's eyes that she had similar thoughts. "Not to change the subject but are you any closer to finding out what Allen was looking for?" she asked as she finished putting in the last sparkplug.

"I wish," Caitlyn said, shaking her head. "I've decided to go back through the computer printouts from where I did a mirror image of the system. I'm hoping that I'll find something there that sticks out. I did run a report on the key logger and it showed that he had tried to gain access to my direct computer system because I saw where he was trying to crack my password." Caitlyn grinned. "He may be smart but he would never crack my password in a million years."

Sydney pulled off her latex gloves and tossed them into the trashcan. "Just be careful and if you do figure it out, I want to know ten seconds after you do."

Caitlyn grinned. "You will know within five seconds."

"Good. So are you looking forward to tomorrow? You have all your Christmas shopping done?"

"Yes, I have my shopping done," Caitlyn said, her eyebrows furrowing into a frown as she looked at Sydney. "And uh no, I'm not looking forward to it. I mean seriously, can you imagine spending all morning with Edward only to leave and go spend the rest of the day with Roberta and Lou?"

"I'm sorry," Sydney said and she meant it. "You know you're always welcome here anytime. If things get too much for you, just come on over."

"Thanks. I appreciate that but you may live to regret giving me that open invitation," Caitlyn chuckled.

"I doubt that and I'll have Edna make a house key so that if I'm not here, you can still come over and hang out."

"So do you have plans tomorrow?"

"Yeah, I will be heading over to my mother's place or what I lovingly refer to as the *Death Zone*," Sydney laughed as she made double quotes in the air with her fingers.

"That bad, huh?" Caitlyn asked, crinkling her nose.

"You have no idea. For some reason, my mother hates me but loves my little sister."

Caitlyn frowned. "Why?"

"Because my sister looks like her but I look just like my dad. When she looks at me, she sees him." It was hard for Sydney to keep the anger out of her voice. Since her mother had learned of her husband's infidelity, she had been taking it out on Sydney ever since and it didn't matter that her dad had now been dead for five years.

Sydney glanced at her watch. "I guess I should go see how your mom's doing. Wanna come say hi?"

"Thanks. Maybe some other time. I really want to get back to the office," Caitlyn answered.

"Okay, I will walk you to your car then."

Chapter 8

Allen leaned back in his chair. With his elbows resting on the chair arms, he steepled his fingers together against his chin. His thoughts turned to Caitlyn and he felt his face flush. *She thinks she is so damn smart when she's nothing more than a snot-nosed teenager. She doesn't belong in the corporate world. The corporate jungle is for men like him.*

He knew what it took to make it and making it meant that you did whatever you needed to do in order to succeed. The saying that "nice guys finished last" was true. The nice ones were swallowed whole but the ones like him; they took what they wanted regardless of what anyone else thought. Either they got onboard or they got run over and if he had to step on a few bodies to get to the top, well that's just collateral damage.

A knock at the door pulled him from his thoughts. Virgil Parsons pushed the door open far enough to poke his head through the doorway. "Hey, Allen, you got a few minutes you can spare?" he asked.

"Sure, come on in," he said, motioning with his hand. "What can I do for you?"

"I found a little discrepancy regarding one of our property acquisitions."

Allen frowned. "Which one are you talking about?" he asked.

Virgil glanced at the computer printout in his hand. "It's an old warehouse just outside of Springfield. The paperwork says it was purchased a little over a month ago."

"For what purpose?" Allen asked, the frown on his face deepening.

"That's just it. From what I can tell, there isn't one," Virgil said, shaking his head.

"We never purchase property without knowing beforehand what we're planning on doing with it. That doesn't make any sense," Allen said.

Virgil snorted. "You're telling me. What I can't understand is why I didn't know about this before now. All properly acquisitions go through me first and quite frankly it perturbs me just a bit."

"I can't say I blame you," Allen laughed. "Have you talked to Sydney about this?"

Virgil shook his head. "Not yet. I stopped by her office before I came to see you and Maureen said she was gone for the rest of the day."

"I'll tell you what," Allen said, nodding at the paper in Virgil's hand. "Why don't you leave that with me and first thing Monday morning, I'll get with Sydney and see if we can't get to the bottom of it."

A look of relief crossed Virgil's face. "That would be great if you're sure you don't mind," he said as he held the paper out to Allen.

"I don't mind at all," Allen said, smiling as he took the paper.

"Well, I appreciate it just the same. I'd do it myself but I am so swamped with lining up all the contractors for Dem and on top of all that, Bev told me that Sydney is thinking about merging Welsh and EMCOR."

Allen's eyebrows rose in surprise. "I didn't know that."

"No one else does either so what I just told you has to stay between us for now."

"I won't tell a soul. Did Bev by chance say why Sydney is thinking about doing this?" Allen asked, his mind and thoughts whirling a mile a minute.

Virgil shrugged. "Not really. Just that the Welsh Programmers had been working on a secret project and if it worked out like Sydney thought and as well as they all hoped, then it would make sense to house the two companies together under the same roof."

Allen felt his temper flare again as he listened to Virgil's explanation. "Well, I'll be sure to talk to Sydney about this," he said, tapping his finger on the paper.

"Thanks again," Virgil said as he walked toward the door.

"Not a problem. Can you shut the door behind you when you leave?" Allen asked and then waited for Virgil to close the door before he fully lost control of his temper. He slammed his fist down on the desk. "Damn you, Sydney," he swore under his breath as he slung the computer printout across the room. "Why did you hire her?"

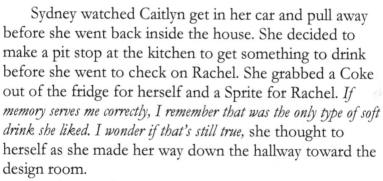

Sydney watched Caitlyn get in her car and pull away before she went back inside the house. She decided to make a pit stop at the kitchen to get something to drink before she went to check on Rachel. She grabbed a Coke out of the fridge for herself and a Sprite for Rachel. *If memory serves me correctly, I remember that was the only type of soft drink she liked. I wonder if that's still true,* she thought to herself as she made her way down the hallway toward the design room.

As she got closer, she could hear the rhythmic clicking of a keyboard. She had expected Rachel to be gone by now, after all, it was Christmas Eve. She hated to admit it, but she had been more than a little happy when she saw Rachel's car still parked in front of the house when she had walked Caitlyn out.

She stood in the doorway for several minutes, mesmerized by the woman sitting at the desk. She knew that the young woman she had fallen in love with all those years ago was long gone but the woman who had replaced her was heart-stopping stunning.

They are so alike, she thought as she watched Rachel's facial expression change repeatedly. Rachel was so intent on what she was doing, she hadn't noticed that Sydney was standing there.

Sydney cleared her throat so she wouldn't scare her. Rachel stopped what she was doing and looked up at Sydney. The look in her eyes caused Sydney to catch her breath. For a small instant, she saw a glimpse of the old Rachel she once knew.

"Hey there. I thought you might like something to drink," Sydney said as she came fully into the room and held the can out to Rachel.

Rachel smiled as she took the offered drink from Sydney.

"Why are you smiling?" Sydney asked.

"I guess it's because I can't believe you still remembered after all these years," Rachel answered as she held the can of Sprite in the air. "Thank you."

Sydney shrugged. "There are some things you never forget and lucky for me some things never change." Sydney smiled and then said, "I guess that includes your drinking habits."

Rachel cocked her head to the side as she thought about it. "You're right," she said finally.

Sydney leaned her hip against the side of the desk. "I half-expected you to be gone by now."

Rachel grimaced. "I kinda lost track of time."

"You do know that it's Christmas Eve, right?" Sydney asked.

Rachel laughed. "Yes, I know what day it is. I just wanted to finish the design changes for the bathroom. You'll be happy to know that I was able to finish all the rooms that you wanted done first." She reached over, grabbed a stack of printouts off the printer, and laid them on the edge of the desk near Sydney. "I took the liberty and made three different variations for all four rooms. So when you get a chance, look at them and decide which ones you like best. Once you've decided, I'll order the materials needed and line up the contractors so I can put a schedule together to implement the changes."

"Sounds like a plan to me," Sydney said, glancing down at the printouts.

They were both silent for several seconds. Rachel shifted slightly in her chair. She looked at Sydney, who now had a strange look on her face. "Are you all right?" she asked.

"Yeah, sorry. I'm just deep in thought," Sydney answered.

Rachel laughed. "I'm almost afraid to ask but here goes, what are you thinking about?"

"I was wondering if you've ever thought about me over the years," Sydney answered honestly.

By the expression on Rachel's face, Sydney's answer is what she expected. "What do you think?" she asked, answering Sydney's question with a question of her own.

"I don't know, otherwise I wouldn't have asked," Sydney said, her eyes narrowing as she studied Rachel's face for some indication of what was going through her mind.

Rachel looked down at her folded hands, which rested in her lap. "The answer is yes. I've thought about you a lot over the years," she answered without looking at Sydney.

"But not enough to want to see me again," Sydney said. The silence in the room was almost deafening and Sydney felt her anger rise to the surface.

"Why would I? You've been out of my life for over a decade," Rachel said, her voice just above a whisper.

"I don't know. How about to maybe apologize for the fucking *Dear Jane* letter you left me. Regardless of why you did what you did, I think ... no ... I know I deserved better than that."

Rachel got up from her chair and grabbed her jacket off the back of the stool. With her back to Sydney she said, "I don't want to get into this right now." She turned and took a step toward the doorway.

"Oh no," Sydney said and blocked Rachel's exit with her body.

"You read my letter, Sydney. So you know why I left."

"You're right, I did." Sydney laughed. "More times than I care to remember actually."

"I need to get home," Rachel said, her voice shaking.

"I just have a few questions for you first. Things I've wondered about for a long time now."

"How long is this going to take? I have plans tonight," Rachel said as she leaned back against the drafting table and crossed her arms over her chest.

"Still doing the midnight mass thingy?" Sydney asked with a smirk on her face.

"It's none of your business what my plans are," Rachel said through clenched teeth as she felt her own temper flare.

"You're right, it's not. So tell me this, Rache, how can you still support a church that hides and condones pedophile priests, yet has the audacity to declare that two women who are hopelessly in love with each other are a sin or abomination? You know what I think is a sin?" Sydney asked but continued without giving Rachel a chance to answer. "I think it's a sin that the Pope tells people they shouldn't be having sex and he's talking about a subject when he's the last person who should know a damn thing about the topic of sex."

The shocked expression on Rachel's face was a clear indication that she hadn't expected to hear what Sydney just said.

Sydney held her hand up in the air. "Never mind but here's a news flash for you, the church, and your whacked out ass parents. Priests who rape children are not homosexual, they are perverts who should have their balls cut off, then shot and then shot again for good measure."

Rachel's right eyebrow shot upward. "Why don't you tell me how you really feel. Are you done now?"

Sydney's eyes narrowed as she looked at Rachel. "Hell no, I'm just getting started and for the record," Sydney said, looking up toward the ceiling as if she were talking to God. "If the church or anyone else wants to worry about the people who molest kids, they should look at good old heterosexual grandpa who likes bouncing little girls on his lap or that stepfather who seems to be so wonderful. It's not us lesbians or gay men who rape their kids, it's the so-called straight men that more than likely turn out to be a goddamned relative. I suggest that you look no further than your own father or Uncle Henry."

"I think someone in this room has some serious anger issues," Rachel said. Her words served only to fuel Sydney's anger.

"I would let a lesbian or gay man babysit my child any day of the week before I would trust them to the care of my so-called *straight* male relatives. Those are the ones the church should be warning people about." She stopped and took a deep breath as she looked at Rachel. Several seconds past by without them saying a word. "Okay, I think I'm done now," Sydney said finally.

"Are you sure, I think you may still have a little more church-anger lurking in there somewhere."

"You're damn straight and I'm not the only one. I have anger issues because I'm fed up with lesbians and gays getting the blame for everything that's fucked up in the world. The difference is that I have the balls to tell it like it is."

"The church doesn't blame you personally." Rachel said the words although she knew what she said was a lie but she was so angry right now with Sydney that she didn't care.

"Give me a freaking break, Rache. You think your church is so great and that you will find all the answers within those four walls. I don't care what you believe or think or anyone else for that matter, something is really fucked up when the church would rather see a woman with a man who beats her every single day of her life, then see her with someone of her own sex who loves her and would worship the ground she walked on."

Sydney took another deep breath. "Tell me, Rache, how could any parent want that for their child? How could you prefer to see your daughters with an abusive boyfriend or husband instead of someone of their own sex who loves them? It's insane!"

"You know what? I've heard enough," Rachel yelled.

Sydney grinned. "You know what you are?"

"I'm sure you're going to tell me," Rachel sighed.

"You're a hypocrite. You, like so many others, have what I call *Doorstep Religion*. You pick it up on the way into the church and drop it off on the step on your way out but you know what's worse than that? You're setting one helluva an example for your daughters." As soon as the last words left Sydney's mouth, she regretted it.

Rachel, with tears in her eyes grabbed her car keys and purse off of the drafting table and brushed past Sydney through the doorway.

Sydney followed her out into the hallway but made no move to stop her from leaving. She knew what she said was hurtful and wrong on so many levels but once she started, she couldn't stop. All those years of hurting had come to the surface and she was unable to stop it. "Go ahead and run away. We both know how good you are at it," she yelled.

She stood there for several minutes, unable to move. She heard the front door shut and then turned and went into her office. She slammed the door shut behind her so hard that several books fell off their shelves, landing on the floor with a thud.

"Damn it, Sydney, you sure know how to make matters worse," she chastised herself as she dropped down into her desk chair. She pulled out her lap drawer. For several seconds she looked at the folded yellow paper lying next to a box of paperclips.

She picked it up and unfolded it. Her eyes filled with tears, the pain she had felt for all these years rushed to the surface. No matter how many times she read the words, the pain in her heart always felt the same.

The tears continued to stream down her cheeks as she read the words aloud.

"My dearest Sydney,

As I sit here, my heart feels as if it's being ripped to shreds. I want you to know that the last few months have been the best months of my life. I love you, Sydney, and the love I feel for you and the love you have shown me is more than I ever hoped to have in my lifetime and I will always be grateful for that and to you.

Writing this letter to you is the hardest thing I have ever done. I wish things could be different. I wish we lived in a different time where the love we share for each other would be looked at as something to be honored and cherished instead of an abomination of Christ.

I'm sorry, Sydney, but I'm not at the same place you are. I know I shouldn't care what people think or care what the Catholic Church thinks, but I do. I can't raise my daughter in a lesbian relationship.

I will never forget you or the love we shared although it would be easier on me if I could. You are a wonderful woman with so much to give. My only wish for you is that you someday find that one woman who leaves you breathless. That one woman who can share her life with you, regardless of what anyone else thinks. I wish it could be me but it can't.

I beg you not to come after me or try to find me because I won't be here. Please remember that I do love you and probably always will.

Rachel

By the time Sydney laid the letter down, her cries had

turned to gut wrenching sobs. She wrapped her arms around her waist as she rocked back and forth in the chair. The more she tried to stop the tears, the more persistent they became.

A knock at the door caused her to try to pull herself together.

"Sydney, honey, are you okay?" Edna's voice asked through the closed door.

"I'm fine, Edna," she managed to choke out as she wiped her cheeks off with the back of her hand.

"I don't believe you and I'm coming in whether you want me to or not," Edna said as she pushed the door open. She took one look at Sydney sitting behind her desk and rushed over to her. "Aw, sweetheart," she said as she rubbed Sydney's back. She pulled a handkerchief from her pocket and wiped the tears off Sydney's cheeks. "It'll get better, hon, these things take time," she said in a soothing voice.

"It's been thirteen-years. How much longer do I have to wait?" Sydney asked through a half-hearted laugh.

"Oh, so Rachel is the woman of your dreams?" Edna asked as her mind finally put two and two together. She leaned back to look at Sydney. "Am I wrong?" she asked.

Sydney looked at Edna with a shocked expression on her face. "How do you know about Rachel?" she asked.

"Hon, you talk in your sleep," Edna laughed.

Sydney grimaced. "I do?"

Edna nodded.

"Well damn, and here all this time I thought you were psychic or gifted with unseen magic powers," Sydney laughed.

Edna placed her hands on her hips and pretended to glare at Sydney. "I am gifted missy and don't you forget it."

Sydney laughed a deep belly laugh. "How is it that when I'm feeling down or sad, you always have a way to bring me out of it?"

"It's just a gift I have," Edna said with a wink. "I think a long, hot soak in the tub will make you feel even better."

"I think you may be right about that. Maybe I'll throw in some bubbles while I'm at it to help me prepare for tomorrow."

"Oh, I forgot that you will be dining with Deidre," Edna snorted, covering her mouth with her hand to keep from laughing.

"Yeah, can't wait to hang out with Mommy Dearest," Sydney chuckled.

"Well, you better get to it then and be sure to say hi for me tomorrow," Edna laughed as she left the room.

Rachel sat in her car for at least fifteen minutes just staring at the Immaculate Conception Catholic Church. She had been worshipping here for as long as she could remember. All her life she had been taught to praise God and live according to the words in the bible and having parents who took everything to the extreme, including church, had made her life a virtual hell.

All throughout her life, she'd had conflicting feelings and emotions regarding the strict teachings of the church.

Sydney was right. She was a hypocrite in the worst sense of the word and perhaps she had known all her life that she was.

She thought about Caitlyn and Alyssa. They were her life and their happiness mattered to her more than anything else in her life.

"Would I care if they fell in love with a woman?" she asked herself. She really didn't have to think about it at all. As much as she hated to admit it, Sydney *was* right. She was setting a piss poor example for her daughters. By staying with Edward, she was in a sense telling her girls that it was okay for a man to beat his wife; she was showing them that it was acceptable and she had done it for years.

"Oh God, what have I done?" she cried out. She slammed her hands against the steering wheel and try as she might; she was unable to stop the tears from spilling down her cheeks. She was angry with herself. She was angry with her parents, angry with the Catholic Church. She thought about all the years she had wasted but she was most angry with herself for not being brave enough to stand up and fight for Sydney.

Instead, she hurt the one person who mattered so much to her. She had no doubt that Sydney had truly loved her. Just one look in Sydney's eyes had told her just how much Sydney had loved her. It was undeniable and she knew that her own eyes had told the same story as to how she had felt about Sydney.

She knew there was only one thing left for her to do. Without realizing it, she had left her car and was now standing in front of the church, looking at the door.

She took a deep breath, counted to ten, and pulled the door open. "You can do this," she whispered as she entered the church. She looked around and was surprised to see that she was alone. It was Christmas Eve and she normally attended Midnight Mass but she had put this off for far too long now. She glanced at her watch. It would be more than two hours before the next service began.

She walked up to the marble stoup, the basin for Holy water and dipped her fingertips in it. She made the sign of the cross in front of her chest and then walked into the nave, the central part of the church. She stopped at a pew near the back, knelt, and made the sign of the cross again before entering. She laid her purse down on the bench and pulled the kneeler down.

With her hands clasped up in front of her, she felt the tears as they continued to stream down her face. She knew this prayer was going to be like none she had ever said before but she needed to do this. It may be too late for her now, but not for her girls.

Chapter 9

Sydney pulled her truck in behind her sister's car and shut off the engine. "I really don't want to do this," she muttered as she took her key out of the ignition. She looked down at the short and sexy, very low-cut; figure hugging black dress she was wearing. She knew her mother was going to hate it and that made her smile.

She barely had time to get out of the truck before her niece and nephew came barreling out of the house toward her. The twins hit her at the same time, nearly knocking her over as they wrapped their arms around her waist.

"Auntie, Syd, what took you so long? We've been waiting for hours," Seth said as he looked up at her.

"Yeah, what Seth said," Sarah chimed in.

"I hardly think you've been waiting for hours. Seems like a little bit of exaggeration to me," Sydney laughed as she hugged them. "You both look very nice today and you are just too handsome in that suit and tie, Mister."

"What about me?" Sarah asked.

"You are as beautiful as ever, sweetie, and you know blue is my most favorite color in the world and ... I absolutely love the lace on your dress."

"Thank you Auntie, Syd, and you look rather fetching, too," Sarah said, grinning from ear to ear.

Sydney laughed. "Fetching? You think I look fetching. Where in the world did you hear that word? " she asked.

"She's been watching shows on the BBC," Seth said as he rolled his eyes.

"Ah that explains it," Sydney chuckled.

"Wait till you see what we got you for Christmas,"

Seth said as he placed his hand in Sydney's hand.

"And we bought it with our own money, too," Sarah said, smiling as she took Sydney's other hand.

"Wow, really?" Sydney asked as she allowed the two kids to pull her toward the front porch. "I'm sure that whatever it is, I will love it."

"It's about time," Liz said from the open doorway.

She looks more and more like mother every day and just as beautiful, Sydney thought as she climbed the steps. She let go of the kid's hands. "Jeesh, I'm five minutes late and not only do I get the third degree from these two little rug rats, I get it from my favorite sister," she said.

"I'm you're only sister," Liz laughed as she hugged Sydney.

Sydney grinned. "Now you know why you're my favorite sister."

"Whatever," Liz said and then punched Sydney in the arm.

"Ouch, that hurt," Sydney whined as she pretended to rub the spot on her arm.

"Merry Christmas, Sis," Liz said as she moved back to allow Sydney and the kids room to come inside the house.

Sydney cupped her hand around her mouth. "Time to face the firing squad," she whispered just loud enough for Liz to hear.

"It's about time," Deidre said as she glanced out the dining room doorway and saw Sydney.

Sydney hung her coat in the closet, walked over to the dining room, and stopped just inside the doorway. "Merry Christmas, Deidre," she said with a tinge of sarcasm.

Deidre finished folding the last napkin and laid it on the table. Her eyebrows pinched together in a frown as she looked up at Sydney. "How many times have I told you to stop calling me that?"

Sydney watched her mother re-arrange the silverware. "And when are you going to get a haircut? You're looking a little scraggly, and do you think you could have dressed a little sluttier," Deidre asked through pursed lips as she looked at the dress Sydney was wearing.

Sydney smiled and then immediately felt her temper flare as her mother made her way around the table, making sure every place setting was just right. "I don't know, maybe I'll get it cut and wear more clothing when you learn to stop being such a class-A bitch to me."

Deidre glared at Sydney. "You need to watch your language young lady. In case you haven't noticed, there are children present."

Sydney shook her head. "You're never going to change are you, Mother?"

"What is that supposed to mean?" Deidre asked, the look on her face saying that she had no idea what Sydney was talking about.

"You know damn well what it means. I can't help it that I remind you—"

"Well, hello there and Merry Christmas," Sydney's brother-in-law said as he came up behind her and wrapped Sydney in a bear hug. He took one look at Deidre's expression and realized that he had interrupted something.

Sydney turned around to face him. "Merry Christmas, Ray," she said as she returned the hug. "Your timing is perfect," she whispered in his ear.

He smiled at her. "You look fantastic and glad I could help."

"You look pretty handsome yourself," she said. He was extremely handsome with black wavy hair, dark eyes, and chiseled features that put him on the cover of GQ. The twins had the best of both parent's genes. They got their blond hair from their mother and their dark eyes from their father.

Liz walked into the dining room carrying two glasses of mimosas. She handed one to Sydney. "Thought you might need this by now," she said with a wink.

"You thought right. Maybe you should just set the pitcher next to my placemat," Sydney laughed.

"Have I told you how beautiful you look today, Liz, honey? I love the new dress," Deidre said as she took her place at the head of the table.

Liz pulled out the chair next to Sydney and sat down. "Yes, Mother, you did."

"Seth, Sarah, time to eat," Deidre shouted.

Sydney glanced at her watch as she took her seat at the table next to Liz. *So much for me spending several hours here hanging out with the twins. I'll be lucky to make it one hour,* she thought as she laid her napkin across her lap.

"Do you need some help, Mom?" Caitlyn asked as she walked into the kitchen.

Rachel smiled at her daughter and placed the plate she had just washed into the drainer. "Not unless you want to help, baby," she answered.

"May I ask you a question?" Caitlyn asked, picking up a towel. She began drying off the dishes in the drainer and placed them on the counter.

"Sure," Rachel answered, handing Caitlyn a glass to dry off.

Caitlyn grinned. "We have a very good dishwasher, so why are you washing them by hand?"

"Because it's relaxing and it gives me a chance to clear my head while I watch the birds eating out of the feeder," Rachel answered, nodding toward the window overlooking the sink.

Caitlyn looked out the window and watched as several Northern Finches, more commonly known as Evening Grosbeaks gathered around the feeder, while a squirrel on the ground happily cleaned up the seeds that the birds had dropped.

Rachel picked up the pan that she had cooked the ham in. She took it over to the trashcan and scraped out the leftover remnants from Christmas dinner. "Did you have a good Christmas?" she asked.

"Yes, I did but then again, any day I get to spend with you and Alyssa is a good day."

Rachel smiled and wrapped her arm around Caitlyn's waist. "How did I ever get so lucky and blessed to have a daughter like you?" she asked.

"I am the way I am because I had a wonderful mom who raised me," Caitlyn said and kissed Rachel on the cheek.

"Flattery will get you—"

"Hey, Mom," Alyssa yelled, running into the kitchen.

"What, baby?" Rachel asked, smoothing back Alyssa's hair from her face.

"Christy just called and asked if I could sleep over tonight. Please, Mom. Please? Can I?"

Rachel looked down at Alyssa's sweet upturned face. "I don't know, can you?" she teased.

"M-o-m," Alyssa said, dragging out the word.

"What did Christy's mom say?"

"She said it was okay with her if it was okay with you. Please? I'll clean my room for the next two weeks."

Caitlyn laughed. "Lyssa, you already clean your room. It's cleaner than mine."

Alyssa put her index finger over her mouth. "Shhh," she said to Caitlyn in a conspiratorial tone.

"Okay," Caitlyn whispered back.

Rachel cleared her throat. She placed her hands on her hips. "In case you two have forgotten, I'm standing right here and I can hear everything you're saying," she said, looking back and forth at her two daughters.

"Oh yeah," Alyssa grinned at her mom. "Does that mean I can go?""Yes, you can go," Rachel said. "Now go get your overnight bag because I know you've packed it already."

"Yes," Alyssa said, making a fist pump in the air as she ran out of the kitchen.

"Mom, I have something important that I need to talk to you about and I think you may want to sit down for this," Caitlyn said, taking Rachel by the hand. "Don't worry, it's not that bad, or at least I don't think it is," she quickly added when she saw the worried look on Rachel's face.

"Okay," Rachel said slowly as she sat down at the table.

Caitlyn pulled out a chair and slid it over next to Rachel's chair. She took her mom's hand in hers. She cleared her throat. "I'm just going to say this. I'm a lesbian," she said and then waited for her mom's reaction.

Rachel looked at her in stunned silence. Several long seconds went by without her saying anything.

"Mom, please say something," Caitlyn said.

"Um ... I'm sorry, baby. I'm just a little shocked, that's all," Rachel said.

"Do you hate me?" Caitlyn asked, a worried look on her face.

Rachel cupped Caitlyn's face with her hands. "Oh, sweetheart. I could never hate you."

"You kinda look a little pale right now," Caitlyn laughed.

"It's just ... I mean ... are you sure?" Rachel asked, her words jumbled as her mind tried to wrap around what Caitlyn was telling her.

Caitlyn smiled. "I've never been more sure of anything in my life."

"Come here," Rachel said, pulling Caitlyn into her arms. "I love you, Caitlyn, and I just want you to be happy. That's all I've ever wanted for you and Alyssa both."

Caitlyn leaned back so she could look at Rachel. "I

have another confession to make," she said a little reluctantly.

Rachel leaned back in her chair. "Don't tell me you've decided to run off and join the circus," Rachel laughed.

"Jesus Christ woman, can a man get a damn drink in this house?" Edward yelled from the other room.

Caitlyn rolled her eyes. "How about getting it yourself," she mumbled under her breath.

"It's okay," Rachel said, her eyebrows furrowing into a frown. "I'll get it for him. Would you mind running Alyssa over to Christy's?"

"I don't think I should leave. Why don't you come with us?" Caitlyn asked, concern etched on her face.

"I'll be all right, baby," Rachel said, reassuringly. *With any luck, he'll drink enough and pass out*, she thought to herself.

"I won't be long and when I get back, I'd like to finish our conversation," Caitlyn said, looking at her mom. She turned toward the doorway leading into the family room, her brows still creased into a frown. "Come on Mini-me," she yelled. "I'm getting old standing here."

"You're too funny," Rachel laughed. She opened the cabinet and grabbed a tall glass off the shelf.

"Are you sure, you'll be okay?" Caitlyn asked again. She didn't want to leave her mom alone with Edward, especially after he had been drinking heavily and lately, that seemed to be from the time he got up until the time he went to bed or passed out, whichever came first.

Rachel smiled. "Yes, baby, I am," she said just as Alyssa came into the kitchen carrying her overnight bag.

"Bye, Mom. I love you," Alyssa said, wrapping her arms around Rachel's waist.

"I love you, too, sweetheart," Rachel said and kissed the top of Alyssa's head.

Rachel waited for the girls to leave and then filled the glass three-fourths of the way full with whiskey, topping it off with a small amount of Coke. "Hopefully, this will do the trick," she said to herself as she picked up the glass and headed toward the family room.

Chapter 10

Christmas and New Years day had come and gone and things at Welsh had returned to normal. Jackie's investigation continued along at a snail's pace and they had yet to discover the identity of the account owner embezzling the funds from Welsh. Sydney liked to think of herself as a patient person but even she had her limit and she had long since reached it. She wanted answers and results and she wanted them now.

She and Rachel had not spoken or seen each other since Christmas Eve. Over the past few weeks, Sydney had thought long and hard about the way she had handled things. She knew she was out of line and that she owed Rachel an apology.

She took her cup of coffee and walked over to the bay window that looked out into the backyard. She smiled as she watched a Northern Harrier bathing in the heated birdbath next to the flower garden.

Her thoughts turned to Rachel. She knew Rachel would be in the design room because she had been in her room when she heard Rachel's car. She had watched through her bedroom window as Rachel parked. The unexpected racing of her heart and the sudden dryness in her mouth had caught her off-guard and her first instinct had been to go to her but something had held her back. She wasn't sure if it was embarrassment for her behavior weeks earlier or if was more out of fear.

She took a sip of coffee. "You're only fooling yourself, kiddo," she said aloud, shaking her head. "I think my little plan may be back-firing on me."

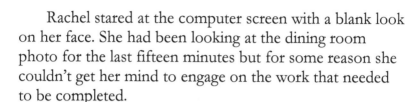

Rachel stared at the computer screen with a blank look on her face. She had been looking at the dining room photo for the last fifteen minutes but for some reason she couldn't get her mind to engage on the work that needed to be completed.

She hated to admit it but she had been disappointed that Sydney wasn't home when she had arrived earlier. The more she tried to focus on the design changes, the more her mind wandered and the more her thoughts repeatedly turned to Sydney.

Over the last two weeks, everywhere she looked she saw Sydney's beautiful smiling face. She had reminisced about the love they had once shared. The thoughts had left her happy, yet sad at the same time. She had dared to let herself dream about the life she and Sydney could have had together.

Although she had been furious with Sydney the last time they had spoken, what she felt now was gratitude. Everything Sydney had said had been the truth and it took Sydney's anger to make her wake up and realize that for the last twenty-five years, no make that thirty-seven years, she had lived her life for everyone else.

After her trip to the church on Christmas Eve, she had left feeling better than she had ever felt in her life. It was as if a terrible burden had been lifted from her shoulders.

"Snap out of it girl," she said aloud, picking up the four printouts that Sydney had selected. She thought it was ironic that the ones Sydney had chosen had also been her picks out of all the samples.

She opened up her daily planner and made notations next to the company names that she would be using to order the fabric.

"Good morning," Sydney said from the doorway, her voice startling Rachel. "Sorry, I didn't mean to sneak up on you."

"It's okay," Rachel smiled and leaned back in the chair.

Sydney suddenly felt a little awkward, unsure of herself even. She shifted nervously from one foot to the other.

Rachel looked at her with amusement. "You have to use the bathroom?" she laughed, her right eyebrow rising upward.

"Uh ... no, um ... I've been doing a lot of thinking over the past few weeks," Sydney said.

"Yeah, me, too," Rachel said, running her hands through her hair. The sexy gesture caused Sydney's throat to tighten. She had hoped that the time away from Rachel would lessen the desire that was steadily building inside of her with each passing day. She couldn't have been more wrong. If anything, she wanted Rachel more than she had ever wanted anything in her life and that scared her.

"Hello?" Rachel said, waving her hand in the air.

Sydney shook her head as if that would erase all thoughts and feelings that threatened to overtake her. "I'm sorry, what did you say?" she asked, her face flushing slightly with embarrassment.

"I asked you what you've been thinking about," Rachel grinned.

"I owe you an apology, Rache," Sydney said, clasping her fingers together in front of her.

Rachel pushed her chair back away from the table and stood up. She slowly walked over to Sydney. She pulled Sydney's hands apart and took both of them in hers. She laughed at the shocked expression on Sydney's face when she brought them to her mouth and gently kissed, first one palm and then the other.

"I'm the one who owes you the apology, Sydney. What you said to me was the truth. Every single word you spoke was dead-on."

Sydney felt a lump rise in her throat. She shook her head back and forth adamantly. "No, Rache, I was so out of line and I had no right to be that rude to you and I'm so sorry." Sydney looked down at the floor. She was afraid that if she looked at Rachel, she would lose it and make an even bigger fool of herself.

"Sydney, please look at me," Rachel said softly. When Sydney made no move to comply, Rachel gently touched her cheek. She used her hand to force Sydney to meet her gaze. What she saw in Sydney's eyes made her heart skip a beat. It wasn't anger, lust or desire, what she saw were years of hurt and anguish but most of all she saw love. She knew what it was because she was sure that Sydney could see the same thing when she looked in her eyes. She felt her heart ache as a lone tear fell from Sydney's eye and ran down her cheek. She smiled as she used her thumb to wipe it off.

"For so many years, I have denied who I was as a person. I lived my life according to how everyone else thought I should live and because of that, I missed out on you and what could have been but more importantly, I missed out on what it meant to truly be in love and to have that love returned ten-fold."

Sydney took a deep breath. Her mind was racing in so many directions that she felt dizzy. She had waited so many years to hear these words from Rachel. "I don't understand."

"I was so angry at you when I left here. I was angry because you were right about everything," Rachel said, caressing Sydney's cheek with her thumb.

"But ... but what changed your mind? What happened?" Sydney asked. Her mind was still having a hard time digesting what Rachel was saying to her. She wanted to believe her but her mind warned her to be careful.

Rachel laughed. "I went to church."

Sydney's eyebrows rose in surprise. "Did you have a spiritual awakening or something?"

"More like a 'Come to Jesus' meeting," Rachel chuckled.

Sydney grinned at her. "Well, that must have been some kind of a meeting."

"It was ... very eye opening," Rachel said, nodding her head.

"What does it have to do with us, though?" Sydney asked.

"I'm not really sure but I do know this," Rachel said as she cupped Sydney's face with both of her hands. Before Sydney could say anything, Rachel pulled Sydney's face toward her and then their lips met with the sweetest abandon.

The soft sensation coming from Rachel's lips, rocked Sydney to the core. She felt the tip of Rachel's tongue push forward and was helpless to do anything but allow her entry. She groaned as she gently caressed, sucked, and tasted Rachel's tongue. She felt her knees weaken as her hands moved up and down Rachel's sides as if they had a mind of their own.

Rachel's deep intake of breath was almost her undoing as her hands found their way beneath Rachel's t-shirt, sliding over silky soft skin as they searched for their desired goal, covering her breasts. She squeezed gently, her thumbs making circular motions over Rachel's nipples. She moaned into Rachel's mouth as she felt them grow harder with each stroke.

Sydney shivered when Rachel's fingers and hands did a tap dance across her stomach. "You're killing me," Sydney groaned as Rachel traced kisses up and down the side of her neck. The tingling sensation ran from the tip of Sydney's head all the way down to her groin. She felt the wetness gather between her legs when Rachel ran her tongue along the outside edge of her ear.

"Do you have any idea how bad I want you right now?" Sydney growled as her lips made their way back to Rachel's mouth.

"Probably as much as I want you to want me right now," Rachel whispered. She slowly traced the outline of Sydney's lips with the tip of her tongue.

The clearing of a throat caused both women to jump apart as if they had been burnt by fire. Rachel felt her cheeks redden as she jerked her shirt down.

"Sorry to interrupt," Edna chuckled, "but there is a delivery man out front. He says you ordered some car parts and he says he won't leave until you've had a chance to inspect them."

"Thanks, Edna," Sydney said as she tucked her shirt back into her pants.

"Don't mention it," Edna laughed as she turned and walked away.

Sydney turned to Rachel, pulled her into her arms, and cupped her face with her hand. "You're still the most beautiful woman I've ever laid eyes on," she said and then kissed Rachel softly on the lips. She looked at her one last time and then left the room.

Chapter 11

Rachel tapped her pencil on the desk. She hadn't seen or talked to Sydney since … since their what? She laughed out loud. She didn't even know what to call what they had done yesterday. She hadn't planned on kissing Sydney. It just happened in the heat of the moment.

"Oh my gosh," she whispered. "You felt her up, that's what you did." She felt the color rise in her cheeks at the thought of what she had done. She had no idea on where they stood or where they would go from here.

All she knew for sure was that she had been unable to get it out of her mind and Sydney had been the last thing she thought about when she went to sleep and she had been the first thing she thought of when she had awoken that morning.

"I think these two belong to you," Edna said, poking her head through the doorway.

"Hey, Mom, what's up?" Caitlyn asked as she came into the room with Alyssa following behind her.

Rachel frowned at the sight of her daughters. "What are you two doing here?"

"Sorry, but I didn't know what else to do with her," Caitlyn said, nodding at her little sister. "Christy's mom called my cell. Seems Christy has some kind of flu bug so I went over and picked her up. I figured Sydney wouldn't mind if I brought Mini-me over here."

"You're right. Sydney doesn't mind at all," Sydney said from the doorway. She walked up to Alyssa and held out her hand. "Hi, Alyssa, I'm Sydney."

"Hello, Sydney. I'm pleased to meet you," Alyssa said

in response and shook Sydney's hand.

"Well, I guess it's settled then," Rachel laughed.

"I guess so," Caitlyn chuckled. "I got a lot of work to do so I will talk to you ladies later."

"I will touch base with you in a little while," Sydney said to Caitlyn.

"Sounds good because I think I may have solved one of our little puzzles concerning a certain exec that we both know," Caitlyn said with a wink.

"Now you've got my curiosity aroused," Sydney said.

"I need to re-check and verify a few things but once I'm done, I'll buzz you on your cell," Caitlyn said.

Sydney smiled at her and said, "Can't wait."

Once Caitlyn was gone, Sydney turned her attention to Alyssa. "So, Alyssa, Caitlyn tells me that she calls you Mini-me. Why is that?" she asked.

"She says it's because she and are just alike," Alyssa answered.

"Is that true?" Sydney asked.

"Yeah in most ways, I suppose. Only she likes computers and I like cars."

Sydney's eyebrows rose in surprise. "Well, if you like cars, then you might like me a little bit, too." She glanced at Rachel and flashed her a broad smile that made Rachel's heart skip a beat.

"You like cars?" Alyssa asked excitedly. Sydney's revelation had obviously pleased her.

"I love, love, love cars," Sydney said and then winked at Rachel.

The small gesture caused Rachel's breath to catch in her throat. She couldn't take her eyes off of Sydney as she watched her interact with her youngest daughter.

"You should see the shelves in my room, shouldn't she, Mom?" Alyssa asked, looking at her mom for confirmation.

"Yes, she should, baby. I think Sydney would be

impressed by your model collection," Rachel said and nodded her head for emphasis, much to Alyssa's delight.

"You build models?" Sydney asked, her eyebrows rising in surprise.

"At least two a week," Alyssa answered proudly.

Sydney smiled at the young girl who looked so much like her mother. "I'll tell you what, how about I take you around and show you the rest of the house so your mom can get back to work."

"Sweet," Alyssa said, her face lighting up with the thought. "Is it okay?" she asked, looking at Rachel.

"Yes, baby, it's more than okay," Rachel answered with a smile. She looked at Sydney and silently mouthed a *thank you."*

Sydney grinned at Rachel and then wrapped her arm around Alyssa shoulders. "Do you like video games?" she asked.

"I love video games," Alyssa replied.

"What about Donkey Kong?" Sydney asked.

"I will kick your butt," Rachel heard Alyssa tell Sydney as the two of them headed down the hallway. She laughed and shook her head. Alyssa definitely marched to the beat of a different drummer just like her older sister.

Hearing Sydney and Alyssa laughing warmed Rachel's heart. "I'm like an emotional basket case," she whispered as her eyes unexpectedly welled up with tears.

Meredith laid down long ways on the couch. She kicked her panties off to the side. She motioned to the little petite, hot looking blonde-haired woman who had accompanied her to Sydney's Christmas party.

"What do you want, sweets?" the blonde asked in a

seductive voice.

"You know what I want, Brandy, honey," Meredith purred as she spread her legs open wide, revealing her completely shaven self.

Brandy smiled as she pulled off her top and unhooked her bra. By the time she made it over to the couch, she was completely naked, having shed all of her clothes along the way.

She licked her lips as she settled between Meredith's legs. "Mmm, you're so damn wet," Brandy whispered as she slid her fingers through the wetness. She lowered her head and simultaneously entered Meredith with two fingers as she ran her tongue across her swollen clit.

"Oh shit," Meredith moaned as her hips began to thrust hard against Brandy's fingers. "I need more," she begged.

"You taste so good," Brandy groaned as she slid another finger inside.

Meredith reached down, pushing Brandy's face into her harder. "Yes, yes, right there," Meredith panted. "Whatever you do, don't fucking stop," she growled. Her hips bucked wildly as the orgasm screamed through her body. She tossed her head back against the arm of the couch and pushed hard against Brandy's mouth. She cried out as the last sensations of the of the orgasm subsided. "No more," she said, pushing Brandy's head away.

"But I was just getting started, sweets," Brandy whined.

Meredith looked at Brandy as if she were something she had picked up off the street. "You know how I hate when you talk like that," she said in a snotty voice. "Hand me my cell off the coffee table."

Brandy did what she was told and tossed Meredith her cell phone. She leaned back on the couch with a pouty look on her face as she looked at her lover.

Meredith glanced at Brandy with what could only be

described as indifference as she punched a number into her cell. She smiled as she waited for the phone to be answered on the other end.

"Hello, Edward," she said, grinning from ear to ear. "It's not important who I am. What matters is that I know who you are and I know who your wife is. Would you be interested in knowing just what that wife of yours has been up to lately?" Meredith laughed. "If you aren't sitting down you might want to think about it but I suggest before you do that you fix yourself a long hard drink."

Chapter 12

Sydney, dressed from head to toe in coveralls and a welder's apron, was so intent on the job she was doing that she didn't notice when the garage door opened.

Alyssa turned her head to keep from looking directly at the arc coming from the machine Sydney was using. She walked up and lightly tapped Sydney on the shoulder.

Sydney looked back at Alyssa and smiled. She switched the torch off, laid it down, and then jerked off her face shield.

"Hi, Alyssa, I didn't know you were coming over today."

Alyssa shifted nervously from one foot to the other. "You don't mind, do you?" she asked.

Sydney frowned. "Of course not, I'm very happy to see you."

"Really?" Alyssa asked, grinning.

"Yes, really and I was hoping you would come over again because I wanted to show you *my* model kit." Sydney pointed at an area behind Alyssa.

Alyssa turned to see what Sydney was pointing at. "Wow. Is that what I think it is?" Alyssa asked as she walked closer to the car that was suspended from the ceiling on a pulley system.

"I guess that depends on what you think it is," Sydney laughed.

"I know exactly what it is," Alyssa said as she circled the car body.

Sydney crossed her arms over her chest. "Okay, tell me what you think it is."

"I don't think, I know, and that is a replica body shell for the Mirage K Lamborghini Countach Kit Car," Alyssa answered.

Sydney shook her head. "How in the world do you know that?" she asked, looking at Alyssa in amazement.

Alyssa laughed. "I told you that I'm a model freak."

"Well, young lady, I am thoroughly impressed," Sydney said, still shaking her head in disbelief. "How old are you anyway, twenty?" she asked although she knew exactly how old Alyssa was.

"I'm only eight years old, silly, but I'm in the seventh grade," Alyssa laughed.

"I must admit that you are pretty incredible for an eight-year-old." Sydney looked at Alyssa. Considering how intelligent Rachel and Caitlyn were, she shouldn't have been surprised that Alyssa would be as well but she was.

"I see that you're using a Pontiac Fiero as the host body for the kit. What year is that '94, '96,?" Alyssa asked as she circled the stripped down car that Sydney had been working on.

"'94 with a ninety-three point five wheelbase," Sydney answered.

"Yeah, the old kits didn't quite fit right and you had to extend the wheelbase on them before the body could be assembled. Automatic or five speed?" Alyssa asked.

"Five," Sydney answered as she watched Alyssa circle the car. The young girl was studying it just like a scientist would study a newly discovered specimen under a microscope.

Alyssa walked to the rear end of the car. "Since you don't need to extend the wheelbase, then what are you welding?

"When I pulled the Fiero body off, I noticed a few weak spots along some of the weld seams, so I'm touching them up just to be on the safe side.

Alyssa tapped her index finger against her chin. She

looked so much like an adult. "That's probably a good idea. Are you using a TIG or MIG welder?" she asked, nodding at the welding machine.

"MIG and just what do you know about welding?" Sydney asked, again surprised by this young lady.

Alyssa shrugged. "Not much really. Just that the TIG uses Tungsten Inert Gases and that a person who uses that type of weld has to have a lot of skill. Most people use MIG though because the Metal Inert Gas is easier to handle since it supplies a continuous metal wire feed and fuses the two metals together. With the TIG, you have to use two hands, one to hold the welder and the other to hold the metal rod for welding."

Sydney shook her head in amazement as she looked at Alyssa. "I thought you said you didn't know much about welding."

"I don't really. That's about as much as I know," Alyssa said with a shrug.

"I think that's enough," Sydney laughed. "So, how would you like to help me work on it?"

Alyssa's eyes flew open wide. "Are you serious?"

Sydney nodded.

"Sweet," Alyssa said.

Sydney laughed. "Well, first thing we need to do is get you some coveralls. I don't think your mom would be too happy with me if you ruined your clothes."

Caitlyn, with a donut in hand stepped off the elevator on the executive floor. She glanced through the open doorway of several offices as she walked toward her office. It was very quiet and she liked it that way. A glance at her watch told her that it was almost five-thirty and she knew that very few employees worked past their scheduled time. She was definitely an exception in that area. More often than not, she was the last employee to leave the building.

She was looking down at her shoes when a movement out of the corner of her eye caused her to look up. She stopped walking. She held her breath, listening for any sign that indicated she wasn't alone and then she heard it.

"Who's there?" she called out as she walked several more feet and stopped. She waited for several seconds and when she didn't hear anything else, she continued down the hallway toward her office.

As she reached her office, she shivered involuntarily. She turned and looked over her shoulder. For some reason she had a strange feeling that she was being watched. She took one last look down the hallway and then went into her office.

She noticed that the red light was flashing on her answering machine, indicating she had unheard messages. She pressed the button to hear them through the speaker and smiled when she heard Janice from Property Records' voice.

"I hope you have the news I'm looking for," she said to the machine.

"Seems you were right, Caitlyn," Janice said through the speaker. "The prior owner of the property you were asking about once belonged to an Allen Carmichael, which he got for a steal if you ask me. Must be nice to buy a property for twenty-five grand and then flip it for three-hundred thousand. Anyway, I just wanted to give you the information. If you need anything else, you know where to find me."

"I knew it," Caitlyn said, shaking her head as she disconnected the line. "Gotcha, Allen!"

Sydney came out of the closet near the back of the garage carrying a pair of dark blue coveralls. She walked up to Alyssa and held them up to her. They were at least two times Alyssa's size.

"I think we're gonna have to modify these a bit for you," she said and handed the garment to Alyssa. She walked over to her workbench and grabbed a pair of scissors.

"Okay hold these up to you like this," she instructed as she knelt down on her knees in front of Alyssa. She used the scissors and cut a good twelve inches off the length on both legs. "Now we need to make them fit your arms," she said and held the coverall arm against Alyssa's arm. Again, she cut off close to the same amount as what she did the legs.

Before she could tell Alyssa to try them on, the young girl had already slipped them over her clothes and zipped up the front.

"Not bad," Sydney said as she admired her handiwork. "Now we got to find you some gloves."

Alyssa frowned. "What do I need gloves for?" she asked.

"I may like working on cars but I can't stand getting grease under my fingernails," Sydney said, crinkling her nose in disgust.

Alyssa giggled and rolled her eyes at Sydney.

"Don't give me that look missy," Sydney said, shaking her finger at Alyssa.

"You can't really be serious about the grease. Part of the fun is getting dirty," Alyssa said as she continued to giggle.

"Uh, yeah ... dead dog serious and if I wanna get dirty, I'll go play in the mud," Sydney said, a grin on her face.

"Dead dog? Really?" Alyssa groaned.

"Yeah, because nothing is more serious than a dead dog, don't you agree?" Sydney asked.

"Oh brother," Alyssa said, shaking her head.

Sydney frowned. "Hey, you wanna help me or not?"

"Of course," Alyssa answered through a giggle.

Rachel had checked the theater room and every other room where she thought Alyssa might be. When she didn't find her, she headed toward the kitchen, thinking that either Fred Rick or Edna would be there and that one of them might know where her daughter was.

She hadn't planned on having Alyssa at Sydney's with her while she worked but Mrs. Novak, the older woman who usually stayed at the house with Alyssa after school, had called off with the flu. Although Edward made it home on most days before she did, with his drinking problem, she just wasn't comfortable leaving Alyssa alone with him. *That should have told you something right there*, she thought to herself. When a mother doesn't trust her husband enough to leave her daughter alone with her own dad, something is very wrong.

She thought about last night and how relieved she was when she got home and found Edward already passed out in bed. She knew she had some major decisions to make and that her life was about to change in the most drastic way. What was odd, was that she wasn't scared at all. It was as if an inner peace had come over her after her trip to Immaculate Conception and when she had left that day, she had known that it would be the last time she set foot in that church.

She knew that her parents were aware of her lack of attendance the past two Wednesday's and Sunday's by the numerous messages, they had left on her answering machine at home. When that didn't get a response, her mother had begun leaving messages on her cell phone voice-mail. As of yesterday, she had twenty-two voice mails and all but three of them were from her mother. She hadn't bothered to listen to a single one, instead she had deleted them. She just wasn't ready to face her parents yet, mostly because she was dreading the confrontation along with the screaming that was sure to come when she laid it all out for her parents.

"Caitlyn, Caitlyn, Caitlyn," she said repeatedly to herself. "You never cease to surprise me," she laughed as her thoughts turned to the conversation she'd had with her daughter in the kitchen when Caitlyn had announced that she was a lesbian. She had made it all sound so simple and in reality, it was. She had hugged Caitlyn and told her how proud of her she was.

After Caitlyn had made her announcement, for a brief second she had felt a tinge of jealousy. It wasn't jealousy in the true sense of the word, but more akin to envy, envy because Caitlyn seemed so at ease with who she was and had fully accepted it and she didn't care what anyone else thought. Caitlyn's biggest fear however, was how she would react to the news.

She had assured her eldest daughter that all she ever wanted was for her to be happy and if loving and being loved by a woman would give her that, then she would support her fully.

The look of relief on Caitlyn's face nearly made her cry and if that wasn't enough, Caitlyn then decided to drop the real bombshell after she returned from dropping Alyssa off at Christy's house.

She had told Rachel that she knew who Sydney was all along and that she had remembered Sydney from when she was a child. She then went on to chastise Rachel for not following her heart but she also eased the sting by telling her that she understood why she had made the choices she had made but things were different today and people were more free to love who they wanted to love.

Caitlyn had laughed when Rachel had groaned about not looking forward to talking to her parents. Caitlyn had shrugged her shoulders and said, "Oh well, if they can't accept you, then it's their loss."

"That's what happens when you have not one, but two prodigious daughters who are a lot smarter than you," she laughed.

Voices coming from the kitchen pulled her from her thoughts. She pushed the door open and immediately saw Fred Rick busily cooking something on the stove.

Fred Rick looked over his shoulder and smiled at Rachel with perfect white teeth. "Good afternoon," he said as he transferred whatever was in the skillet onto a plate.

"Hi, Fred Rick, you wouldn't happen to know where my daughter is by any chance?" she asked.

"I sure don't, sorry but if you find her or Sydney, can you tell them that dinner is ready."

"Have you checked the garage?" Edna asked.

Rachel turned and for the first time, noticed that Edna was sitting at the small table off to the right side of the bar. "Hi, Edna, I didn't see you sitting there," she said as she approached the table.

Edna laughed. "I'm just sitting here blending in with the woodwork," she said, taking a sip of her coffee.

"You may do a lot of things, but I wouldn't say just blending in is one of them," Rachel laughed. "Is there any particular reason why I should check the garage?"

"Just go see for yourself and that's all I'm going to say," Edna chuckled.

Rachel's right eyebrow shot upward, a grin playing at the corners of her mouth. "Okay, I will just go and do that right now."

Edward had been stewing for quite some time after the mysterious phone call about his wife. The more he thought about it, the more pissed off he got. He walked over to the kitchen counter. He picked up the bottle of whiskey and refilled his glass. He tilted his head back, downed the contents of the entire glass in one long swig, and then refilled it.

"Who the fuck does she think she is?" he growled. "She's my damn wife and this shit is going to stop and it's going to stop now!"

He staggered over to the table and snatched up his keys. He nearly fell into the wall on his way to the door. "She's coming home and that's final," he yelled, jerking the door open with a bang.

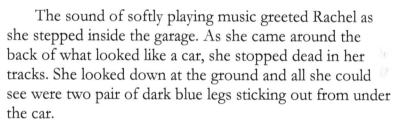

The sound of softly playing music greeted Rachel as she stepped inside the garage. As she came around the back of what looked like a car, she stopped dead in her tracks. She looked down at the ground and all she could see were two pair of dark blue legs sticking out from under the car.

"What exactly do you two think you're doing under there?" she asked, raising her voice slightly in order to get their attention.

She heard Sydney mumble something and then heard Alyssa laugh and then the two of them, slowly slid out from beneath the car and looked up at Rachel.

Rachel covered her mouth with her hand to keep from laughing. They looked like twins. Sydney and Alyssa were each lying on a small rectangle shaped board called a creeper and were dressed in identical dark blue coveralls with grease stains smeared all over their face. They were a sight for sore eyes to say the least.

Rachel placed both hands on her hips. "What do you think you're doing young lady?" she asked, looking at her daughter.

"Having a blast," Alyssa laughed.

"And what about you?" Rachel asked, directing the question to Sydney.

"What she said," Sydney answered, motioning toward Alyssa with her hand.

Sydney and Alyssa looked at each other, then looked at Rachel and then back at each other and then they lost it. Both were laughing so hard that Rachel couldn't help but join in.

Rachel was the first to pull herself together. "Fred Rick wanted me to let you know that dinner was ready."

"We better get cleaned up then, huh," Sydney said to Alyssa, nudging her with her shoulder. "You two are staying for dinner, aren't you?" she asked, looking at Rachel.

"Not tonight but thank you. It's getting late and we really need to be heading home."

"Oh, Mom. Do we have to?" Alyssa whined.

Rachel grabbed a clean rag off of the workbench. "Come over here," she said to Alyssa. She wet the rag with some spit and tried to wipe the grease off of Alyssa's cheeks.

"Mom, you're embarrassing me," Alyssa whispered as she tried to swat Rachel's hand away.

Sydney looked at Rachel and laughed.

"You're not getting into my car looking like that young lady." She stopped to look at Sydney. "And I'm glad you think it's so funny," she said, shooting Sydney a look that was supposed to be menacing as she continued to wipe Alyssa's face off.

"As a matter of fact I do. I think it's extremely funny," Sydney answered with a look of her own that was anything but menacing and it caused Rachel to do a double-take.

"You do, do you?" Rachel asked, her eyes narrowing. She gave Sydney a look that could only be defined as smoldering and full of raw "I want to rip your clothes off" desire.

Sydney suddenly found it hard to swallow as she watched Rachel move slowly toward her, a grin playing at the corners of her mouth.

"You have some grease on your face," Rachel whispered as she used the rag to wipe the smudges off of Sydney's cheeks.

Rachel was so close that Sydney could feel her warm breath on her skin. She reached up and covered Rachel's hand with her own to stop the motion. "If you knew how bad your touch affected me right now, you would stop doing it," she whispered, her voice husky with desire.

Rachel looked at her through heavily lidded eyes. She leaned in so that her lips were touching the edge of Sydney's ear. "I think if I knew how much you liked my touch, the last thing I would want to do is stop doing it," she whispered.

Sydney felt chills start from the bottom of her feet and run all the way to her head. She had no doubt that every single hair on her body was standing on end. A movement out of the corner of her eye caused her to look over Rachel's shoulder. Rachel turned to see what she was looking at.

Alyssa had stripped off her coveralls and was standing there with her hands on her hips looking at them. "You two do know that it's not polite to whisper in front of other people, right?"

"Yes, baby, we do and you're right," Rachel laughed.

Sydney bit her lower lip to keep from laughing and had to turn away from them in order to hide the smile on her face. She stripped off her coveralls and tossed them on the floor next to the one's Alyssa had discarded.

"Come on you two. Let's go before Fred Rick sends out a search and rescue party for all of us," Sydney said as she wrapped an arm around Rachel and Alyssa's shoulders.

Oh no, this can't be good, Edna thought as she looked at the disheveled looking man standing on the other side of the door. She was sure she could smell alcohol dripping from every pore of his body. "May I help you?" she asked.

Edward made a grunting sound and then pushed his way past her, shoving her off to the side as he staggered into the foyer. "Where's my fucking wife?" he snarled.

"I don't know who you're talking about," Edna said, playing dumb as she followed him into the family room.

"I know she's here goddamn it, her car's out front! Now where is she? Never mind, I'll find her myself," he yelled.

"I think you need to stay right where you are," Edna said, trying to reason with him.

"And I think you need to mind your own damn business," he growled.

"I need to find Sydney and find her quick," Edna mumbled as she ran toward the kitchen. She pushed the door open with a bang. Sydney was sitting at the bar with Alyssa. She immediately got to her feet when she noticed the look on Edna's face.

What's wrong?" she asked.

Edna glanced quickly at Alyssa and with her head, motioned for Sydney to come over to her.

"What's going on? You're whiter than a ghost," Sydney said.

"Rachel's husband is here and he's drunk and he's searching for her now. You need to hurry," she whispered franticly in Sydney's ear.

"Are Jed and Frankie still here?" she asked, her mind racing a mile a minute on how to handle the situation.

Edna nodded. "They're working on the pump motor in the pool room."

"Okay, you stay here with Alyssa," Sydney said as she took off out the door.

"You ready to go home, sweetheart?" Rachel asked without looking up from the printout she had lying on the desk in front of her.

"You're the one who's fucking coming home and you're doing it right now," Edward yelled from the doorway.

Rachel jumped up from the desk. She felt the color drain from her face. "Edward ... wh ... what are you doing here?" she asked in a shaky voice.

"Did you think I wouldn't find out about your little secret?" he growled. "You're going to quit working for that dyke bitch and get your ass back home where you belong." With each word, he inched closer and closer to Rachel and with each step, she took a step of her own, backing away from him.

"That bitch may own your company but she doesn't own you," he yelled, causing spittle to fly out of his mouth.

"She is my, my boss and she can have me do whatever job she wants me to do," Rachel said, raising her chin in defiance.

"How dare you disobey me," he said, grabbing Rachel by the wrist. He drew his free hand back to strike her.

"Please, no, Edward," Rachel cried out, jerking her arm free. She held her hands up in front of her face to ward off the blow that she knew was coming.

At that instant, Sydney, followed by Jed and Frankie

ran into the room. Jed and Frankie grabbed Edward by his arms. Sydney rushed over to Rachel and pulled her toward the door.

Edward struggled to break free. "Get your fucking hands off of me," he yelled.

Frankie was a goliath of a woman with brown spiky hair and stood nearly six and a half feet tall. She looked down at Edward and grinned as she tightened her hold on his arm. "We'll be glad to do that just as soon as we throw your sorry ass out the front door."

With Edward struggling and cursing the whole way, Frankie and Jed forcefully dragged him out into the hallway and out the front door.

Once they had him on the front porch, they released his arms.

"Don't ever come back to my house again, Edward, because if you do, you're going to jail for trespassing," Sydney said from the doorway.

He pointed his finger at her. "You're going to be sorry you ever met me and you have no idea who you're messing with," he threatened.

Sydney shook her head. "Oh, Edward, I know exactly who you are, darlin'. As for being sorry I met you, I already am," she laughed. "I know more about you than you think but you know what's funny? Thinking you know someone when you really don't know them at all. I'm not the only one with secrets," she said, a smug look on her face.

"Got to hell, bitch," he snarled.

"Not to be clichéd but ..." She shrugged. "Been there, done that!" She turned to Frankie. "We don't need another drunk on the roads. Take my truck and give the asshole a ride home, please. Jed can follow behind you. If he resists or gives you a hard time, knock him out."

"My pleasure," Frankie said and grabbed Edward by the arm. "Come on powder-puff stud muffin, let's get you home so you can sleep it off."

When Sydney walked into the design room, she didn't know what to expect. Rachel was standing by the drafting table looking out the window.

Sydney slowly walked up behind her and laid her hand on Rachel's shoulder. "Are you okay?" she asked.

Rachel brushed Sydney's hand away and whirled around to face her. "This is all your fault," Rachel said, her eyes were like ice.

Sydney's look was incredulous. "How is it my fault?" she asked. "Is it my fault you married a drunken, pompous, arrogant ass bastard?"

"If you hadn't black-mailed me, I would have never been in this situation to begin with." Rachel said the words although she knew in her heart they weren't true. Sydney was right, she is the one who created this mess but she was too angry right now to admit it.

Sydney felt the stinging threat of tears behind her eyes. "You're the one who married him, Rache, you just remember that," she said, her voice just above a whisper. She turned to leave and stopped. "Our deal is off. You're free to go. No strings attached. I'll have someone else take care of the design changes," she said over her shoulder and then left the room.

Chapter 13

It had been several days since Sydney had left Rachel standing in the design room and since she never came back, it was clear that she had taken Sydney up on her offer to let her out of their deal. Sydney hadn't realized just how much she was used to having Rachel around until it stopped—she missed her!

She had been so depressed that she hadn't bothered to go into the office all week. Thankfully, Caitlyn didn't mind making several visits to the house so they could discuss business and on behalf of Karen, brought along several time-sensitive documents that required Sydney's signature.

On Caitlyn's last visit, which took place earlier in the day, she had informed Sydney that she now knew beyond a doubt what Allen had been searching for in her office and it wasn't good. She had shown Sydney a copy of a deeded property located in Springfield, a property that Welsh now owned and had purchased at a substantially higher price than what they would have ever agreed to pay. Caitlyn had then pulled out another document, which showed that the previous owner of the property was none other than Allen Carmichael.

It took Sydney a little while to understand exactly what had happened and how Allen had managed to pull this off. Once she understood, then she was able to see why Allen was so desperate to search Caitlyn's office as well as his reasons for wanting to hack her password.

Everything came back to the new software system Caitlyn had installed. Using the old system, Allen was able to create a program that would erase the sale so that it wouldn't show him as the previous owner, which would have raised red-flags by sending out an alert for 'conflict of interest'. The conflict of interest clause had been one that Sydney had the programmers set up when she first started Welsh. She was adamant about never doing business in a way that could be interpreted by her investors as inappropriate.

In other words, no one who worked for Welsh was to do business with the company and in a sense be able to double-dip by making a profit off of the association. She even took it a step further by prohibiting Welsh deals with friends or associates of any employee at Welsh. There was also a clause in every employee's contract that stated if they were found to be guilty of such an act, they would be terminated immediately.

Allen's undoing was that he hadn't counted on, nor was he privy to the information regarding the new software system. He only learned about it the day before Caitlyn had caught him in her office.

Caitlyn's take on it was that he was searching through her drawers, hoping that she would make a newbie mistake of writing down her password. He needed Caitlyn's access to the system in order to write up a new program that would hide his deception.

Fortunately for Sydney as well as Welsh, Caitlyn was a lot more intelligent than Allen had given her credit for. Sydney had made the decision to meet with Allen the following Monday where she, along with Caitlyn, would lay out all the evidence against him.

Sydney would relieve him of his position at Welsh and she would give him the option to return the money or she would have him arrested for theft, fraud, and whatever else her attorneys could throw at him. It would be a meeting that she was dreading, yet looking forward to at the same time. She wished she could add embezzlement to the list of charges but they had no proof of that—yet!

Chapter 14

Since the day Rachel left Sydney's house, she had been miserable. Every waking thought seemed to be about Sydney. Everywhere she looked, everything she did, brought up images of Sydney's face. In the time they had been apart, Rachel had done more soul-searching than she thought she was capable of and in the end, she knew it was time to make the decisions she had dreaded and put off for years. One of those decisions now sat directly in front of her. She looked at the small two-story house where her parents lived.

"Now or never," she said as she stepped out of the car and walked up to the front door. She rang the buzzer and waited.

Lou Masters, a portly man with grey hair and kind blue eyes, pulled the door open. He smiled at Rachel. "Well, don't just stand there, come on in," he said, pulling the door open further.

"Hi, Dad, is Mom here?"

"She's in the kitchen. I have to warn you though, she's in rare form, and you not returning her phone calls hasn't helped matters any."

Rachel sighed. "Great, just what I want to hear but I need to talk to both of you and what I'm going to say may push her over the edge, so I want to prepare you now."

"Sounds important," Lou said as he led Rachel toward the kitchen.

"It is. At least for me it is," Rachel said. She took a deep breath before she stepped into the kitchen.

Roberta Masters, wearing a pale yellow smock, stood next to the sink with her hair in curlers. She placed her hands on her hips and glared at Rachel. "Where have you been young lady and why haven't you called me? Why haven't you been to church? Well, what do you have to say for yourself? Let's hear it," she demanded.

Her mother's attitude and condescending voice was all Rachel needed to gather the strength that she had lacked for so many years when it came to her parents. She'd had enough. "First of all, I don't answer to you nor do I owe you an explanation as to why I haven't been to church because quite frankly, it's none of your damn business. What I do and don't do is not your concern."

Roberta clutched her chest as if she were having a heart attack. She looked at her husband. "Did you hear how she just spoke to me, Lou?" she asked, a mortified look on her face.

Lou, with his mouth gaping open, looked at his wife and then back at Rachel.

Rachel grinned at her mother. "Well if you like that then you're really going to love what I have to say next," she said.

"What could possibly be worse than what you just said to me?" Roberta asked.

"I'm a lesbian," Rachel blurted out. She smiled inwardly at the shocked expression on her mother's face.

Roberta gasped. "What did you just say to me?" she asked.

"You heard me. I ... am ... a ... lesbian," Rachel said, making sure to annunciate each word so that her mother would have no doubt about what she was saying.

"How dare you use that word in this house. How dare you. Get out," Roberta screamed, pointing toward the door.

Rachel looked at her mother and laughed. "You remember Sydney Baxter, Mother? Don't answer that because I know you do. I'm in love with her and I always have been and I plan on telling her that myself and just so you know, I will be filing for a divorce from Edward and I don't give a damn what you or anyone else thinks about it!"

All the blood seemed to drain from Roberta's face. She looked at Rachel as if she had suddenly announced she was a serial killer. "Get out of my house this instant, you, you unrepentant harlot," she yelled.

Rachel smiled. "That's probably the nicest thing you've ever said to me," she said and turned to leave. She stopped and looked back at her mother. "When I walk out that door, I can assure you that I won't be back." Without waiting for a reply, Rachel left the kitchen and walked out of the house. When her feet hit the driveway, she took a deep breath and for the first time in years, she actually felt free.

"Rachel, wait," her dad yelled.

She turned to see her father coming toward her. She held her hand up. "Dad, if you're here to ridicule me or tell me I'm going to burn in hell, I don't want to hear it because I can tell you, growing up with that woman was more hell than any person should have to deal with."

Lou's expression softened as he looked at Rachel. "Rache, I didn't come out here to do any of those things. I wanted to tell you that I love you and just want you to be happy and if Sydney is what makes you happy, then so be it." He laughed at the shocked expression on Rachel's face.

"That is not what I expected you to say. Um ... I don't quite know what to say," Rachel said.

He wrapped his arm around Rachel's shoulders. "I know that your mother is extreme and although I tag along, your needs and wants are my first priority."

"She'll never change, Dad," Rachel said, shaking her head.

He shrugged. "It doesn't matter if she does but I want

you to know that I still want to see you and my granddaughters and if I need to come over to your house or Sydney's then that's what I will do. That's if it's okay with you."

"Of course it is," Rachel said with a grin.

"You might not understand this but throughout all the years I've been with your mother, I mostly just went along in order to keep the peace but even I've had enough."

Rachel knew she was standing there with her mouth hanging open but she couldn't help it. She had no idea how her dad had felt, which made her feel bad because she had never bothered to ask him. "I love you, Dad," she said, wrapping her arms around his shoulders.

"And I love you," he said, hugging her back.

"You've got my number," she said with a wink as she climbed into her car.

He grinned at her. "I do and I will be using it. Tell Sydney I said hi," he said as he turned and walked back up to the house.

After Lou went back inside, Rachel sat in her car for several minutes, her thoughts turning to everything that had happened in her life over the last couple of months. She thought about Sydney and hoped that it wasn't too late for them and if it was, she knew she had no one to blame but herself. Regardless of what the future held, the one thing she knew for sure was that there was no turning back now.

Chapter 15

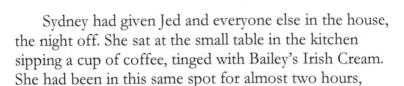

Sydney had given Jed and everyone else in the house, the night off. She sat at the small table in the kitchen sipping a cup of coffee, tinged with Bailey's Irish Cream. She had been in this same spot for almost two hours, seemingly unable to move.

The sound of the doorbell chiming caused her to jerk her head up. She glanced at the clock on the wall. She reluctantly got up from the table and made her way through the family room. It was nearly nine and she couldn't imagine who it might be.

She crossed the entryway foyer, unlocked the door, and pulled it open. What she saw caused her breath to catch in her throat.

A distraught Rachel, with blood on the side of her face looked at Sydney. "I'm sorry and I know it's late but I didn't know where else to go."

"No, no, come in," Sydney said, taking Rachel by the hand. "What happened, Rache? Are you okay?" she asked, kicking the door shut with her foot.

"I told Edward that I was filing for a divorce and he went nuts and ... and ..." she broke down in sobs, unable to finish her sentence.

"It's okay, baby. You're safe now. Let's go get you cleaned up," Sydney said soothingly as she led Rachel toward the bathroom.

She flipped on the light and gently pushed Rachel down onto the toilet seat. She felt anger course through her body as she glanced at the cut near Rachel's eyebrow. She opened the medicine cabinet and took out some ointment, alcohol pads, and a Band-Aid. "Did he hit you?" she asked.

"Yes."

Rachel's one word answer caused Sydney to feel something akin to rage. *I'm going to kill the son of a bitch. That's all there is to it*, she thought as she jerked open a drawer and took out a clean wash cloth.

She knelt down in front of Rachel. She gently laid her hand against Rachel's cheek. "Are you hurt anywhere else, sweetheart?" she asked the question although she was afraid of the answer.

Rachel shook her head. "No but it wasn't for lack of trying. I got out of the house before he could do anything else."

Sydney got to her feet and turned on the hot water. "What about the girls?" she asked as she soaked the washcloth in warm water.

"Caitlyn's still at work and Alyssa had a sleepover at Christy's."

"I'm just going to wipe the blood off, okay," Sydney said as she pressed the washcloth against Rachel's face. She wiped away the blood, trying to be as gentle as she possibly could.

"Mmm, that feels good," Rachel said, leaning into Sydney's touch.

"You might not like me too much after I clean it though," Sydney said as she ripped the package open and removed the alcohol swab. "This may sting a bit."

Rachel groaned when the swab made contact.

"I'm sorry, baby," Sydney said, tossing the swab in the trashcan. She spread a small dab of ointment on the cut, ripped off the Band-Aid strips, and gently covered the small gash.

Without realizing what she was doing, she leaned over and softly kissed Rachel on the mouth. She intended to pull away, but Rachel's arms wrapping around her neck prevented her from doing so. For several seconds they just stared into each other's eyes.

Sydney knew that the desire and hunger she was seeing and feeling from Rachel was also mirrored in her own eyes and body. Her mouth went dry, her heart began to race and she knew that this woman would always own her heart.

"Kiss me, Sydney," Rachel said, her words coming out as a plea.

When their lips met, everything in Sydney's world stopped. She devoured Rachel's mouth as if it were the last thing she would ever taste. She groaned when she felt the tip of Rachel's tongue slide over her lips.

Sydney pulled back to look at Rachel. "I want you so much, Rache, so much that I think I will die if I don't taste you."

"Then taste me," Rachel said huskily and then proceeded to trail kisses up the side of Sydney's neck.

"As much as I want that, it's not the right time or place at the moment," Sydney said.

Rachel laughed. "And here I thought chivalry was dead."

Caitlyn glanced at her watch as she dropped down into her chair. Another late night at the office—*I really need to get a life,* she thought to herself. She heaved her laptop bag up on the desk and unzipped the outside pocket. She pulled a compact disk out and removed it from its protective pink case.

She pushed the button to open the disk drive on her desktop and waited for the tray to slide open. "That's odd," she said, frowning. She looked at the silver colored disk lying in the tray.

"This is definitely not mine," she said and removed the disk. "Where did you come from and what are you doing here? Someone has been in my office when I wasn't here and lucky for me they forgot you," she said, continuing to talk aloud to the disk as if it were a person and not an object.

"Let's see what you have to say little guy." She placed the disk back in the tray and pushed it in. She clicked on the cd drive letter and waited for the contents of the disk to pop up and then clicked on the only folder listed.

"OMG ... I can't believe this." She grabbed her cell out of her purse and hit the speed dial for Sydney. "Come on, come on, answer," she urged as the phone rang in her ear.

"Oh, Sydney, thank God," she said when she heard Sydney's voice on the other end.

Sydney lay on the couch with her cell up to her ear. She smiled at Rachel as she sat two cups of tea down on the coffee table. "Hey there, what's up?" she asked.

"You're not going to believe this. I know who the embezzler is ... It's ... No, don't," Caitlyn's voice screamed through the phone.

Sydney sat bolt upright on the couch, the color draining from her face. "Caitlyn, Caitlyn," she yelled into the phone.

Hearing Caitlyn's name, Rachel stopped in mid-motion. "What's wrong?" she asked with a panic stricken look as she watched Sydney jump to her feet.

Caitlyn's unconscious, crumpled body lay on the floor. A steady stream of blood ran down the side of her face, dripping onto the carpet.

Maureen knelt down beside Caitlyn and removed the syringe sticking out of the side of her neck. She slipped a plastic cover over the needle and stuck it in her coat pocket.

She glanced at the phone laying several feet away from Caitlyn's head. The sound of Sydney's voice filled the room as she yelled through the receiver. Maureen slowly got to her feet, stepping over Caitlyn's body. She bent down and picked up the phone.

She placed the phone against her ear. A sadistic smile formed on her mouth as she listened to Sydney's frantic pleas.

"Hello? Hello," Sydney yelled into the phone. She looked at Rachel as she came out from behind the coffee table. "I know you're there because I can hear you breathing. Answer me damn it," she yelled into the phone and then the line went dead.

"Sydney. Where's Caitlyn? What happened?" Rachel's asked calmly when every nerve in her body was telling her to scream.

"I don't know but we need to get to Welsh now," Sydney yelled over her shoulder as she ran toward her bedroom.

Tears streamed down Rachel's face as she took off running after Sydney. "Oh my God, Sydney, if something has happened to Caitlyn, I don't know what I will do," she sobbed.

Sydney stopped and turned to face Rachel and pulled her into her arms. "She's going to be okay," she said in an attempt to reassure Rachel as well as herself. She knew something was terribly wrong and she fought like mad to keep her mind from creating the worst case scenario of what was happening at this very moment in Caitlyn's office.

"We can't waste anymore time," she said, reluctantly letting go of Rachel. She ran around the side of her bed and jerked open the top drawer of her nightstand.

"Oh no, no. What are you doing?" Rachel cried out when she saw the object in Sydney's hand.

Sydney ignored Rachel's question and slipped the magazine clip into the butt of the gun. She chambered the bullet by pulling back and releasing the slide. She grabbed an extra magazine from the drawer and slipped it into her pocket.

"Sydney, this is not the answer. We need to call the police," Rachel pleaded when Sydney didn't answer her.

"We don't have time for that," Sydney said as she came from around the bed. "They may kill Caitlyn before the police can get there."

"Oh dear God," Rachel cried between sobs.

The sound of Sydney's cell phone ringing in the family room caused both women to run out of the bedroom. Sydney snatched the phone up without bothering to look at the caller ID. "Hello," she said into the receiver as she sat down on the edge of the couch.

"As you know by now, I have your employee," the distorted voice said into Sydney's ear.

Sydney hit the button to put the phone on speaker mode and then laid it down on the coffee table.

"I want two-million dollars in unmarked bills and you have twenty-fours to make it happen," the distorted voice said.

"I can't get that amount of money that quickly. I need more time," Sydney tried to argue.

"Ms. Welsh, if you want to see your employee alive

again, you better make it happen."

"I want to speak to my daughter. Is she okay? Please tell me," Rachel yelled at the phone.

"I will call back in one hour. Keep your phone with you and no police," the voice said and then the phone line went dead.

Rachel dropped down on the couch next to Sydney. With shaky hands, she ran her fingers through her hair. She leaned against Sydney as gut wrenching sobs wracked her body. "I can't lose Caitlyn, I just can't," she cried as Sydney wrapped her arm around her shoulders. With her free hand, Sydney picked up her cell and hit the speed dial. She frowned when it went straight to voice-mail.

"Jackie, it's Sydney. I have an emergency and I need your help now. Meet me at Welsh just as soon as you get this message." She hung up the phone and got to her feet, pulling Rachel up along with her.

Caitlyn's eyes slowly fluttered open. It took several seconds for her vision to come into focus and when it did, she realized that she was flat on her back, looking up at a dingy grey ceiling. Her heart begun to race as images from her office flashed through her mind. She felt something cold against her skin and raised her head slightly to look at her legs. Wrapped around her ankle was a metal cuff with a chain attached to it. The other end of the chain was affixed to a large screw protruding from the wall.

She groggily sat up and then swung her legs over the side of the green-colored cot that she was sitting on. As her feet hit the floor she grabbed both sides of her head to try and stop the throbbing sensation behind her eyes. The pain was so intense, she felt like she might puke.

She looked around the room to try and get her

bearings. It was small, and measured approximately ten feet on all four sides with only one way in and out. The walls were made of large cinder blocks and were covered with chipped lime green paint. There were no windows and she assumed that she must be locked in a basement somewhere. She looked at her only route of escape. A door, with a small caged window, was centered directly in the middle of the wall opposite her.

A movement out of the corner of her eye caused her to jerk her head around. She quickly covered her mouth with her hand to keep from screaming. Two feet away, standing next to the wall, was a rat the size of a house cat. As she glanced around the floor, she felt her stomach heave as she watched several more rats scurrying in different directions.

This time, she was unable to stop the scream that came from her mouth as the rat near the wall ran beneath the cot she was sitting on. She jerked her legs up off the floor and wrapped her arms around her knees. She rocked back and forth, sobbing as tears streamed down her face.

"Oh God, please help me," she begged.

"For heaven sakes, shut the hell up," Maureen yelled as she looked at Caitlyn through the wire window in the door.

Caitlyn looked up at Maureen. "Sydney would have given you anything you asked for. Why are you doing this? I don't understand."

Maureen snorted. "No, I guess you wouldn't. You being little miss perfect and all," she said and then walked away.

Caitlyn frowned as she looked at the door. Although it was muffled, it sounded like Maureen was talking to someone. "She's not alone," Caitlyn whispered. Who else is in on this? she wondered.

"What the hell were you thinking?" Caitlyn heard the second person yell in a mechanically altered voice.

They're using a voice-changer, Caitlyn thought as she listened to their conversation.

"Are you kidding me? You're the one who told me to go get it and if you hadn't left the damn cd there, we wouldn't be in this position," Maureen yelled back.

"She was never part of our plan. She saw your face. She knows who you are and now we have to kill her," the voice said.

Forgetting about the rats, Caitlyn jumped up off of the cot. "Shit, shit, shit. I've got to get out of here," she whispered. But how? How do I get out when there's only one door and I'm chained to the freaking wall. Think, think, she told herself.

"We should have asked for more money," Maureen said.

"Just how damn much more do you think we need? In case you didn't hear me the first time, she was not part of our plan and now we have a mess to clean up. Murder was never part of the fucking deal," the voice replied.

Caitlyn could hear the agitation in the person's voice that was using the voice-changer and the sound of something being slung against the wall told her that this person was not happy one bit.

"We don't have to kill anyone. Don't you see? In two days this building will be demolished for Sydney's precious little project. Our little problem is going to have a very unfortunate accident, so technically it's not murder," Maureen said in a soothing voice, trying to reason with the person she was talking to.

"Call it what you want but I still don't like it. Do you think you can handle things until I get back?"

"How long are you going to be gone?" Maureen asked.

"Couple hours at the most."

"I can handle it but try to hurry, okay?"

"I can't believe all of this has been going on for months and not once did you think to call the police. Were you out of your damn mind?" Rachel yelled.

"Yelling at me isn't going to help and I know you're right. If I could do it all over again I would," Sydney said as the tires on her truck squealed.

"Would you please slow down before you kill us both?" Rachel shrieked as she reached out to grab the handle near the top of the door to keep from sliding across the seat.

"I know what I did was stupid, Rache, and I will do everything I can to get Caitlyn back," Sydney said as she ran through the third red light in a row.

"I swear, Sydney, if anything happens to Caitlyn, I'll never forgive you."

Sydney pulled into the Welsh parking lot and brought the truck to a tire sliding halt right in front of the main entrance. Without a word, she and Rachel jumped out of the truck and ran inside. They took the elevator up to the executive floor.

"Oh dear God," Rachel cried out when they entered Caitlyn's office. The room was trashed. "Oh no, no, no," Rachel kept repeating when she saw the blood smears on the side of Caitlyn's desk. "She's dead," Rachel said when she noticed the small puddle of blood on the floor that had turned the light blue carpet purple.

"Listen to me," Sydney said, grabbing Rachel by the shoulders. "Listen to me," she repeated. She gently shook Rachel in order to get her to look at her. "She's not dead and we are going to find her but you have to help me here. Please, I know this is hard but I need your help."

"I know," Rachel said, laying her head against Sydney's chest. "I can't lose her."

"I promise, we won't," Sydney said and placed a light kiss on the top of Rachel's head.

The sound of Sydney's cell phone ringing caused them

to pull apart. She snatched it off her waistband and looked at the caller ID. She didn't recognize the number.

"Hello," she said after pressing the speaker phone button.

Maureen held the voice-changer to her mouth. "Have you arranged to get my money yet?" she said into the cell phone.

"I need more time," Sydney replied.

"Bullshit! Do you really think I would believe that the great and powerful Sydney Welsh can't get her hands on a measly two-million dollars within twenty-four hours?" Maureen asked.

"I want to talk to Caitlyn," Sydney demanded.

Maureen laughed. "And people in hell want ice water and from where I'm standing, you're in no position to demand anything."

"Please let me talk to Caitlyn. I just want to know that she's okay," Sydney asked in a calm voice.

"With God as my witness, Ms. Welsh, if you've called the police, make no mistake about it, I will kill her," Maureen said, her voice raising several octaves.

"I swear. I haven't called the police. You have my word on that," Sydney said in an attempt to reassure Caitlyn's kidnapper.

"I'm watching you and Ms. Ashburn and if you do, I will know it," Maureen said in a matter of fact voice.

"What do you mean you're watching us?" Sydney asked.

Maureen laughed "Let's see, right now, you are wearing a black turtle neck sweater and jeans and Ms. Ashburn looks ravishing in that cream colored blouse. It really accentuates the curve of her breasts, don't you think?"

Rachel and Sydney looked at each other with shocked expressions on their face. Sydney looked around the room. Her eyes stopped at the small camera on Caitlyn's desk. She casually moved in front of it and turned to face Rachel, her back blocking the camera lens. She placed her finger to her mouth for Rachel to be quiet and not say anything.

"Okay. I got the message. I promise, we won't call the police and I will have your money first thing in the morning," Sydney said to the caller on the other end.

"Please ... please let me speak to Caitlyn," Rachel begged.

She and Sydney exchanged glances at the sound of keys jingling. They heard a door creak open.

Maureen held up the taser gun and pointed it directly at Caitlyn's face. With the voice-changer still in her hand, Maureen spoke into her cell phone.

"I'm warning you. If either of you say one wrong word, I will kill her right where she sits."

Maureen placed the phone on speaker. "Say hi to Mommy, honey."

"Mom, are you there?" Caitlyn asked.

"Oh, baby. Are you okay?" Rachel asked, her voice coming out crystal clear through the speaker.

Before Caitlyn had a chance to reply, Maureen took the phone off speaker.

"Have my money tomorrow or she dies," Maureen said into the phone. Just as Maureen was about to disconnect the line, Caitlyn yelled out, "Two Demo Boro."

Maureen looked at Caitlyn as if she had committed a cardinal sin. "You bitch," she spat, backhanding Caitlyn across the face and splitting her lip in the process, causing her to cry out in pain.

"Caitlyn," Rachel's voice screamed through the phone just as Maureen disconnected the line.

Rachel paced back and forth in front of the desk. She was a nervous wreck. All she could think about was getting her hands on whoever had Caitlyn.

Sydney casually tossed her jacket over the camera sitting on Caitlyn's desk. She reached out to pick up the phone and Rachel grabbed her hand to stop her. "What about fingerprints?" she asked.

Sydney shook her head. "It doesn't matter because whoever the kidnapper is, they are somehow tied to the embezzlement with a link to Welsh. For all we know, they are an employee and their fingerprints will be all over the place."

"I suppose you're right," Rachel said and let go of Sydney's hand.

Sydney picked up the phone on Caitlyn's desk just as Jackie came running into the office. "Sorry it took me so long, Syd. I was visiting my parents over in Sugarcreek when I got your second message and I got here just as soon as I could."

"It's all good, I'm just glad you're here," Sydney said.

"Have they made any other contact?" Jackie asked as she came around the desk.

Sydney nodded. "Yeah and they let Caitlyn speak, so we know she's still alive."

Jackie looked at Sydney with raised eyebrows. "What about the police? Don't you think it's time you called them now?" she asked.

"Thank God. Someone who can see reason," Rachel

said, looking at Jackie. She turned to look at Sydney, shooting her a look that made Sydney want to cringe. "Who are you calling?" she asked.

Sydney shook her head. "I'm not calling the police. I'm calling my banker. I need her to pull the money together as soon as she can and there's no reason she can't do it within the time frame we need."

Ignoring both Rachel and Jackie's protests, Sydney turned her attention back to Caitlyn's phone. Without meaning to, she accidentally hit the redial button. She looked at the display window and quickly disconnected the line. Without looking at Jackie or Rachel, she punched in a number and waited as the line rang through.

"Jen, I'm sorry to bother to you at this late hour but I need a huge favor." Sydney cocked her head as she listened to Jennifer Ogden, her banker; assure her that the late hour was not a problem.

"Here's what I need, Jen. Two-million dollars in unmarked bills," Sydney glanced at her wrist watch, "within the next four hours."

"Sydney, I know you know what time it is and how hard that will be," Jennifer said through the phone.

"Listen to me, Jen, you either get the money and have it ready for me to pick up in the next four hours or I will find myself a new banker along with a new bank," Sydney yelled into the phone right before she hit the button to disconnect the line.

Rachel and Jackie just stared at Sydney as she slammed the phone back into the cradle. Sydney didn't miss a beat, though. "Jackie, see what you can find. Follow the blood and see where it leads," she instructed, pointing at the blood on the floor that showed a clear path out the door of Caitlyn's office.

After Jackie went out the door, Sydney sat down in Caitlyn's chair and turned on her computer.

"What are you looking for?" Rachel asked, coming up

behind Sydney to look over her shoulder.

"I have no idea," Sydney reluctantly admitted. "Do me a favor, look through Caitlyn's notebook and see if anything stands out," she said, pushing a binder over to the side.

Rachel sighed in frustration as she flipped through the pages. "Sydney, nothing in here makes sense to me. It's all gibberish except for something that says Project Burg."

Sydney stopped what she was doing. "Hand that to me, please," she asked, looking at Rachel.

Rachel slid the binder over to Sydney. Using her finger, Sydney scanned the contents on the page that Rachel had open. "That's it," she said, looking at Rachel with a smile on her face.

"I don't understand," Rachel said, a look of confusion on her face. Sydney wasn't making any sense at all.

"See this?" Sydney said, pointing to the line that said 'Project Dem/Burg.

"I don't understand," Rachel said, shaking her head.

"It's a building that I own off of seven-twenty-five and it's set to be demolished in two days. I bought it a few months ago. Welsh is going to use it for our new computer recycling plant," Sydney grinned.

Rachel frowned. "I still don't understand."

Sydney grabbed Rachel and kissed her fully on the lips. "Two Demo Burg," Sydney said shaking her head. "Your daughter is a freaking genius, Rache. That's all there is to it and I think I know exactly where she's being held."

Rachel shook her head. "But all she said was demo burg two. What does that mean?"

"I'm not one hundred percent sure. It could be anything, second floor, two people, second door. Hold on a sec," Sydney said as she clicked the mouse a few times. She opened up a folder from Caitlyn's files. She looked at Rachel and smiled.

"What?" Rachel asked. She had no idea what Sydney

was doing or where her train of thought was leading.

Sydney pointed at the computer screen. Rachel looked at the screen and shrugged her shoulders.

"That building is scheduled to be demolished in two days and based on my update reports, the demolition crew partially rigged the building this morning with explosives."

Rachel unsuccessfully tried to choke back a sob. She shook her head as she covered her mouth with her hand.

Sydney laid her hand on Rachel's shoulder. "We need to get over there, Rache," she said.

Both women looked up as Jackie walked back into Caitlyn's office.

"I checked all the doors, no sign of forced entry. I did find a blood trail on the back stairwell that led to the side parking lot. The trail stopped next to a set of tire tracks. It looks like whoever was here was also in a hurry to leave from the slide marks left on the ice," Jackie said, looking at Rachel and then at Sydney.

It took Sydney several minutes to fill Jackie in on what they found and her opinion about what it all meant. She then voiced her feelings that there might be more than one kidnapper but she wasn't sure. She knew Caitlyn would have put up a fight if it had been just one person and if by chance she were unconscious, the kidnapper in all likelihood would have needed help getting Caitlyn in the car.

"I agree with you one hundred percent," Jackie said, nodding her head. "Just from the little bit of interaction I had with her, I can't see her going peacefully."

"Do you have your gun with you?" Sydney asked, looking at Jackie.

"Oh yeah, never leave home without Bertha," Jackie laughed as she pulled open her jacket, revealing the gun and holster.

Sydney laughed. "Bertha? Really? Couldn't find something a little more original?" she asked.

"Hey, watch it. That was my granny's name and she was meaner than a damned old rattlesnake. So Bertha fits perfectly."

"If you say so," Sydney laughed.

"If you two are done chatting, I think we should call the police," Rachel said, her voice undeniably filled with sarcasm. All she could think about was Caitlyn and what she must be going through. She's probably scared to death.

Sydney looked at Rachel and shook her head. "Not yet, hon. We can't take the chance of risking Caitlyn's life. We're just gonna drive over to the building and if we see any evidence that Caitlyn might be there, I promise, we will call the police. Okay?" she asked, looking at Rachel.

Rachel and Jackie stood next to Sydney's truck. They waited for Sydney to secure the door.

"Follow, behind us," Sydney instructed Jackie as she walked up to the two women.

"You got it," Jackie said, heading toward her own car.

Once inside of Sydney's truck, Rachel turned to look at her. "I don't understand why you won't call the police."

Sydney shifted in her seat to look at her. "You just don't get it, do you, Rache? Caitlyn knows who the kidnapper is and I have a strong hunch that she meant that there are two of them and that's what she meant by the number two."

"How can you be sure?" Rachel asked, slamming her hand on the dashboard in frustration. "Would you please share your fucking thoughts with me?"

Rachel's use of the 'F' word caused Sydney to do a double-take. As long as she had known Rachel, not once had she remembered hearing her ever utter or use that word. She just didn't say it—ever. She looked at Rachel and shrugged. "Because I've been around Caitlyn long enough to know that she wouldn't have said it, unless it was significant."

Rachel took a deep breath and tried to bring her emotions under control. "If she was being held on the second floor, that would be pretty significant."

Sydney looked at Rachel. "Please just trust me on this," she said.

Rachel glanced at Sydney. She shook her head. "Why do I have a feeling that you're hiding something from me? That you're not telling me the whole story?" she asked.

"I don't know why. Maybe its divine inspiration," Sydney said with sarcasm.

Sydney pulled her truck into a parking spot, directly in front of the building and stopped. She unhooked her seatbelt, reached across Rachel, popped open the glove box, and pulled out a flashlight.

They waited for Jackie to park and then got out of the truck.

"I can see why you're tearing it down, it's a mess," Rachel said, looking at the dilapidated old four-story structure that had large pieces of concrete missing along the front.

Sydney turned the flashlight on and pointed it down toward the ground. "I know. We just bought it for the land. Be careful here," she said as they climbed up a set of steps that were in nearly as bad of shape as the building.

"This is definitely not good," Sydney said. The chain that had been used to secure the door had been cut and was hanging off to the side, the padlock still attached. "Once we get inside, try to keep your voice low," Sydney said, looking first at Rachel and then at Jackie.

"We should call the police now," Rachel said, her voice shaking slightly.

Sydney slowly pushed the door open. "I just want to have a look around and if she's not here, then we'll call the police," she whispered.

"How do you want to do this?" Jackie asked, quietly closing the door behind them.

"Do you really think those are necessary?" Rachel whispered as she watched Sydney and Jackie take out their guns and check them.

"It's for our own protection," Sydney said as she used her flashlight to look around. They were standing in what was once the lobby. She shined her light toward the back of the room. On either side of the receptionist's desk were three doorways. Directly to their right, was an elevator that had a "Not In Service" chain hanging across it.

"If I remember correctly, that door," Sydney shined her light on the doorway furthest to her left, "leads to the break room."

Rachel grabbed the back of Sydney's shirt. "I don't like this. It's so dark in here," she whispered.

"Just hang onto me and stay close," Sydney said as she moved toward the second doorway. "Rachel and I will check this side, you take the other one," she said, looking at Jackie.

"You got it," Jackie said and headed toward the door.

"Hey, Jackie?" Sydney whispered.

"Yeah?" Jackie, answered, stopping to turn and look at Sydney.

"Be careful," Sydney said.

"You, too," Jackie said and then disappeared through the doorway.

"I have a bad feeling about this," Rachel said, her voice trembling as she followed Sydney into a dark hallway.

"I promise we'll call the police either way once we're

done here," Sydney said, reaching behind her to briefly squeeze Rachel's hand.

Sydney stopped at the first door they came to. She slowly pushed it open and shined her flashlight around the room.

Jackie slowly made her way down the hallway, turned to her right, walked a short distance and stopped in front of a closed door. She pushed it open. It was a stairwell that only led down. She felt her heart thundering in her chest, beads of sweat popping up on her forehead as she quietly pulled the door shut behind her. Moving as quietly as she could and with her back pressed against the wall, she descended the steps.

"This must have been their call center," Sydney said, shining her light on several cubicles.

Rachel tightened her grip on the back of Sydney's shirt. "This place is creepy," she whispered.

"It's not so bad during the day when you can see your hand in front of your face," Sydney laughed softly. "Come on, we still have a few more places to check," she said, pulling Rachel out the door by her hand.

Jackie stopped at the bottom of the stairs. With her gun aiming forward, she slowly pushed the door open and stepped into a room, lighted by two propane lanterns hanging on the wall.

Maureen looked up from the table where she was sitting. She smiled as she got to her feet and walked over to Jackie.

"I was beginning to worry about you, baby," she said, wrapping her arms around Jackie's neck.

Jackie reached back and unclasped Maureen's fingers from around her neck. She gently pushed her away, holding her fingers to her mouth for Maureen to be quiet.

She slowly raised the gun and pointed it at Maureen's chest. She looked at Maureen and silently mouthed the words, "I'm sorry."

For a split second, Maureen's eyes went wide in shock as her mind registered what was happening. Before she could open her mouth, Jackie pulled the trigger.

The gun recoiled in Jackie's hand, the sound echoing loudly off the walls. The bullet hit Maureen directly in the middle of her chest. Her body dropped to the floor with a thud. The white blouse she was wearing turned pink as blood gushed from her chest.

"Oh no," Sydney yelled when she and Rachel heard the gun go off.

"Caitlyn!" Rachel screamed.

Sydney grabbed Rachel by the hand and pulled her toward the doorway that led back out into the hallway. Still holding Rachel's hand, she took off running in the direction she thought the sound had come from. "Shit, I don't know which way to go," she said in frustration when they came to the end of the main hallway.

"What about that door?" Rachel asked, pointing to the

door located less than three feet in front of them.

"I think it leads to the stairwell," Sydney said. As soon as she jerked the door open, they heard Caitlyn scream.

Jackie hurriedly pulled a gun out from inside her waist band. She used the tail end of her shirt to wipe off her fingerprints. She knelt down next to Maureen's body and picked up her right arm.

"What's going on out there?" Caitlyn shouted. She grabbed the chain wrapped around her ankle and jerked with all her might, trying to rip it from the wall. It didn't budge. "Let me out of here, please," she pleaded.

Ignoring Caitlyn's cries for help, Jackie placed the gun in Maureen's hand, making sure to press her fingers around it, taking extra care to insure Maureen's index finger touched the trigger.

Just as she got to her feet and took several steps back, the basement door flew open and Sydney and Rachel rushed in. Rachel gasped, clasping her hand over her mouth when she saw Maureen lying on the ground. She looked around the room. "Caitlyn?" she yelled.

"Oh God, Mom. I'm in here," Caitlyn sobbed from the other side of the door.

Rachel ran over to the door and looked through the screen window. She was unable to stop the tears spilling down her cheeks when she saw Caitlyn standing next to the cot. "It's okay, baby. It's all over. You're safe now. I'll get you out in a second."

"Don't leave me," Caitlyn sobbed.

"I won't, baby. I've got to find the keys. I'll be right back." Rachel looked around the room. "Keys, where are the damn keys?" she yelled.

"I think that's them laying there," Jackie said, nodding

toward the table.

Sydney walked over to Maureen and knelt down on the floor beside her. She used her fingers to check for a pulse in Maureen's neck. Rachel looked at her expectantly as she snatched the keys off of the table. Sydney shook her head. Although she checked for a pulse, she had known that Maureen was already dead by the fixed position of her eyes, which were now staring blankly up at the ceiling.

"Oh, Maureen. Why? If you needed money, I would have just given it to you. All you had to do was ask," Sydney said, fighting back tears.

Rachel tried several keys before she found the one that fit the door, she unlocked it and ran over to Caitlyn, wrapping her arms around Caitlyn's shoulders.

Caitlyn collapsed against her mom, her body shaking as she cried. "It's okay now, baby," Rachel said in a soothing voice as she hugged her daughter tightly. She let go of Caitlyn long enough to find the key that fit the cuff on her ankle. She released the chain and wrapped her arm around Caitlyn's waist as she led her out of the room.

Jackie ran her hand through her hair. "I had no choice, Syd. She pulled the gun and ..."

"Is, is she dead?" Caitlyn asked when she saw Maureen.

Sydney nodded. "Yeah, she is," she said, getting to her feet.

"Do you know her?" Rachel asked, looking at Sydney.

"She is, was my assistant," Sydney answered. She looked at Rachel. "Do you have your cell with you?"

Rachel nodded. "Yeah, why?"

"Call the police. When you get them on the phone tell them that there's been a kidnapping and a murder and that we're standing here with the person who's responsible for both." Rachel and Caitlyn both looked at Sydney like she had just lost her mind.

"Just do it, Rache," Sydney said when Rachel made no

move to take out her cell.

Much to everyone in the room's surprise, Sydney slowly raised her gun and pointed it at Jackie.

"What the hell are you doing, Sydney?" Rachel asked.

"Damn it, Rache, just do it! Sydney yelled, not taking her eyes off of Jackie.

"No! Not until you tell me what's going on," Rachel said, shaking her head.

"Yeah, Syd. I think we would all like to know the answer to that question," Jackie said with raised eyebrows.

Sydney glared at Jackie. If looks could kill, she would have been dead in an instant. "Shut the fuck up," she yelled. She rubbed her temple with her index finger. "It all makes sense now. How could I have been so stupid?" she asked, shaking her head.

"Damn it, Sydney! Please tell me what's going on? What are you talking about?" Rachel demanded.

Sydney looked at Jackie and smiled. "Jackie is or was Maureen's lover."

"Don't be stupid, Sydney," Jackie said.

Sydney glanced at Caitlyn, being extra careful to keep an eye on Jackie. "Caitlyn, can you tell me if you remember hearing a phone ringing a little while ago. Actually, what I want to know specifically, is if you heard a phone ring twice, say around fifteen minutes apart."

"Yes, it was a weird kinda ringtone," Caitlyn answered without hesitation.

Sydney watched Jackie's facial expression as she flipped out her cell phone. She hit one of her speed dial buttons. "Did it sound like this?" she asked, continuing to watch Jackie.

Inside Jackie's coat, her cell phone rang, producing a raucous kind of beat.

Caitlyn's eyebrows rose in surprise. "Yeah. That's exactly what I heard," she said, nodding her head.

Jackie laughed. "I never did like that ringtone but Mo

insisted on it." She looked at Sydney and grinned. "So hotshot, how'd you figure it out?"

Sydney looked at Caitlyn and smiled. "Actually, Caitlyn did it. It was your clue. At first, I thought two demo referred to the demolition taking place in two days for the Demo Burg Project and it wasn't until I went to your office that it all started making sense. I went to use your desk phone and I accidentally hit the redial button. The caller ID display showed Jackie's cell number and I couldn't figure out why you would have ever called her and then it dawned on me ... All those times Maureen had received roses, they were signed by John. I could never understand why she didn't want to find out who this person was, she didn't need to because she already knew who John was. Calling yourself John was pretty ingenious. Nice word play on the name Jack," she said, looking at Jackie.

She turned to Caitlyn. "See one of the things I knew about Jackie is that she thought JFK was the best president to ever walk the face of the earth. His name was John, yet everyone called him Jack. As for Maureen, she had to have called Jackie from your office after she attacked you and that's how she carried you out. Jackie helped her."

Sydney smiled at Jackie. "I'm doing pretty good so far, huh?"

"You figured it out just from the caller ID?" Caitlyn asked.

"No, it just confirmed what I already suspected. It was that shorthand way of talking thingy you do."

Caitlyn smiled. "I knew you would get it."

"Yes, but when I wrote out the clue you yelled through the phone, it took me several tries to get it right. Two demo stood for the demolition and Mo was short for Maureen, which is what Jackie called her when she was at my office, which I assume was a slip-up on her part. I just assumed the two meant there were two people involved."

"Not bad for an old lady," Caitlyn laughed.

Rachel shook her head. "But how did you know she killed Maureen and that it wasn't in self-defense like she said?"

Sydney looked at Jackie as she spoke. "That's an easy one and Jackie should have known better. She put the gun in the wrong hand."

All three women looked over at Maureen's right hand, which still held the gun.

"She was left-handed?" Rachel asked.

"Yeah, she was. I used to tease her about it all the time," Sydney said.

Rachel took out her cell phone and dialed 911. She waited for the dispatcher to pick up. "My name is Rachel Ashburn and I'm at ..." She looked at Sydney.

"2122 North Third," Sydney said.

"I'm at 2122 North Third Street. There's been a kidnapping and a murder and you need to send someone as soon as you can." She paused to listen to the dispatcher. She shook her head. "No, I can't stay on the line," she said and then snapped her cell phone shut.

Jackie shifted nervously from one foot to the other. "If all of you are done with your little love fest from the admiration society, I'd like to add my two-cents worth."

"I'm not interested in a damn thing you have to say you twisted bitch. If I had a gun I'd be tempted to shoot you myself," Rachel snarled.

"Wow, Mom. I didn't know you could break butch," Caitlyn laughed.

"Baby, you ain't seen anything yet," Rachel said.

"I have a question," Caitlyn said, looking at Jackie.

"Fire away," Jackie said.

"Which one of you wrote the programming codes?" Caitlyn asked.

"That would be me," Jackie said, tapping her chest with her finger. "It was quite ingenious, don't you think?

Like you, computers and programming are in my blood. The only difference is that it was more like a hobby for me." Jackie smiled, obviously proud of herself. She looked at Caitlyn and shook her head. "I have to tell you though, I was shocked and impressed at the same time when you figured out I was using the Salami Technique. I got the idea from a case that I helped investigate in New York. It was so simple and almost full proof." Jackie shrugged. "If it hadn't been for your new system upgrade, who knows how long we could have kept it going."

"But why?" Sydney asked. That was the one question she didn't have an answer for.

Jackie looked at Sydney and shrugged. "Hell, I don't know. Partly greed and thinking you had so much money, you'd never miss it but for me it was more an issue of seeing if I could pull it off. It was one helluva an adrenaline rush. Now Mo on the other hand, had her own reasons."

"And those would be?" Sydney asked.

"Do you remember a company called Hazlo?" Jackie asked.

"Vaguely, why?" Sydney asked.

"You should. It was one of four companies you took over when you first started building your business." Jackie smiled and shook her head as she watched Sydney as she tried to place the name. "Let me help you out. Mo's parents had worked at Hazlo all their lives and when you came in, you stripped the company down to the bare bones, laying off or should I say, firing ninety percent of the workforce. Mo's parents were two of the employees who lost their jobs and because of your greed and ruthlessness, her parents lost their house, the house that Mo grew up in. So when she found out you were hiring at Welsh, she decided to come work for you and get her own revenge.

Sydney sighed heavily. She ran her fingers through her hair in frustration. "I had no idea about her parents."

Jackie laughed. "Of course you didn't.

"It wasn't personal, it was just a part of doing business," Sydney said.

Jackie snorted. "Her parents and the rest of the employees were just peons to you. They didn't matter as long as you got what you wanted and to Mo, it was *very* personal."

"But how did you get involved?" Sydney asked.

Jackie shrugged. "She and I had been dating for almost three months when she told me all about her parents and how she hated you. So, with me having programming skills and her being on the inside at Welsh, we sat down and put a plan together and you know the rest of the story." Jackie smiled. "When you track down the rest of your money, you'll see that some of it's missing. Mo used it to buy her parents a new house and car."

Sydney shook her head. "This is unbelievable."

"Yeah, well it is what it is. I'm sure you'll take their house back now that you know," Jackie said, her voice full of sarcasm.

"No, I won't," Sydney said, shaking her head. She looked at Jackie. "So tell me this. Why didn't you just kill Rachel and me once I figured out where Caitlyn was being held?"

Jackie laughed. "Oh believe me when I say I seriously thought about it but then the logic side of my brain kicked in. I figured it would be easier to make it out like Mo was the mastermind. You know, raise less questions than if I off'd you and your main squeeze."

"And Maureen? Do you not feel any remorse for what you did to her?" Sydney asked.

"Nah, not really." Jackie shrugged. "She was expendable."

Rachel's look was incredulous. "You're insane," she said to Jackie.

"Maybe," Jackie said, grinning at Rachel. She looked at

Caitlyn and then at Sydney. "Why don't you tell dear Caitlyn here the real reason why she got the job working for you?"

Sydney glared at Jackie. "Shut up."

Caitlyn frowned. "What's she talking about, Syd?"

"Go ahead, Syd," Jackie mocked sarcastically. "Tell the kid how you only hired her so you could take revenge on her mother."

"I said shut up," Sydney yelled, pointing the gun directly at Jackie's head.

Jackie grinned wickedly. "Ah, what's the matter, Syd? Cat got your tongue?"

"I mean it, Jackie," Sydney said as she took a step closer.

Rachel turned and looked at Sydney. "What's she talking about, Sydney?"

"Well if you won't tell them I will," Jackie said with a shrug of her shoulders. "Actually, I have something I want to say to you first. Something, I have wanted to say to you since we met. It's your fault that people like me do what we do. You with all your money, sitting on your high and mighty throne, pulling the strings for all of us lowlifes as if you were the puppet master. You use your power and money to fuck with people's lives, and then when things go wrong, you're the first to blame everyone else. Poor, poor, Sydney Welsh, she got her little heart broke and couldn't handle it. Why is that, Syd? Because dear Rachel here, had enough sense to tell you to go fuck yourself?"

Rachel grabbed Sydney by the arm. "Tell me what the hell she is talking about, Sydney?" she demanded.

Sydney felt her heart breaking all over again as she looked at Rachel. She opened her mouth but no words came out.

Jackie laughed. "Wow, the great Sydney Welsh, Ohio's finest millionaire is speechless. That has to be a first."

Sydney's look was incredulous. "How dare you pass

judgment on me after what you've done. For Christ's sake, you killed Maureen, the woman you supposedly loved. You kidnapped Caitlyn and you and I both know that you were going to kill her, too."

"Yeah, well … C'est la vie, enough about me. Let's talk about the last ten years and how you had me help you put together this massive scheme to get dear old Rachel back into your life and …" Jackie pointed at herself and then at Sydney. "How you and I working together as a team, plotted to hire Caitlyn fresh out of high school, and how we worked on your plan to purchase Rachel's company."

With a move quicker than Sydney thought possible, Jackie reached to her right and grabbed Caitlyn. Caitlyn screamed as Jackie rammed the barrel of the gun against the side of her head.

"Don't be stupid," Jackie said as Sydney and Rachel both took a step toward her. "I swear to God I will put a bullet through her pretty little head. So be smart, Sydney, and slide your gun across the floor to me."

"If it's about the money, Jackie, I will give you whatever you want."

"You just think you can buy your way out of everything don't you? I said, put the goddamn gun down, Sydney," Jackie yelled.

Caitlyn shook her head. "No, Syd, don't do it. She will just kill all of us anyway."

Jackie smiled. "I give you my word. I will let all of you go."

Sydney snorted. "Yeah, I know how much that's worth now."

The sound of sirens in the distance caused Jackie to cock her head. "Sounds like the Calvary is coming," she said in a voice thick with sarcasm.

"How can you possibly judge me after what you've done? I don't give a shit what you think about me, or what

I've done. Nothing can justify you killing Maureen," Sydney said in an attempt to keep Jackie talking to buy them more time. "You know, this just keeps getting better. I just now realized that you and Maureen came into my life around the same time." She looked at Jackie and laughed and for a split-second, she clenched her teeth so hard it made her jaw hurt. "My God, that means the two of you have been planning this all along."

Before Sydney knew what was happening, Caitlyn had twisted away from Jackie, shoving her sideways in the process.

Jackie bent over at the waist and laughed. As she stood upright, she slowly brought the gun to her head.

"You aren't getting off that easy," Sydney yelled, pulling the trigger.

Jackie screamed as the bullet hit her right thigh. She fell to her knees, dropping her gun in the process.

"You shot me, you bitch," Jackie cried out as she grabbed her thigh, trying to stop the blood that was now flowing between her fingers.

"You deserve much worse," Sydney said, kicking the gun away from Jackie with her foot. She walked over to the table and grabbed a rag off of it. She carefully side- stepped around Jackie, bent down, and picked up the gun using the rag.

The sound of footsteps running across the floor above their head got their attention. "Let's get out of here," Sydney said, looking at both women.

Rachel and Caitlyn, their arms wrapped around each other's waist followed Sydney out of the room.

"Freeze," a cop, dressed in a Miamisburg's Police uniform yelled from the top of the stairwell.

"We're the good guys," Sydney yelled back, shielding her eyes with her hand from the bright glare of his flashlight. "I have two guns, one is mine, and the other wrapped in this rag belongs to the killer. It's the murder weapon and has her fingerprints on it. I'm going to slowly pull mine out of my pocket and lay it down on the step along with this one."

"I strongly urge you to move very slow," he said, his voice shaking.

Sydney slowly removed her gun and then laid them both down on the step.

Now put your hands up where I can see them," he yelled. It was then that Sydney as well as Rachel and Caitlyn noticed the gun pointing at them.

"Please don't shoot us," Rachel pleaded as she along with Sydney and Caitlyn raised their arms in the air.

"Come on up here and move slowly," the officer instructed as another officer came into the stairwell. He held the door open and as the women came up the stairs, he backed slowly away from them through the open doorway.

"All three of you against the wall, arms over your head," he said, still keeping the light on them.

The other officer quickly searched them. "They're clean," he said.

"You can put your arms down now," the officer who had the gun on them said as he put his gun back in the holster.

"There's a woman downstairs who's been shot and she needs an ambulance. She killed the other woman lying on the floor," Sydney said.

"Who are you?" the officer who had held the door open asked.

"My name is Sydney Welsh and I own the building." She nodded at Caitlyn. "She's my employee and was kidnapped by the two women downstairs and this is her mother, Rachel Ashburn."

"We're waiting for the homicide detectives to arrive but we're going to need a full statement from all of you," he said, looking at Sydney.

Sydney nodded and said, "I understand."

Chapter 16

Sydney stood next to the fireplace in the family room, a glass of Bourbon in her hand. She took a swig, watching as Rachel came across the room toward her. "How's Caitlyn," she asked.

"She's sleeping better than a baby. The doctor gave her a sedative that knocked her out," Rachel replied.

"And Alyssa?"

"She's fine. I'm gonna pick her up tomorrow at Christy's after one."

"I'm so sorry, Rache," Sydney said, her voice just above a whisper.

Rachel looked at Sydney with contempt, her face a blank mask. She felt all the hurt and anger suddenly boil over. In less than a second, she had slapped Sydney across the face before she even realized what had happened.

Sydney stumbled backward from the blow.

Rachel's mouth flew open in horror. "Oh my God," she said, clasping her hand to her mouth.

Feeling beaten and broken down, Sydney dropped her head against her chest. She deserved so much more than just getting slapped across the face. When she looked up, tears were streaming down her cheeks. "When you leave here, I promise to never bother you or your children again." Sydney closed her eyes, turned to walk away but Rachel grabbed her by the hand.

Rachel's expression softened as she looked at Sydney. "I had no right to do that and I'm sorry," she whispered.

"You had every right," Sydney choked out between sobs.

Rachel cupped Sydney's face in her hand. "Please don't go. I have spent too many years away from you and I can't do it anymore. I don't want to do it anymore," she said, her eyes pleading. "I may not fully understand what you did but I know what a broken heart feels like because mine has never healed."

Sydney reached up and covered Rachel's hand with her own. She brought it to her lips and kissed it. "When I first put this insane plan of mine together, I had tunnel vision so bad that nothing or anyone could make me see how crazy it was. I told myself that I was doing it for revenge and that I wanted you to hurt as bad as I had hurt for all these years. I couldn't understand or accept why you wouldn't stand up for us."

"Oh, Sydney, I did hurt, sweetheart," Rachel said as she wiped the tears from Sydney's cheek with her thumb. "You don't need to tell me any of this."

"No, Rache, I do need to tell you this. I want to tell you the truth, a truth that I just recently realized. I was lying to myself. I never wanted revenge and I know I subconsciously thought ... I thought that if you were around, that maybe you would fall in love with me all over again and if you did, maybe we would finally have a chance for a life together."

Rachel thought her heart would break as she watched Sydney struggle to get the words out. The anguish and remorse that she was showing was almost more than Rachel could take. She cupped Sydney's face between her hands. She kissed her softly on the lips. "I am in love with you, Sydney Welsh, and I always have been. I do want a life with you and I don't care what anyone else thinks about it."

"Oh God," Sydney cried as she wrapped her arms around Rachel's waist and pulled her close. She felt like the weight of the world had just been lifted from her shoulders. She rested her forehead against Rachel's, looking her in the eye. Try as she might, she couldn't stop the onslaught of tears falling down her face.

"I've always been in love with you, Rache. From the moment you opened your mouth I was mesmerized," she said through a fresh rush of tears. "Other women have had my body but none of them ever had my heart. It's always belonged to you and no one else and it will be yours until the day I die."

Edward watched Sydney and Rachel through the window and just as Sydney lowered her head to kiss Rachel, he snapped off several pictures using the camera in his cell phone. "You think you're so damned smart, well we'll just see about that," he snarled under his breath. *You don't know who you're dealing with bitch, but you're gonna find out,* he thought as he continued to take more pictures.

"I need to make love with you and if I have to wait much longer, I'm going to die," Sydney whispered in Rachel's ear.

"Oh no, sweetheart, I haven't suffered all these years to have you up and die on me now," Rachel said, sliding her hands beneath Sydney's shirt.

Sydney shivered and groaned at the same time when Rachel's fingers softly grazed the side of her breasts.

"Something wrong," Rachel whispered against Sydney's neck as she lightly kissed her way up to her ear.

Sydney tossed her head back as warm tingling sensations spread throughout her entire body, ending with wet and throbbing pulsations between her legs. "I'm going to pass out," she moaned as Rachel's hands cupped both of her breasts, her thumbs making light teasing circles over her nipples.

"I want to make love with you all night long and I guarantee you're not going to pass out," Rachel said, removing her hands from inside of Sydney's shirt. She took Sydney's hand in hers and pulled her toward the master bedroom.

Sydney stopped walking. The quick move caused Rachel to spin around so that she was facing Sydney, their breasts now firmly pressed against each other.

She looked into Rachel's eyes and every ounce of love she felt for this woman poured out. When their lips met, all the years of pain and suffering and longing melted away. Sydney had never tasted such exquisiteness in her life and she wanted so, so much more. She was unable to stop the moan that escaped from her throat as Rachel's lips parted, allowing her tongue to taste such divine sweetness.

Without realizing how it happened, they found themselves standing next to Sydney's bed.

Sydney's hands moved up and down Rachel's body as if their sole purpose in life was to devour everything they touched. I need to see you, all of you," Sydney said as she slowly unbuttoned Rachel's blouse and slid it off of Rachel's shoulders. She let it drop to the floor without taking her eyes off of the woman standing in front of her. With skilled hands, she unfastened the button on Rachel's jeans and slid them off of her hips and down to the floor.

The way Sydney's eyes caressed her skin as they traveled up Rachel's body made her feel as if she were already completely naked.

"You're absolutely beautiful," Sydney said, her voice husky with desire.

"Thank you," Rachel nervously laughed. She turned her head slightly to avoid Sydney's eyes. She suddenly felt self-conscious, somewhat shy, and she knew Sydney could sense it.

"Are you okay?" Sydney asked softly, her words confirming Rachel's thoughts. "Rache? Look at me, please," she said, cupping Rachel's face with her hands and turning her head slightly so she could see Rachel's eyes. "What's wrong, baby?"

"You're going to think I'm stupid," Rachel answered, her voice just above a whisper. "It's just ... I ... I've never done this before. I mean, I have ... but—"

"Not with a woman," Sydney answered for her.

Rachel nodded. "I ... I don't know what to do," she said, feeling her face flush as she said the words.

Sydney's expression softened as she watched many different emotions quickly flicker across Rachel's face. "Yes, you do," was all she said, pulling Rachel into her arms. "Just do what feels natural, touch me the way you want to be touched."

Rachel smiled. "I think I can handle that," she said. She looked at Sydney's mouth and unconsciously licked her lips. Her heart rate increased. Suddenly a long neglected fire coursed through her veins and she knew Sydney was the only one who could put it out. This new awareness fueled her in a way she never imagined and she wanted nothing more than to make love to the woman holding her. She wrapped her arms around Sydney's neck, pulling her forward.

Sydney lowered her head, devouring Rachel's mouth. She groaned when she felt Rachel slip her tongue inside of her mouth. She slid her hands up along Rachel's back, unhooked her bra, and slipped the straps over her shoulders. She tossed it off to the side as she ran her tongue along Rachel's lower lip, before sucking it gently into her mouth.

"You're killing me," Rachel groaned as she ran her hands up inside Sydney's shirt and with more bravado than she thought she had, slid her fingers under the edge of Sydney's bra. She pulled up, releasing Sydney's breasts into her hands. "Damn," she whispered. She had never felt anything so soft or wonderful in her life.

"And you said you didn't know what to do," Sydney teased, her breath making Rachel shiver as she left a trail of kisses along Rachel's collarbone. "We need to get you out of these," Sydney said as she pushed Rachel's panties off of her hips.

"I think you're a little overdressed as well," Rachel said and pulled Sydney's shirt over her head and then removed her bra.

"I agree," Sydney said and unfastened her pants. She slipped them and her panties off at the same time and tossed them on a chair next to the bed.

Rachel shook her head as she looked at Sydney. "You take my breath away and I know for as long as I live, I'll never get tired of looking at you," she said, a lump forming in her throat. She was unable to stop the tears that fell onto her cheeks.

"Oh sweetheart," Sydney whispered as she laced Rachel's fingers with hers. She pulled her close and kissed the tears away. She slipped her leg in between Rachel's leg and felt her breath catch in her throat when Rachel's desire for her coated her skin. She maneuvered them backward, all the while trailing kisses along Rachel's neck, until they were at the head of the bed. She reached down, pulled back the covers, and then gently urged Rachel onto the bed.

"Sweet Jesus," Sydney groaned as she lowered herself down on top of Rachel, her thigh between Rachel's legs and when Rachel's skin fully touched hers, Sydney knew she had finally come home.

"I want you so bad," Rachel said, pulling Sydney's mouth to hers. She nibbled Sydney's lips as she ran her hands down Sydney's back, cupping her ass with both hands. "Touch me, please," Rachel pleaded, the throbbing in her groin so intense, she squeezed her legs together in order to get some relief, resulting in Sydney's sharp intake of breath.

"You're so wet," Sydney murmured as she used her leg to push Rachel's legs apart. She positioned herself so that she was between them and then raised herself up onto her knees. She leaned forward, her hands on either side of Rachel's head.

Her shallow breath and tongue were hot and wet in Rachel's ear as she whispered, "I'm going to touch and taste every single inch of your body until you beg me to stop."

"Please," Rachel moaned. Sydney had awakened a craving inside of her that reached beyond anything she had ever experienced.

Sydney laced her fingers with Rachel's, she brought first one hand to her mouth, kissing the soft part of her wrist, and then her palm. She kissed the tip of each finger and then repeated it with Rachel's other hand.

Rachel watched as Sydney slowly sucked her pinky finger into her mouth. It was the most erotic and sensuous thing she had ever seen.

"Mmm, you taste so good," Sydney whispered against Rachel's skin, her mouth, and tongue doing a seductive dance, trailing kisses down Rachel's arm, across the soft skin just above her breasts and when her tongue grazed Rachel's nipple, she nearly came undone. All those years of dreaming about this very moment seemed surreal, it was if time was standing still just for them—the universe as they knew it, had stopped.

She pulled Rachel's nipple fully into her mouth and nearly climaxed as she took each breast in her hands. She kissed her way over to Rachel's other nipple. She groaned as she made circular motions, feeling it grow harder with each tantalizing lick. She smiled when she felt Rachel's hands in her hair, trying to push her downward. She bit gently, eliciting an animalist groan from Rachel.

She raised her head to look at Rachel, who's eyes were now closed. "I will never get tired of looking at you," she said, her eyes now looking at Rachel's mouth. Her lips were swollen. They were too inviting and Sydney couldn't resist the temptation. "God, Rache," she groaned as their tongues met in a fiery battle.

Sydney felt Rachel's fingernails lightly rake over her back. She pulled Sydney down on top of her, their breasts melding against each other, sending a new rush of waves of pleasure through Sydney's body, ending with her desire for the woman in her arms, running down the inside of both of her thighs.

"Baby, I swear to God, you're driving me out of my mind," Rachel panted.

Sydney continued her tease, laying little kisses along Rachel's skin as she worked her way down Rachel's body, her hands blazing a trail for her mouth to follow. She ran her hand down along the inside of Rachel's thigh, slowly moving toward what she sought most. She couldn't stand the torture any longer. She had to touch her.

She felt a tear slip silently down her cheek as her fingers found what they sought, covered in wetness that surpassed her wildest dreams. "You feel so good," she said, laying her head against Rachel's stomach.

Rachel moaned, her groin pressing against Sydney's fingers as she slid them back and forth across her clit. She heard Rachel's deep intake of breath as she slowly entered her.

Sydney's breathing grew shallow, then urgent as she moved inside of Rachel. Every nerve ending in her body felt as if they were on fire, her senses screaming as she thrust deeper and with each rise of Rachel's hips, she melted a little more.

Without removing her fingers, she lowered her head,

slowly running her tongue along the sides of Rachel's clit.

Rachel cried out as Sydney took her fully into her mouth, sucking and licking, her fingers and tongue finding a steady rhythm, and loving the taste, the smell, her mind reeling, knowing that Rachel was ready to explode.

"Sydney," Rachel cried out as her hips rose off the bed to meet Sydney's thrusts, shudders coursing through her body as she climaxed, the orgasm rippling from a depth so deep, she thought she would collapse from sheer pleasure.

"Sweet Jesus," Rachel gasped, trying to catch her breath as she reached down, running her hand through Sydney's hair. "I've never felt anything so good in my life," she said huskily when Sydney, resting with her face against Rachel's stomach, looked up and smiled at her.

"I agree," Sydney said as she kissed Rachel's stomach. "I love you, Rache," she said as she slowly removed her fingers.

"I love you, too, baby. Come up here with me," Rachel whispered.

I will never stop loving her, Sydney thought as she moved to lie next to Rachel, her head on Rachel's shoulder.

Rachel, using her index finger, traced the lines of Sydney's face. She turned slightly and gently kissed Sydney's cheek, her eyes, and then softly kissed her lips. She felt a new arousal stir as she smelled and tasted her essence on Sydney's mouth. *I never dreamed it could or would be like this,* she thought as she looked at Sydney's beautiful face.

She brought Sydney's hand to her mouth and kissed her wrist and then her palm. She watched Sydney's reaction and smiled as she ran her tongue between her fingers, causing Sydney to inhale deeply. She shifted slightly, turning so that she was facing Sydney. She lowered her head, groaning as she took Sydney's nipple in her mouth, her hand roaming freely over Sydney's curvaceous hips.

She watched Sydney's eyes as she slipped her hand between her legs. *I've surely died and gone to heaven,* she thought as her fingers were covered in so much wetness.

"And you said you didn't know what to do," Sydney said again through a ragged breath as Rachel's fingers moved back and forth over her clit. She was already so close to the edge that she knew it wouldn't take much more.

"I'm a fast learner," Rachel smiled.

"I'll say," Sydney said as her breathing turned into short quick gasps. "Please don't stop," she begged as she moved her hips urgently against Rachel's hand.

Never," Rachel groaned as she felt Sydney's body tense.

"Oh God," Sydney cried out against Rachel's mouth as her body stiffened, the orgasm ripping through her body in waves. She collapsed back on the bed, gasping for air as she tried to slow her breathing down. She turned her head to look at Rachel. "I love you so much."

"And I will never get tired of hearing you say it," Rachel said as she brushed several strands of damp hair from Sydney's face and then laid her head on her chest.

Sydney wrapped her arms around her and placed a kiss on her cheek.

Within minutes, Rachel's slow and steady breathing told her that she had fallen asleep and for the second time in less than an hour, Sydney felt a tear slip down her cheek. She closed her eyes, thinking she was the luckiest woman on earth

Chapter 17

Sydney opened her eyes. She glanced to her left, noticing that she was in bed alone. "Please tell me I didn't dream last night and that I didn't imagine it," she said as she swung her legs over the side of the bed.

"Damn," she said as she got to her feet, feeling her muscles strain from the movement. "It wasn't a dream," she said, smiling as she slipped her robe on.

She looked up at the ceiling. "Please forgive me for all the crazy shit I've done in my life."

The first thing she heard was laughter when she pushed the kitchen door open. Caitlyn, Rachel, and Edna were sitting at the table eating breakfast. Fred Rick was standing next to the table re-filling their coffee cups.

For several seconds Sydney stood there watching them unnoticed.

Rachel grabbed Fred Rick by the arm. "Will you please sit down and join us? You don't need to keep waiting on us."

Fred Rick smiled at her and pulled out a chair. "I don't mind if I do, Ms. Ashburn."

"And you can knock the formal crap off, too," Rachel laughed.

"Yes, ma'am, Ms. Rachel," he said and chuckled at the look she gave him.

"That goes for the ma'am crap, too," she said.

"Dang. You're tough," he laughed.

Sydney decided to make her presence known. She walked over to the counter and grabbed herself a cup. "Just sit right where you are, I can get my own coffee," she said, waving Fred Rick off with a wave of her hand, as she filled her cup. She glanced at Rachel and smiled. "Good morning."

"Yes it is, isn't it," Rachel said, a smile playing at the corners of her mouth. Sydney felt her face flush as she looked at Rachel's eyes and as she attempted to take a drink of coffee, she choked. There was no mistaking the raw lust and desire she saw and felt as Rachel practically undressed her with her eyes.

"You okay there, sport?" Fred Rick teased as he looked first at Sydney and then Rachel.

Sydney shot him a look. "As for him, trust me." She nodded at Fred Rick. "You haven't seen anything yet," she said, winking at her chef.

Edna picked up the remote control lying on the table and clicked on the TV that was mounted on the wall on the opposite side of the room. On the screen was a picture of the building where Caitlyn had been held hostage along with a picture of Jackie and Maureen.

A male reporter with sandy-colored hair came into view. "We will now switch over to our latest breaking news story. It seems like Ms. Sydney Welsh's problems just keep mounting," the reporter said.

"What the hell?" Rachel gasped, covering her hand with her mouth.

Now showing on the screen was a live news conference. Edward along with a white-haired man sporting a goatee was standing behind a podium covered with microphones.

"As most of you know, my name is Richard Alexander and on behalf of my client, Mr. Edward Ashburn," he placed his arm around Edward's shoulders, "I will be filing a five-million dollar lawsuit against Sydney Welsh of Welsh enterprises. Since Ohio abolished the Alienation of Affection Law, it will be filed under the Ohio statute of Toitus Interference. Ms. Welsh is *thee* other woman, which has resulted in Mr. Ashburn's wife Rachel, asking for a divorce after ten years of marriage."

The screen momentarily flashed and a new picture appeared. It showed Rachel and Sydney standing in Sydney's family room kissing. The screen flashed again, the picture showing Sydney removing Rachel's shirt.

Fred Rick let out a loud cat whistle. "Not bad for a couple of old ladies," he laughed.

"Oh, bite me," Sydney groaned as she leaned forward and pretended to beat her head on the counter.

Caitlyn looked at Sydney and then Rachel and then busted out laughing.

Rachel looked at her. "What's so funny?" she asked, looking at her daughter.

"Um ... uh ..." Caitlyn stammered.

"What?" Rachel asked, her brow creasing into a frown.

"I was just thinking that I wish I could be there to see the look on grandmother's face when she sees this," Caitlyn laughed.

Rachel's eyes flew open wide. She covered her mouth with her hand. "Oh no. I completely forgot about them."

"Well, if you ask me, I think you two look positively radiant," Edna chuckled.

"Radiant?" Sydney asked, looking at her housekeeper.

Caitlyn and Fred Rick both laughed.

"Yes, radiant. You both are positively glowing this morning and it couldn't have happened to two nicer people," Edna said, nodding her head.

"Seriously, Mom, I didn't know you had it in you," Caitlyn teased.

"I could really say something here but I think I will hold my tongue," Fred Rick chimed in.

"Good idea," Sydney said.

Rachel groaned. She looked at Caitlyn. "You're not upset?"

Caitlyn laughed. "Are you kidding? I'm thrilled to death," Caitlyn answered honestly.

Edna looked at Sydney, her expression serious. "That color really suits you."

Sydney frowned. "What color?

"Rosy pink," Edna chuckled as Sydney's cheeks flushed a deeper pink, which only served to make everyone laugh.

With a worried look on her face, Rachel glanced at Sydney. "What are we going to do?" she asked.

Sydney walked over to the table. She covered Rachel's hand with her own. "I will take care of it. Please don't worry."

"I'm afraid that may be easier said than done," Rachel replied.

"Well, the first thing we need to do is go down to the police station and give them our official statements," Sydney said.

Chapter 18

Sydney, Rachel, and Caitlyn walked down the steps in front of the Miamisburg Police Station.

"I have a few things to do and I need to stop at the office and then I will swing by and pick Alyssa up," Caitlyn said, looking first at Sydney and then Rachel.

"Can I speak to you for a second?" Sydney asked, looking at Caitlyn.

"Sure," Caitlyn answered.

"I'll meet you at the truck and then I need to go get my car as well. I need to call my dad, something I'm not really looking forward to doing," Rachel said to Sydney.

"Okay, I'll just be a few minutes." She waited for Rachel to walk away and then turned to Caitlyn. "Caitlyn, you have every reason to hate me but I just wanted to tell you that I'm sorry."

"Apology accepted and I know that you didn't do it for revenge like Jackie claimed. You did it because you never stopped loving Mom and don't tell her I said this, but I think she was a fool for ever letting you go," Caitlyn grinned.

"You're really something else and I love you as if you were my own daughter," Sydney said, pulling Caitlyn into a hug.

"I love you, too and I hope you realize that you won't get rid of us so easily now," Caitlyn laughed.

Sydney smiled. "Getting rid of you is definitely not what I have in mind. You're stuck with me now."

"Before I go to the office, I'm gonna drop a little gift off for you at the house. I'll leave it on your desk," Caitlyn said, smiling from ear to ear.

"What kind of gift?" Sydney asked, frowning.

"Trust me, you're gonna like it. You'll see," Caitlyn laughed.

Caitlyn went into her bedroom and walked over to her desk. She pulled out the bottom drawer, removed several stacks of paper, and then pulled out a small black pouch. She unzipped it and looked at the small mini-cassettes lying inside of it.

"Towanda!" she said with a smile as she zipped the pouch closed and crammed it into her jacket pocket.

Sydney, sitting behind her desk, clasped her fingers in front of her. She looked across the desk at Edward Ashburn. Standing directly behind him, leaning against the wall were Jed and Frankie, their arms crossed over their chest.

"You can't hold me here. This is kidnapping," Edward snarled.

Sydney laughed as she slid the phone on her desk over in front of him. She picked up the receiver and held it out to him. "I think you should call the police then. I'm sure they won't be so inclined to charge me after I give them this," she said, holding a file folder in the air for him to see.

"Wh ... what's that?" he stammered.

Sydney laid the folder down on her desk and opened it. "This, Edward ... is your pathetic life."

"You don't know jack shit about my life."

Sydney's eyebrows rose in amusement. "Really? I guess the first thing would be for me to start calling you by your real name. Dont'cha think, Martin?" She watched Edward's jaw clench as he shifted nervously in the chair. "You've been a very, very bad boy, Martin."

"I don't have to listen to this shit, especially from a dyke bitch like you and the name's Edward," he said defiantly.

Sydney covered her heart with her hand, her expression pained. "Ouch, Martin. There's no need for name calling here."

"I don't need this shit," he said, his voice raising several octaves as he glared at Sydney. He made a move to get up but Jed and Frankie were on him so fast he didn't have time to react. They shoved him back down in the chair.

Sydney picked up a document from the file folder. She shook her head. "Tsk, tsk, tsk," she mocked. With a million dollar bounty on your head, dead or alive, I'd say you must have really pissed some people off, huh, Martin?"

"I don't know what you're talking about," he said but Sydney could tell by his expression that he knew exactly what she was talking about.

She slammed her fist down on the desk and stood up from her chair. "You know what? This has been fun but now it's becoming just tedious, so I'm going to lay it all out in a way that even an idiot like you can understand. I know who and what you are. I know that you changed your name because Jorge Escobar of the Meddain Drug Cartel in Columbia, the man you used to launder money for by purchasing and flipping real estate, has a million dollar bounty on your head because you ripped him off. I also know that you have been physically abusing Rachel for years and now it's going to stop."

He laughed. "You don't know shit about me and my

wife!"

Sydney picked up a black zippered pouch lying on her desk. She opened it, pulled out one of the cassettes, slipped it into a tape recorder, and then pressed the play button. The sound of Rachel's screams filled the room and Sydney felt her blood boil as Rachel begged Edward not to hit her again. She turned the tape recorder off.

"You think I'm afraid of you?" Edward asked in a calm voice as if Rachel's screams didn't faze him one bit.

Sydney shrugged. "I don't give a damn if you are or not but if you have any brains whatsoever, you should be. I'm going to tell you what you're going to do, Martin, and if you don't do it, here's what I'm going to do to you." She picked up an express overnight package that was lying on her desk. She held it up for Edward to see. "This package is addressed to the head man of the Columbia Drug Cartel and I think you're smart enough to know what's inside this envelope. If not, it contains a copy of everything I have on you, including your whereabouts."

She picked up another document and tossed it down on the desk in front of Edward and then picked up a pen and tossed it on his lap.

"What's this?" he asked as he picked up the document.

"Read it!" Sydney yelled.

He read the document then looked up at Sydney. "I'm not signing this. I'm not giving my child away," he said, shaking his head.

"Your life in exchange for hers. It's that simple. If I mail this envelope, you will be dead within forty-eight hours of Jorge Escobar receiving it and you know it."

Edward looked at the divorce papers, which also gave Rachel full custody of Alyssa and relinquished all rights to his child. His jaws clenched tightly as he looked at Sydney. He picked up the pen and signed it. "Now what?" he asked, slinging the pen across the desk.

Sydney pulled out another document from the folder

and slid it over to him. It was a one-way plane ticket to Las Vegas.

"What the fuck am I supposed to do in Vegas?" he asked as he looked at the ending destination.

"I'm sure you will fit right in," she said and pulled open her desk drawer. She grabbed a wad of cash and tossed it on the desk. "Jed and Frankie will drive you to the airport and wait to make sure you get on the plane and if you ever decide to come back here or contact Rachel or her children, you're a dead man and to prove just how serious I am, I will be watching you. You won't be able to take a piss without me knowing about it. Do I make myself clear?" she asked, coming out from around the desk to stand next to him.

"Fuck you!" he snarled.

"Only in your dreams, sweetheart," she said, smiling.

"You can have the fucking bitch. She's nothing but a who—"

Before he could finish the word, Sydney backhanded him across the mouth so hard it split his lip open. "Don't you ever talk about her like that again," she said through clenched teeth.

Edward glared at her as he wiped off the blood running down his chin with the back of his hand.

Sydney took a step back, looked at Jed and Frankie and nodded.

"Let's go slick," Frankie said as she and Jed snatched Edward up by his arms. He gave no resistance as they led him out of the room.

After they were gone, Sydney dropped into her chair and let out a huge sigh of relief. She smiled as she leaned back and laced her hands behind her head.

Sydney grabbed two wine glasses from the cabinet along with a bottle of Martin and Weyrich's Moscato Allegro from the fridge, and placed them on the bar. She pulled out a stool and sat down. She had just inserted the corkscrew into the cork when Rachel came into the kitchen.

Rachel pulled out a stool and sat down next to her. She looked at Sydney and smiled. "Are we celebrating something?" she asked as Sydney pulled out the cork.

"As a matter of fact we are," Sydney said, pouring the wine into the glasses.

"Care to share?" Rachel asked as she picked up her glass.

Sydney reached into her back jeans pocket and pulled out a folded paper. She laid it down in front of Rachel and then waited for her reaction as she picked it up and read it.

"Is this real?" Rachel asked, her eyes searching Sydney's eyes for signs that this was some sort of joke.

"Yes, baby. It's real. You're free," Sydney said as she took Rachel's hand in hers. She brought it to her mouth and kissed it.

"I'm, not even going to ask how you managed to pull this off," Rachel said as she looked at the paper, which granted her a divorce from Edward.

"Probably wise," Sydney laughed. She picked up her wine glass and held it in the air. "A toast to us and our health as we try to make up for lost time."

"To us," Rachel smiled as she clinked her glass against Sydney's glass. "Where are the girls?" she asked as she took a sip of wine.

"Last time I checked they were taking turns diving into the pool," Sydney said as she grabbed the stool Rachel was sitting on and pulled it over so that Rachel's legs were between hers. "You know, this wild journey of ours began right here," Sydney smiled.

Rachel grinned at her. "I know that wicked look,

Sydney Welsh. What's going through that pretty little mind of yours?"

"I was thinking that maybe we should christen it," Sydney said, huskily as she slid her hands up under Rachel's shirt, cupping her breasts.

"Mmm, I think that's the best suggestion I've heard all day," Rachel said, leaning forward to kiss Sydney softly on the lips.

Their love was infinite and this is where Rachel belonged, where Sydney belonged, and both women knew that nothing would ever keep them apart again—soul mates in the truest sense of the word.

EPILOGUE

After things had calmed down at home, Sydney had suggested they could use a nice vacation and Rachel readily agreed. So they packed their belongings into Sydney's truck, hooked up her massive Everest fifth-wheel travel trailer, and hit the road. They decided to take four weeks off from work and travel across the U.S.

They had arrived in Yellowstone National Park the day before and were now enjoying everything the park had to offer.

Sydney, along with Rachel, and Alyssa watched the flames in the fire-ring dance around as a light breeze fueled them along.

Alyssa poked the fire with a stick causing sparks and ember to shoot up in the air. "Were you serious about me getting a car when I'm sixteen?" she asked, looking at Sydney.

"Dead dog," Sydney said, grinning at her. "Have you decided what kind you want yet?"

Alyssa's eye got big. "Oh yeah, I want a 1970 Chevy Chevelle SS454," she said.

Sydney nodded her head in approval. "That's a sweet ride and what kind of specs do you want on this car?" she asked.

Alyssa, with a serious expression on her face, tapped her finger against her chin as she thought about it. "It needs to have a four-fifty-four big block engine with a four-twenty-seven crank. Four speed of course with an oval port and two point three intake valves that open up to a one point ninety-four exhaust," she said finally, rattling off her specs.

Sydney laughed. "What about two-ninety four Hebert hydraulic cam roller tip arms with a five-seventy-five lift?" she asked.

"Definitely," Alyssa said, nodding her head. "I think the intake should be a Pro-comp with a Holley Avenger seven-fifty, four-barrel cfm carburetor."

Sydney leaned forward in her chair. "That would give you quite a bit of horsepower, somewhere around five-hundred to five-fifty, I think."

"Oh yeah," Alyssa said, grinning. "Probably hit around thirteen, fourteen seconds on the quarter-mile."

Rachel looked at Alyssa and then Sydney and shook her head. "Listening to you two talk about cars is like listening to Swahili," she laughed.

Sydney and Alyssa both shrugged their shoulders and then laughed when they both said, "We like cars," at the same time.

"So what kind of rear-end do you want in it?" Sydney asked Alyssa, ignoring the look that Rachel was shooting her.

"Three-seventy-three Posi twelve bolt," Alyssa answered without hesitation.

"That will be a very nice ride. We may have to build it ourselves though," Sydney said.

"Sweet," Alyssa said, grinning.

Rachel cleared her throat. "Exactly how much is this car going to cost?" she asked, looking at Sydney.

"Not much, around forty or fifty grand," Sydney answered, cringing at the look on Rachel's face.

"You are not buying her a fifty-thousand dollar car, Sydney Welsh," Rachel said, shaking her head.

"I'm not," Sydney said. "Alyssa and I will buy all the parts and build it ourselves. If we do it that way, it should cost half that. Besides, she has to pay for it herself."

Alyssa's eyebrows shot upward in surprise. "How am I

supposed to pay for it? I'm only eight years old," she said, looking at Sydney.

"That will give you eight years to save all of your allowance," Rachel laughed.

Alyssa shrugged. "Okay. I can do that," she said, causing Sydney to laugh. "Can we roast marshmallows later and make smores?" she asked, looking at Rachel.

"Yes, baby, we can," Rachel laughed.

Sydney grinned as she looked at Alyssa. It was amazing how brilliant she could be one minute and even more amazing how she could immediately revert to being the eight-year-old child that in reality she was.

Her thoughts turned to all the things that had happened in the last six months. Jackie had been formally charged with kidnapping and murder along with several Federal charges, one of which included wire fraud and once the embezzled money was no longer considered evidence, what was left of it, would be returned to Sydney's bank account.

She thought about Allen and the meeting she and Caitlyn had with him regarding the property in Springfield. At first, he had tried to weasel his way out of it just like Sydney had expected but once Caitlyn laid the documents in his lap, he knew he'd been caught. He had offered little resistance when Sydney told him he was terminated. She also told him that if he returned the money within forty-eight hours, she wouldn't press charges against him and he had willingly accepted her offer. He was then escorted out of the building by security.

After the meeting was over, Sydney called Karen up to her office. She offered her congratulations for graduating with honors, and then offered her Allen's former position as Assistant Vice President of Computer Logistics, reporting directly to Caitlyn since she had also been promoted to President of Computer Logistics.

Karen being true to herself, happily accepted the

position and then proceeded to do a cartwheel in Sydney's office. By the time she had left, Sydney and Caitlyn were practically rolling on the floor with laughter.

Rachel's mother kept her word and had made no attempt to smooth things over with her daughter, but Lou on the other hand, did keep his and called Rachel several times over the past few months. He even managed to have dinner with them at least once every other week. Sydney had always believed that where there was life, there was always hope and she hoped that one day, Roberta would see that not only was she hurting herself due to her narrow-minded way of thinking, she was hurting her daughter and granddaughters as well and missing out on getting to know three really incredible people.

As for her own mother, Sydney held out as much hope for her changing as she did Roberta but that didn't stop her from wishing it.

She thought about Edward, AKA Martin Hollis, and how he had already found himself a new wife but he had not attempted to contact Rachel or Alyssa and Sydney didn't think he ever would. She had decided to keep an eye on him just the same and received monthly status updates. She would keep getting them as long as he remained alive.

She shook her head as she thought about Meredith. There wasn't much to say really. She was still the same woman doing the same things, using women for her own selfish needs and then tossing them away like yesterday's newspaper.

The part that bothered her most about everything that had happened was Maureen. She hated a part of herself for not being more feeling and compassionate all those years ago regarding her business practices. Unbeknownst to Maureen's parents, she had made an anonymous deposit into their bank account for one-hundred-thousand dollars and she kept her word about allowing them to keep their house. She had made a promise to herself to look at the whole picture, to look at the people specifically involved or affected when making business decisions in the future.

What surprised her most was how Caitlyn had figured out that Maureen was the embezzler. The cd Jackie had accidently left in Caitlyn's office didn't just contain the computer code she had written, it also had Maureen's grocery shopping list on it, a careless mistake that unraveled their entire plan.

Rachel reached over and took Sydney's hand in hers, pulling her from her thoughts. "It's beautiful here," she said as she looked around their campsite.

"Yes it is." Sydney frowned. "Where's Caitlyn?"

"I'm right here," Caitlyn answered before Rachel could answer.

Sydney shifted in her chair, smiling as she watched Caitlyn step out of the trailer, holding hands with her new girlfriend of three months—Natalie from the shipping department at EMCOR.

Caitlyn dropped down into one of the chairs, pulling Natalie down on her lap.

Natalie looked at Sydney. "I still can't believe that the trailer has a fireplace and a central vacuum in it," she said, shaking her head.

"My idea of roughing it," Sydney laughed as she got up from her chair. She looked at Rachel. "I'll be right back," she said and went inside the trailer.

"What's she up to?" Caitlyn asked, looking at her mom.

"Knowing her, it's hard to say," Rachel laughed.

Sydney came out a few minutes later. She kept her hands behind her back as she squatted down in front of Rachel. "Umm ... I was thinking since you're legally a single woman now ... that ... um ... I would love to make an honest woman of you." She brought her hand out from behind her back. She was holding a black velvet box.

Rachel gasped as Sydney flipped back the lid. Laying in

the box was the most gorgeous diamond ring she had ever seen, lying next to it was a channel band wrapped in diamonds. "Will you be my wife, Rache?" Sydney asked.

"Oh my goodness, Yes! Yes," Rachel yelled as she jumped up from the chair and proceeded to knock Sydney backward on her butt. Rachel pushed her back further so that Sydney was laying flat on her back. She fell down on top of Sydney and with tears streaming down her face, she kissed Sydney on the mouth. "Yes, I will marry you."

"About time," Caitlyn laughed as she did a fist pump in the air.

"Uh, Mom, what about the neighbors?" Alyssa asked. "They're kinda watching."

"Let 'em, watch," Rachel said as she kissed Sydney again.

"Do you think we can roast hotdogs now?" Alyssa asked in a serious tone, causing everyone else to burst out laughing.

"Yes, baby, we can roast hotdogs now," Rachel laughed as she helped Sydney up off the ground.

THE END

Author Bio

Trin Denise lives with a house full of rescue pets, which all happen to be physically challenged. She is a huge advocate against bullying, especially when it comes to physically challenged children and she also writes children's novels under the name T. Denise Robinson. Her writing career began eight years ago when her love of movies led her to write her first screenplay. Since that time, she has become an award winning and produced screenwriter and multi-published author.

Find out more about the author at: www.trindenise.com

If you have the time, friend her on Facebook or follow her on Twitter. She is always happy to meet new people.

Web site: www.trindenise.com

Facebook: http://www.facebook.com/#!/trindenise

Twitter: @trin_denise

Listen To Her Heart

Due to be released late 2012

Yalen Martinez is a bestselling author of lesbian fiction. She has thousands of fans that come from all walks of life, yet she is alone.

Since the breakup of her ten-year relationship two years ago, there has been no one special in her life. She just doesn't have the time or energy for it.

After countless attempts by her two best friends to set her up on blind dates, she decides to use the internet to get to know a few women because she thinks it's safe and she can do it anonymously. They don't need to know who she really is or what she does for a living, thus eliminating her constant worry of whether the women in her life will like her for her, or for what she can give to them materially.

She joins a lesbian dating site called, "Lesbian Neveah" and soon finds herself on the receiving end of several beautiful women who would love to get to know her better. One in particular named Emily gets her attention and they begin conversing.

Over several months, they develop what could be viewed as a romantic relationship but then something goes terribly wrong. Being an author, Yalen has a way with words and when Emily sends her a poem that she supposedly wrote for Yalen, alarm bells go off. The poem is just too perfect.

Being somewhat internet savvy, Yalen copies the poem that Emily wrote and pastes it in the Google search engine. What she finds, turns her world and her stomach upside down. The poem comes up under a website detailing copies of letters used for online dating scams. Part of the scam Emily is running, leads Yalen to believe that she's from California and is away in Japan at chef school. To make matters worse, Emily claims to be hearing impaired, therefore, Emily's often chopped vocabulary never sent up a warning sign.

Yalen chastises herself for not doing a more thorough investigation and everything she thought she knew about Emily, is now a lie. She's not even sure that the pictures that Emily sent of herself are real or if Emily is even female. Not only is she hurt, she's pissed off and is now determined to discover Emily's true identity.

Yalen's curiosity gets the better of her and she starts an investigation by tracking the IP addresses from Emily's emails. Lo and behold, the emails are originating in the United Kingdom and being rerouted through San Francisco and they are being sent by a Blackberry.

Without letting Emily know that she suspects that she is a con artist, Yalen hires private investigators in Japan and the United Kingdom to track down the owner of the Blackberry, and once she knows their identity, she is determined to confront them face to face. Her investigators determine that the woman running the con is not the same woman shown in the pictures that Emily had sent and that the chef school is not a chef school at all. It's a cooking school that offers one and two days classes for those interested in learning Japanese cuisine.

Yalen, though disappointed, becomes obsessed with finding out who the woman in the picture is and she's willing to go to any length to get that information, starting with posting the woman's picture in all the major newspapers in the U.S. and on Billboards. She anonymously offers a $50,000 reward for any information that will lead to the woman's identity. After only two days, she gets the call she's been waiting for and passes the information onto her investigator. The report comes back that the woman is a former Victoria's Secret model, single, and a lesbian.

Armed with the woman's name and address, Yalen boards a flight to Tennessee without any idea as to how she plans on approaching this woman. She's just going to have to wing it and hope like hell that the woman doesn't think she's some kind of psycho head-case.

Determined to get to the bottom of the online dating mystery, Yalen and her new found friend in Tennessee, set out on a high-risk adventure that will have them criss-crossing the globe and risking their lives repeatedly as they come face to face with a million-dollar, underworld crime syndicate that specializes in on-line dating scams.

Is it possible that two women who live very different lives who never knew the other existed can meet after being forced together due to unforeseeable circumstances, only to discover that they were brought together because it was their destiny? Sit down, buckle up, and hold on because Yalen Martinez is about to find out the answer to that question.

Note from the Author

about

Worth Dying For

I'm often asked where I come up with the ideas for my stories. I guess the easy answer would be to say "everywhere". Well, that answer is the truth. I get ideas from watching the news, reading the newspaper, and sometimes I overhear a piece of a conversation and the idea is sparked. However, the answers above are not how I came up with the idea for Worth Dying For.

I'm sure that most of my readers have heard about or watched American Idol. Well, the year I wrote WDF, was the first year I ever watched AI. It was the year that Carrie Underwood beat Bo Bice. For the finale song, Carrie sang a song called "Inside Your Heaven". It was the most beautiful song I had ever heard. The lyrics took my breath away. As she sang the song, I thought to myself, *"This is exactly how I want to feel about a woman someday."* I turned and said to a friend of mine, "That song would be so awesome for a movie." As I said the words, scenes immediately began to form in my mind.

The very first scene to come in my mind and the first scene I wrote was the beach scene when Caroline discovers that Rheyna isn't dead. I could clearly hear, "Inside Your Heaven," playing as Rheyna lifted Caroline off the ground and spun around in circles with her in her arms.

I was a screenwriter before I became a novelist and I still am. I knew I had to write WDF as a screenplay and so, I started writing my scenes down on index cards as I saw them happening if WDF were a movie. I've always had a fascination with the Mafia and somehow I knew I wanted to incorporate that into my screenplay. After I laid out all the scenes on index cards, I sat down and did approximately two weeks of solid research on the mob and the FBI. Once my research was complete, I sat down and three weeks later, I had a 120-page screenplay. I took this screenplay and entered it one of the top screenwriting contests in Hollywood. On my very first try, I made the quarterfinals and I thought, maybe I'm not so bad at this writing thingy after all.

A friend of mine who read the script told me that I should turn it into a novel because this was the type of book she would buy. I told her that I had no idea how to write a novel and that I was a screenwriter. Thank goodness, she didn't give up. She harped on me for a month about turning it into a novel. I finally gave in and agreed to do it just so she would stop riding me about it. So, I spent about a week learning everything I could about writing novels. Using the screenplay that I wrote as an outline, I laid out the chapters for the novel. Five weeks later, I had a 85,000-word novel. As you can tell, I'm not like most writers. Usually a book is adapted into a movie, not the other way around. I do it just the opposite and do what is known as a reverse-adaptation. All of my novels begin their lives as a screenplay first and then become novels. I figure that if my stories aren't good enough to be movies, then they aren't good enough to be novels.

After several re-writes, I submitted WDF to publishers. I was very fortunate and only received three rejections before the fourth publisher loved it. Several months later, in 2009, Alpha World Press released the first edition.

Since the release of WDF, I have gone on to write award winning screenplays as well as novels. Not too many people get to do what they love when it comes to their career. I am very fortunate and grateful that I am one of those lucky few. I love writing almost as much as I like breathing... LOL

Thank you for your support and if you have the time, shoot me an email or friend me on Facebook. I would love to hear from you!

Note from the Author

about

She Left Me Breathless

I'm often asked where I come up with the ideas for my stories. I guess the easy answer would be to say *everywhere*. Well, that answer is the truth. I get ideas from watching the news, reading the newspaper or I may overhear a piece of a conversation and sometimes something personal that happens or has happened in my life sparks the idea.

As with all stories I write, I find songs that inspire me as well. With this novel, the artist just so happens to be Adele. Her songs, *One and Only, Rolling in the Deep, and Set Fire to the Rain* were the songs that I listened to as I wrote this novel.

With *She Left Me Breathless*, this story just so happens to hit a little closer to home and is somewhat personal to me although it is a work of fiction.

When I was twenty-one years old, I fell in love with my best friend, who also happened to be *straight*. At the time, she was married and going through a painful divorce. She was also the mother of a beautiful, seven-year-old little girl. However, twenty-years ago, being an out-of-the-closet lesbian like I was, just was not as acceptable as it is today. The woman that I had fallen in love with couldn't get past what her mother, society, and the church thought about homosexual relationships. What everyone else thought about us being of the same sex was more important than how much she loved me. The day I walked out of her life was the day she told me that she could not raise her daughter in that kind of an environment, meaning a lesbian relationship. It was as if being in a relationship with me was worse than being a serial killer.

There is a scene in this novel where Sydney loses control and she talks about how some parents, society, and the church would rather see a woman be with a man who physically abused their daughter, than see her with a woman who worshipped the ground she walked on. Twenty years ago, I yelled those exact same words because the woman that I loved was indeed in an abusive marriage and that was more acceptable than being in a relationship with me.

I am so grateful that I no longer have to live under those type of circumstances. I have all of the lesbian and gay men who came before me to thank for fighting for, and giving me those rights, rights that now allow me to openly love whomever I choose regardless of the fact that my lover is a woman. I say to hell with what anyone else thinks about it. You only get one life, so enjoy it!!! :)

After twenty years, me and my old love have reconnected and once again we are friends. We both realize that we can no longer look back at the past with regret and instead, be grateful for the friendship we now share in spite of it.

The only words of advice I can offer is to never ever live your life for someone else

Free Signed Copy of WDF or SLMB

Contest

Let's Have Some Fun

In WDF and SLMB I refer to some things that you will find in both books. These things can be an object, person, place, thing, or phrase. If you can spot what two of these commonalties are and email them to me, you will be entered in a drawing and win your choice of a signed copy of either book. These drawing will be held every 3 months.

Proof

Made in the USA
Charleston, SC
30 June 2012